TATA

ALSO BY

VALÉRIE PERRIN

Fresh Water for Flowers
Three
Forgotten on Sunday

Valérie Perrin

TATA

Translated from the French
by Hildegarde Serle

Europa
editions

Europa Editions
8 Blackstock Mews
London N4 2BT
www.europaeditions.co.uk

This book is a work of fiction. Any references to historical events, real people, or real locales are used fictitiously.

First publication 2026 by Europa Editions

Translation by Hildegarde Serle
Original title: *Tata*

A catalogue record for this title is available from the British Library
ISBN 978-1-78770-646-0

Perrin, Valérie
Tata

Cover design by Ginevra Rapisardi

Cover photo: Toni Frissell, *Un baiser à sa mère – capturé à Berlin-Est.* Allemagne, octobre 1961. Library of Congress, Prints & Photographs Division, Toni Frissell Photograph Collection, LC-F9-1961-10-21, frame #16.

Prepress by Grafica Punto Print – Rome

The authorized representative in the EEA is Edizioni e/o, via Gabriele Camozzi 1, 00192 Rome, Italy.

Printed and bound in Great Britain by Clays Ltd, Elcograf S.p.A

CONTENTS

To Claude Lelouch

For my brother Yannick

To those absent, Jérôme Chaussin and Jean-Paul Didierlaurent

TATA

2010. Samuel Paty, Simone Veil, Milos Forman, and Elizabeth II were still alive. Barack Obama was president of the United States, and Vladimir Putin was behind the murder of Anna Politkovskaya four years earlier. That particular year was declared France-Russia Year. I don't know what that signifies.

The Taliban hadn't regained power in Afghanistan.

Kathryn Bigelow became the first woman to win the Oscar for Best Director, for *The Hurt Locker*.

It's also the year in which Meryl Streep was nominated for the sixteenth time in the best actress category. The tallest skyscraper was inaugurated in Dubai, global production of CO_2 rose by 6%, and it was the hottest year ever recorded. Since then, that last record has been beaten.

In France, Nicolas Sarkozy was president.

TikTok didn't exist. Adele wasn't yet singing "Someone Like You," or Clara Luciani "*La grenade*."

2010, it was the year of Damien Saez's song "*J'accuse*."

2010, it was the year my aunt died for the second time.

Part I

1

October 21, 2010

Hello?"

"Good morning, ma'am."

"Good morning."

"Are you the niece of Colette Septembre?"

"Yes."

"It's the gendarmerie here. The gendarmerie of Gueugnon. I'm Captain Cyril Rampin. I'm calling to give you some bad news."

". . ."

"Your aunt has died."

"My aunt?"

"Colette Septembre. I'm with the first responders. Her body has just been discovered at 19, Rue des Fredins. It would seem that she died in her sleep. Her body is being taken to the mortuary for forensic confirmation."

"My Aunt Colette has been buried at the Gueugnon cemetery for three years. She lived on Rue Pasteur."

"I have some ID right here; it's Colette Septembre, born in Curdin on February 7, 1946. She's younger in the photo, but it does look like her."

"It must be a mistake. Probably just the same name."

"In her wallet, there's a note saying, 'In case of emergency, contact my niece Agnès at 01 42 21 77 47.'"

". . ."

"It also says that she wants to be cremated. And laid to rest with Jean Septembre."

"Jean?"

"Yes. Do you know him?"

"He was my father."

"Your aunt's brother?"

"Yes. But my Aunt Colette died three years ago, I tell you."

"Where do you live?"

"Paris."

"Does your aunt have any other close relatives?"

"I'm . . . the last one. I'm the only . . . and then my daughter . . . But—"

"My condolences. When are you thinking of coming to identify the body?"

2

In 2000, my aunt disappeared for a week after the match between FC Gueugnon and Paris Saint-Germain. It was the first time a second-division team reached a League Cup final. A team known as "*les Forgerons*"—the Foundrymen—that she'd worshipped all her life.

Match score: 2-0. A fixture that seemed to be a mere formality. The small fry against the big fish. The match took place at the Stade de France and was broadcast on Channel 3. Richard Trivino, goalkeeper. Amara Traoré, captain. Alex Dupont, coach.

My aunt had hung a portrait of Alex Dupont in her home, and one of Émile Daniel, too. She owned all the team photos and would circle some faces with a red felt-tip pen, like men wanted by the Mafia.

At the sixty-fifth minute, a first goal was scored by Trapasso. In extra time, a second by Flauto. Never had Paris Saint-Germain lost in a final. The cheering went on for ages; many tears were shed. The victory was toasted from plastic cup to plastic cup. Dozens of coaches had been required to ferry the supporters to Paris. My aunt had sat up front, alone, to see the road. On the stands, thousands of splashes of color—yellow for the players' shirts and blue for their shorts—were chanting: "*Et un et deux*!"

When it was time to go home, the driver of Colette's bus, a certain Éric, looked everywhere for her. She was missing. They waited. They called her. She never showed up. They phoned my mother, Colette's only family by marriage: "Your sister-in-law has gone AWOL." And Mom told them not to worry.

Colette only reappeared three days later, back in her shoe-repair shop, bent over a pair of size-42 loafers belonging to Christian Duclos, the right heel of which was particularly worn due to its owner's slight limp, the legacy of falling off a bike.

No one ever knew where she'd been. No one asked her the question. No one ever asked her questions.

On the day of the victory, I learned for the first time, from my mother, that Colette did sometimes disappear, but always returned. My mother said it as if talking about a mutt that runs away but finally comes home when hungry.

3

October 21, 2010

I feel like phoning him. I need to phone him. I imagine what I'd say to him. I imagine how he'd reply. His hello.

"Pierre?"

"Yes."

"Is that you, Pierre?"

"Yes. It's me."

His voice, the tone of his voice, annoyed, hurried. He always answered the phone like a guy who's just leaving. Who already has his coat on. Who dashes back to the phone to answer it. Answering it to get rid of it.

"It's Agnès."

How would he react? I wouldn't give him time to say "Agnès?" or "Agnès." Or "Why are you calling me? Has something happened?"

"Believe it or not, the police have just phoned me. The Gueugnon police. Colette is dead."

No, I wouldn't say "believe it or not." I'd say:

"The police in Gueugnon just phoned me. They've found the body of a woman and claim adamantly that it's Colette."

No. Not adamantly. I never say "adamantly." He would reply:

"She's already dead . . . Have you been drinking? Are you drunk or something?"

And I would hit straight back:

"That would suit you just fine, wouldn't it? Like that, you and your slut could have sole custody of Ana."

And I'd hang up.

I've never used the word "slut." When I'm angry, I shout "bitch" or "stupid cow." Which of us would hang up first? At what stage would the conversation turn nasty?

Three years without hearing the sound of his voice on the phone, but that's ancient history now. Colette has redied. There's no such word. Redying, no such thing.

At the beginning, the beginning of my end, it was Cornélia, the nanny, who would take our child to his place, well, their place. And it was Cornélia who would bring our child back to mine. The child is now fifteen. She travels by metro, or taxi if it's late.

My last movie wasn't my biggest hit at the box office. And yet it did receive the most enthusiastic reviews. And it is the most widely distributed, globally.

Why am I thinking about that? I was peacefully dead. I was doing nothing anymore. I was making do with my dividends, under the duvet one week in two, and now I'm being forced to come back to life and buy a train ticket and book a room in a town at the back of beyond, in Burgundy. To go identify a dead old lady I don't know.

The last movie I directed was a love story. I was so very inspired.

4

Single and childless, Colette is the sister of my father, Jean. Since the day her brother died, she'd been in mourning. It took up all the space. All her shrunken space. Her thin, small body, her big dark eyes that dominated her face, her shoe-repair shop, her bed, the air she breathed. She never accepted his death, "because there's nothing to accept," she would say, sweeping the air with the back of her hand.

Until I was seventeen, my aunt remained pretty silent with me. She would occasionally exchange a few words with the neighbors, storekeepers, customers, and footballers, who revered her the way an Italian reveres the Blessed Virgin. But not with me. With me, it was a monastic silence.

As a child, I'd have had to hide behind the doors of her shop to hear her saying words other than: "Did you sleep well? Are you hungry? Are you thirsty? Aren't you finishing that? Are you hot? Good night . . . " Words cast in my direction, always at the same times of the day.

But I never did so. She didn't interest me. I thought she had nothing to say, nothing for me. I hated my vacations, her house, the smell of her house. The flooring, the furniture, the narrow windows, the room that was allocated to me and smelled of mothballs.

At ten years old, I would cut photos out of magazines and stick them in exercise books with grid paper, photos of young girls who made me dream of having the same haircut, same mouth, same blue mohair sweater. How could I possibly be interested in a woman who'd never worn makeup, or cared a fig about her appearance? She was the type of woman who made people think: if she fixed herself up a bit, she'd be pretty. Her clothes were far too big for her. It was like she bought the wrong size on purpose, made the mistake so as to disappear a little.

To keep the shopkeepers of Gueugnon busy, she would give me three blank checks before I went back to school. One to buy something to wear at Shopping, a second for something else at Causard, and the third to pick a fine pair of shoes at Madame Bresciani's. For my aunt, a fine pair meant top quality. And you had to pay the price for that. The kind of leather shoes that cut into my feet.

I was entitled to this sentence at the end of August, always the same one, with no particular sign of affection: "Here, go fit yourself out for the new term."

5

Three years ago, I was still living in Los Angeles when Colette died in her sleep. She's died twice in her sleep now. I didn't go to her funeral. A fifteen-hour flight. "It's not worth it," Louis Berthéol whispered to me. Formerly a baker in Gueugnon, he was a close friend of my aunt.

Louis took care of everything. I wrote a check for the burial costs. Like when my aunt would "fit me out" for the new term. I didn't even have any forms to fill in. He organized her funeral for August 13, 2007.

When I did return, he gave me a box containing family photos, football-club pennants, and a few scarves. He'd donated the clothes to the *Secours populaire* charity.

I went to the cemetery on foot. It was early January. The air was freezing cold. I looked for her grave, found it on Avenue 7. No flowers, no wreaths, no plaque, as she'd apparently instructed Louis. Only a pair of shoes had been placed on the gray marble. Kickers style, in dark blue leather. Out of curiosity, I checked the size: 37. My aunt's size was 36. I asked Louis who had left the shoes there, he couldn't tell me.

In 2007, I'd been living in the US for four years. Throughout that time, I'd phoned Colette every Tuesday. Why Tuesday? I don't know. With some habits, one can't remember how they started. We would talk about the same things, almost word for word, the weather, health, the worsening quality of shoes, mass-produced by miserable workers, with stitching unworthy of the term. And my aunt would tell me the ranking of her football team, which I didn't give a hoot about. The transfers of such and such players, those who were promising, those who partied too much, the triers, the duds. The death of a former player, the birth of the son of a supporter. And she'd always wrap the conversation up with the same words, her voice uncertain: "And your work, going well? Are you working on a movie? And Ana? And Pierre? Are they well? It isn't too big over there?" And I'd say: "All's well." At the end of our exchange, there was no "lots of love" or "big kiss." I don't think she'd ever uttered those words. She'd whisper, "Bye for now." And I'd say, "Until next Tuesday." I think, as time went on, I must have added a "look after yourself" or "take care of yourself." That kind of thing.

6

October 22, 2010

Hôtel Monge. Room 3. A bag, hastily packed after Captain Rampin's phone call, thrown on the bed. Formerly the Hôtel du Centre, the Monge has just been entirely refurbished. I've been going to this establishment's restaurant since I was little. For every Christmas Eve dinner, with my parents and Colette. And I sometimes had lunch there with some football officials, but I don't know which ones. They would come and fetch my aunt at the shoe-repair shop, all smelling of fine cologne, and say: "Madame Septembre, we're lunching at Georges's, be our guest." It was Georges's after Georges Vezant, the former owner and chef. The food was seriously good. The thought still makes my mouth water.

When they would invite her, she would abandon the shoe in her hands. Quickly come and pick me up, wherever I was, often roller-skating on Place de l'Église, sweaty and with grazed knees. I'd wash my hands, brush my hair, and off we'd go for lunch. For me, it was literally a feast day. Lovely white tablecloths, crystal glasses, escalope à la crème, sautéed potatoes, fried fish, cured ham, Burgundy-style snails. And my aunt would tuck into her mashed potatoes with a special sauce prepared by Georges, bowed over her plate, intimidated and silent. Proud, too, that *those men* should invite her, consider her an important part of the club.

The hotel and restaurant have now been taken over by Leslie, a small, bubbly brunette who talks to angels and heals ailments. She's not here today. Shame. I would have asked her to communicate with my aunt who died three years ago, so she could tell us about the woman on Rue des Fredins. The one in possession of Colette's ID, her final wishes, and my Paris phone number. A number that was assigned to me after Colette's death.

Since yesterday, I've been trying to get in touch with Louis Berthéol, but he's not answering. Upon arriving in Gueugnon, I asked my taxi driver to go past his house. All the shutters were closed.

I have an appointment at 2 P.M. to identify the body. Rampin's coming to fetch me at the Monge hotel. I have two free hours ahead of me. So I walk over to the house the body was found in. I make a detour to go past the shoe-repair shop on Rue Pasteur. When my aunt died, the shop was taken over by a couple.

Colette owned neither her shop, nor the house beside it. She paid a token rent to Louis. "A pittance," she would sometimes say, when talking to the shoes and handbags she was mending. She used to put her money into a metal cashbox. I remember the banknotes she would smooth down with the palm of her hand. One day, one of the neighbors had whispered to me that the rumor around Gueugnon was that my aunt had a "woolen stocking" stuffed with money. I'd replied, "Yes, probably," pretending I understood. When I got back to the shoe-repair shop, I looked at her legs, and she was wearing pantyhose. After she died, Louis told me that nothing had been found of her imaginary hoard. There was something like two hundred euros in her bank account. I asked him to keep that money for all the services he'd rendered. He replied: "Being your aunt's friend isn't a service, it's a blessing."—"Fine, but keep the money."

The shopfront hasn't changed. But gone is the sign saying: "Closed due to football." She would hang it on her door every other Saturday, if the match wasn't scheduled for the evening.

The new owners have had a more modern shop-sign installed. They've removed the stone planters Colette grew geraniums in, to keep the flies away and look pretty. Still the same gravel in the courtyard. The adjoining accommodation, and the stairs going up to the entrance. The elementary school a hundred meters away. I hear the cries of the children in the playground. How many times had I gone over there to imagine what the place would be like with pupils in it? I'd always known it deserted. Off-season.

It's midday. The siren blares across the town. For a century, it has heralded the exodus of workers from *l'usine des Forges*—the ironworks. Two simultaneous outflows, as the barriers lifted, one on the bridge side and one on the Place des Forges. Fascinated, I used to watch, from the bottom of the bridge, the herd escaping from work on bikes and mopeds, or on foot to reach the cars parked along the Arroux, the river that runs through Gueugnon. Workmen, managers, technicians, foremen, office staff, inspectors. The siren sounded for a long quarter of an hour on May 8, 1945, the day Germany surrendered.

I find myself in front of 19, Rue des Fredins in a matter of minutes. On the way, I was sad to notice that the handsome old storefronts in the town center have turned into banks, insurance brokers, opticians, or medical labs. Only a few store owners are holding out.

Impossible to access the courtyard; a high, double-locked wooden door stands in the way and tall privets surround the garden, some three-hundred square meters in size. I push hard, turn the handle back and forth. Impenetrable. As I step back, I catch a glimpse of some cement roof tiles. No mailbox. That's the most I'll know. I shiver, as if seized by a sudden fever.

7

October 22, 2010

Today's my birthday. Today, I was supposed to celebrate my thirty-eight summers with my daughter, Ana, at a restaurant in Paris, but fate has decided otherwise.

The gendarmerie captain, Cyril Rampin, is driving an unmarked police car. Tall, young, light-brown hair, close-shaven. He seems to take his work seriously and says very little. So much the better. After greeting me, he told me that he'd been transferred here two years ago and was originally from the Somme. And then he went quiet. I don't know the Somme; I've only seen it through the battlefields in movies about the Great War. The captain looks me straight in the eye when addressing me and has a firm handshake. Polite and respectful toward others, he's likeable and inspires confidence.

It's 2:30 P.M. when we enter the hospital's morgue. And everything unfolds just like in the movies, including one of mine called *Les Silences de Dieu*—The Silences of God. We have to show some ID and then walk up and down basement corridors. Dead people are never seen in rooms bathed in natural light. As if death has to be hidden in the bowels of buildings.

"Have you had lunch?" Rampin asks me.

"A snack on the train."

He must fear that I'm going to faint.

A body, covered in a sheet the same color as the walls, lies on a table under a halo of cold light, between gray and blue. A forensic pathologist greets me and lifts up the sheet. I'm incapable of uttering a word. Her face, her neck, her shoulders. She's lost a little weight. She's aged. She's dead. She's cold. Her eyes are closed. Her lovely complexion is now but a waxen mask. It's her, without being her. But it is her. I identify her. The captain asks me if I'm sure. I say yes.

All I can think of is that pair of blue shoes. Are they still there, on the grave of the unknown woman in the Gueugnon cemetery?

The last time I saw a dead person, it was a dead woman, and it was Mom.

The day before yesterday, my aunt, Colette, was alive, and I didn't know it.

"Do you recall any distinguishing feature?" the pathologist asks me.

I shake my head.

She had so many, but none that could be seen on her poor emaciated body. She walked fast, she had style, she was clever, she never married, I never knew her to have a lover, she never had children, she was secretive as a tomb, so secretive that I don't know who's been lying in *her* tomb for the past three years, she had pretty hands, she was good with her hands, she was a fan of the Football Club of Gueugnon, the novels of Agatha Christie and Pierre Bellemare, and of Inspector Maigret. And that's when I realize that I'm a total idiot. I turn toward Rampin and mutter to him:

"I'm a total idiot."

8

I think I've always written stories because I spent all my school vacations at my aunt's. When normal life started up again, I was elsewhere, far away, in another town, another place, with other friends. Throughout my childhood, I was always the absent one. From the first day of the holidays, the children at my school stopped seeing me, and the children in Gueugnon saw me once again, as soon as the bell announced the start of their freedom.

She's arriving tomorrow.

The adults called me "the vacation girl" or "Colette Septembre's niece." The kids my age called me by my name.

People would set off for Fréjus, Quiberon, or Spain. For the sea, for the mountains. And me, for Gueugnon. My parents rarely departed from the rule. Even after the death of my father. Until I came of age, I got landed with the shoe-repair shop, the Rue Jean-Jaurès, the Rue de la Liberté, the Place de l'Église, the footbridge, the municipal swimming pool, the matches at the Jean-Laville stadium.

"Where are you going?"

"To Gueugnon. Saône-et-Loire."

"Is that far?"

"Not very."

I was never very far from Colette. My friends in Gueugnon could be counted on the fingers of one hand. Hervé, Adèle, and Ilyas. The children of storekeepers, who'd meet up during the day while their parents were hard at work. The hours had to be filled. We'd split up for lunch. Half an hour, and we were done. At the end of the day, we had to be home at around six. Have a wash, maybe lay the table while awaiting parents. At Colette's, I only had to jump into her hip bath. Then, I'd dive into her collection of Tintin books, which I adored. She'd order them for me from the *tabac.* I was forever rereading

The Castafiore Emerald, because it's the only one that's set entirely in Marlinspike Hall. I found that reassuring, somehow. I don't know why. And when I needed to travel, when boredom and missing my parents became too oppressive, it was *Tintin in Tibet*, *The Blue Lotus*, or *Prisoners of the Sun*.

On summer evenings, Ilyas, Adèle, Hervé, and I would go back outdoors until nine. And on really hot days, we were allowed an extra hour. We'd hang out on the banks of the Arroux, near the footbridge. We'd skip stones. We'd listen to the radio or to music from my cassette recorder. We'd imagine our futures. Me, I wanted to be a reporter. Ilyas, a professional footballer and to play for France. Adèle, a *Médecin du Monde*, a doctor of the world. Hervé, an explorer.

"What d'you want to explore, Hervé?"

"Don't know yet."

"Why a doctor of the world, Adèle? Why not just a doctor?"

Sometimes, Mom and Dad would come and fetch me in the middle of the vacation, like picking at a plate of food, to take me somewhere for two or three days at short notice. Otherwise, Ilyas and I would spend the month of August together. His father didn't close his grocery store, and my aunt didn't think it possible to leave Gueugnon, except when the team played away.

Hervé and Adèle would be off to spend three weeks by the sea with their parents, who would pull down the shutters and hang up the "Annual vacation" sign. Not the same sea. The Mediterranean for Hervé, the Atlantic for Adèle.

"You could never bump into each other swimming," Ilyas would say.

In August, Gueugnon was empty. A dead, hot, deserted town, like in the Westerns, when the hero or villain rides into town and everyone's hiding.

They're there. All three of them. Sitting in the entrance hall of the Monge hotel. Lightly dressed because it's still warm for October. Adèle, Ilyas, Hervé. We'd lost touch. A word on Facebook every now and then, a "like" or a heart emoji on a comment about some photo that touches us.

Apart from Hervé, who has broadened out, whose features have thickened with age, they haven't changed. Adèle still has a youthful figure, and Ilyas a childlike beauty.

It's Adèle who speaks first. The opposite of when we were young. She was the one who said nothing. "We heard you were here. News travels fast in this place." She stands up and hugs me. She smells of honeysuckle. Like before. I'm in a complete daze. Instead of saying hello or good evening, nice of you to come, how are you, I blurt, right out of the blue:

"My aunt who's buried, it isn't my aunt. Mine died two days ago."

The two boys look questioningly at me as they stand up. They hug me in turn, silently. Ilyas has a whiff of ambergris about him, Hervé of vetiver cologne.

"I should have realized when I collected her belongings back then, there was almost nothing to do with her football team, the FCG. And mainly, not a trace of her collection, which included dozens of scrapbooks. She'd cut out all the articles in the newspaper. Had done so for decades. Do you think that's normal? What a total idiot I am . . . Can you believe that you went to my aunt's funeral three years ago, and it wasn't her?"

"Impossible," they all reply, in unison.

"I've just seen her at the morgue!"

"You're sure?"

"Sure. I spent enough years with her to recognize her . . . Even dead."

They remain silent. Lost in thought.

"But then, who is it? In the cemetery?" Hervé asks.

"It's a mystery."

"D'you think the coffin's empty?"

"No idea. The captain from the gendarmerie told me they're going to compare Colette's DNA with mine, and they'll be exhuming 'the person.'"

"It's not right to disturb the dead," Adèle whispers.

"But we need to know the truth."

Adèle shrugs.

"For all that the truth can tell us."

"What are you doing this evening?" Hervé asks.

"It's your birthday," Ilyas chips in.

"We must do *something*, we're not leaving you all on your own."

"I'm not in the mood for celebrating."

"All the more reason," Hervé says, smiling.

"I have an appointment tomorrow morning on the Rue des Fredins. At the house Colette apparently lived in for the past few years . . . "

"Rue des Fredins? Whereabouts?"

"At No. 19 . . . "

"This is completely insane."

"You lot, did none of you ever come across her? See her again?"

"Never," Adèle replies.

"Maybe we don't see the dead. I mean, when we think someone's dead, even if we come across them somewhere, we can't see them. Our brain isn't ready."

"Shall we go have a drink? We don't need to stick around here."

"Should we book a table here for later?" Adèle asks.

"No need to book, not a soul around."

*

My first crush was called Jacques Daubel. It was summer 1985. Jacques was Hervé's cousin. His father was Vietnamese, his mother French. Perfect profile, straight nose, fine features, nice mouth, and dark almond-shaped eyes. On vacation, like me. We'd swim in the municipal pool and ride our bikes. He'd go to the football matches, like everyone did. It was an outing for the locals. Sometimes, there'd be TV coverage from the press stand, Canal+, Thierry Roland commentating. Which made it even more of an event.

Sandwiches, cola, merguez sausages we'd wolf down at the stall run by supporters. In-shell peanuts that Monsieur Dollet would sell out of a basket, from stand to stand, at half-time.

When the Gueugnon team scored, we'd scream. From a distance, I'd see my aunt standing up. She'd suddenly seem taller to me. Unlike the rest, she never shouted. An inscrutable smile would play on her lips and her big eyes would light up. And then she'd sit back down, hands gripped together. Sometimes she'd mouth words, her eyes fixed on the players as if praying. When the opposing team scored, she froze and turned pale, as if all life had left her, right there, on her cement stand.

I saw tears in her eyes when Gueugnon suffered a defeat. Tears that didn't fall, that stayed put, at the corner of the eye, so as not to disturb or draw any attention.

*

We're all at the age of having teenagers. That is, at the age of having some time to oneself in the evening, even when it's not really late. No more bathtime, supper to prepare, homework to supervise. Our offspring know how to warm something up and shut themselves in their rooms to pretend they're studying.

"And with mobile phones, it's handy, we can reach them everywhere," Adèle murmurs. "We can even track them."

Adèle has seventeen-year-old twins, away in Dijon for their studies.

Instead of becoming a doctor of the world, she's a visiting nurse. "Which comes to the same thing," she quips. She set up her own practice. Divorced when her girls were ten years old, has a boyfriend, but doesn't live with him every day.

"Each to their own evening," she says with a smile.

"Nice expression, each to their own evening."

"Will you put it in a movie?" she asks me.

"What I'd never have dared put in a movie is what—"

My voice cracks.

"Why my aunt let people believe she was dead. Why was she hiding? There are, what, eight thousand people in this town? Don't tell me that no one knew! And then, on Rue des Fredins, nearly all the houses are occupied. She didn't live as a recluse, for goodness' sake."

"Old Berthéol!" Hervé cries out. "He's bound to know something. He and your aunt were as thick as thieves."

"He's not at home. Doesn't answer the phone. I went to his place again this evening, on my way back from the morgue, no one there. Everything's so weird. I feel like I'm dreaming."

"As for me," Ilyas says, "I attended your aunt's funeral. There was a good crowd. Smaller than normal because it was summer. Lots of football people, some players, and some store owners. I saw the coffin going down into the hole. Saw it with my own eyes."

"What a crazy story. It's like my love life, one lost, one found, and then lost, and then another one found!"

Smiles all around.

Hervé is an insurance broker. He's had three children with three different women. The youngest is seven, but he and her mother have just separated; "It's the pits," he groans. But he can't help it, he just has to date, to love, to cheat. Only Ilyas hasn't had children. "Not to my knowledge, anyhow," he says with a smile, pouring himself another glass of soda. He gave up on his sporting career and went to the factory's training center to qualify as a process operator.

"The little one," Hervé continues, "I see every other weekend. My eldest daughter lives in Lyon, like you when you were a kid, Agnès. She has a boyfriend. And my son lives with his mother, not far from here. He's sixteen. We go eat at McDo's, do stuff like that. He's still keen on cars and football . . . Fuck, all this makes me want to go up to the cemetery and find out who's buried under there."

"The dead mustn't be disturbed," Adèle says, again.

"Oh, quit going on about that, when you're dead, you're dead. No one's disturbing anyone."

"I'm impatient for tomorrow, to get inside the house on Rue des Fredins."

"Want us to come with you?"

"I don't think that's allowed," Ilyas cuts in. "Are you going there with the gendarme?"

"Yes."

"How long are you staying in Gueugnon?"

"I've no idea. It'll depend on all that stuff. It was so un . . . unforeseen. I think that's the word."

"Have you seen the journalist?"

"What journalist?"

"Nathalie Grandjean."

"Really? She's a journalist?"

"Yes, and you'll be granted the full attention of the press. Even of the TV! A dead woman who isn't dead, that'll hardly go unnoticed! Especially the aunt of a local celebrity."

"Shall we share a cheese board?"

"Forget the cheese board, Adèle! It's the birthday of a great lady, we're going to stuff ourselves!"

"And otherwise, Agnès, how are you? Living the good life?"

9

October 23, 2010

Flanked by two gendarmes, Cyril Rampin opens the high wooden door that conceals the property from the street. I discover a small, 1950s-era house, single-story, surrounded by a more-or-less maintained garden. The privets haven't been trimmed for ages, wild grasses are invading the flagstones of a one-time terrace. And yet, some gravel paths have been raked. As if care had only been taken of those close to the residence. How to imagine that we're entering the home of a dead woman? Boots wait patiently beside the door. I glance at the size: 36. My aunt's size. The captain hands me some latex gloves. "It's preferable."

A corridor with a whiff of ammonia, reminiscent of an elementary-school classroom. Everything is clean. A peg, a gray raincoat. I can't resist sniffing the collar to get her vanilla scent back. She'd buy it in little bottles, and the liquid was slightly oily. The fabric smells of roses.

To the left, a kitchen, Formica table, two chairs, cooktop, small fridge. Some slippers neatly set aside, dishes done, a plate, cutlery, and a glass drying at the edge of the sink. Lemon-scented dish soap, a carefully folded cloth. The furniture is clean. I open the fridge: butter, three plain yogurts, three eggs, a jar of jam, carrots in the vegetable drawer, leftover soup in a saucepan, covered with a plastic lid. Curtains at the windows. A door on the left, allowing a glimpse of a sitting room with a TV in pride of place, a small two-seater sofa, three cushions. I recognize nothing. Apart from the *France Football 2000* magazine—"Gueugnon, victory for the *Forgerons*"—placed like a trophy on the coffee table. The shock knocks me for six. I shrink back.

As we approach the third door, the one to the bedroom where Colette was discovered in her bed, I get the most awful shivers. The sheets are barely rumpled, as if even in death she didn't want to disturb, make any wild gestures. My aunt never made any wild gestures, not to my knowledge, anyhow. At this moment, I realize that I don't know her. Or rather, not anymore. Her trust in me must have been seriously lacking for her to let me believe she was dead. I don't enter the room.

At the end of the corridor, a final room, in which some plastic boxes are stored. I recognize the old ottoman from the shoe-repair shop. Beside it, a table and an iron, a modern sewing machine, and also a cupboard. What throws me is a telephone and an old directory in one corner. I pick up the receiver. A ringtone. She had a phone. But who would phone her? Who knew? Whose name is the line under?

"We have to start with that."

"Start with what?" Cyril Rampin asks.

"With the phone records. So we know who she was calling, and who was contacting her. We'll know who knew."

"That's considered to be the private domain. Unless the death seems suspicious, which doesn't seem to be the case, I don't think I'd be allowed to access that data."

I call my cellphone from the landline phone. A number appears, I save it.

"The prosecutor called me. In the light of the circumstance surrounding this death, the pathologist has reported a forensic obstacle. An autopsy will be carried out on Madame Septembre. We'll have to wait a few weeks before the body is returned. Then we'll proceed with the exhumation of the body buried in the cemetery. It's likely to be a lengthy inquest."

I'm not listening to Cyril Rampin anymore. Instinctively, I've just half-opened the right-hand door of the cupboard. Some piled-up cardboard boxes. I grab hold of one: inside, some large books, lying one on top of the other. Covered in brown paper, with labels, like on school exercise books: 1982, 1983. I flick through the pages, knowing that I've just found her collection. She used to cut out any articles about matches, team formation, and substitutes. I recognize the journalists' names at the end of the articles. Their faces come back to me. "The good one and the bad ones," Colette would say. "The ignoramuses who are jealous of the players, and the guy who supports them and knows what he's talking about: a former footballer." On one shelf, the LPs of my parents' performances. And finally, shoved down below, the funeral plaques and club pennants that she must have removed from "her" grave.

"This is why, at the morgue, I realized that I'm a total idiot," I say.

"Sorry?"

"When Louis Berthéol gave me her belongings three years ago, I didn't twig, even though I know this collection and that she was far too attached to it to part with it. Ditto for my parents' LPs."

I find a box full of photos. Portraits of me at every age. From a baby to a twenty-year-old. I'm beyond moved. I ask the captain if I can keep them, and he replies:

"Later. For now, we must leave everything as it is."

One last door. "And the tour is complete," a real-estate agent would trot out. A spartan bathroom, tiny bathtub and shower, sink, medicine cabinet, washing machine. The walls smell of fabric softener and *savon de Marseille*. Everything is clean. Everything shipshape. I feel as if someone's going to appear and ask us: "What are you doing in my home?"

A rose-scented eau de toilette. Colette must have changed perfumes at the end of her life. Out with vanilla. A hairbrush. She had a mop of hair that would fall out in strands if you brushed too hard. My hair is still dark; hers had turned white. We had that in common, our manes of hair. A toothbrush and toothpaste. I open the medicine cabinet; on a box, someone has written "painful joints." I recognize her handwriting.

"Who does this house belong to?"

Cyril Rampin consults a register he's holding and replies:

"The owner is called Louis Berthéol."

"Who informed you about Colette? You didn't find her body by chance."

"An anonymous call from that phone."

"A man's voice, or a woman's?"

"A man's. We must go," he adds.

"I'd like to stay. Sort things. Gather things. Try to find a diary or some letters, or whatever. The contents of the boxes might end up revealing something, and . . . "

"Not just now," the captain interrupts me. "You can come back here alone once the doctor certifies that your aunt died of natural causes."

"How long will that take?"

"A few days."

In my hands, I have Colette's ID. It was issued in 2000. I also have a handwritten note: "I wish to be cremated and for my ashes to be placed with my little brother Jean Septembre and my sister-in-law Hannah. I would also like a handful of me to be scattered at the Jean-Laville stadium. Please pass this note on to Agnès Septembre, my niece. Colette Septembre."

10

I live in the house opposite.

She arrived with the gendarmes. She hasn't changed, her hairstyle maybe, shorter, although she still gathers it up into a weird kind of bun. And anyhow, I'd see her, from time to time, on TV when she was plugging one of her movies. I read in a magazine that she'd separated from the actor. Personally, I thought it a case of pearls before swine.

When she turned up here, she was white as a sheet. Like when she was little and would arrive for the vacation. For the first few days, she'd be pale as anything, then would get better colors from running around with the other kids.

The gendarmes will probably come knocking on my door. Neighborhood enquiries: "Who lived there? Who would visit there? You didn't notice anything?" I will reply: "Nothing at all." I don't spend my days at the window, checking on the neighbors. I've got my housework, my shopping to do, my crosswords, and, crucially, my lessons to prepare. This morning was out of the ordinary. It's not every day that three police cars park on my sidewalk. This morning, Gueugnon seems more like America, like we see it on the TV.

Yesterday, when I saw the first responders and gendarmes bringing someone out on a stretcher, when I realized it was a lifeless body, I cried a lot.

Sometimes, in the *Journal de Saône-et-Loire*, one learns about terrible things, with headlines one has to read several times to understand them, well, not to understand them, rather to accept them. Like "Discovered in his apartment, he had been dead for several months." And each time, I find it dreadful, really dreadful.

If they come to question me, I'll say I had no idea who lived behind that hedge of trees that was never trimmed. Who was lying on that stretcher. That I've only just learned that my neighbor across the street was a woman. A single woman, rumor has it. And again, according to the gossip, it was Colette Septembre.

Colette has been resting in the cemetery for a few years now. Unless it's what I'm thinking it is. What only I know. Unless it's connected.

Apparently, my neighbor passed away in her sleep and was still warm when they came to certify her death. I know perfectly well who called in the cavalry. Who found her lifeless.

The people I saw going into the house opposite, I'll never say who they were. If I'm asked, I'll explain that that house is invisible from the street, that it was silent. No lawnmower, no cat, no dog, no music. No banging of shutters. That in the evening, I would glimpse a light through the tightly packed branches. So tightly packed, you'd think they'd been grafted to each other for a century. Unless it's Agnès who's asking me questions. In that case, I will answer.

11

1956

Jean! Jean! Hurry up, we'll be in trouble."

He runs toward her, gurgling with laughter. A spray of stars up into the low, dark sky. Wrapped in a coat that was once Colette's, he waddles up to her. A small green overcoat that still does the job, whether you're a girl or a boy. Jean is also wearing a red balaclava that's tight around his throat. "It's scratchy," he moans again to his sister, on the path leading to the farm. His small hand in hers, which isn't much bigger. Colette's hands with their black fingernails. The harder she scrubs them with brush and soap, the more the soil seems to sink in. At school, kids mutter "bumpkin" as she goes past. But not too loud, because Blaise de Sénéchal, the son of the marquess who owns the land farmed by Colette's parents, is three heads taller than the others. Blaise is the guardian angel who's often right behind her.

Colette is ten, Jean six. She loves this child with the spring-green eyes, fruit of the union of their parents, Robin and Georgette. A union she finds unlikely. Two ugly faces. Colette can't understand by what miracle her little brother is so beautiful. An angel who's landed in a family not his own.

Colette has but one fear, that Georgette, their mother, might fall pregnant again. She keeps as close an eye on her belly as on milk on the stove. She already has to miss school often, told she must help on the farm; with a third kid, they'd end up removing her from school for good. *A farm girl, a beast of burden, that's all I am.*

Her source of joy is her brother. And hugging the lambs until they doze off in her arms. Secretly, because there's always work to do. Always. Her hands, they're extra help, free labor. Her hands are those of the elder sister.

They never hit her. Neither the father nor the mother. But they never kiss her, either. Neither the father nor the mother. Apparently, her parents met at the July 14 dance in Gueugnon. Whenever Colette asks questions to understand—"But what was the music like? Did you dance together? How did Robin get to talk to you? What did he say?"—the mother shrugs her shoulders, blushing, and says: "Haven't you got nothing better to do? It's not with your questions that the critters and us lot'll get fed."

Haymaking in summer, sacks of spuds to lug down to the cellar before winter, helping the father push the plow pulled by the horse, Bijou. Makes your back ache like hell. The beans to be bottled, the lettuces to water, hoe, plant, weed, toss, bringing the animals in and leading them out, fifty-odd rams and ewes, helping with the milking. And all that before and after school. In the evening, as the mother's tired, Colette must "put the littl'un to bed." So it's she who watches over Jean until he falls asleep.

"Sleep, little brother, close your eyes."

"Will you tell me a story?"

"I've just told you 'Sleeping Beauty.'"

"Another story!"

Colette breathes in the smell of his neck. She senses him laughing.

"Jean, please, sleep. I still have work to do."

"You have work, Coco?"

"Yes. Coco has to help."

"A little story?"

"One last one, and then you promise? You'll close your eyes?"

"I promise. The piano?"

"Again?"

"Yes."

Colette fetches her math exercise book from her satchel. On the last two pages, Blaise has written a story, in pencil, for Jean, a short one that he particularly likes:

"There was once a tiny piano that lived in the pocket of a little boy called Jean. Every evening, the child would take the instrument out, hold it close to his ear, and listen to it improvising the most wonderful music. Jean would close his eyes and fall asleep. The music would accompany him in his dreams, and the piano would get bigger, taking up all the space as the night went on. Sumptuous sonatas lulled the nights of his childhood. But one morning, he couldn't find his piano anymore. He searched in all his pockets, but he'd lost it. He opened the sitting room door and saw his instrument. It had gotten bigger, like in his dreams, and now had pride of place in the middle of the room, black and glossy like a thoroughbred. The piano was back. But unlike the other one, it didn't play on its own. The music had to be found on the keyboard. Jean lifted the lid and began to play, randomly. It was hopeless; all he could get were sounds without harmony. His erratic fingering couldn't guide it. The sonatas were dead. But because he kept searching, practicing, listening to what the piano had to say to him, he finally found the melodies again, his melodies. And Jean became a great pianist, even greater than his piano. The two were never apart and traveled together to all the countries of the world."

Colette kisses her little brother. He's warm. Smells of milk and almonds. She leaves the room, goes to the shed. A ewe looks up at her, watching out for her lamb. The mothers know that, one day or another, human hands take their little ones from them. They are never at ease. It's the hand that feeds and that takes away. Colette buries her fingers in Bijou's mane and can feel him shiver; she kisses his shoulder.

Colette walks across the kitchen. Robin is snoring, nose buried in his newspaper, while the mother is sleeping upstairs. All the better, she thinks, it's the same every night . . . her up there, him down here. At this rate, no risk of him getting her pregnant. She pushes the lingering embers to the back of the hearth and does her homework at the table. She'd like to become a teacher. But to do that, she'd have to continue her studies after elementary school. Move on to secondary school with Blaise, keep going to the baccalauréat. And not follow the path already chosen for her, leading only to the post-elementary school certificate. The path that means that, at fourteen, you start work in a factory or stay on the farm. But her own choice seems impossible. Her parents will never allow it.

Blaise interrupts her thoughts by throwing little stones at the window. She silently joins him to wish him good night. He hands her

Bel-Ami, the novel by Maupassant. He sneaks books out of his parents' library. Colette doesn't really have time to read, barely a few minutes before dropping off, but she likes to take the words with her into that deep sleep. She hides the novel under her sweater.

"My father says that it's just for grown-ups."

Colette stifles a giggle with her hands.

"Thanks."

"See you tomorrow. Good night, my Colette."

Colette often tells Blaise that, one day, he'll be a great writer like Victor Hugo.

12

October 23, 2010

"D'you want me to come?"

"You've got school and piano, darling."

"But Mom, you can't stay all alone in Gueugnon."

"I'm not alone, sweetheart. I met up with Adèle, Hervé, and Ilyas."

"The friends in that photo in your bedroom?"

"Yes."

"They haven't moved away?"

"Not everyone leaves. Sometimes, people stay where they were born and grew up."

"What are they like now?"

"The same. They're exactly the same."

"And you still don't know where Louis is?"

"No."

"Mom, this whole story is freaky. Seriously, why did Coco do that? And why has Louis vanished? D'you think she was being pursued or threatened, like by the Mafia?"

"Ana, my aunt was a shoe-mender."

"That might have been a cover. Maybe she was a member of the secret service . . . Why didn't she tell us anything, not even us?"

" . . . "

"It's 2010 now, and I hadn't seen her since Christmas 2006, d'you remember? We did the round trip with Dad to spend Christmas Eve with her . . . And eight months later, she was dead . . . "

The mention of Pierre chills my blood.

Get a grip, Agnès, for god's sake, get a grip.

"Have you seen her?"

I mishear and think she's asking me about her father.

"Coco. Have you seen her?"

"Yes . . . yesterday, at the funeral parlor."

"How does she look?"

"Like you remember her, she hasn't changed. Maybe aged a bit, but I recognized her. There wasn't a doubt in my mind."

The first time I presented Ana to my aunt, I thought Colette was going to pass out. She was behind her key-duplicating machine. It made a terrible racket. She looked up at us, switched off the machine. Ana was in my arms, asleep, Pierre was pushing the empty baby carriage just behind us. My aunt turned paler than when Gueugnon let in a goal. I saw her eyes changing, glazing over. She took a few timid steps toward us without saying a word. She looked down at the baby, who instantly awoke, as if her great-aunt's eyes had brushed against her. Colette wiped her hands on her apron and, clearly moved, said: "She looks like Jean." It's true. Ana resembles my father. They have the same distinctive green eyes. Fringed with eyelashes so long, you'd think they were blackened with mascara.

"Would you like to hold her?" Pierre asked.

"Yes," she murmured.

She sat down on the old ottoman. The one I recognized at the house on Rue des Fredins. I placed my daughter into my aunt's arms. I'd never seen her with a baby. I remember that Pierre took a photo. I was surprised he had a camera on him; he took so few photos.

Colette watched Ana for a long while in silence, her dark, inquiring eyes lost in those of my baby. Ana fell asleep, fists clenched. Colette sat stock still. A customer came into the shop. Colette barely looked up, whispering to her to come back later. She asked Pierre to lock the door and close up shop.

When she found her voice again, it sounded younger. As if she'd drawn strength from discovering her great-niece. Then the usual questions came, like a litany: "Are you sleeping at mine? Oh, right, yes, of course, the hotel is better, more comfortable. Are you staying long? Oh, just until tomorrow, really? Of course, work. Does she sleep through the night? Jean cried a lot at first. Are you working on a new movie? Writing one? That's good, that is. Writing. Ana's a lovely name, it's your mom's name, but not written the same way. It's simple, it's really lovely when it's simple. Do you think she'll come to mine for vacations? Will you start her on the piano?"

13

1957

Blaise plays an F sharp. Jean plays the same note with his eyes closed. Whatever the note, Jean replicates it instantly.

It's hot outside. All the shutters are closed. Summer is at its height. The marquess and marchioness have gone out. Colette is helping her parents and the laborers in the fields; it's haymaking season. Since Jean is still too little for this hard work, Blaise, at Colette's request, is watching over the Septembres's youngest.

Since last spring, with Colette's help, Blaise has been sneaking Jean into the château. Apart from the servants and the Germans during the Occupation, no one gets past its walls. On hunting days, the men remain in the lodge. As for Robin and Georgette Septembre, who thoroughly disapprove of the friendship between Colette and Blaise, they would be beyond angry or ashamed if they learned that their son was playing the piano. God, how heavy human stupidity is to bear!

Blaise is teaching Jean the sound of the piano. He has just played the *Minuet in G major*, then attributed to Bach, a simple piece aimed at beginners. Jean has memorized it with eyes closed. Now, he's playing the piece flawlessly.

Blaise has never heard of absolute pitch. He read somewhere that, in 1770, the fourteen-year-old Mozart had heard Allegri's *Miserere* at the Vatican and had apparently been able to reproduce the work from memory: a work for two choirs and nine individual voices. But that was Mozart, the greatest genius of all time. For someone with absolute pitch, music is like a second language, and already, Blaise thinks Jean grasps and can master that language. It's like a kind of reincarnation. Maybe Jean was a musician in a former life? "Who on earth could believe such claptrap?" Blaise's father would say.

It had started with a radio that Blaise had given Jean and Colette for Christmas 1955. Jean had heard some musical pieces on it for the first time and hummed them back to Blaise. Intrigued, he sat Jean at the piano when his parents were away and realized that the little boy could reproduce, on the keyboard, the music he'd heard the previous day. Without ever having any lessons.

What should be done with this innate talent? The question obsesses Blaise. Keep quiet about it, or reveal it? In whom can he confide, apart from his mother? But the marchioness is afraid of her husband. What will she say when she finds out that Jean plays on the château's Steinway?

14

October 24, 2010

In just over two months, we'll be celebrating eleven years since 2000. I barely noticed them passing," I say, finishing a second glass of champagne.

We're alone, Ilyas and I. Alone at the Petit Bar, and, don't ask me why, I'm sipping champagne. It just happened, when the owner asked:

"Agnès, what can I get you?"

At first, I didn't dare ask for alcohol. Ilyas ordered:

"Water with lemon, as usual."

"And a coffee for me."

Then, without thinking, I added:

"With some champagne, please."

Vincent, the boss, went into the storeroom, saying that the last time he'd brought bubbles up from his cellar had been for a silver wedding anniversary. A group had booked the whole bar.

"Got something to celebrate?" he asked me, smiling.

"Not remotely. I just feel like being a bit tipsy."

"I couldn't care less about time passing," Ilyas declares. "For me, it stopped in the changing rooms of a stadium when I was seven."

"What d'you mean?"

"Charpie, remember?"

"No. What's Charpie?"

"A director. He had no business being in the changing rooms, but I can tell you, he spent a lot of time in the boys' showers. He got an eyeful over three generations, frequently. Not to mention the inner thighs and balls he'd fiddle with on Wednesday afternoons."

". . ."

"He was brazen about it. A medical check-up, so he said. And he'd leave with a kid. Alone with a kid."

"Shit, that's horrendous. Was he arrested?"

"Never. It was hushed up. Charpie was a bigwig, a director at the factory. An influential man. He was protected. And the children said nothing. Boys, what's more, so you can imagine . . . He finally cleared off, from one day to the next, like a thief in the night, to settle in the South of France. Where, apparently, he started up all over again."

"Someone must report him."

"He's dead. May God never rest his soul. You don't report the dead. You bury them."

"The Nazis, even the dead ones, were reported, Ilyas. Even judged in court."

"What's the point?"

"Why did you say that time stopped when you were seven? What did he do to you?"

"Can we move on? Like, hey, what did you do to bring in the year 2000?"

"How on earth can we move on, Ilyas? It's appalling, what you're saying. Why did you never tell me before?"

"Do you know many victims who actually speak out? And then, I was the handy Arab. Can you imagine if my parents and sisters had found out about it? They might have shipped me back to North Africa . . . But life goes on. Look, I've gone on. So have you. We've all gone on. Hey, I really loved your last movie!"

"That was ages ago."

"Doesn't matter, movies are the only things that never grow old. When a movie's good, it stays good for eternity."

I gaze at him and find him handsome.

"Why did you stay here?"

"Here or elsewhere . . . I have my part-time job at the factory. A nice pad. Not huge, but nice. You must come see it. A bit of a garden for barbecues. My motorbike, a Méhari jeep, my pals. A chick every now and then. I've got it all."

He hands me a fob before getting up.

"The key to my Méhari, it's parked outside. It's yellow. You can't miss it. Keep it, I don't need it, and you can't spend your life here calling taxis or walking for kilometers on end."

"What about you?"

"I've got my motorbike."

He plants a kiss on my hair.

"I'm off to work. See you . . . "

"What was his real name, that Charpie?"

"I'm not uttering his name ever again."

15

October 24, 2010

Do I go back to Paris, or do I stay on a few more days? I'd so like to search the Fredins house. Stretch out and doze off within its walls. Dream about my aunt. Hear her talking to me in my sleep. Find notes she might have left for me. I need to understand; it's visceral. How did she live her final years? Did she try to contact me? Did she want to protect herself, or protect someone else?

I drove to the cemetery in the yellow Méhari. Dad loved these jeeps. I understand why. There's something poetic and nostalgic about them. Like a Chopin sonata. My father didn't live long enough to buy himself one.

I'm in front of the grave of the unknown person. Who lies within it? The blue shoes are still there. Not even damaged by the passing years, the inclement weather. Like new. Like Ilyas's face. So handsome. I keep thinking about what he confided in me. What did that monster do to him? Why only talk about it now?

My cellphone vibrates in my pocket, an unknown number; I answer it. Nathalie Grandjean, the journalist from the *Journal de Saône-et-Loire*, wants to see me. I suggest the Petit Bar in an hour.

"You're staying at the Monge?"

"Yes."

"Then I'd prefer to meet there; it'll be quieter for us."

My name is Agnès Dugain, née Septembre. I'm the daughter of Hannah Ruben, violinist, and Jean Septembre, pianist. I've kept the surname of my ex-husband, Pierre Dugain. Officially, to keep my professional name, unofficially, to piss off his new partner. I was born on

October 22, 1972. Now it's 2010, I've just had my thirty-eighth birthday, I have a fifteen-year-old daughter. At the ballot box, my heart has always tilted left. I believe in God.

I could say that my ex-husband was an actor, magnificent and mercurial. That I loved him madly and don't love him at all anymore, when in fact he's neither magnificent nor mercurial, and I still love him. Pierre is incredibly charming, what our daughter calls "the charm of intelligence." I no longer have a mother or father. My aunt has just died for the second time. I haven't written a word for months, I've drawn a blank. The white page. No desire at all anymore to direct movies, put on makeup, get a team together, some co-authors, nothing to say, no need. I'm alone. Divorced. I feel as if I don't have any desires anymore. As if I loved too much, so much, so badly that I've used up all my emotional capital. That my heart is worn out and full of holes, like an old pair of jeans on a stand at the Saint-Ouen flea market. That I only aspire to be alone and talk to a passing dog, a stray cat, to the birds in the sky, or to a ladybug that mistakenly lands on my sweater.

I've directed five movies, including a short. My first feature film garnered what's known as unanimous approval. Five Césars, two Oscar nominations in the Best Foreign Language Film and Best Original Screenplay categories, three Golden Globe nominations, among other accolades. I went all around the world with *Le Banquet des anciens*—The Banquet of the Elders. My ex-husband had one of the main parts; he played the favorite son. He was marvelous. Subtle. Very moving. He won five international Best Actor awards.

In *Le Banquet des anciens*, the action takes place over one day, from ten in the morning to seven in the evening, as four generations of the same family gather around a table to celebrate the birthday of its oldest member. I could have called it *Un dimanche à la campagne*—A Sunday in the Country—like the wonderful movie by Bertrand Tavernier, but that title was already taken.

The weather had to be good; I filmed in June, in the area around Giverny.

Naturally, lots of Bach (my parents' favorite composer). My movie begins on a clear morning. "Looks like fine weather." Everyone gazes up at the sky. Verdant countryside surrounds them. Waiters fuss around the large table, some instructions given by the "old man," and his wife like a shadow behind him, breathing the air that he breathes, seeming nice but isn't. Being oppressed can make one monstrous. And then the family gradually arrives, cars are parked in front of the house. At a distance, too. Seeing where people park is crucial. The way people position themselves to stay or leave, even escape.

Each person, child, nephew, cousin, arrives at the table, delighted or constrained, trying to get a particular caress or a glance from the "old man," all dragging their faults and their wounds with them, happy to meet up again but, inevitably, afraid of being assessed, of feeling judged. The children scuttle off to be together and finally laugh, smoke, talk of their loneliness, of the loneliness of their parents, whom they no longer admire; and, around the table, with the help of alcohol, voices rise, then fall, and there's some singing—Charles Trenet, Jean-Jacques Goldman, Jane Birkin, and Jean Ferrat. A few speeches are made, emotions loop the loop. The landing can be happy, funny, failed, or miserable.

Aperitifs, appetizers, mains, crystal glasses, red wines, carafes, bunches of pink and white peonies, cake. "Happy Birthday" sung by everyone: out of the five weeks, I spent one filming each face singing it, the expression, the look in the eyes. Coffees, sepia-stained tablecloths, the presentation of gifts.

At the time, I was compared to Jane Campion. "The French Jane Campion" was the headline in several newspapers. That really made me laugh. Why not the French Michael Jackson? Human beings are always compared. Put into boxes, drawers, types. All the same, thanks to that movie, I was able to find the financing to make others. I was courted. I had the most wonderful time, I worked relentlessly with Pierre. We discussed things together, I wrote for him, he was my source of inspiration. We shared everything. House, love, work, our adored child, vacations, plans. He made me laugh and made love to me. He didn't look at other women, but other women looked at him. Had looked at him for years. Increasingly frequently, we were going up on stage to receive awards, me in divine black dresses lent for the occasion, him in elegant tuxes. We'd "made it," as they say.

And my husband was funny, too. Not only with me, naturally; when you're funny, it's with everyone. It's second nature. With his dark, intense gaze, his sardonic, but never disdainful, smile, he became irresistible. And me, I was tired. That's the price of success: the terror, ever increasing and oppressive, of having nothing left to say. What am I going to convey in the next movie? That feeling of serving up the same soup.

Among the other women that my husband didn't look at, there was one who did more than look at him; she threw herself at him. She smelled nice, she was gentle and sugar-sweet. She desired, she prompted desire. And he, being easy-going, went along with it, at first to know, to understand, to taste someone else. He'd known almost only me, despite our age difference. When there's space for someone else, it means there's space, period.

After that first time, he swapped pastries pretty swiftly, desserts at any rate, swapped lives. He moved in with her. Ana spends every other week at their place, and half the vacations, too. And that's how a good cake fucked up my life. But then, I'm actually the type who thinks that you fuck up your own life, all by yourself. That it's never the fault of the other one, the loved one. You can't be constantly vigilant. Otherwise, life would be like some hideous dictatorship.

16

October 24, 2010

I went by the public records office—Noëlle Pic works there now, don't know if you remember her—and I asked her to check whether, by any chance, your aunt had a twin sister. She was born in 1946, just after the war, and babies were sometimes separated back then, to have fewer mouths to feed."

Sitting in front of me, Nathalie Grandjean hasn't changed. Hasn't gained a gram or a wrinkle. She has swapped her teen gear—ripped jeans and grunge tees—for a blue flannel suit. A tall redhead with pale skin and square shoulders, she's clutching a small notebook and, like Lieutenant Columbo, frantically writing down her own observations, since, so far, she hasn't asked me a single question. She smells of Elnett hairspray, like my mother used to. When Nathalie arrived at the Monge and kissed me, I felt dizzy. The smell reminded me of Mom before her concerts. Just before joining the orchestra onstage, she'd spray her hair with it, making it look like nylon and stiffen under my fingers. She'd say: "Agnès, stop it, you'll mess up my hair." And as soon as she turned her back, violin and bow in hand, I'd linger in the musicians' dressing room and spray some onto my own hair. It would stiffen my knots. I've always had long and tangled hair. Much as Mom would brush it every morning and evening, there were always shrieks. And when I'd go to my aunt's, Mom would threaten to chop it off on my return if I didn't keep it untangled. I was terrified at the thought of having short hair, of being mistaken for a boy. Then she'd say to my aunt: "Please, Colette, a detangling shampoo every three days."

Nathalie turns a few pages of her notebook and reads out loud:

"Colette Septembre, born February 7, 1946; Jean Septembre, born March 7, 1950. No trace of twins."

Instead of responding, I blurt out:

"You stole my sweetheart."

She has no idea what I'm on about.

"Jacques Daubel, one day at the pool, you kissed each other behind my back."

I can see her thinking about it, the memory coming back to her, it shows in her eyes. Her in a red two-piece swimsuit, him in navy-blue trunks with three green stripes down the side. Her with the toned body of a swimmer, milky skin, taller than him; him with golden, glossy skin like a caramel choux bun. They're in the shade, behind the building where we'd buy candies and ice cream. They'd rested their cones on the wall, the raspberry ran onto the plaster, a small pool of blood. Now Nathalie is turning bright red.

"That's ancient history," she mutters.

"It's never ancient history when it comes to betrayal."

"Agnès, are you joking now?"

". . ."

"You mean Hervé's cousin? The show-off with the motorbike?"

"Yes."

"How old were we?"

"The age for kissing. Thirteen. Summer 1985. I thought I was going to die when I saw the two of you."

". . ."

"Did you know I was going out with him?"

"Yes," she admits, without batting an eyelid.

"That evening, I was devastated, in tears, when I got home, and my aunt really spoke to me for the first time. So thank you."

She closes her notebook, uncomfortable but reassured. I'm not about to give her a hiding.

"I wrote my first screenplay with that story. Three adolescents at a swimming pool. A handsome boy, a beautiful girl, and a shadow, a skinny kid. I set it at the pool in L'Isle-Adam. D'you fancy something to eat? I'm hungry."

I get up without waiting for her reply and find the person who looks after bookings and any orders when the restaurant isn't open. A young, very thin woman with a long braid down her back, relatively disagreeable, who rolls panicked eyes at the smallest request. As if ordering a tea or a glass of wine was wildly eccentric.

I return to Nathalie in the hotel hall's tiny salon; she hasn't moved. Like a porcelain doll propped there, on the edge of the sofa.

"I loved your last movie," she tells me.

"That was ages ago."

"How long?"

"Four years."

"Are you making another one?"

"No. In your opinion, who is buried instead of my aunt?"

"You'll have to dig into her past to find out."

"Into whose past?"

"Your aunt's."

"I'd like to, but I can't enter her last residence."

"Why not?"

"There's going to be an inquest. Access is prohibited."

She reopens her notebook to jot something down.

"Are you married?"

"I live with my female partner. Since the swimming pool, things have become clearer. Guys aren't my thing."

"Oh, shit, so I really was unlucky back then."

We burst into laughter at the same time.

"I've thought of something. Since you work at the newspaper, would you be able to find Colette's death notice? The one from three years ago."

"Of course. Would you like me to write an article about the double death of your aunt?"

"Yes. An article could loosen some tongues . . . or not. We'll see."

From the very next day, Nathalie's article was picked up on the *Parisien/Aujourd'hui en France* website. And magazines of the *Détective* kind embroidered it, imagining a body-snatching scenario. My aunt, so discreet, who spoke quietly so as not to disturb anyone, who never made any noise, even when pulling out a chair, my aunt, so careful, who seemed to walk, and generally move, in silence, would've hated all of this. Well, I think so. She must have known, all the same, that her second death wouldn't go unnoticed. Even if, according to her, what went on in Gueugnon stayed in Gueugnon. "Apart from a few players, no one's heard of us," she'd often say. Or maybe she thought she'd die later.

When a certain sector of the press learned that "the woman who died three years ago" was related to Pierre and Agnès Dugain, the famous actor and the director, a sidebar appeared in a tabloid. In the column called "*Pas glop*"—Not cool—with a very old photo of me and Pierre to illustrate three lines: "They discover that a dead member of the family wasn't actually dead. But who's hiding in the tomb? It's enough to make your flesh crawl and prompt a new screenplay."

17

1958

Colette has seen ewes lambing since forever. She helps them when the lambs are awkwardly positioned. She gets hold of the little one, turns it around and pulls it toward life. Births are part of her everyday routine.

As she walks along the corridors of the maternity hospital, she remembers Jean's birth eight years ago. The mother's cries. Her contorted features, the redness of the cheeks, that of pain, the blue veins under the bulging eyes. She was four years old when Jean was born—at the farm, not in this kind of hospital, with its clean, white walls. She can see herself passing towels to the midwife while her father boiled some water. She wonders why all those towels and liters of water. With animals, no need for all that gear.

She watches the gestures of the woman leaning between Georgette's thighs. They're all in the parents' bedroom, a dirty room that Colette never usually enters. The expulsion. The baby's coming.

"Push, Georgette! Push!"

Colette stands at the back of the room, the better to see the midwife delivering the mother's baby.

The baby is crying. A lamb never cries when it sees the ewe. It calls out to her. She licks it. Colette gazes at the slimy blue form.

"He'll be called Jean, like my father," Robin whispers.

A neighbor has just arrived. She takes the baby and plunges him into a bowl of fresh water. Out of the shit and blood, Jean appears. Handsome and hearty. Colette is at once overwhelmed and filled with wonder. A little brother. Robin is beside himself when faced with the baby. The joy in his eyes: it's a boy.

"My son."

That was eight years ago.

What Colette had dreaded had finally happened: Georgette's belly had started to swell. The blow of a third child that dashed any hope of going to high school. The sentence was pronounced: after elementary school, just the certificate. It was inevitable. She hadn't dared voice her desire to teach.

Danièle, the little sister, is born on March 13, 1958, not at home but in a maternity hospital. Upon pushing open the door, Colette finds her in a white room. The baby is already washed, dressed, in a cot, her little pink fists side by side, her eyes closed. This little princess-like sister seems modern to her. Not born in the same century as her and Jean. She's wearing new pajamas. The mother is dozing. Jean grips Colette's hand.

"She's called Danièle," she tells him.

"Danièle," Jean repeats, touching the baby with his fingertips.

"Want to give her a kiss?"

"Yes."

He plants a kiss on Danièle's temple.

"She stinks," he whispers in Colette's ear. She bursts out laughing.

The mother wakes up, the baby starts to moan, and Robin, the father, immediately ushers the children out with a firm hand.

"Gotta leave yer mother and the littl'un in peace."

All three of them climb into the truck. All three in front.

Gradually, Colette can feel the anger rising up inside her. Something really intense. She tries breathing into her little brother's hair, but something bursts because, with a rage unknown from the one who never makes a fuss, she blurts out:

"I want to stay on at school."

The father, behind the wheel, looks at her as if she wasn't talking to him. Stubbornly, she says it again:

"I want to stay on at school. Anyhow, it's compulsory."

The father finally reacts, realizing that his daughter's words are addressed to him:

"You'll do like me," he says, without anger or sadness, "you're the right age to help yer parents."

"I'm not you."

"Is that how you speak to yer father?"

"It isn't inevitable."

"What's that mean?"

"Like fate."

"School's putting ideas into yer head . . . and that Sénéchal son is, too. You talk like some book, and I ain't got time, everyone's gotta be fed now there's the littl'un. You're the eldest, you'll work like everyone else."

Colette swallows her tears. She knew it would happen. She knew that this new child spelled the end for her. That a birth can mean that, at the same time, someone else dies. On the day the new lamb is born, its older sibling has already gone to the abattoir.

18

October 25, 2010

I have the privilege of having a fairy who manages everything at home, for whom nothing is ever a problem, and whom I love. Apparently, that's not the done thing; everyone must stay in their place, employer, employee. But me, I love her, because Cornélia *is* my home.

When Ana started school, Cornélia should have left us. She's a trained pediatric nurse. We solved the problem. She became my personal nanny. Why shouldn't an adult be allowed to have one?

Ordering paper, printer ink, making medical appointments, doing tax returns. Preparing meals when I'm away, vacuuming and loading the washing machine. Cornélia is my fairy tale, she manages daily life like a Mary Poppins. A daily life that, until four years ago, was just made up of work, writing, rereading, filming, editing, location-finding, and traveling.

When I was abroad or away on business, Cornélia would sleep at the house. I'm not traveling anymore, but she has her room close to Ana's. She sleeps there whenever she wants to. No one's waiting for her back at her place. She was married, badly, and has a son who lives in Belgium. She goes to visit him regularly. For a few months now, I think she's had a lover, but she remains secretive. I tease her: "Cornélia, who are you all made-up for? Cornélia, who's that new dress for? Cornélia, why are you humming, have you got a date?" She cracks up laughing, but doesn't answer. I think she's too tactful to tell me about her happiness. She's mistaken; her happiness would do me so much good.

To simplify our lives, since our return to Paris, I've been renting an apartment for her two buildings away from the one I share with Ana.

We live in Montmartre, above the Villa des Abbesses restaurant, top floor. Her father and "the other one" chose the Marais neighborhood.

I've decided to return to Paris for a few days; I feel like being back with Ana, Cornélia, in my own room, with the scent of the candles in the sitting room, in my own kitchen. I need to wash my clothes and to reflect while hanging it to dry in the laundry room. There's no housework to do at a hotel. That's what depresses me most about hotels.

I parked the Méhari outside the station and jumped on a train. It's all happened too fast. All I can think about now is my aunt. The enigmatic way she'd look up at me when I'd enter the shoe-repair shop. Was she happy to see me? Did she want to kiss me? Speak to me? Say things to me that she never said?

As I open the door to my apartment, I hear voices that sound familiar, including Cornélia's, and when I find her sitting beside Louis Berthéol on my sofa, I think I'm hallucinating. It's not possible. My aunt's Louis beside my Cornélia. I'm stunned. They'd never met. Two of my worlds brought together.

"But Louis, I've been searching everywhere for you over the past four days!"

He stands up and walks toward me.

"The other morning, when I saw that she was dead . . . I called the gendarmes. And then I left."

He bursts into tears. Cornélia now stands up and lays a hand on his shoulder.

"So you're the one who informed them?"

"I'm going to make some tea," Cornélia breaks in, kissing me on her way. "Are you okay, sweetie? You're looking a bit rough. Been drinking, or what?"

"Like a fish. Have you heard?"

"Heard what?"

"About my aunt."

"Yes. Nana and Louis told me."

Cornélia has always called Ana "Nana." The first time she saw my three-month-old baby, she said to her, "*Comme tu es jolie, petite nana.*"—How pretty you are, little lady.

At the mention of my aunt, Cornélia crosses herself. Since when has Cornélia crossed herself? It's the first time in fifteen years I've seen her make this religious sign.

"Cornélia, where's Ana?"

"At school. Where else would she be?"

I sit on the sofa, and Louis joins me.

I feel as if what I've been living through for the past four days is unreal. Like when I would confuse what was happening in my movies with reality. I think back to Adèle's words, "for all that the truth can tell us."

"Louis, there's a lot you need to tell me."

I want to give him a hug and to knock his block off. How can he have made me believe that Colette died three years ago? How can he have given me her belongings in a cardboard box while looking me straight in the eye? Why had he hidden her in that house?

"That's what I'm here for," he whispers.

He indicates something to me with his eyes. I turn my head and instantly recognize Colette's big suitcase, standing in the hall. It was stored in her shop, beside the hammers. Took up too much space in the cupboards of her house. Its only journey had been from goodness knows where to a dusty shelf, from which it never moved again. When Colette would go to away matches with the club, in the supporters' coach, they would never sleep the night there. They came home after matches. I wonder where that piece of luggage originally came from, I'd never asked the question. I ask it now, out loud:

"Where did it come from, that suitcase?"

Louis could reply to me: "From the shoe-repair shop," but he understands and comes straight out with it:

"It's the only thing she took when she left the farm. And the worst of it is that, apart from the hope and the toothbrush she threw inside it, it was empty. Her mother refused to let her take her clothes."

"Why?"

"They had to be kept for Jean and, even more, for Danièle, the little sister . . . Now . . . what's inside the suitcase now is for you."

I can't move. Can't get a single word out anymore. What am I so scared of?

Cornélia is back with some cups and a teapot.

"Do you take sugar, Louis?"

"No thanks. I don't drink much tea," he says, apologetically, tugging on his shirtsleeves as if they were too short.

"Would you like something else?"

"No, that'll be fine, that'll be fine."

Cornélia looks at me, concerned.

"Why are you so pale?"

Now it's my turn to indicate the suitcase with my eyes.

"What's inside it?" she asks, anxiously, staring at Louis.

"Cassettes. Lots of cassettes. And your thingy, y'know."

"What thingy?" I finally manage to say.

"You used to make cassettes with the other kids, you'd all mess about with that thingy. And then it went out of fashion, after that you had your camera, y'know. You were forever filming us."

"My camcorder?"

"Yes, and the thingy, you left it at your aunt's. And she, well, she carried on."

"Carried on?"

"Recording. Everything. People, birds, her wee garden in summer. 'I listen at night, Louis,' she'd say. Sometimes, she'd record the matches, she carried her thingy around everywhere. She'd say to me: 'Speak, Louis, go on, speak into it.' But I had nothing to say. 'Everyone has something to say," she'd reply. And she'd speak into it for hours, all alone. Like some ninnyhammer."

"What's a ninnyhammer?" Cornélia asks.

"Someone with bats in the belfry."

Cornélia remains silent. Louis notices her bafflement. He tries again:

"Someone a bit crazy, y'know . . . One day, her thingy, it broke down. Colette, she became like a person possessed. A bit like that Madeleine."

"Who's 'that Madeleine'?" Cornélia asks, again.

This time, it's me who answers:

"She's a lady who'd wander the streets of Gueugnon alone, in her slippers. She wore a stained nightdress under a grimy old overcoat.

She talked to herself. As kids, we were scared of her, so we'd snigger stupidly when she went past. People said she could fly into mad rages. I think that was untrue. And I still feel bad about it. She didn't smell great. The storekeepers, the mocking sort, would open the doors wide after she'd been in their store, to air the place out. She'd play at being a customer, like kids play store, she'd pretend to be interested in different items on display without ever buying a thing. She owned nothing. I remember her so clearly, her features, her fine hair, her gentle face, an elderly child's face, she was heartbreaking. Sometimes, she'd swipe some fruit from Ilyas's father's stall, and he'd pretend not to notice. Occasionally, she'd come into the shoe-repair shop; she'd gaze at the tins of polish, murmuring inaudible words. My aunt would say to her: 'How are you today?', and Madeleine wasn't able to answer her, or even look at her. I wonder if she was really called Madeleine, or if people had just decided to call her that. She lived in her own world. I seem to recall that she stayed at her sister's. A woman who resembled her like a twin but was 'normal.' With smart clothes, a job, a car, a house. One day, I saw her and was flabbergasted. Like another version of the wandering one, of Madeleine's solitude. A restored version. I realized that I preferred the first one, the original, more poetic, one."

Louis nods in agreement.

"The thingy had to be mended, urgently. I had the right person at hand. A nephew who knows his way around those machines. It was just a 'winding problem,' so he told me."

"The thing you're calling a 'thingy,' that was my recorder, Louis. A cassette recorder."

"Yes, that's it."

This Louis says like someone accused of a crime finally confessing. Then he continues:

"What's more, she had a hell of a job finding new cassettes. Haven't been around for a long time. All got chucked out at one stage. About ten years ago, one of Colette's customers came across a box of around a hundred new cassettes in a dumpster. Invaluable stock. Invaluable only to Colette. They were C-120s, that I do remember! 'Two hours of recording, Louis,' she'd say, 'one hour on each side.'"

"That makes twelve thousand minutes of recording."

"How d'you know that, Cornélia?" I ask.

"Well, I can count: a hundred cassettes of two hours, that makes two hundred hours. So, twelve thousand minutes."

"But those cassettes, did Colette use them?"

Louis again indicates the suitcase with his eyes.

"They're inside that?"

"Yes," he whispers.

"All of them?"

"Yes."

"Are you telling me that my aunt, the most taciturn person I've ever come across in my life, has recorded . . . how many minutes, Cornélia?"

"Twelve thousand."

"Twelve thousand minutes' worth of tape?"

"Yes. Even a bit more."

"A bit more?"

"Yes."

"Why did she do that?"

"For you."

" . . . "

"She'd say it was for you."

He's crying again, and repeats:

"I'm sorry, I'm sorry . . . *je m'excuse . . .* "

And I recall my French teacher in eleventh grade, Madame Petit, who'd once retorted to a pupil who'd said "*Je m'excuse*" for being late: "Well, if you excuse yourself, I've nothing more to say."

But why am I thinking of my teacher? Why does my mind take me elsewhere when I'm facing a situation that's terrifying me?

"I picked them up the other morning," Louis says, sniffing into a handkerchief. "Didn't want the police to come across them."

"But what on earth are you telling me, Louis? What on earth are you telling me?"

He hangs his head.

"Why didn't you tell me that she was alive?! Why?! Why did she make me think she was dead?! Three years of lies! Three years of silence!"

"I merely respected what your aunt wanted."
"But what did she want?"
"Go and see Jacques Pieri."
"Doctor Pieri?"
"Yes. It's him who signed the death certificate."

19

October 28, 2010

It's been three days since I returned to Paris, three days that Colette's suitcase has been sleeping at the foot of my bed. I haven't opened it. It would be like opening Pandora's box. I'm scared. It's massive. Dizzying. It's her. It's for me.

Ana is off to Mauritius for a three-week vacation with her father and the other one. During this abyssal absence, I've decided to go back to Gueugnon. Back to childhood to listen to the recordings. I need to do it over there. Where I was close to my aunt.

Twelve thousand minutes, which apparently equates to eight days of listening. One thousand four hundred and forty minutes in twenty-four hours, Cornélia calculated. That must be about eight days and eight nights. I don't know, Cornélia, I don't know, I've never been able to count.

The gendarme Cyril Rampin phoned me; I'm now allowed into the house on Rue des Fredins. I'm going to stay there, and if I get spooked, I'll call Ilyas. Colette Septembre died from a cardiac arrest in her sleep. *Aunt Colette, your heart stopped. Why? What, or whom, were you dreaming about?*

I'll receive a burial permit soon, since I'm the closest living relative. *But before organizing your funeral, I want to see Dr. Pieri.* I'm seeing him tomorrow at his office in Gueugnon. I phoned a secretary to make an appointment, without introducing myself.

"We're not taking any new patients," she told me, unpleasantly.

"I'm not a patient. I'm Colette Septembre's niece and I have some questions to ask him."

"I don't know if that will be possible; his schedule is full."

"Well I *am* sure it will be possible, seeing as he signed a death certificate for my aunt three years ago, when she was still alive. I'm coming tomorrow morning at 10."

And I hung up.

*

I had my attorney stand in for me at the conciliatory hearings for the divorce. It was explained to me that not showing up would complicate the division of property, but I didn't give a damn, I wanted nothing. Not compensation, not alimony . . . Nothing. March 23, 2009, 11:30 A.M., the seventh arrondissement court. Family division. It was raining. It was cold. A rubbish spring. To justify my absence, the attorney said it was due to circumstances beyond my control. I had just been admitted to the ER. And didn't wish to postpone the hearing. At six in the morning, I'd turned up at Bichat hospital bent double, claiming to have unbearable pains in the stomach, or kidneys, or thorax, you choose. My pain really was unbearable. I could have banged my head against all the walls, but my vital signs were good, my blood pressure and heartbeat okay, an ultrasound normal. No presence of poison in the blood. And me, I was still doubled up, in tears, under the dubious gaze of the doctor. A broken heart.

"You're sure you haven't suffered an emotional shock?"

At this question, a violent spasm made me heave, and I vomited all over his sneakers. I now had the right to written proof for the court: "We are keeping this patient under observation; she also seems confused." When the nurse gave me a morphine drip, I could have kissed her. I gently floated, until I was finally thrown out.

"Everything is fine, madame, everything is normal."

Everything is normal except me.

I don't want to see Pierre anymore. He's supposed to be collecting Ana, here, at our home, any minute now. He left me no choice: "We'll pick her up in our taxi, it's on the way to the airport." Cornélia told him the code and the floor. She's the one who deals with him, never me. I shut myself away in my study. I should have gone out for a quick walk before he arrived. Now it's too late. The worst thing would be bumping into him on the stairs.

The bell rings; I hear Cornélia opening the door. Churning stomach. But why, when I haven't seen this man for months, does he still have this tsunami-like effect on me? Pierre is my disaster. I allow him to be my disaster. Since this morning, I've been working at my desk. Answering emails, invitations: "I won't be attending, I'm away, currently abroad" . . . For the past half-hour, I've not moved.

From the sound of Cornélia's voice, I can hear that something abnormal is going on. I rush to the hall and find myself face to face with Audrey Tudor. My ex-husband's new pastry, who stammers that she's come to fetch Ana. Ana, my daughter. Audrey Tudor, actress. An appalling chill descends on the apartment. *So you're not embarrassed, turning up here, babe. You've got a nerve.* But right now, it's me who's struggling to breathe. In a cloud of Guerlain perfume, dressed all in red, headband holding back dark hair, eyes and mouth made up, she looks like a doll with features drawn by Raphael or Renoir, I can't decide. She looks better than her age, ten years younger than me.

Ana appears, holding her traveling bag. We bought it together at Monoprix; it's navy blue. I'd wanted to buy her the same one but in pink. "Oh no, Mom, not pink, Barbie's *so* over." She's in jeans and sneakers, free, frank, fifteen, a touch of gloss on the lips.

"I thought Dad was supposed to pick you up," I say, a hint of annoyance in my voice, when I'm actually holding back my rage.

An ocean of rage. Inside my head, it's *The Shining*. As I hear myself saying that to Ana, I know she's the one who'll feel uncomfortable. The other one, in red, couldn't care less. And Cornélia's mind is elsewhere. Thinking of "her little girl's" vacation, off to swim with dolphins. I hate myself for being such an idiot. For holding my child hostage.

"Right, I'm off," my daughter says, with a nervous smile.

Ana kisses Cornélia, who whispers, "Happy vacation, my Nana," in her ear. I hug Ana tight.

"Enjoy, enjoy, enjoy, love you, love you, love you. Will you call me from time to . . .?

"Yes, Mom."

The pastry greets my daughter with a kiss. I feel hatred. Feel like beating her up. Her mouth on Ana's cheek. Fuck, I'm going to die. But my parents brought me up well. So I keep my mouth shut, squint my eyes to conjure a fake smile, which can't look great.

"Happy vacation."

Once I hear them walking down the stairs, I burst into tears and throw myself into Cornélia's arms.

"I've messed up my life!"

"How old are you again?"

"Thirty-eight."

"So what d'you mean?"

"Thirty-eight. I still love Pierre. Pierre is the man of my life. And he's going off with our daughter and the other one. Their bedroom will be beside our daughter's. It's unbearable."

"Yes," Cornélia says, "it is unbearable. But you'll have to bear it. For yourself and for Nana."

20

October 30, 2010

Get on the train at Gare de Lyon. Get off at Le Creusot-TGV. Just one turn of the key and the Méhari starts. When Colette died in 2007, I was sure I'd only ever return to Gueugnon to visit her grave. Thought my LA-Burgundy flights would be few and far between. I didn't know she wanted to be laid to rest close to my parents rather than at the Jean-Laville stadium, which is clearly visible from the cemetery. Some round trips from time to time, diminishing over the years.

When she died in 2007, I was sure I'd live the rest of my life with the father of my daughter in the States. That we'd continue making movies together until our golden years. We'd dream of Italy, too. Of moving close to Naples. Our years didn't get the time to turn golden. We sold the lovely house and pool, and the bougainvillea that came with them. I settled back into an apartment in Paris. And now here I am, parked outside the medical office on Gueugnon's Rue Danton, to have a few words with Dr. Pieri. Colette's suitcase and mine on the worn-out back seat.

Before getting out, I listen again to Ana's message, just to hear her voice: "Momma, I've arrived, it's dreamy, so, so beautiful, love you."

It's strange. Whenever Ana is with her father, she has lunch and supper with *them*. Breathes the same air as *them*. But knowing she's on vacation with "the other one" torments me. The thought that she dips her ass in the Indian Ocean with my daughter beside her destroys me.

As I enter the medical office, no chance to be greeted by the sour secretary; I come face to face with Captain Rampin.

"Good day, Madame Dugain. Are you well?"

"I've come to talk to Dr. Pieri. It's him who signed my aunt's death certificate three years ago."

"His secretary informed me. You can't investigate for me."

"But . . . "

"The inquiry is ongoing. Shall I drive you to Rue des Fredins?"

"No thanks, I've got my car . . . I'm not allowed to talk to the doctor?"

"It's preferable to wait."

He ushers me to the door and then reappears beside me.

"I'll wait outside the house to give you the keys."

He makes sure I get into my car and then sets off in his own vehicle to follow me. The cops are tailing me like I'm a wanted criminal. I can't help laughing out loud, despite the situation; I'd rather like to be wanted, at least that would mean someone's interested in me.

I drive through the deserted streets. I think of Louis Berthéol, who appeared on my sofa only to disappear again, of Colette's suitcase he'd placed in the hall. Since then, he's been on voicemail. He had warned us, Cornélia and me, that he was going traveling for a few days.

When I asked him what my aunt had lived on for the past three years, with what money, he told me that her stuffed "woolen stocking" was no myth. And that in 2002, she'd changed around ten thousand francs into euros every month. For just over a year. The banker on the Rue de la Liberté, who was very fond of her, had turned a blind eye. She also did some sewing for a store. "It kept her busy, she liked that, still feeling useful. Colette had worked all her life." She would make curtains and do all kinds of alterations. It was Louis who would pick up the garments, fabric, measurements, and patterns from a workshop on the edge of town, bring them to Colette in her "hideout," and then deliver them to the store once the work was complete. It was all paid for in cash. No one asked any questions, the finish was impeccable.

It's crazy how organized her disappearance had been. She could have lived like that for much longer without anyone knowing except Louis. I wonder whether she ever went out, for a walk, to visit the cemetery.

I park in front of the "hideout."

The trees surrounding the house seem to have grown even taller.

The neighbor opposite lifts a curtain and waves at me. I must go and visit her. Captain Rampin tells me that they went right around the neighborhood, and no one knew that Madame Septembre lived here.

"Not even the lady who lives opposite?"

"She moved in recently. And she'd have needed a crane to see what was going on inside."

Cyril Rampin gives me some duplicate keys.

"For the big door on the street and the house door. The small key is for the garden shed."

"There's no mailbox here."

"No. We found neither letters nor junk mail."

"Not having a mailbox, that's not existing."

Silence intrudes for a few seconds.

"If there's the slightest problem, don't hesitate to call me."

I loathe his paternalistic tone. I see him off and close the heavy door behind me. The moment I turn the key, and the house releases a smell of mustiness, coldness, and bleach, I can't understand what I'm doing here. It's a bad idea to sleep here, in the house of a dead woman. Would've been wiser to book a room at the Monge and come here for the day. In fact, I probably should've listened to the cassettes at home, in Paris, with Cornélia nearby. I'm making nothing but bad decisions. My daughter's swimming with dolphins, her father's slathering suncream on "the other one," and me, I'll be spending the week in a sordid little house.

I must stop feeling sorry for myself, quit being hard on myself. I must summon up the joyful strength I used to have. That joy that was part of me for so long. And that anger that made me swear like a trooper, I must get that back, too. *Sort yourself out, for fuck's sake Agnès, sort yourself out.* I can't have lost everything. What was inside me must surely still be there. Just like my eyes, hands, mouth, stomach. Nothing's changed. I can't be empty. I must put some music on. Open the windows, throw everything into the washing machine. Must scour the tiles. Must talk to my aunt. Out loud, before listening to her voice on the cassettes.

I have the strange feeling of having arrived at a disappointing vacation rental. What else did I expect, choosing to stay here?

Come on, once it's aired, the house won't be too far from the sea anymore. I dash out to the mini market to buy the cleaning products I'm used to, wine, apricot juice, sparkling water, rice, sweetcorn, three tomatoes, balsamic vinegar, a bag of chips, and candles.

When I get back, I find a pot of vegetable soup on the doormat. With this note, "From the neighbor at No. 21," scribbled on a scrap of paper. That's the lady I saw earlier. And what if the soup were poisoned? Ridiculous. I'll go and thank her later. I do two hours of cleaning in a house that wasn't dirty, but seems to be getting its color back, all the same.

I take my inflatable mattress out of my suitcase. An antediluvian thing. Pierre and I would keep it in the back of the car and inflate it when we stopped somewhere in the wilds to spend the night or have a nap. We made love on it so many times. But I don't want to think about that. I want to think about now. Possibly about later, but not too much. Already, thinking about now isn't so bad.

I wedge the mattress between the TV and the sofa. I'll sleep there, in the tiny sitting room. I've washed some sheets that are now drying. Those on the bed I threw away. And I'll donate the two pillows and the blankets to Gueugnon's animal shelter.

I open Colette's suitcase, which I've laid on the floor in the corridor. I find my black cassette recorder. The red push-button to record, the others for playing, winding and rewinding, left, right. It was Dad and Mom who gave it to me. Christmas 1985. Since Colette's house was too small, all four of us would go for dinner to Georges Vezant's restaurant. And when we got back, we'd find our presents in the kitchen. No memory of a Christmas tree. Or of Christmas decorations. Only a string of lights around the window of the shoe-repair shop, which would flash occasionally, as if by mistake.

When I'd unwrapped my state-of-the-art auto-reverse recorder, I'd shrieked with delight. We spent the evening recording our voices; Colette laughed a lot that night, amazed at being able to hear her own voice. She kept saying to my father: "I have a weird voice, don't you think, Jean?"

Alongside my recorder, audio cassettes. All stored in their transparent boxes. And numbered in blue ink. From 1 to 119. Without comments or names. I close my eyes. I don't want to choose where to start. I mix them up, keep one in my hand. I open my eyes. Chance has gone for No. 19. I take the cassette out of its box, slide it into the recorder. Then her voice, a light voice. The words spoken softly, interspersed with silences, with breaths.

21

Cassette No. 19

Colette
Recording of Jean's story. For Agnès. Today is . . .

I hear her footsteps, she opens a drawer, closes it; I try to guess which room she's in, she returns to the recorder.

Colette
. . . September 5th, 2005.

A pause, a breath.

Colette
It was your mother who told me. Hannah was screaming and repeating: "Jean has gone." I thought she was accusing him. That my brother had gone off with another woman. He was handsome, and genial. He bewitched pianos, so why not someone's heart? Someone else's.

Then your mother said: "There was nothing they could do." It's that "they" that caused me more pain than anything else in my life. I had a vision, I saw people frantically working around him, on him, on his heartbeat. I saw his metronome fall to the ground. I understood that "they" were neither you nor her. They were passers-by or paramedics. But at the same time, a voice kept repeating inside my head: "He's too young, he can't die before you. You repair shoes, you're less important than him, who makes music."

Agnès, have you seen the look in the eyes of the audience during concerts? It's far more beautiful than the look in my customers' eyes when they collect their shoes. Afterward, I cried so much I could have drowned in my tears. And then I thought of you, Agnès. I wasn't going to leave you all alone with Hannah, who was really nice, oh, yes, really nice, but alone with you and her violin, I couldn't quite see how she'd cope. Musicians are slightly maladjusted, you know. Your mom, apart from playing the violin, she didn't know how to do very much, and your father was lost without a piano. When Jean passed away, I bought black clothes and stopped listening to the radio. Do you remember? Before, in my shop, there was music. After Jean, I stopped for a long time. I turned my back on songs.

A long silence.

I press pause. I can't get over what a treasure that big suitcase contains. I stand up to fetch a glass of water. I open the kitchen cupboard. I'm surrounded by Colette's things, I'm surrounded by her voice, by her final walls. Did she know that one day I'd be here? Why had she waited to die in order to speak to me? I grab the sponge from the corner of the sink. How many times did she use it to wipe up crumbs on the table?

I return to the small sitting room, sit down on my mattress, and press play.

COLETTE

For you to understand, I have to go back in time. The nice things began and the nasty ones ended . . . when my father died. A year after the birth of Danièle, the little sister, a year after taking me out of school. A kick of a hoof to the head. It's me who found him, lying in the straw, all stiff, with blood in his hair. That's what shocked me the most, that blood in his light hair. He was all stiff. Cold. I was really scared. I cried out. When the mother saw him like that, she began to scream, with her strange accent, a bit Burgundian, a bit dialect, a gibberish from I don't know where: "Wha'ever'll becom'a us?"

The marquess and marchioness de Sénéchal, who owned all the land, looked after the widow and the three orphans. I, as you know, was friends with the son, Blaise. And I liked his mother. She'd give us sweets, scarves, lemonade.

They employed the mother in their service and housed her, Jean and

Danièle in an outbuilding. Me, I went off to do an apprenticeship. I wanted it, that opportunity. I'd never have dared hope to leave like that. I'd stopped dreaming; becoming a teacher, no chance! But then, doing anything at all just to leave and live in town, that was like a fairy tale.

No more animals, farm, shit, spuds, plow, work that makes you ache all over. What remained of our livestock was sold. Except Bijou, the draft horse. Blaise persuaded his parents to keep him. I've never loved an animal so much . . .

Those that were sacrificed, their panic when loaded onto the trucks. A lamb cries like a child. And Jean cried like a lamb when he saw me taking up my big empty suitcase. I hugged him for a long time, explaining that I'd come back every Sunday of my life to see him. All my life. And that I'd be learning a trade. But now I'm not explaining things clearly . . . My brother's tears gave me courage. For the first time, I entered the courtyard of the château with him, when the mother had forbidden me from doing so. For us lot, the Septembre family, the château was out of bounds. It was Monsieur de Sénéchal who opened the door and looked at us as if Jean and I were two little heaps of still-steaming dung. But I didn't lower my eyes; I said, "Good day," and asked if Madame de Sénéchal was at home. He was about to slam the door in my face when Blaise appeared. He'd been waiting for me. He was like the angel in the Gueugnon church. The sculpture at the back, on the left. Go and look. You'll see how it resembles him. I still have a photo of us two. We must be about twelve in it.

She stops speaking for a few minutes; in the silence, I can hear her breathing.

COLETTE

"Ah, Colette," Blaise said when he saw me. He feigned surprise. "Are you well?" I said yes and that I'd like to see his mother, the marchioness. "Follow me." His father went off, pulling a strange face. With Jean's hand in mine, we went up the stairs; everywhere smelled of perfume, of jasmine and beeswax. I was very careful with my movements, where I put my feet, so scared of breaking something. Jean didn't bat an eyelid, sticking close to my legs. At nine, he was knee-high to a grasshopper and light as a feather. The parents sometimes wondered what they'd do

with him, since he didn't have the build of a farm boy. You can bet the mother would fill him to bursting with soup. On that day, he didn't ask any questions; he always trusted me. He always followed me.

I can hear the humming of the fridge behind her. And I picture her sitting in her kitchen.

COLETTE

Blaise entered a room and said: "Mama, Colette Septembre would like to see you." He used the formal vous *with his parents. The marchioness appeared with a smile, as if just roused from sleep or a bit feverish, wearing a pale dress, and with a touch of pink on her cheeks and lips. She didn't look much like other people. Always seemed to have stepped out of one of the novels Blaise took from the library to lend me.*

"Good day, madame, sorry to disturb you, but as you know, I'm leaving to do my apprenticeship and I can't take my little brother with me . . . Before I go, I wonder if . . . could I see the big piano?"

Her eyes widened a little, and she said yes.

"Could Jean see it, too?"

"Yes."

We followed Madame de Sénéchal and Blaise, crossed two light-filled reception rooms with paintings on the walls, and then we saw it. Like a king, gleaming, in the middle of a huge room. A Steinway. A masterpiece. More beautiful than all the paintings on the walls, the carpets, the furniture. The marchioness said:

"The Germans requisitioned the château during the war. The piano arrived in a truck for a high-ranking officer. After they were routed, they left it here . . . I don't know where it comes from . . . To whom it belonged."

I press stop. I take a deep breath and go out into the garden. A ray of sunshine greets me. My thoughts are very much with my parents. People don't talk about it enough, the horror of losing one's parents and finding oneself alone in the world. I return to the recorder; I have to keep going. To understand.

COLETTE

When I saw my peasant reflection in that lacquered black surface, I forgot Madame de Sénéchal, I forgot Blaise, I forgot good manners, and I said to Jean:

"It's yours, Jean. This piano, it's yours."

Jean let go of my hand, moved closer to the instrument without touching it, then started to laugh. I always wanted to keep his laughter. I'd have liked to put it somewhere, in a jewelry box. I've never forgotten it. I still hear it. Several times a day. I carry it with me.

The marchioness smiled. Meanwhile, Blaise had lifted the lid and raised the piano stool. As he did that, I've never wanted to cry as much, far more than when the father died. You see, Agnès, I don't know why certain people are kind to others, why they're born to be generous, but Blaise de Sénéchal was one of them. Jean sat at the piano. I saw his eyes light up.

"We'll pick up where we left off," Blaise told him.

Then he said to his mother:

"Mama, Jean has a gift. Jean, play Bach's minuet for us, the first one we worked on together."

When my brother placed his little fingers on the keyboard, I was overwhelmed. I felt good and bad at the same time, overcome by emotion. As they say. Emotion like I'd never felt before.

Agnès, can you imagine, it was 1959, I'd grown up in shit, and my little brother held Bach in his hands, his arms, his whole body. Blaise said to his mother:

"He's never studied musical notation, but as soon as he hears any music, he can reproduce it."

Children depend on their parents. If Jean had depended on the marquess, on the mother, on the father, he'd have become a worker at the Gueugnon ironworks. Nothing dishonorable about that. I've known and liked many foundrymen. But it's the marchioness who took Jean under her wing. Only large birds can take you under their wing. I didn't have to ask for anything else. Didn't even have to do any begging for my brother. Moved by Jean, Eugénie de Sénéchal herself decided that my brother would learn musical notation, would have lessons with Blaise. And that she would make sure of it. At all costs. That's what she said: "At all costs."

I left to learn my trade. I knew that Jean wouldn't miss me. That the piano would take up all the space and there'd be none left for anything else.

She stops speaking. I hear her standing up, lowering the stylus of her hi-fi system onto a record. Dad's first studio recording. Some Chopin nocturnes. My father gave her that Pioneer system in the eighties, so she could listen to him whenever she liked.

Dad rarely spoke about Colette to me. Between them, things were mellow. I never saw an argument, the slightest implied reproach, or a brusque gesture. There were many exchanged looks and silences between them. I paid no attention. Guys on their motorbikes interested me far more than the relationship between my aunt and my father.

My hands are shaking. I'm going to draw this out. Discover these cassettes little by little. Like a present. Close my eyes to let chance take over. I won't listen to them all in one go. Like when I'm reading a book I don't want to devour but rather savor. I have plenty of time.

I was desperate for my first success. Then for another success. Today, nothing and no one is waiting for me anymore, and I'm not waiting for anything from anyone. Maybe that's what luck is. Or freedom, at least.

22

Cassette No. 7

Colette

It's January 7, 2003. I'm going to talk to you about Blanche. The first time I see her, I'm six or seven years old. She's sitting on the bench at the back of the classroom. The bench that's free all year. She's the daughter of circus folks.

"This is Blanche," the teacher says. And the others, instead of looking at her, they look at me, the bumpkin. Even Blaise.

Colette calls out to someone: "Blanche! Blanche! Come here!"

I hear footsteps and a woman's voice: "I'm coming, I'm coming." A gentle voice like my aunt's. My heart races; I feel like I'm dreaming. I listen to that bit again, and again: "I'm coming, I'm coming." My aunt wasn't alone at the time of the recordings.

Blanche
I'm here.
Colette
I'm recording things for Agnès. Would you like to say something?
Blanche
For Agnès? . . . Things?

An angel passes, and takes its time.

Blanche
Isn't that dangerous?
Colette
We'll be dead when she listens to us.

BLANCHE
Are you sure?
COLETTE
Yes, come on, over here.
BLANCHE
I don't know.
COLETTE
Tell her about the first time you saw me.

A long silence.

BLANCHE
Hello Agnès, my name is Blanche. I would have liked to meet you. I so would have wanted to meet you.

She switches off the recording. How long did she pause it? Impossible to know.

BLANCHE
The first time I saw Colette was at elementary school. The École Pasteur, which still exists. 1953. I'm sure of the year because Naja was still alive. She died a few days later. When we left for Clermont-Ferrand. I didn't manage to get her out of her cage. To give her back her freedom. My lioness came from Africa, she was old, worn-out, broken. Her stomach became twisted. A nasty man had sold her to my genitor for a song.

I stop. Silence all around me. What time is it? These cassettes are addictive. And I realize that I haven't thought about Pierre since I've been listening to Colette. So it is possible not to think about him.

Blanche's voice has the same tessitura as Colette's, and she has the same way of pronouncing words. It's as if they've spent their lives together. Like those couples who end up talking the same way. I try to imagine her face.

BLANCHE
Personally, I didn't question anything when I saw you. I didn't think

it strange. I was born into a traveling circus and grew up in the arms of Natalia, a bearded lady, with Fabrizio, a man just a meter tall, with Nestor, who lifted anvils, and with Vlad for as long as he lasted—he suffered from macrocephaly . . . had an enormous head. My genitor ended up abandoning him at the entrance to a hospital.

In our circus, there were many unfortunates who didn't look like other people. But we loved each other. The public would come to applaud us and to see "monsters" or freaks. The more terrifying, deformed, they looked, the more satisfied people seemed to be; they'd gotten their money's worth. Poor Vlad suffered the consequences. But the real monster was my genitor. He spoke just one language, that of blows. As much to the animals as to us.

Strangeness was my everyday life. So you, sweetheart, when I first saw you, it had no effect on me; you'll always be my loveliest childhood memory. My only childhood memory. I didn't have a childhood. I started working young. The booming music that heralded our arrival was the opposite of how we felt. Ta-da, ta-da, ta. Lights and oompah-pahs. But the reality was awful. I would tremble, my stomach would go crazy, I was scared of that thrill-seeking audience and its sick curiosity. I only liked having the eyes of the children on me, because I could make them dream. I was a high-wire acrobat.

"Roll up, ladies and gentlemen, roll up!" my genitor would roar. "Come and discover the unimaginable! The exceptional . . . "

Her voice cracks.

BLANCHE
I'll stop there for now. Is that okay? Did I speak well?

I switch off the recording. "Sweetheart" Blanche called my aunt "sweetheart."

There's a knock on the door. Shit. I forgot to lock it. I'm not expecting anyone and don't wish to speak to anyone. I don't move, plunged in semi-darkness. Hunched up.

"Agnès!"

I instantly recognize Ilyas's voice.

"Are you there?"

And Nathalie Grandjean's, too.

I don't move. My phone vibrates in my pocket. It's Ilyas; I don't answer. Then there's a message from Nathalie that I read straightaway: "I didn't find your aunt's death notice." I jump up and dive toward the front door, fearing they've already left. They're still on the doorstep. I startle them.

"You okay?" Ilyas asks.

"Yes."

They daren't move.

"Were you sleeping?"

"No, I was concentrating. I'm listening to some recordings."

They come inside.

"So this is where Colette was found?" Ilyas asks.

"More importantly, this is where she lived."

"Jeez," he hisses.

"Will you stay long?" Nathalie asks, concerned and horrified. "This place gives me goose bumps."

"I have twenty days ahead of me."

Nathalie stares at me.

"Come to my place."

"No, really, it'll be fine. If it gets too oppressive, I'll go to the Monge."

Ilyas looks at the inflatable mattress in the middle of the sitting room, the cassettes and the recorder.

"We played with a thing like that when we were little."

"That's the one. My aunt kept it."

"After that you had your camcorder. You were forever filming us. Did you keep the footage?"

"I think the camcorder got stolen. Along with the video cassettes. I noticed far too late. Or maybe it got lost during a move. What time is it?"

Nathalie checks her watch.

"Six twenty."

"I have some apricot juice and some nibbles. Any interest?"

We go into the kitchen, sit around the table. I put out three of those glasses mustard's sold in, and the chips in a salad bowl.

"I searched through the archives, no trace of a death notice," Nathalie says, after taking a handful of chips.

"And yet," Ilyas objects, "I attended her funeral. Which means that I knew about it. And I wasn't the only one. We gathered at the cemetery in the morning. There were at least fifty of us. Louis Berthéol read something, can't remember what. But it was nice. And she was buried. Now that I think of it, it's Louis who told me about Colette's funeral, and who gave me the date and time. And Pascale, too."

"Pascale?"

"The florist on Rue Jean-Jaurès. I don't read the newspaper, let alone the death notices. 'Radio Gueugnon,' it's just like everywhere, news of your aunt's death spread like wildfire."

"Louis was late in telling me that she'd died, because of the time difference. He said the funeral would take place right away—it was the middle of August, and it was the only slot the undertakers could find. He told me that by the time I'd caught a plane back to France, Colette would already be in the ground. To be honest, it suited me. Ana wasn't happy that we weren't going. I fed her some lines like: "What counts is that she's in our hearts and our thoughts." We went together to light some candles in St. Sebastian Church. Candles in America for my poor aunt who'd died in Burgundy."

"The shoe-repair shop changed hands pretty quickly, and we didn't question any of it. You lived a long way away back then; I sent you a message, and that was that."

"And now here we are, in this house, gobbling up chips. When I say that life is strange . . . "

"Who do you say that to?" Ilyas asks Nathalie.

"I say it to everyone, all the time. You know, I'm a journalist, I come across tons of weird stuff."

"I didn't know the two of you knew each other."

"Nathalie's like my sister," Ilyas replies. "We've known each other since nursery school. I didn't like her at first, thought she was a show-off."

"And I thought he was a pathetic druggy."

"I was. We met again when we were twenty. A boozy party. Right place, right time. We got talking. And we've been close ever since. She's into chicks, so we can just be friends. We're good."

Nathalie looks at Ilyas with real affection.

"It's me who took him to detox. Several times. Until the right one. There's always a right one."

"She's as stubborn as a mule, wouldn't let up on me."

"For years, I've been encouraging him to write. Ilyas is a great writer, but he doesn't have any faith in himself. Charpie frazzled his brain."

An angel passes. My aunt, perhaps. Or my father. Or my mother. Or Blanche. Or the four of them, hand in hand.

"At what stage were there doubts about that guy?"

"Personally, I heard talk once he'd already left for the South of France," Nathalie says to me. "There were rumors. I realized that he'd been dismissed. Not one victim spoke up or made a formal complaint, though. Not to my knowledge, at any rate. Later, I learned that the kids would just laugh about him among themselves, they'd snigger, tease each other: "So you were treated to Charpie check-ups, too?"

I close my eyes. An urge to vomit.

Nathalie is seriously wound up. Anger makes her go red. Her neck is crimson.

"He coached the junior league," Ilyas says. "The ideal scenario. But he had no business being in the changing rooms, and what's even more staggering, he wasn't even a doctor . . . I can't really explain it to you, but he was arrogant, sure of himself. No one would have intervened. It was a different time, a time when the directors laid down the law. The hierarchy at the factory was replicated within the club. He ruled over his little world. He ran the IT department. He had a stranglehold on the football and the factory."

"It's different today. Men in suits and boss-types, they seem less scary to people, to children . . . although that's debatable. There'll always be adults who have power over the innocent."

"How many years did he run the club?"

"Are you ready?"

I nod.

"From 1956 to 1980."

"Twenty-four years," Nathalie stresses. "Twenty-four seasons, many of them with the junior league."

"Was he married?"

"Never married."

"Children?"

"No children."

"When did he die, again?"

"Last year," Nathalie says. "I went down there to investigate."

"Investigate?"

"Accident or suicide, no one ever knew. Part of his face was messed up, as if he'd been struck, and I needed to know. They found his body in the sea off Cannes, three days after he disappeared. The forensic pathologist couldn't establish whether it was from falling accidentally, jumping, or if someone had wounded him. Had a boat bumped into him after his fall? What's certain is that he wasn't dead before entering the water. He had water in his lungs. So he drowned. He must have been struck before falling into the water."

"Did you discover anything else down there?"

"Nothing at all."

"Did the cops know he was a suspected pedophile?"

"I don't think so. But I passed myself off as a provincial journalist looking into a former resident of Gueugnon. I said nothing. Didn't want to attract any attention. The cops concluded that it was a 'slip' on the seafront. On the day he disappeared, there'd been some fierce winds over the Mediterranean."

"I guess the sea took revenge for the kids," Ilyas adds, helping himself to more apricot juice. "This juice of yours, it's really gross. I'm starving. I'll go get some pizzas at Joseph's."

"Joseph still exists?"

"Of course. Joseph is eternal. And may I remind you, he's Jesus's father," Ilyas quips. "There's lots of talk of the mother, but so little of the father in the Catholic faith."

Joseph is the boy who's been making pizzas on the Place de l'Église for a very, very, very long time. It seems like I've almost always known, seen, his truck in the same spot. About a hundred meters from Colette's former shoe-repair shop. As if his vehicle, with its integrated wood-fired oven, is as old as the Romanesque church that gives it shade on summer evenings. Ilyas stands up and says:

"I'll be back."

"Take some money from my wallet on the console thingy in the hall."

"It's fine, I'm not poor. I can afford three pizzas. Which flavors?"

This question makes me laugh. And reminds me of the best pizza I've ever eaten in my entire life: at Marinella's in Ajaccio. In fact, I think the pizza was called La Marinella. So I suppose it's not that silly, I could talk about flavors, tastes, about that shady, open-air terrace over the Med, about Pierre who's eyeing me hungrily, about us, in love, crazily so, about the promise of a dirty siesta, as he'd say, and about that thin pizza, huge like they make them in the South, fabulous, that turns up at our table on a large stainless-steel tray. I'll go back to Corsica. I'll go back to Marinella's. This is the first time in three years that I have a plan.

"For me, tomato and cheese! I never know if that's the margherita or the regina."

"Same here!" Nathalie cries.

"Okay. And don't say terrible things about me while I'm gone, now."

Ilyas closes the door behind him.

"Did you come by car?"

"Yup," Nathalie says. "I don't like riding his motorbike, it terrifies me."

She stands up.

"Gotta call my other half, tell her I'm staying here a bit longer."

She goes out into the garden, cellphone in hand.

Since I'm not alone, I dare to go into the room with the sewing machine. The one with the ironing board and the cupboard containing my aunt's collection. The collection that tells the story of the Gueugnon Football Club from 1965 to 2000. For thirty-five years, she cut out every single article, and then she stopped. Why? What can make someone stop from one day to the next? A bout of flu that keeps you stuck in bed? Meeting someone? A new interest? Just getting sick of it? Strange for a fanatic like her.

I decide that I must donate this collection to the club, to the fans who have virtually given their lives to the story of football in Gueugnon. I'll have a chat with Michel Chaussin, a friend of my aunt's. He's the one who keeps the heart of the club's story beating on Facebook. I'm a follower of his there. I look at the photos of former players he posts, of classic matches, of current sporting events. I love the fans' fervor. I wonder if my aunt was waiting for me to do a movie on football. The best one is *Coup de tête* by Jean-Jacques Annaud, with Patrick Dewaere. It's never crossed my mind before. I must have disappointed her. I must have disappointed her badly.

Nathalie returns. She joins me in the sewing-machine room.

"Did Ilyas tell you about Charpie?"

I understand her question instantly, from the way she looks at me, the tone of her voice.

"Yes. The vile medical check-up that turned into a nightmare. He was seven years old."

"I don't think he was the only one. I'm investigating secretly. I don't want to talk to him about it. He's suffered enough. I meet people, ask questions, everyone seems embarrassed. Many had no idea. When you're besotted with a sport, you can't necessarily see the evil lurking around it. And then there are those who did know. The other day, I go to buy some paint at a friend's store. A lovely guy who's around the same age as Ilyas. And we get to talking about life, and for some reason I question him, I ask if he used to play football, if he remembers Charpie. He turns white and says to me: 'He was filth.' 'What makes you say that?' I ask. And then he told me everything . . . that Charpie would never have laid into him, the rebel, that he'd pick out the shy boys, the vulnerable ones, the ideal victims. And that every day, Christophe Delannoy, a friend of ours, a guy who's a bit nutty, a bit of a misfit, walks past his store, and every day it brings back the memory of that bastard . . . He said to me: 'Do you hear me, Nathalie? Every day, when I see Christophe passing my store, I think of Charpie. I'm sure he abused him. At the time, Christophe tried to talk to me about it, he stammered: "He touched my balls." And at the time, I made fun of him. We were idiots. We didn't talk about stuff like that . . . A trip to Manosque with other kids, for football training, we must have been around ten, I was there. When we got back, Christophe had changed; it was after that he started to isolate himself. I never dare leave my store to ask him what that man did to him, but I know, I can sense that he abused him.'"

"How many Delannoys would there have been?"

"Hard to know. There are some guys who refuse to talk to me. I tried to get in touch with Ilyas's childhood friend, but he just ignored me."

Nathalie glances at the collection that I've spread out on the ironing board.

"What's that?"

"That's the light. The light from the football stadiums that my aunt collected for years. It's the opposite of Charpie. It's the beauty of the game. The beauty of the teams. It's what made millions of Gueugnon locals flock to the stadium for matches. It's what made hearts beat for years. It's what made my aunt tremble when the team conceded a goal or scored one."

"I didn't know you liked football."

"Neither did I," I hear myself respond.

23

1959

The man she's apprenticed to is called Mokhtar Bayram. When Colette pushes open the door to the shoe-repair shop, she discovers another world from that of the farm and the school. A universe of tools and hammers, pliers, brushes and cloths, of nails and sandpaper. A smell of leather, oil, glue, polish, metal, and grease. She's carrying her big empty suitcase in one hand. Mokhtar, with his dark, mischievous eyes, asks her what she's hiding inside it.

"My toothbrush," Colette tells him.

"That's all?"

"I have nothing else."

Mokhtar smiles at her.

"Have you got what it takes?"

"I think so, monsieur," she stammers, a little embarrassed.

"How old are you?"

"Thirteen."

Colette has never seen so many shoes side by side. She's always owned just the one pair, for both winter and summer, a single pair that had to last as long as possible. At first, they were far too big for her, and by the end, they were so much too small that they cramped the arches of her feet. She prefers the clogs elderly peasants wear. The wood is hard, but in summer, she'd slide her bare feet into them.

"Are you good with your hands?"

"I don't know, monsieur. But I can deliver lambs."

"Call me Mokhtar, m'dear."

Mokhtar had agreed to take on an apprentice at Madame de Sénéchal's request. He refuses nothing to the marchioness, repairing and reinforcing the soles and seams of the shoes of the entire Sénéchal family. The condition being that Colette must get her vocational training certificate by taking classes at the École Sainte-Cécile, which is three minutes away from the shoe-repair shop. A private school of which Madame de Sénéchal is the trustee.

Mokhtar had replied: "No problem, madame, I'll teach her the craft if she's a hard worker; if not, I won't keep her on."

Three meals a day, a thousand francs a month, when the minimum wage of a workman is thirteen thousand, a shed with a window, bed, stove, logs, running water, a quilt, and two pairs of clean sheets. For Colette, this is unheard-of luxury. The toilet is at the back of the garden. Mokhtar has already had several apprentices, but never a girl. It's labor he can't do without, and he's keen to pass on his skills.

Mokhtar, Blaise, and Colette stand at the door of what will be "her room" for two years.

"Put your suitcase down," Mokhtar says. "We'll see what you need later. This place, it's your home. Me, I'll not set foot in it. You'll be the one keeping it tidy. It needs to stay clean for whoever comes after you. Always think about that person following on behind you. Wherever you may be. If everyone did that, the Earth would turn more smoothly."

He points at a structure made of dark wood, a few meters away from them.

"Go there whenever you like. It's always open. Inside there's a block of soap and a tub for washing your clothes."

Blaise slips a few banknotes into Colette's pocket before leaving and plants a furtive kiss on her cheek. Colette doesn't know what to say, daren't move anymore. Those banknotes deep in her pocket feel heavy as an anvil. She can feel tears coming because she has dirty hair and Blaise is as handsome as they come. Her only support in this life, the only person she's been able to count on since she was born. A single friend is enough to make up for the silence and all that's missing. Starting with her parents. The mother didn't shed a tear when Colette left with Blaise earlier, clutching her suitcase. A suitcase as empty as the mother's heart. She merely checked that Colette wasn't taking away anything that Jean and Danièle now needed more than her, since she'd be getting board and lodging. "And your thousand francs, they'll be for me. With children, that's how it goes. Specially the eldest with her mother." Board and lodging, but she'll have to work like an adult and study. Colette knows that girls her age play after school, meet up on Sunday to laugh, dance, dream. All she's known is working after school, and if the father hadn't died, she'd never have gone back to school at all.

"See you Sunday," Blaise whispers to her. "I'll come and fetch you on my bike."

I mustn't be sad, Colette thinks. *I brought Jean and the piano together. It'll be okay; it'll all be fine . . .*

"What's your name, m'dear?" Mokhtar asks.

"Colette. Colette Septembre."

He smiles into his mustache.

"Your name's like the summer."

Colette hesitates, then says:

"My surname's more like the autumn."

"Oh no, m'dear, September's still mostly summer, with just a teeny bit of early autumn."

*

Mokhtar is Tunisian. Growing up in Tunis, he wanted to learn a skill. He became an apprentice during school vacations. The first thing he learned was delivering shoes in the souks. Then he went up the ladder, as he says, and began to make shoes, then to do the finishing touches. By the time Colette turns up in his life, he's had his shoe-repair shop on Rue Pasteur for twenty years. He arrived in France in 1936, with his brother. He'd contracted an illness and lost part of his leg at the age of six. Since he walks on a stump of wood, he says he has a little tree instead of a shoe. He tells Colette that that's why shoes are his life. Through the life of others, those who walk with both feet and don't know how lucky they are. He owns two pairs of shoes, one for winter and one for summer, and the right-hand shoes sleep on a shelf. His passion is shoe-mending and leatherwork. He says to Colette: "I like shoes, I respect shoes, they take you everywhere in life, they carry your memories. I'll tell you the truth, Colette, I'm a shoe-mender, and the first thing I notice about a person is their shoes; if their shoes are well-kept, I move up to their face; if not, I stop right there. There's a difference between protecting and repairing; you have to protect before you repair. Like with your body, m'dear. Don't drink alcohol, don't smoke cigarettes, don't speak ill of people. You've gotta find a little pleasure everywhere. There's pleasure everywhere."

Colette doesn't always understand what Mokhtar is saying. But it comes out of his mouth with kindness when he's addressing her. And it's her that he addresses, no one else. So she feels a bit important. Like with Blaise and Jean. Mokhtar has a very different accent to the Burgundians, and sometimes confuses masculine and feminine nouns, singular and plural.

"What happens to the shoes if no one picks them up?"

"I give them to the Red Cross, and occasionally to the church. But you know, the ways things are now, few people forget. Your pair of shoes, Colette, they're the most precious thing you've got."

She looks down and contemplates her dark-leather clodhoppers. They were suitable before, on the dirt tracks. Right now, they're clean. When Colette leaves the shop, it's to return a pair of shoes to someone elderly, who struggles to get about.

"With customers I don't know, I ask them to pay in advance. And surprise, surprise, they never forget to come back. I have other customers who are so regular, I don't even give them a ticket. You'll see, I have a lot who send their children: 'Mom sent me.' I know everyone in Gueugnon. Except the racists. They wouldn't set foot in an Arab's place."

"Why?"

"We don't have the same God, that bothers some people."

"What's he like, your God?"

"Like yours, 'cept he doesn't speak the same language."

"How d'you know? God doesn't speak to anyone."

"Oh yes he does, m'dear. Listen to God, he speaks . . . What d'you want to do in life, apart from repairing shoes?"

"I want my little brother to be a musician, a pianist."

"And for yourself, what d'you want?"

"My brother to be a musician."

"God will answer you, you'll see, he'll answer you."

Colette also goes shopping for Mokhtar, at Madame Courault's hardware store. She arrives with a list, products with tricky names that he's scribbled on a scrap of paper: creams, varnishes, dyes, nails, and rivets.

"You know, during the war, we were allowed one pair of shoes a year for a ration ticket. I'd make soles out of wood. The Krauts requisitioned any leather."

The first thing Colette learned was how to use the big sewing machine. Before working on pieces of leather, she stitched together meters and meters of fabric. Until moving her fingers on either side of the needle became second nature. Until she could think about something else, could sew as easily as breathing. Next, Mokhtar showed her how to select the right needle for using on leather. How to stitch small offcuts of leather with the machine. The different stitches—cross, saddle, straight. To familiarize herself with the threads, nails, zippers. For cutting to shape, Colette practiced on pieces of cardboard.

"Cardboard doesn't behave like leather, but it's not the material you need to learn about, it's the handling of it. Also drawing lines, circles. You'll be spending your entire day looking at what you're holding in your hands, yes, yes, absolutely."

"With the fine leathers, I feel as if I'm causing pain. Inside my head, I can hear them crying . . . "

"Who d'you hear crying?"

"The lambs. When they're separated from their mothers, they cry. Fine leather, it's lambs' skin."

"You're cracked, m'dear."

"What does 'cracked' mean?"

"It's your ideas. When it rains, they get watered."

Before Colette, Mokhtar had never really thought of leather as skin. For him, it was a tool, basic to his work, a tanned material, of good or bad quality. He'd never thought of the living being, of the life it had had, and what remained of it in his hands. Colette often speaks to him of her connection with the animals when she lived on the farm. It's the first time Mokhtar is dealing with a girl at work. It unsettles him. He finds her more sensitive, more meticulous. More curious, too. She asks more questions.

His little sister, Nadia, lives in Tunis. He hasn't seen her for decades, but they write to each other in their mother tongue. She's married and has two boys, one sixteen, one eighteen; apparently, the younger son looks like him. Mokhtar puts money aside. "That's to pay for my trip." Not a day goes by without him saying this in front of Colette as he slips a coin or a banknote into an iron box.

"Where is your brother? The one you arrived in France with?"

"He died, m'dear. The family had his body brought back to Tunisia."

"Did he die in the war?"

"No. In the hospital."

"Well, if I lost my brother Jean, I'd be even more cracked."

At twelve every day, Mokhtar lowers the metal shutter halfway, so the light still filters into the shop, and brings out a cold lunch that they share: salad, bread, cheese. Occasionally, a nice slice of pâté, or some hard-boiled eggs. They each eat in their own corner. Mokhtar turns the radio on, sometimes swears when listening to a politician's opinions or an ad for mass-produced shoes, then stretches out on his old ottoman behind the till and closes his eyes for a quick quarter of an hour before raising the shutter once again. During that time, Colette goes out if the weather's nice, rereads a chapter of a book or one of her lessons. There are only five girls in her class. The other four are learning dressmaking and are apprenticed to local spinning mills. They tell her she's doing a man's job, that a *cordonnière*, a female shoe-mender, doesn't exist.

"It does exist because it's in the dictionary. Everything that's in the dictionary exists. It's proof."

With the money Blaise gave her, Colette treated herself to two dresses and two sweaters from the market. And a ribbon to tie up her hair. Sometimes, certain customers leave her a tip, a few centimes. She puts them away carefully in a button tin that Mokhtar gave her. Sometimes, too, when she's done some shopping, he says: "Keep the change, m'dear." That money will be for her. Or for Jean. But not for the mother. It amounts to very little. Barely enough for a soda on a café terrace, but for Colette, it's precious. Something that won't be stolen from her.

Even though she misses her brother, the bedtime stories, his smell, his little hand, her days are far brighter than they used to be. She likes working, living in the center of town, she appreciates the presence of Mokhtar, who calls her "m'dear," and not having to be up at four in the morning for milking. She feels as if her days are gaining color, like Madame de Sénéchal in the middle of the afternoon.

24

October 30, 2010

This morning, when I opened the door, I gulped the cold air in the corridor. The silence of a tomb in the depths of winter, in this soulless three-room house, as if death had disembodied my aunt forever. As if she'd never set foot in here.

And then she reappeared. Her voice on the cassettes, filling the space between the walls. Her collection on the ironing board, her articles cut out from newspapers under her kitchen light, the Colette of before, the one from the shoe-repair shop. I remember it so clearly. Her scissors, the glue, the fountain pen, the big albums on the waxed tablecloth, the piles of newspapers.

I would watch my aunt without seeing her. I took this passion for football as the fad of a misfit. A woman without children or a husband who did a man's job. Yes, when I was a teenager, I thought women without children or a husband were a bit weird, those who loved a boys' sport even more so. One can be young and backward.

Tonight, there are five of us. The voices, the gesticulating, Hervé's heady cologne, the bare lightbulbs, the wine and apricot juice, they all raise our spirits. Hervé had bumped into Ilyas at Joseph's pizza truck. So Ilyas got one for him, too. Then he phoned Adèle to invite her along: "Oh, right, you're home alone? In your pajamas? Throw on a coat. What flavor pizza for you? See you at Agnès's place? The Fredins one. Yes, well, her aunt's, yes, she got the keys. See you there!"

The boxes spread out on the kitchen table, chili oil in plastic sachets, Adèle, Nathalie, and I devour our slices as if starving as we discuss our mutual love of *Sex and the City*. Nathalie likes Samantha best, Adèle goes for Charlotte, and me, I love all four characters. But if pushed, Carrie Bradshaw!

In the adjacent room, the boys are poring over Colette's collection, commenting on every article and every match, oohing and aahing, and shouting, "This is amazing, it's insane—jeez, Agnès, you gotta donate this to the club!"

We couldn't be more clichéd. Boys on one side, girls on the other. The blue of the footballers' kit, the pink of Carrie Bradshaw's outfit on the side of New York buses.

"My favorite bit is when Big marries Natasha and the four girls meet up in a café near City Hall."

"Mine is on Brady's birthday, when Miranda admits to Steve that she's always loved him."

"Oh, yes! I love Miranda's wedding!"

"I remember that player. He was the best. Him, not so much. Dragged his feet, played alone. I was jealous of Aimé Chauvel, he was so good-looking. And a great footballer, to boot. So classy! Still lives in Gueugnon I see him around sometimes, he married my first love," Ilyas suddenly reveals.

At this confession, we girls all look up, forget our pizzas, and promptly join the boys in the room next door.

"Really? And who was that?" Nathalie asks.

Ilyas glances at her and smiles.

"Oh, it's not that interesting."

"Not that interesting? You've either said too much or not enough."

He looks down.

"Isabelle Émorine," he admits, already seeming to regret it.

"What? You were with Isabelle?"

"No, I was never *with* her. We kissed one evening at Tacot's, that's all. And it was lovely. I always loved her . . . But she married Chauvel."

"Was he older than her?" Nathalie asks.

"No, she must have been around his age. But more to the point, Isabelle was ten years older than you, Ilyas," Adèle jumps in.

"I couldn't compete. Too classy, the guy. Next to him, I was a dead loss."

"It's funny," I say, "I remember Chauvel. D'you think my aunt mentions him in the cassettes she left for me? Aimé Chauvel?"

They all stare at me with the same curiosity in their eyes. It's Hervé who finally says:

"We'll just have to listen."

"You think my aunt would agree to that?"

"We'll just have to ask her," Adèle suggests, taking a euro coin out of her pocket. "Tails it's no, heads it's yes."

They stare at me, waiting for my approval.

"Okay."

She tosses the coin in the air, slaps it down on the back of her hand. Tails.

"Your aunt says no."

After a silence, disappointment written on everyone's faces, we return to the tiny kitchen to finish our pizzas and drinks.

"Won't you be scared, sleeping here on your own?" Nathalie asks, concerned.

"Not if I sleep on my super-mattress in the sitting room."

"All the same, Agnès! You're loaded, but you're staying here. If I were you, I'd treat myself to the hotel, room service and all," Hervé says.

"How do you know she's loaded?" Nathalie asks, annoyed.

"Her movies," Hervé snaps back. "Come on, Agnès, your movies, they must have made you a pretty penny."

"Yeah. It's true, I could go to the hotel, but I prefer to stay here. Over the past week, I've realized that I overlooked Colette. By living here, I can find her a little."

*

Cassette No. 20

COLETTE
Aimé, my dear Aimé.

Those are her first words. I can hear her hesitation, as if she's about to throw herself into the void. Colette never mentioned any young love, or any love, period. My father never knew her to have a fiancé. Neither did my mother. One day, when I asked my father why she didn't have a husband or a child, he answered with a vague, "That's life."

COLETTE
Right, so . . .

She drops something, which shatters on the floor, and curses: "Blasted thing."

COLETTE
The first time I see him, it's just before the Gueugnon-Louhans match. Gueugnon's playing at home. He's on the bench, beside Novo, the coach. His name was Nowotarski, Casimir Nowotarski, but everyone called him Novo. You don't care about coaches, but me, there were two that I adored. Émile Daniel and Alex Dupont. There was also Briet, who was really good, for sure, he was good. But maybe too candid.

Have you seen the movie Coup de tête, *Agnès? We never talked about it. I saw it on TV. On Channel 1, one Sunday evening. Yes, it was a Sunday. And then I saw it again, several times. Whenever it's on, I watch it. What a fine movie.*

I stop the recording. Return to the kitchen to sob, letting my tears flow. I blow my nose on the paper napkins scattered among the empty pizza boxes. All my friends have gone home.

My heart's moved out
My vacations, always Paris
My plans, to keep going
My loves, to make them up
Yes, Mom, yes,
Yes, Mom, yes,
Mom, if you saw my life.

So now the singer France Gall is inviting herself into the kitchen.

I return to my mattress in the middle of the sitting room. Colette's voice, once again.

COLETTE

He's waiting. For the first time in my life, I don't watch the match. I watch him, him and his every movement. He warms up at the side of the stadium. He runs, does chassés, swings his arms around. He's wearing a hat; I don't know yet that he has thick brown curls. I'll find that out later. I'll also find out that he has caramel skin. Right now, I can't see any of that.

He's slipped a jacket on, over his football shirt. It's cold. He's seventeen years old. It's January 1976. I'm thirty, but I'm well aware that I look older. The players like me because I'm ageless, because I don't look like much. If I was pretty, dolled up, it wouldn't work. They'd trust me less, or then try to get me into bed. It's as dumb as that, life.

I think of the photo that Ana got enlarged to pin on the wall of her room. Colette is posing between Dad and Mom, who've only just met. They're beautiful, all three of them.

COLETTE

He joins the game during the second half, twenty minutes from the end, and it's announced on the PA system: Aimé Chauvel, No. 11. It's funny, before him, I'd never come across that first name.

Right away, I don't understand the coach. Why had he left this player on the bench for all that time? As soon as Aimé steps onto the pitch, it's obvious that he's a cut above. He's a team player. He's everywhere, very responsive, attentive. He's really tall. It can be tricky for tall players, they have more to drag around, but not him.

He ends up passing to Gabriel Duch, who scores in the top corner of the net. The fans are ecstatic. As a debut for Gueugnon, it's some debut. I can still hear the applause now, as I speak.

Someone knocks on the door, and I reluctantly pause the recording. Probably one of my friends who's left something behind. It's Dr. Pieri. I'm in shock. His hair and beard have turned white, but his eyes are still as bright, gentle, and reassuring. He took care of me when I was a child. He was full of humor and music. He'd whistle all the time, like he'd swallowed a bird and its orchestra.

"Hello, Agnès, they said you came by the office this morning. But we'll be better off talking here, away from prying eyes. And we've got the cops on our backs, too," he says, with a sad smile.

"But Jacques, how did you know I'd be here?"

"I saw a light on. I came here regularly to see your aunt, these past few months."

25

1960

For twelve months now, she's been Mokhtar's apprentice. Twelve months during which, every Sunday morning, Blaise comes to fetch her. Going back up to the château takes twenty minutes by bike. Colette sits on the rack. The final hill is so steep, they get off the bike and walk alongside it, quickening their pace.

Colette and Blaise make the most of the Sénéchals being at Mass to go into the château. As she walks up the stairs, Colette can hear the music in the distance. It's a sweet ascent before finding Jean again, sitting at the piano. Pushing open the heavy door that separates him from the rest of the world. Over the past year, she's being gauging his progress. She grips the guardrail to stop her hands from shaking. No need to know about music to recognize her brother's talent.

As soon as he notices her, he throws himself into her arms.

"Listen, Colette, Chopin. 'Nocturne in E-flat major, opus 9, No. 2.'"

Solemnly, he opens his music book, places it in front of him, focuses, then starts to play. His tongue moves from the left corner of his mouth to the right, and he keeps his eyes fixed on the score. Blaise doesn't know whether he's pretending to read the music or playing by ear. Jean would have preferred to just keep replicating the notes. But if he wants to pursue it, to progress, he must learn musical notation.

"What's progressing? I want to play, that's all."

"You want to play every day?" Blaise asks him.

"Yes!"

"Well, then, sight-read this score."

And every evening, after school, they go over it. Eighth note, sharp, triple time, sixteenth note, sixteenth rest, whole note. When

Jean, tired, loses heart, Blaise explains to him that this is a universal and splendid language.

"What does 'universal' mean?"

"That you can play on the moon."

Fascinated, Colette watches her brother's hands running over the keys, his fingers touching them lightly, like drops of rain.

Madame de Sénéchal has already said, several times, to the mother: "I need to talk to you, Georgette; your son is a child prodigy."

The mother half-opened her mouth, not understanding what Madame was telling her. She didn't dare ask what that word meant, so merely replied:

"It's true he's a bit of a fidget, I'll 'ave words with 'im."

At which, without mockery, the marchioness smiled at her, showing all her lovely teeth, as white and perfectly aligned as her pearl necklaces.

"No, Georgette, I mean that Jean is hugely talented, musically."

"Oh, that," she snapped, ashamed, wringing her hands, not knowing what to say anymore.

But why, the mother asks herself, *why would my son be talented musically? Is it some spell, some curse? The devil?* She fears folks from the lower orders drawing attention to themselves. It's the bosses who have the right to do that, it's the marquess and marchioness, not the Septembres, not them. And Jean does nothing but that, draw attention to himself. She curses the piano. Curses the fact that her son goes into the château every day as if it were his home, while she polishes the furniture and washes the dishes, soaps the tiles, scrubs the kitchen. While he's behaving like a prince in his domain. She wants her son to keep his nose clean, learn normal things, do manual work, like Colette, wants him to stay in his place, in the service accommodation meant for them, on the other side of the high walls.

"Jean is a textbook case, Georgette. You see, the war had one good aspect, the piano a Kraut left in the château. You know how I believe in God? Your son has a gift from God."

Eugénie de Sénéchal can see the panic in Georgette's eyes. They seem to seek and see something that terrifies her, whenever the subject comes up. So she doesn't push the matter. But she can't bring herself to abandon Jean. He must make progress, probably go and stay with a teacher, but how to persuade his mother? And then there's her own husband, who's finding the presence of the little musician increasingly intolerable. Her husband who's increasingly morose and taciturn. Ranting when he hears the piano:

"Is this racket ever going to stop? Can't I live in peace, without having to suffer someone else's brat? As it is, my own son, the only one we managed to produce, puts on airs—well, you know what I mean . . . He was far too coddled."

"Blaise is just sensitive."

"Too sensitive . . . "

When he says these words, she's mortified.

"He's top of his class."

"That's not what makes a man."

She thinks back to their wedding, to his fine dark eyes looking deep into hers. How can her gentle husband have changed to this extent? And why? Unless she'd just never paid enough attention to his mood swings?

Jean has to leave the château, and she must find him a music teacher to prepare him for the Conservatoire National. She must support the young boy's talent; otherwise, it would be like slaying God. She feels she's been given a mission. It will cost money, but she needn't tell her husband she's taking charge of Jean Septembre's studies. She has personal savings. Her notary could transfer the funds without her husband knowing a thing.

The marchioness will be meeting with a friend in Lyon in three weeks' time, an extraordinary teacher she met after the war. She lied to the marquess, pretending she had to go there for medical tests, and said Georgette and little Danièle would accompany her on the train. He shrugged his shoulders, growling:

"As you like."

But then tried to do better:

"Are you unwell?"

"Recurring headaches. The doctor wants me to consult a neurologist, to put his mind at rest."

"It's that blasted piano the kids won't stop playing."

"Not at all, their music enchants me."

"If you say so."

She and the marquess have slept in separate rooms since Blaise's birth. Occasionally, he knocks on her door in the middle of the night, asking for a cuddle while muttering inaudible words. He returns to his old gentle self. They make love in silence, and he, so boorish, softens, kissing her lips, her nape, her thighs voluptuously. Then, once dressed, he leaves the room without looking back, almost ashamed of his proximity to a woman. Even if she's his wife.

That Sunday, after listening to Jean play, Colette, moved and buoyed by her brother's genius, wants to find the mother. Blaise accompanies her, abandoning Jean at the keyboard, but he barely notices their departure. Blaise leaves Colette outside the kitchens, where Georgette is helping to prepare the Sunday lunch. Colette greets her, then peels vegetables, gets plates and cutlery ready, and lays trays. Danièle, who's now two, never leaves the mother's skirts. Colette holds out her arms to her.

"Going to come and give your big sister a kiss?"

The child snivels. Which makes Georgette smile.

"It's your mop of hair what frightens her."

Mother and daughter have nothing to say to each other. Colette makes an effort, giving news of her work, of the vocational-certificate exam coming up, but never reveals her terror at time passing. She'll have to leave Mokhtar after her apprenticeship. To go where? He'll never be able to keep her on. Pay her even the smallest wage. So she talks about Jean, gets fired up, announces that he has a great future, that he'll play around the world, but the mother grimaces, as if the passion and talent of her son were some serious illness. Danièle looks like the father; she has his big nose and jutting chin. Danièle is so different to Jean. The mysteries of genetics fascinate Colette. Do fairy godmothers really lean over certain cradles?

On Sunday afternoon, Georgette gets time off. After the meal, she takes a nap with the little one. It's the day when Jean isn't supposed to play the piano, the marquess has forbidden it. So he listens to his radio program, amazed at the sounds produced. Sonatas, musical excerpts, symphonic concerts, pre-recorded and live. Or then, depending on the season, the cold, the fading light, he, Blaise, and Colette swim in the small pond down below, go for a walk, pick flowers, mushrooms, blackberries, go cycling . . . It's on Sunday afternoon that she finds Jean's hand back in hers, and now, that hand seems enchanted.

When it's time to go home, Blaise cycles with her perched on the luggage rack of his bike, back to the shoe-repair shop. And if it's raining or icy, it's the marchioness who gets the car out to drive her there. Before she leaves, a kiss on the cheek and some words, whispered in her ear, from Jean:

"I think I don't love Mommy very much. Can that bring me bad luck?"

"Love can go away and then come back. Don't you worry. See you next Sunday."

26

October 30, 2010

Three years ago, your aunt phoned me during the night. She said: 'Jacques, you have to come and sign my death certificate.' I recognized her voice. She didn't seem to have gone mad, but sounded very anxious. I went to Rue Pasteur and found her, she was waiting for me on the sidewalk outside her shop, with Louis Berthéol beside her. When I saw their two silhouettes in the dark, frankly, it gave me the willies. They looked like two ghosts. We went into the house without exchanging a word. Your aunt was really pale. I'd never seen her in that state. She didn't want to tell me anything about the woman, whose death I could certify, in the room you always slept in. I'm not sure if the term 'niece's room' is appropriate. But a woman had died right there, in your bed. She was under the sheets. Probably cardiac arrest. Absolutely nothing to suggest a suspicious death. Not a drug-induced death, and no trace of any blows. I'm used to it, you know. I've signed so many death certificates and burial permits. And seen so many fishy things, so many folks who 'fell down the stairs.'

"She was a woman of around sixty. Same age as your aunt, I'd say. But the main thing . . . And I don't think I've ever been so scared in my life. Or maybe not scared, but ill at ease. And you know me. A provincial doctor has known everything, seen everything, been through everything. He goes into everyone's homes, at any hour, day or night. He sees chests, asses, fevers, throats, cancers, denials of pregnancy, raging toothaches, dislocated shoulders, old folks, babies, desperately lonely, destitute people . . . and so on. I started in 1974, under President Giscard. I could write my memoirs, but they'd bore everyone stiff, and no one would believe me, anyhow.

What I'm trying to tell you is, what made me feel ill at ease that night was that the woman lying in the bed, it was Colette. And her double was staring at me, standing near me, her eyes vacant. I had to sit down to avoid passing out. Which has never happened to me. After a moment, all I managed to say to your aunt was: 'Explain.' To which she replied: 'There's nothing to explain. I died tonight, in this bed. Louis will take care of my funeral.' And then she went up to the deceased, kissed her tenderly, and whispered: 'It'll be fine, don't worry anymore.'

"She left your room to go into hers, and started to pack her suitcase, like an automaton; she was alive, but drained of all vital substance. I followed her. I watched her for a long time. 'Colette, do you realize what you're asking of me?' She turned and looked at me beseechingly. And so, for the first time, I signed a death certificate and burial permit without seeking to know more. In any case, and I say this in all honesty, I didn't know, on that night, whether I was signing the death certificate of Colette, or of an unknown woman. I remember asking her: 'Do you have a twin sister?' And her looking at me as if I'd lost my marbles. It was the world upside down. I was the one going mad.

"I didn't hear anything for a year. After 'Colette's funeral,' which I attended, and at which I wept—you see how crazy it was—I phoned Louis Berthéol several times, to get some news. He admitted to me that she was still in Gueugnon. That she lived at a new address. I found that totally insane. It was like the witness to a crime changing their identity to disappear because of the price on their head. But we were talking about Colette Septembre, the shoe-mender of Gueugnon, supporter of the football club . . . 'And Agnès,' I asked Louis, 'does she know her aunt is alive?' He told me that no one in the world, apart from him and me, knew. I sensed that the unknown woman had been living at Colette's for a long time."

"What makes you say that?"

"The woman had hung photos on the walls of your room. Photos of funfairs, portraits of strange or disfigured people. And one of a lion. When your aunt put photos on the walls, they were of footballers, of you, or of your parents. And I caught sight of some clothes hanging in your half-open wardrobe. Colorful dresses. Colette never wore colorful dresses . . . There's another thing that struck me. In the woman's room, I'm sure some photos had been removed before my arrival, so I wouldn't see them. They'd left behind slightly paler rectangles on the wallpaper. When your aunt herself departed for good, she took her mystery with her. Why hide a dead woman? You can hide a threatened or wanted person, but why continue hiding her once her life is over? Once she's dead, she's dead."

Dr. Pieri stands up, goes into the sitting room, where the cassettes and recorder are lying on the inflatable mattress.

"What's all that?"

"Cassettes that Colette recorded for me."

He stares wide-eyed, then pulls open a kind of secret compartment under the TV cabinet and takes out a bottle of whiskey.

"My favorite. She kept it for me," he admits, with a smile.

He returns to the kitchen and pours himself a little before continuing:

"No news for a year. Finally, one evening, she phoned me. I was still at the office: 'Jacques, something's wrong.' She gave me this address, reminding me that she was dead. So it had to stay a secret. I shouldn't write it down. Just commit it to memory. Frankly, at that moment, I thought she'd lost it. And that's how I turned up here, one evening, at around eight. It was dark. Colette was in agony. Renal colic. I gave her a jab to reduce the pain and warned her that a hospital stay might be necessary to break up the stones, if she didn't pass them. She replied: 'You should put me down like an old animal, because I'll never set foot in a hospital.' I managed to treat her. And came back regularly. For a long time, I would observe her and wonder whether it was Colette or her double. You don't need me to tell you that she was never talkative. To say the least. And then one Sunday, I dropped by unexpectedly. She was watching *Téléfoot*. At that moment, I knew that Colette was alive. And it was definitely her I was treating. And so I couldn't help myself, I poured myself a small whiskey, like tonight, and we watched the program together, and I asked her: 'Colette, what's this all about? Who is that woman, buried in your tomb? Why are you hiding like a thief?' And she said: 'Jacques, the less a secret is known, the more it's worth.'—'Fine, but just reassure me: you're not being threatened by someone, are you?'—'I can't be threatened, seeing as I'm dead.' And she said nothing more. So I followed normal procedure, checking her blood pressure before leaving, and then went home to my wonderful Hélène."

"Hélène?"

"My beloved. Could you pop the bottle back in same place for me? I'll be coming again to see you. How are you feeling? Do you need anything, while the good *dottore* is here?"

"No, I'm fine."

"Are you staying long?"

"Until I get the burial permit . . . I've told stories all my life. Well, not for four years. But discovering that my aunt wasn't dead the same year that my husband left for good, and for another woman, well, that story beats them all . . . "

"Maybe he didn't leave for someone else, maybe he's waiting for you."

"Yeah, well, right now, he's in Mauritius with his new nymph and our daughter . . . Unlikely he's waiting for me."

"You don't know."

"Stop, Jacques, I'm not ten anymore, when you'd say to me: 'It'll only sting a little' . . . "

He kisses me goodbye and heads for the door.

"Jacques, you didn't by any chance take any photos of Colette, these past few years? Just like that, casually, with your phone?"

"She'd never have allowed it. And I'll admit that, even on the sly, I wouldn't have done so. I decided that, by saying nothing to anyone, not even to you, I was protecting her."

"How did you manage for her medication?"

"I always have supplies in advance, from the labs. I brought some by regularly. She had no specific problems. Slightly raised blood pressure toward the end. Osteoarthritis, inevitably. And I'd give her something for the circulation, a little paracetamol, well, you get the picture."

"Yes, I get the picture. But she died for real, this time."

He smiles sadly at me.

"Call me when you receive the burial permit."

"What are you going to say to the cops?"

"That when I arrived at Colette Septembre's in 2007, I certified the death in her bedroom, her bed. But I'll never say that she was standing beside me at the time. Never."

27

I put the No. 20 cassette, on which I'd written "Aimé Chauvel," the footballer with the ebony curls, back into its plastic box.

Basically, Colette had put together collections all her life. First the football one, and later, these cassettes. She had a visceral need to record the present, and events, somewhere.

I don't close my eyes to pick the next cassette. I want to listen to the rest of No. 7. The recording concerning Blanche. Because that unknown woman, that woman who died in my room at Colette's, it was her. The photos on the walls, the picture of the lion, doubtless Naja, the lioness Blanche talks about, and the "monsters" are all proof of that. I reinsert the cassette.

COLETTE
It's January 9, 2003.

So, she waited two days before continuing with the recording. Is Blanche by her side again?

COLETTE
You see, Agnès, people don't really look at us. When people ask you how you are, most of the time, they're not interested in the answer. And if a girl looks like another girl, well that suits them fine, they think it's just chance. A lot can be blamed on chance.

The phone rings. She lets it ring without stopping the recording. I picture her face. I wonder if it's me who's trying to call her from America and if she's thinking: "Agnès will call back later; right now, I'm recording these words for her." Did January 9 fall on a Tuesday? How could I have imagined that, when I phoned her, another woman was living with her, in "my" room?

COLETTE

So people aren't that interested in what might be extraordinary in life, they're not curious. They just get by. Blanche and I, we always looked alike. From head to toe. At ten, we had the same appearance, the same size, the same hair, dark brown and slightly curly. And the same hairstyle. A ponytail. At school, girls had to have their hair tied back, boys had to have it short. We have the same light skin, thick lips, almond-shaped brown eyes, black lashes and eyebrows. I never understood my brother's beauty. Where it came from. The ugliness of my parents and of my sister Danièle, and even less, my dark looks, coming from who knows where. After Jean's death, since I was always dressed in black, some people in Gueugnon started calling me "the Corsican."

I never believed for a second that the mother might have sinned. Neither in Jean's case, nor in mine. And anyhow, when? Where? For all those years, she never left the farm. Except to go to market with the father. The only other man she came across was Sénéchal, who was a shithead but not a skirt-chaser. And it has to be said, the mother wasn't that alluring. And she never seemed drawn to anyone. Not even the father. I never saw them kiss or say anything loving. Nothing. At our house, everything was rationed.

She stops speaking for a few seconds. Is she crying? I can't detect any particular emotion in her voice.

COLETTE

Already, at ten, there's something much harder in Blanche's eyes than in mine, or rather, how can I put it, the top of her face, her forehead and eyes, they're already defined, like those of a . . . (she looks for the word) *. . . woman. Unlike me, she doesn't look like a little girl. My childhood at the farm, compared with what she went through at her circus, was easy as pie. And then, I was saved, I had Blaise and Mokhtar. Not to mention what my little Jean brought me. I was lucky, Blanche wasn't. Her father didn't die.*

She shifts a little on her chair, then continues in a hushed voice.

COLETTE

And he's still alive. Anyhow, I see her again three years after she first came to my school in Gueugnon. We're in fifth grade. Her family's big top is on Place de Gaulle, like last time, and Blanche will spend two weeks in our class. The teacher presents her to the other pupils and, exactly like three years before, all eyes turn to me. How come the gyppo looks like the bumpkin, like peas in a pod?

Put yourself in my place, Agnès, I don't know if you've ever come across a person who looks like you, but I can tell you that, after a kind of apprehension, you gravitate toward that person because you recognize yourself. The other person draws you in as if you were in front of a mirror. It's the other you. I wanted to touch her. With Blanche, the first thing we did was to compare our hands. And check whether we had beauty spots in common, or identical birthmarks. She has a star-shaped one on her knee. I don't. We were almost disappointed. How to explain it to you . . . I was never pretty; she was. If you'd done a close-up of each part of our faces with your camera, you'd have seen our differences. It was just about general appearance. At ten, Blanche already attracted the boys, but they didn't look at me. There was already desire in the older boys' eyes as they watched Blanche, her movements. Even the teacher. That really struck me. In class, he didn't behave the same with her as with us. He spoke to her as if she was fifteen, when she was no taller than us, or even more developed. Which goes to show, everything depends on people's perception. And on their shoes. But that's another story.

The phone rings again, and unlike last time, I hear her getting up and answering it: "Hello? Ah, is that you, Pierre?" A brief silence ensues. Something changes in her voice, I detect joy. "Hang on a minute," she says to her caller, "just coming." I hear her scurrying back to the recorder. She's wearing slippers. She stops the recording.

Pierre. Which Pierre? My Pierre? My husband? My husband phoned my aunt? No, it must be another Pierre, a customer. No. She didn't use the informal "*tu*" with her customers. Didn't with many people. Pierre who?

I phone Jacques Pieri, who'd given me his cellphone number before leaving. I check the time: 11 P.M. After all that the doctor had confided to me, he can't be sound asleep already, things must be churning around in his head. Our memories are our sleepless nights. He answers immediately:

"Yes."

"Tell me, Jacques, did my aunt have a friend called Pierre?"

Long silence.

"Your husband, the actor."

His answer annoys me. Pierre, Colette's friend? He was her nephew-in-law. Or whatever the husband of a niece is called.

"Aside from my husband. Here, in Gueugnon."

A pause.

"Take a look among the footballers."

"She'd never have said '*tu*' to a footballer."

"A junior?"

"Perhaps."

"A customer?"

"Or then a child."

"A fellow fan?"

"Yeah. Could be."

"Otherwise, apart from Louis Berthéol, the storekeepers' kids who came to wish her a happy new year, and your old friends, I don't think she saw many people. She'd leave her shop every other Saturday to attend matches . . . Pierre's a common name, it's not like Amalric . . . And anyhow, considering the mysteries she's left us with, I think anything's possible."

"Yes, the mysteries . . . What time d'you think it is in Mauritius?"

"Um . . . I'd say one or two in the morning. I can't remember if it's a two- or three-hour difference from us."

"You've been there?"

"Yes."

"How come?"

"On honeymoon with Hélène."

"Ah, of course."

"Goodnight, Agnès."

"Goodnight, Jacques."

On honeymoon. Mine I spent in a cutting room, wading through kilometers of film.

Pierre and I got married once the shooting of *Le Banquet des anciens* was over, in 1993. We had a wrap party, with actors, crew, producers. We didn't yet know that the movie would be such a resounding success. At the time, Pierre was already well-known; he'd been in a few notable movies. Me, not at all. First feature film at twenty-one. I'd been writing screenplays for ten years. That one had caught the eye of my producer.

Surrounded by a phenomenal technical team, I managed to "commit" the miracle of the first movie, which itself became miraculous in myriad ways. By making it, I gave myself a magic carpet.

A year before, I'd made a short, "*Au piano*." It was selected at lots of important festivals. And, with unbelievable luck, garnered numerous prizes. Awards are reassuring.

It was for the making of "*Au piano*" that I met Pierre. A friend of a friend knew him personally and arranged for me to have coffee with him in Paris. At the time, I still lived in Lyon.

I'd seen him "not acting" in movies, and I liked his strong features, those "of a wandering Jew," as Georges Moustaki sings. His sincerity, his smile, his lilt. He was like no one else. I didn't want a fashionable actor. Despite my total inexperience, I knew what I wanted. I was looking for a man who would exude the same thing as my father, a thing that smells true, that smells good. A whimsicality hidden behind an almost austere face. I wanted to be bowled over. I'd just written the story of a pianist in a bar who falls in love with a customer who's having her bachelorette party there, with friends. It's Mathilde Seigner who plays the bride-to-be. Marvellous Mathilde, then unknown, whom I'd noticed playing a tiny part in a play. There are no small parts for great actors.

I met up with Pierre one morning, in his neighborhood near the Champs-Élysées. I had a strawberry milk, to stand out a bit, from what I still don't know, and he had a stiff double espresso. When he turned up, he was polite but grumpy. Looking a bit rough. He told me he'd been up late. The first thing he asked was: "But how old are you?" As if my youth was suspicious.

I was immediately impressed by him. I told him the story of my pianist, to make myself seem important and to convince him he could have faith in me. Exactly as if I were asking for his hand for the duration of a movie. Me, the glorious unknown, I wasn't lacking in chutzpah.

"So, my pianist, well, you, if you accept the part, as soon as he sees this young girl entering the bar, where he plays every evening and no one really listens, he completely changes his usual repertoire. As if he were suddenly bewitched, possessed by popular songs the moment he sees her come through the door. Usually, my pianist, well, you, you play jazz standards without ever turning your mic on; you're a purist, only Coltrane and Fitzgerald count."

When I mentioned those two names, I glimpsed his smile for the first time.

"And when you see that girl surrounded by her friends, you start singing the kind of hits one hears on Radio Nostalgie. Which makes the bar owner groan and rather surprises the group of girls sipping champagne. The one who's taken your fancy is heavily made up and sporting a tee shirt that says: 'Almost married, final fling.' And you, well, my pianist, it drives you crazy with love. Like Dustin Hoffman in *The Graduate*."

When I mentioned Radio Nostalgie, I saw him wince for the first time. But I thought I'd lost him for good with Hoffman. I heard him thinking, yet another female who fancies she's the old wave and thinks she's original. The old wave, that's what he called the New Wave, with a serious aversion to Jean-Luc Godard, apart from two of his movies, *Pierrot le Fou* and *À bout de souffle*. Personally, I liked *Le Mépris*, or *Contempt* in English. And he'd shout at me because I liked it. "It's him who's contemptuous of you!" he'd keep telling me.

Pierre continued to pretend he was listening, while gazing benignly at me. He checked his watch, paid the check, screenplay in hand. Mumbled: "I'm not that free at the moment, I'll read it and get back to you." Sure of never seeing me again. He told me that later. Except that he called me that very evening: "I'll do it, your movie."

The innocence of youth meant that I didn't even think, that's insane, this well-known actor has agreed to do a short with me.

We filmed for three days in a piano bar near l'Opéra, with Pierre and Mathilde. Without a doubt, the best memory of my professional life. I think my strength is having always been well supported. I've only ever worked with good people. My cinematographer, Guillaume Schiffman, who was also my sound engineer and cameraman on "*Au piano*," is a wonderful guy. Highly acclaimed today. He could always grasp the shots I had in my head. He's my best translator of light, emotion, and movement.

Pierre admitted to me later that he'd laughed so much while reading my screenplay, he'd decided he couldn't miss working with a chick who could write something that wacky. I even managed to get him to sing Richard Cocciante's "*Le Coup de soleil*" and Diane Tell's "*Si j'étais un homme*." Fortune favors the innocent.

Thanks to my zany rom-com, I was able to find financial backing for *Le Banquet des anciens*, and I, the child of a pianist and a violinist, met the man of my dreams . . .

It was after reading the screenplay of *Le Banquet* that Pierre proposed to me. He said:

"My love, if we do this movie, if we make it to the end, I'll marry you on the day of the wrap party."

"But will I get to have a wedding dress?"

"You'll get to have all the dresses you want."

"But will we be marrying for real?"

"We'll be marrying for real, living together for real, and maybe even, if we don't become too annoying, growing old together for real."

The mayor of a town close to Giverny, where we were shooting, stretched the rules, since we weren't residents, and got us a special dispensation. He married us on a Saturday morning. Louis Berthéol came with Colette, my mother with her best friend, a conductor. I'm sure he was her lover, but she never broached the subject with me. Sometimes I'd tease her: "Mom, is he your boyfriend?" She'd roll her eyes with a smile, so I'd leave it at that.

We rented a *gîte* in the countryside, laid out a buffet like in my movie, and we drank and danced all day long. We mixed up our lives, the real ones and the fictional ones. All exhausted after those intense weeks of work, the crew members didn't seem to know whether we were still in the middle of a shoot, or in the middle of a wedding. Did I see Pierre as my actor, the man who'd given me far more than expected in the leading role of my movie? Or as my husband, my ideal, the man I was marrying for life? Inevitably, a bit of both. What's certain is that I loved both of them; I loved everything about that man.

It was the first and only time I saw Colette dance. She waltzed with my script supervisor and my cinematographer. It was also the first time I'd seen her in a dress. Blue with butterflies fluttering all over it. A bit too wide, a bit too big. And white pumps. Were they Blanche's? Was she already back in contact with her in 1993?

Colette and Mom seemed happy for us. They must have felt a bit excluded from the group, isolated, even though everyone was sweet with them. Being back with a team at a wrap party is being back with a group of people who've just lived a life at full speed in a timeless bubble, a life that others can't possibly comprehend.

"Hello?"

"It's me."

"I know. Names come up on phones now."

"And how does mine come up? Just Agnès? Agnès Septembre? Agnès Dugain? Ana's mother?"

I hear him sighing.

"Are you aware of the time difference?"

"Yes. Ever since you left me."

He moves, goes into another room. I wonder if he sleeps naked with the other one.

"I have a question to ask you."

"I'm listening."

"When we lived in the States, did you ever phone my aunt behind my back?"

"Why behind your back?"

He stresses the word "behind," annoyed.

"Well, because she was my aunt, not yours."

I hear him lighting a cigarette.
"Yes."
My blood turns cold.
"Yes what?"
"Yes, I did phone Colette behind your back."

28

Cassette No. 7
Continuation of "Blanche" recording

How long did Blanche and Colette live side by side? In the early days of my relationship with Pierre, we would sleep at Colette's. After that, we'd stay at the hotel so as not to disturb her, even though we didn't disturb her. Quite the opposite, I imagine she must have loved having us in her home. But she never let anything show. The truth was, we sought comfort, and to escape the narrow bed I'd slept on as a teenager.

When we left for the States, Pierre had suggested buying her a plane ticket so she could come visit. She always turned it down. He even offered to buy two tickets, one for her and one for Louis, so she wouldn't be traveling alone. She never accepted because of her shoe-repair shop. "Couldn't you close it?"—"Oh no, certainly not!"—"Get someone to replace you."—"Who?"—"A shoe-mender, Colette." I remember one of her extraordinary explanations, which had amused Pierre: "I don't do the same kind of work as you, Pierre; you can be replaced by another actor, but that's impossible for me."

BLANCHE

The second time I came to the École Pasteur in Gueugnon, we were in fifth grade. School is mandatory, and my genitor feared getting into trouble. Otherwise, he couldn't have cared less whether I attended. As soon as we went past the road sign for Gueugnon, I thought: "This is where that girl who looks like me lives . . . The one with the kind eyes." I'd hoped to see you again, Colette. It had been three years . . . And there you were. Sitting in the middle of the class, like a sister who was waiting for me, in clothes that were too big. You smiled as soon as you saw me. Do you remember? I'd stay with you during the lunch hour. I loved staying with you. We'd spend hours talking, sitting on the same bench.

COLETTE

Since your pockets were empty, mine were full of apples for you. And my satchel was packed with bread and hard-boiled eggs, which we gobbled up.

BLANCHE

You'd ask so many questions about my acrobatics. About the spectators all watching. If I was scared of falling. How old I was when I learned to do rolls, the splits, to juggle. You'd imagine my costumes and makeup. I gave you the impression of being a princess in sequins.

COLETTE

Yes, and I'd never seen a real princess.

I pause the tape to boil some water. When I open the cupboard, I find two little packs of Colette's herbal tea, *Nuit tranquille*, her sugar lumps, her coffee filters, and her two mugs, one of which is cracked. I picture her living here. A recluse. Separated from Blanche. What sadness and what appalling solitude. What did she think about? About us in the States? About Pierre, who would secretly phone her before her supposed death? About the League 3 matches? The players? Did Louis bring her the newspaper every day?

It must be one or two in the morning now, and Ana is sure to be sound asleep on her island. After hanging up, Pierre went back to "the other one" in their bed. I couldn't get out a single word once he'd admitted to calling Colette behind my back. Dumbstruck. Stupefied. Furious. Intrigued. I'm not sure. What could an actor living in California and a shoe-mender working in Gueugnon possibly have to talk about?

I return to the recorder, cup in hand, and press play. Once again, Colette's and Blanche's voices ring out between the walls. I hear them burst into laughter at the same time. What's disturbing is that they have the same way of stifling their joy. Their laughter is almost muted.

I imagine them, side by side in front of the recorder, same figure, same face.

BLANCHE
The princess of a realm where the king was an ogre. Which is why I kept you away from the big top. Until that day when . . . You tell.

COLETTE
During the second week, four days before you were set to leave, you said to me: "Colette, I'm going to show you my family. I warn you, it's strange, it can seem scary. But no one is nasty, quite the opposite. The most important thing is that my genitor never sees you, and he's away for the day."

BLANCHE
I didn't want him to find out about you. He was capable of snatching you away from your parents to exhibit the two of us together. Two fairground freaks who look alike without being related.

COLETTE
If I hadn't had Jean, I'd have left with you . . . When we arrived at the square, we met Nestor, a giant with a lovely smile. His hands were as big as rackets. "This is my friend Colette." He said: "Looks like your sister."—"Yes, I know, but she isn't my sister. And don't tell Soudoro you saw us." He joked: "I see nothing, I'm too high up." I asked you who Soudoro was. You whispered in my ear: "My genitor."

BLANCHE
I wouldn't have let him take you away. Those who followed him suffered too much.

COLETTE
I asked you where you lived. You pushed open the door of a caravan, there was a big unmade bed, a corner with a coffee pot, some crockery, and a cupboard. There was also a huge poster with a lion on it. It took up all the space. As you showed me the bed, you said: "This is our

home." And then you took three colored balls out of your pocket and started to juggle. I was spellbound. But what amazed me most was when you showed me your costumes. A blue leotard with a tulle skirt and lace sleeves, the same in white, and a pink sequined dress. Tights, shiny shoes, and a spangled jacket. How I envied you! They were like a doll's clothes . . . Like those in the window of the Galeries Modernes, on Rue Jean-Jaurès . . . You put on some strange slippers and led me into the big top. A vast forsythia-yellow and poppy-red circle. You climbed a ladder, lithe as a cat, and started to walk on your wire. I was scared you'd fall. I'd never seen an acrobat in real life. The other girls of my age weren't nice, but you, you were unique, with a unique life. I think that right then, I already loved you. You were my reflection who lived a different life to mine. And you smiled all the time, though your eyes told a different story. They were solemn.

I watched you, balancing on your wire. A girl tightrope-walker. A girl-bird. I'd never seen anything as beautiful as you, apart from Jean.

Then you slid back down and asked me which of your costumes I'd like. At first, I didn't understand. You insisted: "Choose one, I'll give it to you. We're the same size."

Silence.

BLANCHE
You took the blue leotard. I know you dreamed of picking the pink ballet dress, but didn't dare. I saw it in your eyes.

Silence.

BLANCHE
My costumes were worn-out. Patched up, and then some. They made an impression, but the fabric wasn't good quality. But you, you gazed at them as if they were treasures.

COLETTE
Until I was fourteen, I slept in it. To hold on to you a little. After you left, you sent me two postcards at the address I'd given you. Blaise's

address. And then nothing. No one knew that I was wearing the blue leotard under my clothes when I arrived at Mokhtar's.

Silence.

COLETTE
One day, Agnès came across it. When little, she'd rummage in my drawers, hoping to find I don't know what. She was always disappointed. Except for the day when she found it, wrapped in tissue paper. I gave it to her.

They stop the recording. And I put it on pause. I remember wearing that costume. It's a distant memory. I thought it was a fairy's dress that had turned up at Colette's by magic. That it could never have belonged to her. It remained in my fancy-dress box for a long time.

BLANCHE
As you came out of the caravan, you bumped into Fabrizio, who was holding Noé by the hand.

COLETTE
A small man and a Siamese monkey . . . Your life was like a fairy story.

BLANCHE
A story with two sides to it. One, very beautiful, the other, very dark . . . After the lioness died, we stayed in the south of France. My father wanted to buy another big cat, "a tired old one at a knock-down price," he'd say. He went from illicit zoo to traveling circus. But he had no luck, until one day, he heard about a Siamese monkey named Noé. Can you imagine? He waved a bag of money under its owner's nose and away it came with us. But as I've said, the animals were nothing but window-dressing.

Wherever we went, my genitor would hunt for fresh meat. He'd lurk around hospitals or asylums to root out people suffering from rare conditions, whether congenital or genetic. Disfigured humans he could exhibit and make money out of. And as soon as he'd "worn them out," he'd throw them onto the side of the road.

One day in 1959, with the excuse that she was old and of no interest to anyone anymore—"You're losing yer feathers, me old bird"—he sent Natalia, his bearded lady, packing. I loved her like a mother, and he was jealous of my love for her. I don't know where or when he "disposed" of her behind all our backs. I never heard another word about the gentlest person I knew during my entire childhood.

Silence. I hear Colette getting up, leaving the room, then returning to Blanche, who picks up where she left off. I wonder what Colette went to do. Or look for.

BLANCHE
I'm only saying all this so that Agnès knows that such a thing really existed. It was illegal to exhibit "fairground freaks." Human zoos had been banned before the war. But Soudoro was well aware of his fellow men's morbid curiosity. He'd hide his "monsters" behind heavy drapes and make those who wanted to see "the grotesque with their own eyes" pay under the counter.

I'm not exaggerating. They were shut away in an isolated caravan that no one was allowed to enter. I remember the syringes in the trash cans; I think he pumped them with sedatives. But as soon as the police got wind of what he was doing, we'd pack up and go.

COLETTE
Before heading back to school, we went past a stand that was closed. You lifted a board and, with a mischievous grin, swiped two sticks of barley sugar . . . I'd never seen or eaten any before.

BLANCHE
You saved it for your brother.

Silence. I imagine them gazing and smiling at each other.

COLETTE
As we walked back to school, I asked you: "Where's your mother?" And you replied: "My mother's just fine where she is." I persisted: "She

doesn't live with you?" You took out your three colored balls and started juggling again. One ball fell and bounced on the sidewalk. I ran to catch it. It was soft, like velvet. "She hit the ceiling."—"She's a trapeze artist?"—"No, silly, the ceiling's the sky, heaven, she died."

Blanche

I was the child of a ghost. I owned nothing of hers. Only these words from Soudoro on my fourth birthday: "She died in an accident . . . Can't remember where she's buried. Never speak to me of her again."

29

October 31, 2010

I fell asleep, and the cassette kept playing. It's now nine in the morning. Time to take a shower and tidy up a bit. Back to reality in this 1950s house, and I feel like I'm on the most extraordinary voyage.

I pull on my sneakers and cross the road to knock on the door at No. 21, the door of the neighbor who left the soup. I knock, walk around the garden: no one. I leave the clean pan on the doormat.

I'll come by another time.

Back at the house, I check my phone for the hundredth time, no missed call. Pierre didn't call back.

*

After shooting "*Au piano*," after those three crazy days in that bar near l'Opéra with Pierre, Mathilde, and the crew, after getting him to sing: "*J'ai attrapé un coup de soleil, un coup d'amour, un coup de je t'aime*" . . . I heard not a word from him. I tried calling him, in vain; on his answering machine, "It's Pierre, leave me a message." No hello, thanks, please, I'll call you back. A cold, detached message.

First week:

"Yes, hello, Pierre, um, well, it's Agnès here, Agnès Septembre, I hope all's well. That you were pleased with the shoot. Call me back. I'm just editing. I'd like to show you the clips. I think it's going to be good."

Second week:

"Hello again, Pierre, it's Agnès here, I don't know if you received my last message; call me back . . . I wanted to show you some clips from the film."

Third week (tipsy):

"Yes, Pierre, it's Agnès here, I was just trying you, on the off-chance, I'm not far from your place, out with friends on the Champs-Elysées, just in case, call me back, you're wonderful in my movie. Wonderful."

Then I stopped; I felt ashamed. My actor, on whom my first story, my first images depended, despised me.

I phoned my aunt. Why did I call Colette when Mom was still alive? She was probably giving a concert somewhere. I was in tears when Colette answered.

"I've heard nothing from my actor! I'm useless, I want to die, stop writing shit stories, stop deluding myself, go and keep goats in the Larzac."

Colette's first, panicky response:

"Where's the Larzac?"

"Tata!?!" I screamed, exasperated.

The call was cut off. I thought she'd slammed the phone down on me because I'd called her *tata*, auntie. But she called me straight back:

"Is your movie good?"

I thought for three seconds.

"Yes. Well, I think so . . . I haven't totally finished it."

"Well, he'll come back then. He's an actor. When you film them well, actors come back."

"How d'you know that?"

"In football, when a manager trains his player well and he scores goals, then the player stays in his club. Folks always stay where work is well done. Look at my customers. They know that once I've repaired their shoes, they'll last a long time. So they come back. Life's as simple as that."

"But what should I do? Call him again? He doesn't answer the phone anymore."

"Stop with this business of calling him. What's the point? Are you listening to me? He'll come back . . . The sea, it always comes back."

"Have you ever seen the sea?"

"Yes. What's his name, your actor?"

"Pierre. Pierre Dugain."

She seemed to think awhile.

"Like one of the Saint-Étienne players. He did at least four seasons over there."

"Right. And after that? What did he do?"

"After, he left for Sochaux. And achieved nothing more at all."

"Why?"

"I'm telling you, that's life. Sometimes, a player can be good at one club, and then at another achieve nothing more. Your Pierre, he'll be back. He'll keep working with you. I can sense it. And if one day he does a movie with someone else, you'll see, he'll be less good than with you."

Straight after, I phone Pierre one last time:

"It's Pierre, leave me a message."

I said:

"It's Agnès, leave me a message."

And I hung up.

I finished my image editing, sound editing, color correction, and sound mixing, trying not to think of him. But how could I avoid thinking of him when, in every shot, it was his face I was scrutinizing, his voice I was hearing, the lighting on him I was tweaking?

I reassured myself by telling myself that, basically, he was a total idiot. That I really must learn to differentiate my character from the man. It helped me to keep going. To convince myself that I had to continue.

My producer told me that Pierre was unreachable. All the same, he organized a screening for the actresses and some people in the business, who responded with incredible enthusiasm. "*Au piano*" was selected by the Clermont-Ferrand International Short Film Festival. The second most important French festival after Cannes. We celebrated the event without Pierre.

And then I returned to Lyon, to my studio just by Place Bellecour. To earn my living, I worked three days a week at a Maison de la

Presse store. Which left me time to write my stories, and I liked being surrounded by newspapers, celebrity magazines, novels, and postcards.

One morning, before we opened, I was alone, arranging the dailies and periodicals on their stand, when I caught sight of him through the window, beyond the books. Pierre was watching me. He looked like a ghost. He'd lost weight. He smiled at me, gave me a vague wave. The shutter over the main door was still down. I turned the key to bring it up. It grated so much, it was like it was screaming, an unholy racket. And yet all I could hear was my heart pounding. I was expecting the worst. He'd come to admit to me that he'd found the shoot a trial due to my lack of experience. To the extent of disappearing. He'd come to tell me the truth.

"How old are you again?"

"Twenty?"

"You're not sure?"

". . ."

"Hello."

"Hello."

"What time d'you finish?"

"Three."

"D'you have plans . . . after?"

"No."

"Then I'll come by later. See you at three."

"Okay."

"See you later."

He turned on his heel and disappeared as abruptly as he'd appeared. I was shaking as I finished setting things up. That day, the headlines were back on the contaminated-blood scandal and the indictment of Laurent Fabius, Georgina Dufoix, and Edmond Hervé, as voted for by the Senate. It was a few days from Christmas. So I was a few days from being back with Colette and Mom in Gueugnon. After Dad died, we'd kept up the tradition of dining at Georges Vezant's on Christmas Eve.

The morning went by in slow motion. Each time I took the money for a daily paper with headlines reminding me of the "contaminated-blood scandal," I thought to myself that Pierre had poisoned *my* blood, and if every actor I worked with put me into such a state, the Larzac and the goats wouldn't be such a bad idea. And so I'd never be able to direct again. But I already knew that the only person I wanted to work with was Pierre, hence my despair.

At 2:55 P.M., he was waiting for me on the opposite sidewalk. He was wearing a navy-blue coat and was fifteen years older than me. I crossed over. I stood right in front of him without touching him. He was chronically shy, stammered something, grabbed my arm, and we went into a brasserie.

"Have you eaten?"

"No. But I'm not hungry."

We sat facing each other, on the side, against a street-facing window.

"A strawberry milk, is it?"

"No thanks."

"Oh? What will you drink then?"

"An apricot juice. No one knows it, but in seventeen years' time, a boy named David will write the story of a girl who's called Nathalie and who drinks an apricot juice."

"You're a clairvoyant?"

"A scriptwriter."

He smiled, and relaxed.

"Is that your next screenplay?"

"Yes. The story of a boy called David; he's just eighteen and will become a famous author."

"So I won't be in it."

"No."

"Shame."

"I thought that . . . Why did you disappear for four-and-a-half weeks?"

"Because you're twenty years old."

The waiter arrived. Pierre ordered an apricot juice, then another apricot juice.

"Let's drink to David's good health."

"I thought you'd hated shooting '*Au piano*.'"

And at that, I dissolved into tears. It had just popped out. Pierre looked concerned. He held my hand between his hands as if it were a bird that had just struck a window.

"I'm so sorry . . . I never . . . "

He squeezed my hand really hard to force me to look him in the eye, and once he'd caught my gaze, said:

"Never, ever have I enjoyed a shoot as much as yours."

"Are you making fun of me?"

He reacted as if I'd just slapped him in the face:

"I have many faults. I'm touchy, cowardly, quick-tempered, short-fused, a liar, self-centered, proud . . . in short, an actor. But I never mock. I don't even know how to; it's just not me."

Some fifteen minutes went by without either of us saying a word. I wiped away my tears with the cotton tablecloth. It was blue-and-black checked. I'd never seen one like it, and still remember it today. Finally, I was the one to break the silence:

"The truth is that in my next movie, you have the leading role."

He started laughing. I desperately wanted to kiss him.

"You learn fast. All directors make actors believe they've got the leading role."

". . ."

"What shall we do now?"

"Tomorrow morning, I'll still be twenty."

"We're in the shit."

"Mom says that when you're in the shit, you should go see a movie. And that after the movie, you'll find solutions."

"What does she do, your mother?"

"She's a violinist."

"Let's go see a movie, then."

We walked to the CNP Bellecour theater. It was showing *Un coeur en hiver—A Heart in Winter*—directed by Claude Sautet. Pierre said:

"Sautet's good."

I said:

"Sautet's wonderful."

"Aren't you a bit young to like his movies?"

"I think you're obsessed with my age."

"Possibly," he replied, grimacing.

Throughout the movie, I was perturbed by Emmanuelle Béart, who plays a violinist like Mom. I cried as I thought of my parents, majestic on the concert stage. I was perturbed by Pierre's presence beside me. I found it hard to breathe. To concentrate. I kept thinking of what he'd said: "Never have I enjoyed a shoot as much as yours." I wondered if he was going to kiss me. And if so, when. He didn't even move. I focused on Daniel Auteuil, who, apart from my ex-husband, is still my favorite actor. This magnificent movie explores, in a masterly way, the impossibility of loving. When we emerged from the theater, we didn't say a word. We walked for a long time, aimlessly, looking down at our shoes. At a red light, Pierre stopped and murmured:

"It's too awful, missing out on the love of one's life."

I replied:

"Yes."

The light turned green, but we didn't cross; he kissed me.

*

I check my messages again, nothing from Pierre. Why would he call me back? But Ilyas is suggesting a coffee at the Petit Bar.

I must find out Blanche's surname, and whether this father she calls her genitor, or Soudoro, is still alive. In the 2003 recording, Colette implies that he is. But that was seven years ago. I need to talk to Nathalie about it. She works at a newspaper; maybe there are some archives to root out.

30

1960

The train pulls into Lyon station. Eugénie de Sénéchal alights, with Jean's hand in hers. She's followed by Georgette, who's carrying Danièle in her arms. Surrounded by the crowds, Georgette's eyes dart around, two panicked marbles. Really, Jean never does nothing like other folks. She'd be better off at the château, polishing the copper pans.

Georgette has never taken the train. Never seen any towns other than Gueugnon, Digoin, and Montceau-les-Mines, twenty-odd kilometers from the village she was born in. The farthest destination she knows.

They get into a taxi and head for the Conservatoire National Supérieur. Silently, Jean practices in his head. He must play a Chopin nocturne for the teacher who might then prepare him for entrance to the conservatoire when he's fourteen. A teacher he'll board with, in Lyon. Who's a friend of the marchioness. "You'll get a few minutes to sight-read some music before playing it to him," Blaise explained.

He's been working on his musical notation for weeks now. At the Sénéchals', and in the evening in his room, on a keyboard Blaise drew for him on a piece of cardboard, to keep his fingers supple.

Eugénie de Sénéchal has asked Georgette to lie:

"Don't tell the marquess about Jean's audition. If he asks you any questions when we get back, tell him you accompanied me to the doctor's. Today, Jean will be assessed."

An audition, what's that? Georgette hates the idea of lying to the boss.

The taxi travels along the Rhône, and Georgette watches the

well-dressed passersby rushing in all directions. City people. Madame de Sénéchal's perfume is overpowering, Danièle is sniveling; her mother finally pinches her, gently.

"Behave yerself, don't shame me."

Her son is shaming her enough as it is. She watches him out of the corner of her eye, he's sitting straight as a prince, who on earth does he think he is? Yet Jean weren't born with no silver spoon in his mouth. Really, he's only attached to Colette, taking her for his mother. Their eldest was the first to put crazy ideas into his head. Yes, it's Colette's fault, all this.

The world is conspiring against her, when she just wants to be left to her widow's plight in peace. At night, she prays to the Blessed Virgin for Jean not to get bad ideas into his head. Like that Lulu, a mutt that only sniffed the asses of male dogs. Bitches could flaunt themselves at him, tails in the air, he'd only chase after the males. Deviance, that's what the marquess calls it when going on about his great lump of a son. She heard him saying that to his wife, who was weeping into a handkerchief with her initials embroidered on it. Deviance. She stifles her nausea at the thought. Her poor Robin had finally done away with the mongrel. It was worthless, couldn't even produce puppies. They'd buried the body deep, topped it with quicklime, and pretended that Lulu had run away. Colette had looked everywhere for it, yelling its name in the meadows and all over the forest. Jean, then only small, had wept. "A brat that blubs soon as a mutt dies and his sister's out the door, it don't bode well at all," Robin would say.

The taxi parks outside a large building. All four of them go inside, and the place sure takes the cake. Rooms three times bigger than the castle's. Massive paintings on the walls. Georgette inspects the dust on the furniture; she can't help it, that's her job. Madame de Sénéchal introduces herself, and then Jean. Of Georgette and Danièle, she says: "They're accompanying us." *I'm still the kid's mother, you know,* Georgette silently harrumphs.

They walk up three floors, marble steps, can't be easy to clean, all that. She spots traces of dirt and wear on the chandeliers and can't help but smile; that'd never happen at the château.

The director of the establishment bows before the marchioness, asks her how she is. Observes Jean and puts his hand on Danièle's head as if patting a little pet. He shakes Georgette's hand when the marchioness announces to him: "Jean's mother." And here's shame again, taking over her, rising to her face; she goes red. What's she doing here? This man staring at her, what'll he think of her appearance, her maid's hands, her clothes? The marchioness has lent Jean some of Blaise's old garb for the occasion. He looks like the Sénéchal's son. He's standing nice and straight, at ease, as if he's sprouted up here, in this very building. The director asks him to follow him; he's going to introduce him to Monsieur Levitan, who might be his future piano teacher.

"He'll begin by listening to you and asking you some questions. I've seen your school report; you'll have to improve in some subjects to apply to the conservatoire one day."

The director turns back to Georgette and the marchioness.

"I'll take him from here. You may wait in the adjoining room, first door on the left. Some hot beverages will be brought for you."

Georgette, with a sleeping Danièle in her arms, follows Madame. They sit on a bench, close to each other. It's the third time they're seated side by side on the same day, train, taxi, conservatoire, when up until now, it had never happened. *If Robin saw this, he'd be furious. He always said: "To each their place."*

Suddenly, Georgette stiffens; she hears the piano. Damned piano. Damned Colette. Instrument of woe. Load of nonsense. As for the marchioness, she's smiling, showing all her pretty teeth; she opens her hands, runs her fingers over her skirt, seems to be playing along with Jean. The diamond on her ring finger flashes like a sun. Is it the music that has this effect on her?

Just as suddenly, Danièle starts to writhe like a Fury and scream. The marchioness's fingers instantly freeze and her face darkens. The embarrassment has just changed sides. Georgette springs up, quick as a jack from its box, charges along the main corridor and hurtles down the three flights of stairs. Why had the marchioness brought her? She could have come on her own with Jean. What an idea! She finds herself back on the sidewalk, like some beggar, the little one bawling in her arms. They get sidelong glances, her and her tot, but curiously, as soon as she's far from her son, the shame melts away.

*

Before taking the train home, they'll have "a bite to eat," as the marchioness says, gaily. She's spoken with Jean's future teacher, a delightful man, really enthusiastic about his abilities . . .

"That said, we mustn't delay, the sooner he gets started, the better, don't you think, Georgette? Don't fret about the money, I'll take care of everything."

God, how uncomfortable Georgette feels about eating at the same table as Madame. How's she going to cope? Damned piano, damned boy . . . her only boy. How happy they'd been when Jean was born! A son to keep the farm going, strong arms to ease the daily burden! She can feel tears welling up in her eyes. And what about her? How much money will she get for losing her son?

If Robin could see the four of them, sitting around a table side by side! She'd like to disappear under the table and slap Jean for giving himself airs. He's barely opened his mouth since leaving the conservatoire, but his eyes say it all; he's already changed.

The marchioness gently chides him:

"You heard what your future teacher said: your math grades have to get better. Blaise will give you some help to improve them."

As for Georgette, she's never told him he must work hard at school, since in life, what counts is learning a proper trade. Who cares if you're good or bad at math.

They catch the train. What a relief. This long day is finally coming to an end. Georgette dozes off. Danièle is behaving herself. Jean is gazing at the clouds with Madame, and they're finding animal shapes in them.

When they get home, the marchioness gives Georgette the evening off. She's not hungry, and Monsieur is dining in town with friends.

Tomorrow, Georgette will tell Monsieur de Sénéchal everything. Lyon, the piano, the teacher, the Conservatoire. The shame must switch sides.

They have their soup around the table. Danièle is on her

mother's knees. Georgette speaks to her son for the first time all day as she dunks bread into her bowl. All this commotion has made her hungry.

"So, what'd they say to you, them folks?"

"That in the morning I'll have normal school, and in the afternoon, piano and notation. I'll have a room at their place. My teacher's called David Levitan, he's married."

Georgette can't hold back a grimace. Strange name, that, Levitan . . .

"And how long'll that last?"

"A long time. Until I'm grown up. Until I get into the Conservatoire National."

"Did you tell 'em I were yer mother?"

"Yes."

"What'd you say?"

"That my father's dead and my mother works in a château. And that Colette mends shoes."

"But where's all this malarkey leading? How'll you earn yer money?"

Jean scratches his head. It's a habit he's had since he was very small. As if his thoughts were itchy.

"By playing in an orchestra that gives concerts."

"Why *gives*? It's not paid?"

"It is."

In reality, he has no idea. He's never asked himself that question. He plays the piano like he breathes.

"You don't look sure."

"I am."

"But who's in these 'orchestras'?"

"Musicians."

"Girls or fellas?" she persists, suspiciously.

"Both, I think."

"And how'll you get yerself hired in these orchestras?"

He shrugs, not knowing the answer.

"And where'll you live?"

"With the Levitans. In Lyon."

"And when these shenanigans are over, where'll you live then? It's not yer piano that'll be a roof over yer head. You think I have the means?"

Jean seems lost. She instills doubt in him. His mother's eyes say the opposite of Colette's, Blaise's, and the marchioness's. Beady eyes, wary and fearful.

"You're ten, and I'm still yer mother. Me, I'm not keen on this whole business. Tomorrow I'll talk to the marquess. I'll tell him that the marchioness, she's doing this behind his back."

"But if you say that, I won't be able to play the piano anymore!" he exclaims, on the verge of tears.

"Stop that whining. A man don't whine."

Jean is distraught. He's afraid of Monsieur. Creeps along the walls of the château, head down, so as never to meet his eye. If the marquess knows, he's had it.

"I would like Colette."

He says this out loud, like a prayer.

"She'll come on Sunday, like every Sunday," Georgette snaps, while peeling an apple.

"You're nasty."

"For poor folks like us, life's not playing, life's working! Go to bed now."

"But I'm just working on my notation!"

"Go to bed when I tell you to!"

Jean stands up and goes to his room. Danièle will sleep in her mother's bed, as usual. He takes off the clothes the marchioness lent him, as if removing a skin that isn't his; tomorrow he'll have to give them back.

Poor, his mother never stops saying that word, like some curse. Every time she says it, Jean feels as if she's pressing down on his head as hard as she can so he drowns. And yet they sleep in the warm and eat their fill. They lack nothing. But he sees Colette handing envelopes of banknotes to her mother, who hides them away in her room.

Life before did feel harder, but since his mother's been in the Sénéchals' service, nothing about daily life seems wretched to him.

This evening should be a happy evening, because he didn't play a single wrong note this morning in front of Monsieur Levitan, who watched him but didn't smile, not like Colette, Blaise, and the marchioness do, but he feels overwhelmingly sad. He's missing his sister, having his hand in hers. Jean hugs the piece of cardboard Blaise had adapted for him, the drawn keyboard; no one will take it away from him. It's his only companion in this house.

31

October 31, 2010

Seated at the back of the bar, he seems to be dreaming. As he brings the coffee cup to his lips, he looks vacant. When he sees me walk in, it's like he comes back to life.

"Were you dreaming, dear Ilyas?"

"Yes."

I kiss him.

"Your cheeks are cold."

I order a stiff espresso from Vincent, who is wiping glasses behind the bar while chatting to a customer about odds on the next races.

"Have you listened to any cassettes?" Ilyas asks, before I've even sat down.

"Yes. The ones with Colette and Blanche talking side by side."

"Who's Blanche?"

"The woman who's lying in the cemetery instead of Colette. Well, I think so."

"Totally insane!"

"Yes. And we still don't know why they did that."

"A woman from Gueugnon?"

"No. Passing through. She was born into a circus that stopped at Gueugnon in 1953 and 1956. Blanche briefly attended the École Pasteur. That's how she met Colette. After that, I don't know if the wretched circus returned. Its activities were more or less illegal. Ostensibly, it was all candies, fire-eaters, and acrobats. But for those who paid under the counter, Blanche's father, called Soudoro, would display 'monsters' who were held in appalling conditions. People suffering from malformations or mental disabilities . . . "

"Like in *The Elephant Man*?"

"Yes, except that in the fifties, such 'freak shows' were already outlawed."

"Never heard of that going on in Gueugnon."

"Some older folks must remember."

"Yes, bound to."

"I don't know Blanche's surname. Maybe one of them will mention it in another recording, but I'd be surprised."

"Get Nathalie on the case. She can find articles from back then in the newspaper's archives."

"Yes, I'll call her."

"Life's strange, without your aunt's second death, I probably never would've seen you again. You'd never have come for no reason. No one comes here for no reason. Or maybe for another funeral, one of ours."

"Hey, you're really cheerful this morning."

He smiles, his lovely, sad smile.

"We're all just passing through, don't have to be in a traveling circus for that."

"Why didn't you ever tell me that you were in love with Isabelle Émorine?"

"Because you never asked me. Another coffee?"

"Yes."

"I sometimes come across her, behind a shopping cart, when I'm at the store. We talk for thirty seconds. When you've missed out on someone, on a possible life with someone, you have absolutely nothing more to say to them. Everything is dead. And anyhow, she had children, a good marriage, a dog. All I've got is my motorbike."

"Nathalie's right, you should write."

He bursts out laughing.

"There are enough scribblers in the world. Publishing doesn't need me."

"It's not publishing that needs you, it's the readers."

He grimaces.

"No one needs me."

"Everyone needs someone. It's a peculiarity of mankind."

"And you? When's the next movie?"

"Probably never."

"You're joking?"

"Do I look like I'm joking?"

"But why?"

"Pierre, my husband. Well, my ex-husband."

"There are other actors in the world."

"Sure. Like there are other husbands. But right now, I'm a blank page, and that suits me."

"Don't believe you. A girl like you has plenty of tricks up her sleeve. Just look at your last movie."

" . . . "

Vincent is back with a tray and a third coffee.

"It's on the house!"

"Thanks Vincent. I'm going to be a live wire."

"Better to be a live wire than dead."

His riposte makes me laugh, and Ilyas, too.

"I have a proposal for you," he says. "I write a book and you write a screenplay. We give ourselves . . . "—he thinks about it—"a year, and we see what we've got. Today is . . . Vincent, what's the date today?"

Vincent glances at his watch.

"October 31."

"We'll reconvene on October 31, 2011, here, at the Petit Bar, at Vincent's."

"And what if my screenplay is blank?"

"And what if my book is? We'll wait and see."

We shake on it.

"D'you want to write about Charpie?"

He doesn't take time to think before answering. As if he'd been carrying a story, his own story, for too long.

"Among other things. All the finesse and joy there is in football, but also the misery of silence. My immigrant parents, my wings clipped one Wednesday afternoon, my feet that keep on carrying me. The fear of having a love affair. No, not the fear, the terror of having a love affair. Forever finding the wrong person, the fake blonde, the one who's married, in love with someone else, twisted, a liar . . . The loneliness of giving up alcohol. What it feels like to live without drinking, to be lucid again all the time. No longer floating in a permanent alcoholic haze. Becoming attractive again. It's not nothing, becoming attractive again. Not being parched anymore, or having a beer belly, or a bloated face upon waking. The first telltale signs that appear on the face, the nose, and the hair falling out. Kissing someone on the mouth without thinking, I smell of alcohol. Wanting to kiss someone on the mouth, because before, you only wanted to kiss the neck of bottles. Meeting shrinks or addiction experts who are even more smashed than you are. The contempt in the eyes of some medics, in short, a long, long, long journey until you find the right team, the right listener, the one who helps you find the answers."

Overwhelmed by what he's just confided to me, I can't speak anymore. When Nathalie makes her entrance, I'm almost relieved, thinking that Ilyas has already started to write. She kisses the guy sitting at the bar, "Alright, pet?" Kisses Vincent, "Alright, sweetheart?" And then joins us, all smiles. This morning, she smells of the beach, of monoi oil, despite the chill coming from the coat and hat she pulls off. I look at her hair, static electricity. Her perfume wafts me to Mauritius; Ana hasn't called me again since she got there. And Pierre must be wondering if I was sloshed when I phoned him last night. A man who leaves his wife must imagine her drunk rather than swooning in the arms of another man.

"It did me good, that pizza evening. You must all come and have supper at mine. So, my friends, what's new?"

32

1960

It's eleven in the morning. Mokhtar comes down to get the newspaper he left on the shop counter and does a double take when he sees Colette. She shouldn't be there on a Sunday. She's sobbing in front of the sewing machine, head down on her forearms. Standing in the doorway, Mokhtar daren't move. He didn't think Colette cried. Why? Everyone cries, even those who never cry. It looks like grief, real grief. When he's sad, he hides like a wounded animal. Because he misses his sister too much, his loved ones are far away, his brother is no more. Colette senses his presence, looks up, and roughly wipes away her tears.

"Why on earth are you here, m'dear?" he finally asks. "Did you hurt yourself?"

Colette stands up, looking solemn—a look he's never seen from her—and straightens a pleat in her skirt before answering him:

"The mother has denounced Eugénie de Sénéchal."

She says these words as if spitting them out. Mokhtar frowns and rubs his mustache with his thumbs . . . Denounced, the word takes him back to the war. The Gestapo, the French police, and the traitors. He witnessed, powerless, the arrest of a Jewish family in 1942. That same year, he, the foreigner, was beaten up by three masked men who burst into the shop. They left him for dead. Two broken ribs, bruises all over his body, a head injury. A miracle that he survived. He's never spoken of it to Colette. What would be the point?

"Jean isn't allowed to play the piano anymore. The marquess has forbidden him . . . Do you know any insults?"

Mokhtar thinks about it.

"In French?"

"Yes, in French."

He hesitates before taking the plunge:

"Shit, son of a whore, stupid bitch."

"What's a stupid bitch?"

"I think it's a stupid woman, but far worse," he ventures.

"The mother is the queen of stupid bitches."

"Your mother?!"

"No, *the* mother. I hate her. Starting today, I never want to see her again! She's never kissed me. How many moms do you know who don't kiss their children? Even heifers and ewes nuzzle their little ones. It's only the youngest, little Danièle, that she covers in kisses all day long. But I'm not jealous. I wouldn't want her to touch me, she stinks of garlic! And her skin's rough as sandpaper."

"Perhaps she doesn't know how to tell you things . . . and doesn't do it on purpose."

"No, I don't think so. Jean went to an audition in Lyon to study music with a top teacher. The mother's so spiteful that she told the marquess all about it. It was the marchioness's business, introducing Jean to this teacher. She knew that if her husband found out, he'd stop her . . . because of the money! This was the best teacher to prepare Jean for the conservatoire. The old marquess, he flew into a mad rage when he heard about it. He called his wife a liar and a thief. Blaise told me. Since then, she's kept to her room, and my brother's not allowed to set foot in the château. Apparently, Sénéchal's looking for a master to take Jean on as an apprentice: he's only ten, and already the marquess and the mother want to get rid of him by putting him to work! But Jean, he's made for the piano, he can't become someone else. He's a pianist like you're a shoe-mender. Like God is God, like old François is a mailman!"

"And like you should have been a teacher . . . "

She slumps onto her chair, disheartened.

"I'm happy being here with you. Blaise told me that my brother has been in bed since Thursday. He's refusing to get up for school . . . He's just going to let himself die . . . I'm sure of it!"

Mokhtar goes to sit behind his counter. He lightly strokes his mustache again while thinking.

"If I understand correctly," he says, "your brother needs a piano . . . Well, you can just have Jean here, with us; he can play every day in the church across the street."

"But how will we manage to live?"

"Like everyone else does."

". . ."

"Like everyone else, m'dear. We'll get by. And anyhow, I have the money I put aside for the trip."

"But that money, it's . . . "

Colette doesn't get to finish her sentence. Mokhtar has already gone.

*

At the table, Georgette stares into space as she mechanically spoons down her soup. It's been a good day, lunch service went smoothly. The marquess loved the rabbit stew she'd made for him. It's the first time she's seen him almost smile since the marchioness has been sulking in her room. He had three extra helpings and mopped up the sauce with hunks of bread, repeating: "Damned good." When Colette had heard that she'd told Monsieur all about Lyon and the piano, she'd refused to come over. When it's Sunday! What had she done to the Good Lord to deserve such children? The eldest, forever spouting criticism, the son who wants to live like he was born with pockets full of gold. She pats Danièle's head as she's nibbling a crust of bread and playing with the crumbs. Thank goodness she's got this one.

She starts when she sees Mokhtar standing in the doorway. They've already crossed paths in the town center.

"Has that Colette messed up?" she asks, before even greeting him.

"Good day, madame. Colette never messes up. She's a good little worker."

Georgette frowns, warily, as if hearing praise for her daughter is suspect.

"Where is Jean?" Mokhtar asks, abruptly.

"In his room."

"Is he unwell?"

"He'll get over it."

"Are you sure of that?"

She purses her lips, feels strong. It's clear the marquess respects her, ever since she told him the whole truth. Mokhtar observes this woman at the table, and her daughter clambering on her knees, worried by his presence. Colette isn't like this little one, he thinks. The opposite of her big sister.

"It seems you're looking for someone to apprentice Jean to?"

The woman's eyes light up. Not like a bonfire, more like dying embers. Doubtless the most they can express.

"What'll the pay be?"

"I'm not allowed to hire a child, madame. He'll keep going to school for now."

"And what'll be the gain?"

"For you, one less mouth to feed. And when he's old enough to apprentice, you can agree to terms with him."

"And that Colette, does she agree with the idea?"

"Yes."

"And the piano?" she asks, suspicious.

"Jean can play in the church, the priest's my friend."

Georgette eyes him, still wary. The marquess has had enough of Jean. More than he can take of him. It starts with the kid, and then she might get the blame. The boss could dismiss them, her and Danièle, because of him. Whereas like this, without the brat . . . It could be a blessing, this whole affair. No more piano. Yes, it really is a good day.

"Jean will come see you every Sunday, with Colette," Mokhtar quietly assures her.

Colette's right, he thinks. This woman is a stupid bitch, seems worse than dumb. He thinks of his own mother, gentle and loving. How sweet she smelled. Not everyone's created equal when it comes to their mother.

He'd like to speak to Jean, to reassure him, but he doesn't dare say anything else, ask for anything else. He's scared the "stupid bitch" will change her mind. He doesn't know the little boy. Can only imagine him through his big sister's love for him. He feels almost ashamed now, him, the Tunisian, at the door of this house, in front of this stranger who's staring at him.

"Have a good Sunday, madame. If you agree, it'll all work out for the best."

Georgette says a barely audible goodbye. Before letting Jean leave, she thinks, better talk to Monsieur about it.

She doesn't get the chance. About an hour after Mokhtar's departure, Colette and Blaise enter the house like a draft. Georgette is dozing. From her room, she hears Colette going into Jean's room, telling him to gather his few belongings, and announcing:

"You're leaving to live with me, at Mokhtar's!"

The mother, who hasn't really given her assent, doesn't stand in their way. She doesn't move from her bed, doesn't join them, as if they were to be avoided like the plague. As if disaster struck whenever she breathed the same air as them.

Her son and daughter leave the house without a word. Without calling out to her or looking into her room. She hears their voices. Blaise attaching Jean's bag to the rack on his bike.

"It's only temporary," Colette assures her little brother. "One day you'll go to that teacher to prepare for the Conservatoire. In the meantime, you'll play in the church."

"There's a piano?"

"An organ. It's the same."

"It's the same?"

"Yes."

Then she says to Blaise:

"Tell your mother I'm taking Jean to Mokhtar's."

"I'll tell her."

The three of them set off. Georgette can hear nothing now. Only Danièle's breathing and a magpie in the big tree that separates the château from the building she's lodged in.

33

October 31, 2010

"What did you say? Soudoro?"

Nathalie is jotting things down in her Columbo notebook.

"Yes, that's what Blanche calls her father in the recordings. I have two dates at the moment, 1953 and 1956. She went to the École Pasteur. And according to the recordings, the circus was set up on Place de Gaulle."

"I'll look in the paper's archives and ask my pal Steph, who works at the town hall. He knows the agent."

"Agent for what?"

"For locations for stallholders and traders on market days, and for any temporary installation. He also collects the money for those locations."

"I need the surname of this Soudoro . . . I'd like to know if he's still alive."

"And then we'd also know Blanche's surname."

"Yes. I found nothing in the Fredins house. Colette could've hidden her identity papers, letters addressed to her, an admin form, personal documents, or whatever. But no, nothing."

"You might find something in the coffin. Maybe Colette hid some stuff where no one would think of searching."

Her suggestion leaves me speechless. How on earth could she come up with such an idea?

Nathalie smiles.

"Don't look at me like that; you'd be amazed at the things that can be found in coffins."

"How d'you know that?"

"My father's best friend was a gravedigger for thirty years at the

Gueugnon cemetery. I heard him tell all kinds of stories, especially about exhumations."

I'd never thought of that. When Mom died, I didn't slip anything into her coffin. I gave her violin to Ana. I gave her personal effects to charities. All I kept was her bottle of perfume, her scarves, and the family photos.

"But . . . what can be found in coffins?"

"Records, jewelry, books, photos, letters, wallets, sweets, cigarettes, matches, lucky charms."

". . ."

"Where are you with the burial permit?"

"I need to call Cyril Rampin. Colette wanted to be cremated . . . And if it is Blanche, I really don't want to exhume the body anymore."

"You won't be given the choice, Agnès."

"Adèle says that the dead mustn't be disturbed, I think she's right."

"I agree. But the prosecutor is sure to ask for the body to be identified. For the circumstances of the death. It's serious, what happened."

"Yes, it is serious . . . "

My eyes fall on Ilyas's empty cup. The grains he'd swept with the back of his hand form a tiny mound of sugar.

"You told me you went to Cannes when Charpie died?"

"Yes. Here, it's the omertà. No one wants to talk about it. As soon as you mention his name, there's this deafening silence. I'm absolutely convinced that he did extensive harm. That certain people knew about it. I've heard a few accounts corroborating that the guy was a pedophile, but no names of victims. Apart from Ilyas, I only have one witness account . . . "

"Whose?"

"A friend of my brother's, who's ten years older than Ilyas. Apparently, Charpie didn't touch him but did ask him to pull down his underpants. He didn't tell me if he complied. I think he did, but forty years on, over the phone to me, he'd never have admitted to it. When it's the guilty party who should be admitting to it, confessing, not the victim."

Thousands of needles prick my spine. Nathalie continues:

"I almost think we should do an appeal for witnesses in the paper

. . . but since the predator is dead . . . And I wouldn't be allowed to reveal his identity in the appeal."

"But you, personally, what do you think about it?"

"Me? I think that those who knew, who suspected the guy was up to no good and represented a danger to children, are bedridden or dead by now. But the fact that it happened needs to be stated. There needs to be a record. Some inquiries are reopened fifty or a hundred years after the event."

"Do you think he could have killed?"

"From the moment someone touches a child, they kill a part of that child. In Cannes, he lived in a blue apartment building on the seafront. The old pervert was living in a little paradise. Top floor. Know why?"

"No."

"For the view. But not the one you'd imagine."

She takes a deep breath as if preparing to dive. We're still in the Petit Bar. I've stopped counting the coffees and liters of water we've been drinking. Nathalie takes another gulp of water. "Never tap water, it's poisoned, you know that, Agnès, hey?" She puts down her glass and clenches her fists as if trying to dig her fingernails into her skin.

"He spent his days with a pair of binoculars screwed to his eyes."

"Binoculars?"

"To ogle the little boys on the beach."

34

1960

Mokhtar is sitting on a bench outside the church. The square is deserted. He listens. He prefers to remain on the threshold. Every morning, he meets up with Father Aubry on Place des Forges for a coffee, but never enters his "workplace." It's been like this for four Sundays. Mokhtar counts the weeks in Sundays. It's been seven Sundays that Jean's been living with them, and four that the priest has asked Jean to play an organ piece by Bach, of Jean's choice, after his homily.

The first time Father Aubry had heard the organ, he was in his presbytery, chopping leeks for his soup. He thought it was a miracle, divine intervention. It was 6 P.M., a Monday, and Madame Feuillée never played at that time. He rushed over to the church, climbed the steps four at a time, and discovered a young boy. Concentrating. Enraptured. Colette had in fact told him, but he'd forgotten that the boy would be coming to practice his scales. Standing nearby, Madame Feuillée, the church's organist since 1937, turned to the priest, raised her hands heavenward, and whispered in his ear: "There's no fighting against this competition."

Mokhtar listens to Jean's music. This boy must be a kind of djinn, some supernatural creature come to Earth to spread beauty. Repair the living. Inside the building, Colette is beside Blaise. His parents are sitting in the front row, the Sénéchals' family pew for the past century.

Blaise gazes at his mother's nape. She seems to be praying. What's hidden in her prayers? What are her wishes? What does she expect of life?

She seems so unhappy since the trip to Lyon. How could she be happy with a husband as obtuse and overbearing? What does she think about as she listens to Jean playing as if he's been a master of his art for a thousand years? Blaise could feel pride for having been his teacher, but he takes none of the glory. Jean was born a musician. He'd merely taught him how to decipher the notes on a score.

The marchioness had finally come out of her room, once Jean left for the shoe-repair shop. She's resumed eating meals at the table, speaks to the marquess again, and to Georgette, as if nothing had happened, as if the woman hadn't betrayed her. Georgette whom Colette no longer helps to prepare lunch on Sunday, Georgette whom Colette hasn't visited since Jean's hasty departure.

For the sake of peace, Colette gives the envelope containing her wages to Blaise, who passes it on to his parents' employee. Tranquility can be bought, particularly when dealing with a mother who has every right over her children. Including that of removing them from Mokhtar's, if she decides to do so.

As the congregation leaves the church, Jean is playing the final notes of the hymn, "Glory Be to God in Heaven." Colette is the first to emerge, followed by Blaise. She spots Mokhtar, clutching his cap, and cheerfully joins him.

"He's playing better and better, don't you think?"

"It sure is impressive, m'dear."

Colette doesn't smile, but Mokhtar detects a glimmer of pride in her eyes.

"What kind of music do you have in your churches?" she asks, point-blank.

"They're mosques. And there's no music. With us, it's silence in prayer."

"Silence?"

"Yes."

"This is thanks to you, Mokhtar, you're the one who thought of the organ in the church for Jean."

"Oh, sure, I do occasionally have flashes of genius," he quips, amused.

Colette and Mokhtar bid farewell to Blaise and return to the shop with their heads down, stealthy as thieves. Colette doesn't want to encounter the marquess. She thinks that if he doesn't see them, her and her brother, he'll end up forgetting they exist. And the marchioness hasn't said a word to them since she was denounced by the mother. Just a few little friendly signs behind her husband's back. "She's afraid of him," Blaise says, his loathing of his father running deep.

Jean will join his sister in about half an hour. So as not to disturb Mokhtar, who has only Sunday to rest, they'll have lunch in Colette's room.

She walks beside Mokhtar and would like to hold his hand, like a daughter with her father. She'd like to, but doesn't dare; he'd surely turn bright red. Colette knows that blood ties are "a load of crap," as Mokhtar curses when repairing a cheap shoe. "These seams, a load of crap, this leather, a load of crap . . . I can't work miracles."

Who will work a miracle for Jean, Colette wonders. Since arriving at the shop, her brother has all he could desire, the presence of his sister and a keyboard. A strange-sounding piano, but a keyboard is still a keyboard; though he no longer has a soft or sustaining pedal for support. The only way of playing more or less loudly is to choose the pipe, or combination of pipes, he'll send air to, to produce the sound.

Jean has got Colette's hand back, as he closes his eyes at night and sinks into a deep sleep. He doesn't worry anymore. His sister takes care of everything. He barely thinks about the vocational certificate she'll be examined for in a few weeks, and even less about afterward, when she'll have to give up her position to a new apprentice. Where will she go? What will she do with him?

She's never brought up the subject with Mokhtar. He's so keen on fairness. He's always given the opportunity to a new young person, once their predecessor clinches their diploma. His mantra is, "No string-pulling, no privilege; got to be fair, balanced, like a good pair of shoes. Look, m'dear, one heel is rarely higher than the other."

Next Sunday, they'll go swimming, Colette promised Blaise she'd go with him to the banks of the Arroux. He'd like to take her mind off things. Take her for a swim, and then a doze in May's tall grasses.

She wonders how and where she'll live after the summer. And Blaise will be gone, too. Is it normal to be fourteen and to fret like this?

*

Cassette No. 11

COLETTE

"It'll take your mind off things," Blaise would say to me. But I had just one idea in my mind, placing Jean with a teacher who would prepare him for a music school. That was my idea. An idée fixe. As if my own existence was of no importance. I never thought of myself, only of Jean. So, in 1960, to keep him close to me and to stay with Mokhtar, I did the unthinkable. I went to my vocational-certificate exam and handed in blank pages in every subject. And at the oral exams, I answered nothing. To each question, I replied: "I don't know." And the teacher questioning me persisted, got annoyed. She tried everything, but all she got in reply was: "I don't know." She ended up throwing me out, grunting, "It's your loss."

I thought, if I haven't got a diploma, Mokhtar will have to keep me for another year. When he received my results, I thought he was going to kill me.

She pauses a moment. I hear her sigh. Then she starts to shout, imitating Mokhtar.

COLETTE

"You've betrayed me, m'dear! You've shamed me! People will think you learned nothing with me! That I'm a bad boss. You didn't trust me! I would never have shown you the door! Who do you take me for? A German? And stop putting on that dumb expression! Yes! I said it! A dumb expression! You deserve a good hiding! Oh, yes, you do! A good hiding! You're reckless! Zero in everything! In everything! Do you hear that???"

He turned to the shoes and started talking to them: "Zero in everything! She makes me ashamed! Shames me! Shames you! Shames my shop! Shames my family and my ancestors! Even my sewing machine is ashamed!!! Look at it! The machine is blushing with shame!"

Colette starts chuckling to herself.

COLETTE

And meanwhile, Jean was calmly playing the organ in the church, never suspecting that Mokhtar was giving me a roasting. He sent me to my room: "Away with you! I never want to see you again!"

She pauses once more.

COLETTE

I never tried for my certificate again. And I never left Mokhtar. Or, until 2007, the shoe-repair shop. I've been called Colette Septembre all my life, but in 1967, Mokhtar officially adopted me at Gueugnon town hall, once I turned twenty-one. I kept my birth name. But if you check my official record, you'll see that my surname is Septembre Bayram. Basic adoption combines two ties. To one's blood family and one's adoptive family. I chose my family. But I did want to keep the same surname as Jean. Mokhtar understood that. And he also told me that some people's minds are so warped, they might have imagined that he'd married me. I remained his employee when, in reality, I was his daughter.

My phone rings, I switch off the recording, totally stunned. Where else will it take me, this discovery of Colette, whom I'd believed to be almost devoid of mystery, of complexity? A life that I thought was simple and linear, punctuated by football matches on Saturday or Sunday. And then, when I look at my phone screen, my heart stops. Everything goes haywire. Everything goes crazy. It's Pierre.

35

After the international success of *Le Banquet des anciens* and our wedding, I got back to work. I never stopped working once I'd met Pierre Dugain. I wrote and directed *La Fenêtre*—The Window. I was in the mood for something lighter. Not dealing with families and their neuroses. Not serving up the same story in a second movie. Although I do believe that one makes the same movie throughout one's life.

So I thought up the story of a forty-something would-be delinquent, not malicious, just lacking love and a decent shave, an idealist if anything. A crook who'd received a suspended sentence of several months. In summer, when Paris empties out, he hangs around Montmartre at night, where the buildings are smaller and the ground floors of apartments and houses rub shoulders. He looks out for open windows, takes advantage of them to get inside, swipes a wallet, a pack of cigarettes, a crystal ashtray, or a gold chain bracelet, which he promptly sells.

The movie opens with a scene of theft. That day's plunder is a kid's piggy bank, which he's desperately trying to break open with a knife inserted into the slot. When that doesn't work, he throws it on the floor, but the piggy bank remains in one piece. The smiling porker seems to scoff at him. He stamps on it, in vain, and ends up hurling it against a wall, where it shatters, making an almighty racket. Finally, the pig is in pieces.

As he picks up the few banknotes and coins a child must have patiently saved from Christmases and birthdays, he finds a little handwritten note: "I love you, Granny." He stares at the paper for a long while. Then, while gathering up the shards, he cuts his finger, so he runs some water on it. Improvises a dressing with some cotton wool. The scene is so pathetic that he doesn't even cry with shame. He registers his failure in life with indifference.

And then one night, having pushed open the window of a small apartment, he comes across a photograph of a woman hanging on a wall. He stands transfixed by her face. She's posing on a beach, smiling straight at the camera.

He rummages in a cupboard and finds a photo album that records her life, tells her story. In it, she appears with her parents, her friends, at all ages, in all seasons. And in several of the photos, she has her arm around our thief. Side by side, all loved-up. They're both around twenty.

He tidies everything up behind him. Even does a spot of cleaning, sweeps up some crumbs that have fallen on the floor, rinses two plates and two glasses left in the sink, leaves through the window he'd come in by.

The vision of this ghost that has resurfaced from the past will dramatically change his existence. He decides to set up a security firm for private properties. He hires two former crooks, struggling like him, would-be delinquents, and they go door to door, offering their services. And do well. They know more than most how to turn any residence into a fortress.

One evening, bucked up and feeling brave, he again pushes open the window of his former love, enters clutching a bouquet of flowers, sits on the sofa, and waits for her in the half-light, full of apprehension. But she isn't the one who turns up; instead, it's the cops, alerted by the neighbors, who'd seen him lurking for months outside their place and stopping in front of the same window.

As he read the script, Pierre kept repeating the same thing, after every scene:

"This is great, this is great."

I was sitting beside him, heart pounding. I always felt untold apprehension at the thought of him not liking my proposals. Of him rejecting them. Once he'd finished the screenplay of *La Fenêtre*, he said:

"All I can do now is give you lots of children! I'm living with a genius, if I give you at least four kids, you'll never be able to leave me, you'd feel too guilty."

"Hello?"
"All well?"
"Ana?"
A sudden pain in my stomach. If he's calling me, something must have happened to my daughter.
"She's at the beach."
It takes me a moment to say anything else:
"She's okay, then?"
"She's sunbathing. I have a go at her every day because she doesn't slap on any sunscreen, the one that's factor God knows what."
". . ."
"What are you up to?"
It's been three years since he's asked me that banal question that every couple surely asks each other daily.
"I'm listening to Colette."
". . ."
"She left me some cassettes."
"Cassettes?"
"She recorded herself. Before dying. To tell me certain things."
His voice changes.
"What things?"
"Things about her life."
"So it's true?"
"What's true?"
"It wasn't her who died three years ago?"
"Colette died last week."
"Fuck." I hear him lighting a cigarette. "Who did die, then?"
"Probably a friend of Colette's, someone she'd have wanted to protect. That's all I know."
"Where are you?"
"Gueugnon."
"Wow, what fun."
"You never used to say that, before. You liked coming here."
"That was before. And no, no, I didn't particularly like *coming here*, as you put it. I liked Colette. And anyhow, Gueugnon's not exactly the Bahamas."

"Not everyone has started a new life with a mermaid to drag around the Indian Ocean . . . I bet she never puts her head under water so as not to ruin her blow-dry."

"Don't start, Agnès."

"Oh yes, I do start, and then start again. Seeing as I never finished. Didn't see the end finishing—coming, rather. Yes, that's it, I didn't see the end coming."

". . ."

"Why are you calling me, Pierre?"

"To be honest, I've no idea. I was wondering the same thing. Why on earth am I calling you? To hear some news? But what news? You have nothing new, Agnès! You rehash! You ramble on! You're still stuck in the past!"

"The past? What past?! It's a pretty recent past! It was only three years ago that you abandoned me like a piece of shit! Three years!!"

I hang up on him, after screaming: "Leave me alone!" And I hurl my phone at a wall. Like the kid's piggy bank in my movie. It falls behind the TV that I never switch on.

La Fenêtre was a resounding success. Once again, Pierre got several prizes for his performance, and me, I accumulated best-director awards and trophies. We burst the box office. That's what Pierre would say: "My wife bursts the box office!"

I had Ana a few months after the movie came out. Upon arrival, she removed all hope of another child. But no matter; on her own, Ana is all the children I hoped for.

36

November 1, 2010

I've been in the Fredins house for three days now, and yet I feel as if I arrived here a very long time ago. The cassettes I'm listening to slow down the hours, plunge me elsewhere, into before. I've lost my points of reference. I keep wondering what day it is. *It's Sunday morning and you blubbered all night.* Instead of retrieving my phone from behind the TV console, where it landed last night, I opened the console drawer and finished Dr. Pieri's whiskey, while weeping like a calf being separated from its mother. I now feel hideously sad and hungover.

The first time my aunt really talked to me, after I saw Nathalie kissing Jacques Daubel at the pool, she said: "Why do you have sadness?" With Colette, one had sadness the way one had joy, a sore throat, a headache, good or bad news. She'd told me it was a remnant of Mokhtar's way of talking. She rarely spoke of him to me. I sensed that it was a delicate subject. She'd become somber as soon as a customer mentioned him, instantly close up. I'm still stunned at the discovery that he'd adopted my aunt! What else will I discover as I listen to her cassettes?

I decide to get my phone back. I wince as I pull on the TV console; it's heavier than I thought. I crouch to pick up what's left of the device, its screen smashed. I try switching it on: a dead, cold rectangle. It's Pierre who gave it to me, back in 2007, in the States, just before leaving me. "State of the art." He never said that kind of thing: state of the art, technology, virtual, system, progress, technical. He wasn't remotely interested. He jotted things down in notebooks with a fountain pen, ordering the cartridges from a stationer in Paris's eighth arrondissement. He'd held the phone out to me.

"Here, state of the art. Apparently, the quality of photos and videos is mind-blowing."

I thought, since when does Pierre talk about mind-blowing quality? I thought it without listening to him. If I'd really listened, I'd have understood that a part of him had already left.

"But I can still make phone calls with it?" I asked, with a touch of irony.

My quip didn't make him laugh at all. He snapped back:

"You're an idiot, cost me an arm and a leg, that thing."

And he told me the price in dollars. Since when does one reveal the cost of presents one's giving? Another guy, yes. Any other guy, yes. But not him. Not Pierre. Not "my" Pierre. And he'd never told me I was an idiot, either.

My "state of the art" phone heralded my first howl. Bark. Bellow. Wail. No memory of how I expressed myself in the months that followed. No differently than a mortally wounded animal.

Two weeks later, he was packing his bags. I only took a few photos of him with the smartphone, that first evening, once I'd finished setting it up with Cornélia and Ana. And not one video. I made feature films with him in the leading role that were shown around the world, but I possess no amateur footage of him. Oh, the irony of life.

On September 1, 2007, he came home as usual. I'd just finished writing a new screenplay. I remember it like it was yesterday, but wish I could remember it like it was a century ago. I barely looked at him, barely kissed him; I left my study and—to please him? Seduce him? Keep him close to me for eternity?—because it was a kind of unspoken rule of the game between us, because we'd functioned that way since first meeting, I said to him:

"Sit down, I'll tell you about our next movie."

I was wearing a red cotton dress, slightly low-cut, long, which I threw away that very evening, as if it were covered in blood. The jinxed dress. The one I could never have looked at again. Even on someone else. That day, Pierre was in jeans, his long-sleeved black tee, and his favorite sneakers, the gray ones. He sat opposite me and I dived right in. Excited, stammering, dead nervous, feverish:

"It's the story of a winemaker in California. He's inherited a vineyard. He's an only son. None of his marriages worked out. All his love affairs ended disastrously. He had no children, so no heir. One day, he receives an anonymous letter. Who's it from? Why? This letter incriminates his business partner, his right arm, his long-time friend. The person he most trusts. And it's full of details the winemaker will investigate, discovering some unbelievable things! He'll realize how blind he's become to the rest of the world, because between him and the world, there's this man . . . I wanted to tackle a story like Daphne du Maurier's, but the other way around. It's not about Rebecca, the bride; it's about the winemaker. And the business partner is the opposite of Mrs. Danvers . . . He's affable, funny, likeable . . . But that wasn't very well explained . . . I'm explaining this badly, but I wanted to write a slightly diabolical movie, like Clouzot's *Les Diaboliques*, in fact . . . I'm dying of thirst, want something to drink?"

I didn't wait for his answer, went off to the kitchen to pour us two iced teas. I'd prepare some every day, with slices of lime. Pierre followed me without my noticing. He pressed himself to my back, placed his hand on my stomach, and whispered:

"I'm leaving."

Nothing more happened after that. I didn't turn around, smiling inanely, to get him to repeat it, to look him in the eyes, to silently question him. His words immobilized me. As if he'd shot a bullet into my nape, or a paralyzing arrow. Like when animals are knocked out for treatment. For a long time, I remained with my hand on the handle of the fridge, without moving. He about-turned as soon as he'd said those words. Then he disappeared. *I'm leaving.*

Suddenly, like a breaking wave, a downpour in a storm, I could see him again, kissing the actress I'd hired for my last movie. A small role. I saw Pierre the actor kissing the other one, the actress. Not my husband kissing a pretty young woman. No, I didn't see it when I was filming it; I saw it right then, with my left hand gripping the fridge handle and my mouth dry. A pretty girl I'd cast myself. "It's a small role, my dear Audrey. But important, you'll see. I make sure all my secondary roles matter." And I hired her. We shook hands. The shoot went well. She was at the wrap party. And just like their kiss that I'd filmed, I saw nothing.

When I returned to the sitting room, he was gone. His car had disappeared from its space down below. The bougainvilleas were dazzling, reflecting their vibrant color across every wall of the property. I went up to our room like a zombie. He'd taken some things from the dressing-room, as if just going away for a few days.

I feel like going to the church, closing my eyes to find Dad's ghost back at the organ, and Colette's. And also, I need to see that angel, at the back, on the left, that was supposed to look like Blaise de Sénéchal, according to Colette on the cassette.

Something falls at my feet when I push the TV console back. It's an envelope. I kneel down to figure out where it's come from. It was wedged under the bottom drawer, intentionally, along with another envelope that didn't budge when I jolted the console toward me. I grab that envelope, too. My hands are shaking. "Colette, what is this?" I ask out loud.

Two brown envelopes. With nothing written on them. I unseal the first one. First shock. Then the second one. Second shock. *Fuck. I can't believe this.*

I go to the landline phone, dial 118, the new information service; I get the number I'm after, I'm put through. Nathalie answers immediately. I'd feared she be away, covering some Sunday-morning event with her Columbo notebook.

"It's Agnès. I've broken my cellphone. D'you fancy going to Mass with me?"

37

November 1, 2010

Préfecture of Savoie
Identity Card Issued to French Citizens
No. 98761
Surname:——————————
First name: *Blanche*
Born on: *March 7, 1946*
In: *Flumet*
Département: *Savoie*
Domicile: *Flumet*
Description:
Height: *1.43 meters*
Hair: *chestnut brown*
Eyes: *brown*
Nose: *average*
Shape of face: *oval*
Complexion:
Distinguishing marks:
Fingerprints (both thumbs):
Signature of holder:
Chambéry, January 3, 1958
The Préfet

"But why was her surname crossed out?"

Staring in disbelief, Nathalie reads and rereads every word, studies the official stamps, the affixed postage stamp, runs her fingertips over them. She doesn't take her eyes off the piece of paper she has in her hands, then finally says:

"Have you seen her signature? It's an X."

"She was twelve when it was issued to her."

"There was nothing else inside the envelope?"

"Nothing."

I refrain from mentioning the other envelope. The one in which I'd found an article about Blanche's father. I'll tell her about it later.

She studies the photo of the little girl.

"I have no memory of your aunt young."

"Look," I say to her, placing a photo of Colette on the table.

She's around the same age as Blanche on the ID. My aunt is holding my father by the shoulders, and the Château de Sénéchal can be seen in the background. I think it's a snap taken by Blaise, who owned a camera. I've always kept it in my wallet. Mom gave it to me when I was the same age as Colette in the photo. Dad is so cute, he looks good enough to eat.

"Fuck," says Nathalie, in a hushed voice.

"I said the same thing when I found the ID hidden under the TV console earlier. It's completely insane."

"They could have passed themselves off as each other. They're like twins."

"Apparently, we all have a double somewhere in the world."

"Yeah, apparently."

"Have you seen *La double vie de Véronique*?"

Nathalie looks doubtful.

"What's that?"

"A movie by Kieslowski, with Irène Jacob. It's a magnificent movie, dazzling. The story of Weronika and Véronique. One's Polish, the other French, they're not related, have never met, and yet they're alike in every way. And they sometimes feel the same emotions at the same time."

"I have seen it! There's a puppeteer, too."

"Yes . . . Played by Philippe Volter."

"You're blushing, Agnès."

"I adored that actor. I wanted to hire him, but he died shortly before I began my last casting. You know, I have to love someone to film them. Especially when it's a man. That's why . . . anyhow. Not interesting."

"So interesting! Tell me all about your conquests!"

My conquests, what conquests?

"Let's get back to our subject."

Nathalie looks disappointed that I've nipped that topic in the bud.

"Why did Colette make out she was dead when Blanche died?" I plow on. "What bound them together?"

She raises her hand and orders two espressos. We're in the café opposite the church, and the place is filling up as people are emerging from Mass.

"You really believe that we all have a double?" she asks me.

"Well, I would hope that certain people are one-offs."

She bursts out laughing.

"It's crazy that your aunt hid this ID. Particularly since it hasn't had any legal value for decades."

"Seems like Colette wanted it to be found the day her Fredins house was cleared out. To leave some trace of Blanche's existence, but not one that someone might find before her death. I'm convinced that she was protecting Blanche from her father."

"What makes you say that?"

I don't have time to take the second envelope from my bag. Ilyas, Adèle, and Hervé have turned up.

"So, girls, checking who's coming out of church, are we?"

Ilyas immediately spots the old ID card lying on the table.

"What's that?"

"The find of the day, my aunt hid it under the TV console."

Nathalie hands it to him.

"Is this the circus girl you told me about the other day?" he asks.

"Yes."

"Well, perfect timing," he says.

Ilyas goes off to fetch someone from the back of the bar, while Adèle and Hervé sit down with us. Adèle asks me if this is the woman who's buried instead of my aunt; I reply that there's almost no doubt about it now. The yellowed ID card passes from hand to hand. Hervé seems tired. "A short night," he tells me, with a wink. Adèle ask me if I'm going to tell the cops about it. I don't know. I haven't heard from Captain Rampin since I got here. And I'm too anxious to give him a call. I'm afraid he'll tell me I can have my aunt's body back. Will I have the strength to organize her funeral? Pierre's words are reverberating in my head like the sound of a drill, piercing, painful, permanent.

Ilyas returns, along with an elderly man who walks with the aid of a stick.

"Agnès, this is Monsieur Aubert, he's a keeper of Gueugnon's memories. He worked at the town hall, in several departments."

I stand up and shake his hand.

"Agnès Dugain, pleased to meet you."

The old gentleman is handsome, with those laugh lines around his mouth and eyes. His blue eyes are still bright. Ilyas pulls over a chair so he can sit with us. He leans his stick against the table.

"I've just asked Monsieur Aubert if he remembers Blanche's father's circus. And believe it or not, he does. Could you tell them about it?"

"A little over fifty years ago," he begins, "I'd just started working in the public-records office. One morning, I replaced a colleague at the reception desk. Madame Fernandez called the switchboard. I knew her well, she was a friend of my mother's. She sounded panicked, I struggled to understand what she was saying. An animal had escaped from the circus across from her house and taken refuge in her garden. When I asked her what kind of animal, she replied: 'A monster. It's up my cherry tree.'

"I called the local police, in vain. So I decided to go there myself. I found Madame Fernandez in a complete state, still in her dressing gown, it must have been around ten in the morning. And there, in the garden, I saw the unbelievable, a kind of monkey with two heads hiding in the upper branches of a tree. The creature was screaming. A scream that could rend the heart, even one made of a stone. I thought it was wounded. As I left the garden to go to the big top, about 200 meters away, I came across a little girl. From the look in her eyes, I knew immediately that she was part of the circus. Don't ask me why. Just a look unlike that of other kids. When I explained to her that an animal had escaped, she replied: 'Yes, I know, it's Noé. It's me who opened his cage. I wanted him to go far away.' 'But to go where?' I asked her. 'He can't live in the wild, it's impossible.' She nodded.

'You're probably right.' She seemed to ponder for a long while, before announcing that she was going to fetch him. And she followed me to Madame Fernandez's house. I scolded her, insisted that he must never be let out again, that her parents could get into serious trouble if she did so. 'I don't have any parents, monsieur.' I can still hear her saying it with me. 'I don't have any parents, monsieur.'

"She only needed to call the primate with a few foreign words, Slavonic-sounding, for him to come down and take refuge in her arms. Madame Fernandez screamed like she was seeing the devil. The child reassured her: 'He's dirty, but not nasty. Don't be afraid.'

"I followed her. I'll never forget that image, her straight back and the two heads of the monkey resting on each of her shoulders, like two little children. She went to an isolated caravan and put the animal inside. A man rushed toward us, foaming with rage: 'What the hell did you do with that creature?' He was shouting and swinging a blackjack around. The little girl didn't flinch. Didn't even look scared. I ordered him to calm down. I was only young, but brave enough to put myself between that brute and the child. 'Who are you?' he barked, crimson with rage, ready to hit me with his horrid truncheon. He was short, sturdy, very muscular, and his eyes, slightly slanting, were full of hatred. He had thin lips and a long nose. His skin was pockmarked. He had several tattoos on his arms: daggers of various sizes. That wasn't common back then. Only sailors got tattoos before taking to sea. Their tattoos, they were their identity. But all those knives inked on his skin, it sent shivers down my spine. I stammered my name and said I was there on behalf of the town hall. He immediately calmed down. Seemed scared, or very wary. 'Are you the manager of this circus?' I asked, in a ridiculously solemn voice to seem important when, in reality, forgive the expression, I was crapping myself, the guy was so scary was the guy. He exuded . . . serious violence. Aggressively, he replied: 'Yeah, that's me. And the she-devil behind you, who's got it coming to her, is mine.'

I turned to her, and she looked at me with a strange smile. At once hard, amused, and sad. Like someone who's seen it all before, though she was knee-high to a grasshopper. 'I don't have any parents, sir.' I asked the brute where the child's mother was. Probably because knowing that the little girl had a mother would have reassured me. He replied that she'd been dead for donkey's years. And that it was him who'd settle the score with that one, who was no kid anymore, but a devious bitch, who struck on the sly. What did he mean by 'settling the score' with her? I'd rather not know. He then added that he was striking camp that very day. That he'd never set foot in 'this hole, not enough people' again. He didn't speak, that guy, he hurled abuse.

"The story could end there. The girl ran off somewhere, her father rejoined the men dismantling the big top, blackjack still in hand, and I returned to the town hall.

"But two days later, in the town hall's mailbox, I received a postcard of Gueugnon. Written in capital letters, it said: 'The girl's mother is alive. She was born in Flumet and is called Marie Roman.' Marie Roman. I've never forgotten her name. The card wasn't signed. It took me a few minutes to make the link between these words and the girl from the circus. Who sent me this postcard of Gueugnon's Romanesque church under a summer sky? I never found out. I returned to Place de Gaulle; they'd disappeared. I never saw them again. Neither the father, nor the little girl. I phoned the town hall in Flumet that same day. Said I had doubts about someone's identity, and was looking for a certain Marie Roman, a resident of their district. They said they'd get back to me that day, but didn't. I called again the following day. Landed on a very unpleasant woman who also said she'd get back to me, and didn't. And then I forgot about it, gave up on it, dropped it. I started to ask myself, what good would it do, telling this Marie Roman that I might have seen her daughter one day in Gueugnon? What then? That was a little over fifty years ago. I kept the postcard on my desk for a few years, before finally either throwing it away or losing it. I can't be sure anymore."

38

November 1, 2010

There's a program on the radio about the actress Simone Valère. She met her future husband, the actor Jean Desailly, on a shoot in 1942. I loved that charming couple, saw them on stage three times. Three times the joy. Her beloved passed away two years ago. When will she rejoin him? And me, which beloved will I rejoin when I'm eighty? Pierre and I won't grow old together. What will be said of us when we die? Which of us will go first? The actor or the moviemaker? Which of us will appear on the TV news to talk about the other?

"Can I ask you a question?" Ilyas asks me.

I thought he'd dozed off in the passenger seat, apparently not.

"Of course."

I switch off the radio.

"Why d'you still use your ex-husband's name?"

My hands tighten on the steering wheel. We're about fifty kilometers from Annecy. The sun's still high. I want to get there before nightfall. We've borrowed Adèle's car. "Friends, I have a Citroën sleeping in my garage. I take it out once a year, if that."—"Do I look like a Citroën driver?" Ilyas joked. And went off with her to pick up the car.

In the bar, Ilyas said to me:

"Come on, we're going to Flumet. We've even got wheels!"

I objected that there was no point, it was fifty years ago, Marie Roman was bound to have died. But to no avail.

"Someone must remember her, and anyhow, I feel like moving, come on. I've got three free days off. So have you."

"Ilyas, it's early November, the mountains now are like the end of the world."

"Come on, Agnès! Let's go, we'll pick up clean briefs and a toothbrush, and off we go. It's not even 300 kilometers away. You do realize that, on the ID card, it says Flumet?! And did you notice the look on Monsieur Aubert's face when he saw the photo? I thought he was about to kick the bucket."

We left Hervé and Nathalie on the sidewalk.

"You will call us?" Nathalie implored.

"Of course. We're not leaving for good, y'know," Ilyas replied, "just one or two nights, max . . . Love you."

I packed my bag in a jiffy. I came out, then, with a sudden intuition, went back in to get the recorder and suitcase of cassettes. I waited for Ilyas outside the Fredins house, thinking that this escapade would ease my pain. The woman in the house opposite opened her curtains and gave me a little wave.

"Hello!" I virtually screamed. "Thanks for the soup! It was delicious!"

"I'll make you some more!"

Then she closed her curtains again. And I told myself that, when I got back, I'd go and knock on her door again. Perhaps she'd at least seen Colette. Perhaps she knows something, even if she's only just moved onto the street. Whenever I've thought about going over there, it's either been too early, or too late. Listening to the cassettes is time-consuming and swallows up my days and nights.

Ilyas arrived in Adèle's gray Citroën, which smells new and of leather, I put the suitcase on the back seat, and off we went.

"D'you know how they work, these things?"

I fiddled with the GPS and watched the last destinations entered scroll by, then patiently typed in the address of the hotel.

"I'll do the first 200 kilometers and then hand the steering wheel over to you?"

"Okay."

I fell asleep as we were leaving Gueugnon, only waking when Ilyas stopped to fill up, 200 kilometers later. I had some sleep to catch up on.

I finally answer Ilyas's question about my surname:

"To bug the other woman."

"And you don't think it's more you, yourself, that it bugs?"

"Possibly."

"Hearing his name come out of your mouth every time you introduce yourself, when you're separated."

"Possibly."

"I liked it when you were called Agnès Septembre."

I go silent for a while, then change the subject:

"Look inside my bag."

"What?"

"Take my handbag. There's an envelope inside, open it. You need to read what's in it before we get to Flumet."

As he opens the zipper on my bag, Ilyas spots my smashed phone.

"Did you drive over it?"

"A conversation that spiraled a bit . . . I threw it at the wall. But it's thanks to that, at least, that I found the two envelopes hidden under Colette's TV console."

"But why? Costs an arm and a leg, a smartphone like that!"

"I know. That's what my ex-husband, whose name I still use, told me when he gave it to me . . . "

"They say all the data is stored in the chip."

"Yes. The contacts, the memory. I just need to change the shell of the phone. It's like us when we die, have to change the shell, but the soul remains intact."

"And you think that all our memories are in our souls?"

"Yes."

"Well, I sure hope not. If I have to come back one day, I'd rather do a reset first . . . And be blond with blue eyes. I'm sick of my Arab-looking mug."

"Ilyas, you're great-looking."

"Sure I am . . . Why *did* you smash your phone?"

"It was Pierre. He called me. The conversation started nicely, then went seriously wrong. Especially for my phone. And for Dr. Pieri's bottle of whiskey, which I knocked back . . . I'm sorry."

"Sorry for what?"

"For talking to you about whiskey."

"So what? You can talk to me about vodka, beer, getting plastered. It's the other way around. People who daren't have an aperitif in front of me do me far more harm than those who are relaxed about it. It's me who quit drinking, no one else."

Ilyas falls silent. He still has my bag on his knees and what's left of my phone in his right hand. He stares at the road, lost in thought. The sky is pale blue. The light is white. The mountain peaks are snowy, but the meadows are still green. If starting to brown a little. In a few weeks' time, the first snowflakes should fall. I've always loathed winter sports. Living in Lyon, I often went on school skiing trips. Packing my suitcase was a nightmare. I have a fear of heights and speed. I hate ski boots and skis, which I always get crossed or lose altogether, the skisuits that stifle me, and the cold that creeps into me, the chapped skin, the chairlifts, the frozen kids crying, and those slopes. Vertigo I can't shake off. All I like about the mountains in winter is the hot chocolate with whipped cream and the fondue. I remember hiding behind a pylon to avoid following the others. "Where were you, Agnès?" I'd be asked when, in the evening, I was finally found at the bottom of a slope, runny-nosed and white as a sheet, when the others all had bright red cheeks. "I got lost."

"I got lost," I say out loud.

"No. It's the right exit, we'll be there in just over half an hour," Ilyas tells me.

"I got lost in that love story, I mean . . . well, the one from before."

I can feel his questioning eyes on me.

"You still love him?"

"Even more with every hour . . . Well, I think so, anyway. Look inside the envelope."

Ilyas goes ahead, realizing that I'd say no more on the subject. He takes it out of my bag and opens it. Starts to read.

"Fucking hell, it's him!"

The article was cut out from an edition of *Le Dauphiné*. Someone has crossed out the date of publication. There's a photo of a man (head bowed) flanked by two gendarmes in the dock of a court. In the caption, the surname and first name of the accused have been crossed out with the same red ballpoint pen, along with the name of the town:

> "Since yesterday,——————has appeared in the court of————. He risks receiving a ten-year prison sentence."

The article begins as follows:

> "Monsieur————left his ex-wife for dead in————, in the commune of—————. The police, alerted by neighbors, discovered the body of a woman, lying in a pool of blood, in her own home. Her aggressor had run away but was identified as the ex-husband of the victim, thanks to a witness statement. After breaking into Florence's[1] home, the aggressor battered her with uncommon violence, including several stabs with a knife. The victim, in life-threatening condition, was transported by helicopter to the hospital in—————. She remained in a coma for several months, suffering from multiple fractures of an extremely serious nature, including one of the spine. The victim has lost the use of her legs permanently since the attack. She does not wish to attend the trial, but will be represented by her attorney,—————."

[1] Name changed for confidentiality

39

November 2, 2010

There are some answers that raise even more questions. Why cross out the names and the date of the article? Why hide it under some furniture? Why, why, why? To protect whoever found it? So as not to lead directly back to *him*? And yet he's elderly now. An old man is harmless. This thought reminds me of Klaus Barbie, during his trial in Lyon. He was an old man with eyes dark as hell and a fixed smile. I'll never forget it. It was the smile of the devil.

After our first night at the hotel, close to Flumet's lake, Ilyas and I are wandering around the small cemetery near the church.

"Why so many flowers, is that normal?"

"Yesterday was All Saints' Day, Ilyas. When people put flowers on graves."

Ilyas is convinced that, if Marie Roman is dead, she'll be buried here. If Blanche was born in 1946, like Colette, as it says on her ID card, her mother must have been born between the two wars, and would now be between eighty and ninety years old. Ilyas reads the names inscribed on the tombstones, studies the various fading portraits, bends down to straighten any overturned vases. Some names have disappeared from the surface of the stone. Moss invades, wind blows away, rain erases, sun and snow burn. No trace of a Roman family.

We enter the town hall and head for the public records department, where we come across a sign: "Births, marriages, deaths."

"Life summed up in three words," Ilyas murmurs to me.

A young woman with a delightful smile appears, and her doe-like eyes suggest she's the kind to simplify things.

"Some days I believe in God," Ilyas says to her, before even greeting her.

This remark seems to disconcert both of them. Usually so timid with strangers, Ilyas appears not to understand what's come over him.

"Can I help you?"

He tells her about Monsieur Aubert's phone call, fifty years ago, when he was still employed at the Gueugnon town hall, in Saône-et-Loire, and was looking for a woman named Marie Roman. Ilyas spares her no detail: my aunt, Blanche who is probably buried in the cemetery in Gueugnon, the circus, the manager of the circus, the article with names crossed out. Staring wide-eyed, the young woman laps up everything he says. Her eyes sparkle and cheeks flush as my childhood friend speaks to her. Is it Ilyas having this effect on her, or the story he's telling? Or both? Admittedly, he's very handsome, with his swarthy complexion, piercing eyes, and brown curls. He has the slender stature of a former sportsman. He wears an amber-based cologne and a leather jacket. If I didn't think of him as a brother, I'd fancy him. But it's Ilyas, so I can't fancy him. To me, he's an asexual being.

Ilyas finally asks the town-hall employee if she has any memory of a woman who was gravely assaulted, an event that might have taken place in the region and made the news, a woman who had to use a wheelchair afterward.

She is adamant:

"In this village, impossible. I'd remember, I was born here. Grew up here. I did my higher education in Sallanches, then Chambéry, but I always came back. Follow me."

We accompany her into a side office smelling of paper, mothballs, and ammonia. As we watch, she phones her mother:

"Mom, do you remember a woman being assaulted, in Flumet or the region, and left for dead by a violent ex-husband?"

The answer is: "No, doesn't ring a bell. I'll ask Robert." Robert is her uncle who's a cop. She sits down in front of her computer and searches for a file, which isn't really allowed since we're not related to Marie Roman, but she doesn't seem to care at all, determined to help us.

"Everything was computerized twenty years ago," she explains.

"Bingo! Roman, Marie Madeleine, born in Flumet on July 24, 1929: could that be her?"

I don't get time to respond. An unbearable heat overcomes me; I feel the ground giving way beneath my feet and the walls collapsing in on me.

I come to, lying on the floor, head resting on Ilyas's jacket.

He and the young woman are leaning over me while an unknown man is checking my blood pressure.

"You fainted; Lina called a doctor."

I then realize that Lina is the radiant young woman who'd been helping us. The doctor takes over:

"Blood pressure's fine. I can't find anything abnormal. When did you last eat something?"

"This morning, at the hotel. I had some fruit . . . and two coffees."

"Are you particularly stressed at the moment?"

I'm incapable of answering. All the images come crashing into my head, preventing me from articulating a single word: my aunt in the morgue, her voice on the cassettes, Mokhtar who adopted her, Louis Berthéol, Dr. Pieri, the Fredins house, Pierre on the phone, Blanche, Marie Roman lying in a pool of her own blood, the cemetery this morning. I can feel tears welling up and the heat returning in my head, ominously. I look imploringly at Ilyas to answer for me.

"Yes," he answers, sharply. "She's going through a difficult time."

"I'm going to prescribe something for you, but come to my office; we'll take some blood and do some tests. Here's my address."

No, doctor, my heart isn't normal, never has been. And right now, it's broken. That's right, doctor, my heart can't take it anymore, because it made a mistake. My heart's a traitor.

"Okay," I say, staggering to my feet like an old lady.

"It's probably a vasovagal syncope. Or a severe attack of spasmophilia. Do you suffer from that?"

"I don't think so."

"You're the movie director, right?"

"Yes."

"Or should that be 'directress'?"

"As you like."

"In any case, your movies are really good. And your husband, what a great actor."

I can't help but smile at the furious expression on Ilyas's face, as he looks daggers at the poor doctor. Seems like he's about to faint now. What a right pair of broken hearts we are.

Ilyas suggests that the three of us have lunch together, and before he's finished his sentence, Lina says yes.

She takes us to the only restaurant on the main street, and we sit in the room at the back, looking over the river Arly. It's a pretty place, welcoming. All the tables are occupied.

"Locals. For tourists, this is the off-season. They'll be back for the Christmas holidays," Lina explains to us. "The food's good here."

Having printed out Marie Roman's personal file, she takes it out of her handbag, while checking with me if that's okay, if I'm not going to faint again at the mention of her name.

"It's fine, that's over. Just a little fatigue."

"But do you know her, this woman?"

"Yesterday, I didn't even know she existed."

Lina starts to read out loud:

"Surname, Roman, first and second name, Marie Madeleine, born July 24, 1929, in Flumet, daughter of Roman, Alphonse, and Mangel, Pascale."

"Mangel!" Ilyas cries out. "I saw that name in the cemetery!"

"The word 'husband' has been crossed out," Lina continues. "It says, 'Divorced from Soudkovski.' There's no first name, only that surname: Soudkovski."

"Soudoro . . . Soudkovski! That's it," I exclaim, "we finally know his name! The name of Blanche's father and Marie's torturer . . . "

I clasp Lina's hands in mine and thank her.

"Thanks to you, we've just taken a giant step forward."

"But then, that means that Blanche's surname, the one that's crossed out on the ID card, must be Soudkovski, too?"

"Yes. Ilyas, when we get back to Gueugnon, will you come with me to see Captain Rampin?"

"Sure."

"Are you two married?"

"Friends," I say, amused.

"I never married," Ilyas admits.

"Why not?" Lina asks him.

"Because the opportunity never arose. And you, Lina, are you married?"

"An unhappy story that ended just over a year ago."

Ilyas's face lights up. "In that case, can I invite you to dinner?"

I've never seen him like this. Chatty, jokey, almost beguiling. Lina blushes, then looks at me, embarrassed.

"Don't worry about me. I have to go to that doctor's office, and after that, get some rest at the hotel."

I leave them on the sidewalk. Ilyas wants to accompany Lina back to the town hall, so I make myself scarce. I return to the cemetery. There's an icy wind blowing now, I turn up the collar of my coat. I walk up and down the paths again and finally find Marie's parents. Alphonse and Pascale, née Mangel. It's strange, the name Roman doesn't appear. Only the maiden name of her mother. Other names are inscribed: Ernestine, Martin, Léontine. But not the name Marie.

As I stand there, lost in thought, someone brushes against me and then stops close by, in front of the grave. I jump, holding back a shriek. It's an elderly lady, dressed all in black. From hat to shoes. Small. Slender. Almost a shadow. Just like Colette was. She bends down to pull up some moss from the crack in a plaque, which I can just make out: "To my adored aunt." Numb with cold and shock, I manage to get these words out:

"Excuse me, madame, would you know what has become of Marie Roman?"

40

November 2, 2010

"Come," she said to me.

I followed the lady in black to her home, two streets from the cemetery, in silence. She lives in an apartment within a farm building. Inside, it smells of wood, cow, and coffee. She seized the coffeepot and poured the tepid, dishwater-like dregs into a dirty cup, which I didn't dare refuse. She took off her hat and jacket, put on some glasses, and, on the crumpled envelope of a mail-order catalogue, jotted down, "Éloïse Cardine, 47 Rue des Écoles, Sallanches," then handed it to me, looking me straight in the eye. With her fine features and the half-smile that lit up her eyes, she reminded me of the actress Suzanne Flon.

She asked me nothing, simply wished me a good day. Did she know who I was? Had she understood my question? What did this Éloïse have to do with Marie? Everything between us had taken place in silence.

Sallanches is twenty kilometers from Flumet, and I didn't feel like finding Ilyas to get the car keys. He wouldn't have let me go there alone. He was probably with Lina, and I decided that, when for once he was enjoying the company of a sweet woman, I'd leave him in peace. So I went back to the restaurant we'd had lunch in and asked the waitress if she knew of a taxi company. She phoned a friend, who turned up five minutes later in a kind of Range Rover. When I gave him the address, he said:

"That's a home for old folks, that is. I often do runs over there."

"Would you be able to wait for me, and then take me somewhere they sell phones, please?"

The taxi driver is right. No. 47 is a lodging establishment of sheltered housing for the elderly called "*Tous les soleils*"—All the Suns—which sounds a bit like the title of some vintage TV series. Except that inside, there's no seaside. At reception, I ask for Éloïse Cardine, who takes a good while to appear. The young woman, around thirty with blond hair and blue eyes, cheerful and friendly, is in a pink smock and smells of orange blossom. I introduce myself. She looks perplexed when I explain that a woman I don't know gave me this address and her name. That I met her at the Mangel family grave, because I'm trying to locate Marie Roman. By way of reply, she says the same enigmatic word as the lady in black:

"Come."

Then, in the elevator:

"I've seen you before, on TV. What is it you do again?"

"Movies. I make movies. Well, I did."

"That'll be why, then," she says, adding nothing else.

On the third floor, we walk along a few corridors, passing residents, some clinging to frames, others to the arm of a carer, and then Éloïse opens the door to a room in which an elderly woman sits, facing the window. I immediately clock the wheelchair in a corner of the room. For the second time that day, an unbearable heat overwhelms me, and I sit down on the bed, muttering:

"Please forgive me, it's all the emotion."

A whiff of hospital and cauliflower makes me feel nauseous. Éloïse hands me a glass of water, and the lady turns her eyes toward me.

"Let me introduce you to Marie. She isn't registered under the name Roman. She's under legal protection. Here, she's called Amélie Andrieux. I'm the only one who knows her true identity. Along with the police and Jeanne, her sister. It's her you met earlier, at the Flumet cemetery."

"Her sister?"

Éloïse walks over to Marie/Amélie and leans closer to speak into her ear:

"This person is looking for you. I think it's related to your daughter."

Marie Roman's face lights up.

"How do you know that?" I ask Éloïse, astonished.

"Lina, the girl who works at Flumet town hall, phoned her mother, who phoned Robert, who's a cop, to ask him about the assault, and Robert alerted me. Here, everyone knows everything. And Marie, well, Amélie, is still under legal protection."

"But surely he must be dead!"

"Who?" Éloïse asks me, with surprise.

"Soudoro . . . Soudkovski."

The old lady panics at the mention of the name. She becomes agitated and starts to moan. Lets out some barely audible but pained sounds. She stares straight at me, terrorized. How could I have uttered the name of her torturer? How can I behave so badly? And what am I going to tell her? Announce to her? That her daughter died and was buried three years ago instead of my aunt? For god's sake, what on earth am I doing here? I take her hand.

"I'm so sorry. Sorry to have alarmed you. I'm deeply sorry."

She gradually calms down. Looks hard at me for a few long minutes, then murmurs:

"Is it you, Blanche?"

"Blanche?"

"Is it you, my child? You've come, my angel?"

She reaches out to caress my face, forehead, cheeks, nose. Then seems to be as deep in thought as I am.

"You mustn't worry, Blanche lives with my aunt, who's protected her for years."

Marie/Amélie smiles. Her eyes become cloudy.

"I knew my daughter was protected by someone. But I didn't know who . . . You look like her. Well, I think so."

Éloïse leaves the room so the two of us can be alone. Silence descends for a good while. I observe the old lady. I still have her hand in mine. Her slender, cold hand. Why do old people always feel cold? She's wearing clean, high-quality clothes. She smells of perfume. Her white hair is neat, held by a black barrette. Marie/Amélie is eighty-one, according to her birth certificate. I realize that Blanche died prematurely. Like Colette. Neither of them allowed any extra time. And Dad and Mom even less so. The people around me die young.

"Where does she live, your aunt?"

Her voice jolts me from my thoughts.

"Gueugnon. It's in Saône-et-Loire. Blanche met her at elementary school. When the circus came to town."

"So she had a friend?"

"Yes."

Relieved, she closes her eyes. Two tears roll down her hollow cheeks, slide into the furrows of her skin. I daren't speak anymore. The tears of an elderly person are as unbearable as they are chilling.

"When the French were liberated from the Germans, for me, it was the opposite . . . The enemy occupied my territory. I met Levgueni at the end of the war."

"Levgueni?"

"Soudkovski. Levgueni Soudkovski. But everyone called him Soudoro."

When she says his name, she grips my hand really hard. I'm surprised at her strength. She seems so frail, just skin and bone.

"What is it that attracts misfortune? The first time I saw him, he was doing these amazing moves, hanging onto a rope. I found him handsome, incredibly talented, and brave. The halo of light directed at him deceived me. The spellbinding music that accompanied his acrobatics did, too. After the show, our eyes met, and I felt desired, flattered that a great artiste like him should be interested in a girl like me. He followed me home to find out where I lived. I was with two friends and it made us laugh. Then he came back the following day, and the day after that. Until I responded to his advances. I'm not sure I loved him. Even at the beginning. I was scared. Being scared of someone, that's not loving them. I was sixteen, he was seventeen."

I'm bowled over by how she expresses herself. It all seems so clear in her mind.

"I lived with my parents," she continues. "We saw each other in the evening. He stayed in the region for more than a year with his circus. Annecy, Albertville, Chamonix, all around there. He always found a way to join me in my bedroom in the middle of the night. He didn't have a license but drove all the same. At the time, I was working as a linen maid; it was tiring, but I didn't mind it. I really liked my colleagues. He'd just lost his father and had to take charge of everything. He ruled with a rod of iron. I thought of escaping, admitting everything to my sister and parents and then disappearing, but I said nothing. And believe me, silence can kill. Soudoro continued to join me every night. He'd fall asleep for a few hours and then leave before dawn, like a thief. I fell pregnant. I hid my pregnancy from my parents and others close to me. On March 7, 1946, I gave birth to a little girl in my childhood bedroom. I'll never forget the look on the faces of my father and mother when they saw me with a newborn baby in my arms, in the early hours of the morning. I'd given birth all alone. In silence. It was Blanche's crying that woke them. At that time, when he saw that I was 'preggers,' as he put it, Soudoro had disappeared. He'd called me a slut, saying that the child couldn't be his. That I was a bitch who deserved to be abandoned. I went back to work, leaving Blanche with my sister Jeanne, who was a childminder, and picking her up every evening. My parents agreed to keep the two of us under their roof. During that time, I was almost happy, but it didn't last. God knows why, he came back when Blanche was six months old. My life would've been so different if he'd continued on his wretched path without us. He put on a whole performance for my parents, asking them for my hand in marriage, claiming that he couldn't live without us, that he was sorry, that he'd shower me with gold . . . and they gave us to him. The baby and me. We were married in Flumet, with my sister and parents as witnesses. I thought it was better for my little one to have a father, not to be seen as the kid of an unmarried mother. How could I have been so naïve? The following day, Blanche and I joined the circus, the life on the road, cold in winter, oppressively hot in summer, hell on earth. Soudoro soon made me his slave, never hesitating to slap me, or to beat me like the workers and animals in the big tent. I was scared for the little one. I hated seeing him hovering around her with his ever-present truncheon in his hand. Still today, when I think of it, my flesh aches. The blows he delivered with that thing were like burns that left marks on the skin. The more the months went by, the more he imposed a reign of terror around him. It made him proud, being respected and feared. In hindsight, I also think he started to hate me once he realized that I'd never be an artiste. He tried to train me, but my body wasn't up to it. All the hopes he'd pinned on me had been dashed, and he started calling me 'the useless one.' I lasted for two years, eight seasons, before running away with Blanche. I stole money from the till and got onto the first train. We were in Reims and, like an idiot, an absolute idiot, instead of going somewhere he wouldn't find us, I went home to my parents with my daughter, begging them to keep us. The following day, Soudoro was there, crying his eyes out in front of my father, promising me that he'd make an effort to provide for our comfort. And my parents gave in once again. My sister had moved out, and I sometimes think that had she been there when I returned home, she wouldn't have let us leave with him. When I'd shown my parents my bruises, my tortured body, they'd just asked me to be brave. On the journey back to hell, Soudoro swore that he'd kill me the next time I ran away, and then feed me to the lioness. He added that I could die for all he cared, but he'd never let me have the child. She belonged to him. He had plans for her. What plans? I should have protected her."

She asks me for a glass of water, which I bring her, and then continues her horrifying story:

"At the circus, there was Natalia. A good woman whom Soudoro exhibited because she had a beard. She told me I should leave before it was too late. She sensed that my husband was pouring all his hatred onto me. That his madness was intensifying. He'd spend hours bodybuilding in front of a mirror, strengthening himself physically. He had a knife tattooed on his forearm. That dagger terrified me. He had others tattooed over the years, but those I only saw much later. I obeyed like a trained animal, but everything was an excuse to thrash 'the useless one.' Until the day he sold me. Yes, sold, to a pimp. He left without a backward glance. Totally deaf to my pleas. I remained locked up in a house for several months. A house near Strasbourg of which I remember everything. The mattresses on the floor in rooms the size of cells, the sheets, the genitals, the washbasin, the bolts, the blocks of *savon de Marseille*, the cologne, the other girls, the smells of bodies and cooking. We were all made to eat together in the evening, the way dogs are fed in kennels, carelessly. We were given pills to stop our periods, and doubtless so we wouldn't fall pregnant. What did they force us to swallow? There were around a dozen of us girls, young. Some didn't speak a word of French. The clients were laborers, not nasty, not warped. I managed to escape. One night, the torturer who guarded us was so drunk, he forgot to bolt the main door. Never have I run so fast. I had a knife on me. I'd sworn I would kill myself if he found me, rather than return to the house of the devil. I didn't go to the police, even though I'd just been held hostage and raped. I had just two things on my mind, escaping Soudoro and getting Blanche back. Two conflicting things, impossible to achieve. In my despair, I knew that Natalia would be looking after Blanche. But I didn't know if 'the monster' knew that I'd escaped from my jailers. All I had on was a prostitute's dress, ballet shoes, and a blanket around my shoulders. It was the middle of winter, bitterly cold. I was spotted by a woman in the street, a woman called Aline who worked for the Salvation Army. I said nothing, didn't tell of my escape, of my months of prostitution, but I did accept some warm clothes and a meal. I claimed to want to return to my parents, in Savoie. Where else could I have found refuge? One always ends up going back home. She helped me by putting me on a train with a valid ticket, a bag of provisions, and a few francs. I arrived in Sallanches on January 5, 1949, at 8 P.M. But I didn't go up to Flumet, to my parents, who had betrayed me on two occasions. And I didn't know where my sister was living. I knocked on the door of a former colleague from the linen room. She ushered me inside, horrified by the state I was in. She put me up for a while. I was too scared that Soudoro would be waiting for me at my parents' house. Him, or the fellow he'd sold me to. My friend begged me to lodge a formal complaint to get my daughter back, but I never dared. Doing so would have been signing my own death warrant. I found a job in a book-cum-stationery store in the center of town. In the stockroom. I wanted to live nowhere but in cellars or stockrooms. I wanted no one to see me. I only spoke to my new colleagues when it was about work. I lied to everyone, claiming to be an orphan, originally from Le Mans, unmarried and childless. If I could have disappeared, I'd have become invisible. I unpacked boxes of books and notebooks, put them on shelves, moved on to the restocking and orders. I lodged in a small room just beside the store. I paid my rent on the nail to the landlord, in cash. No delay. No debts. I learned to melt into the crowd. To hug the walls. I'd made my former colleague and friend promise never to speak of me; she kept her word. The years passed by. I literally drowned myself in books. In other people's stories, so as never to think about my own story. As soon as I closed my eyes, I would see my child; I was dying from missing Blanche. Where was she? What was she doing? Was she suffering the violence of her father, or did he spare her? He'd never been brutal toward her, but she was still so little when he'd taken her from me. I knew, I sensed that Soudoro had told her that I was dead. Ten years went by without my returning to my parents, when I was living just twenty kilometers away from them. I didn't go out. I walked the path between the bookstore and my room head down, never making any detours. I spent time with no one and, apart from reading, had no pastimes. I lived as a recluse, terrified at the thought of him finding me. I finally told myself that I'd have to wait for Blanche to be older to get her back. And try to run away with her, somewhere abroad. Would she come with me? During those years of solitude, the devil had had plenty of time to get into my head. I would wake up increasingly often drenched in sweat, in the middle of the night, with this terrible voice telling me: 'Your daughter is like him; Blanche and Soudoro are as one. She'll never love you.' I'd see my little girl, her distorted features those of her father. On March 7, 1958, her twelfth birthday, I did go up to Flumet. My parents thought I'd died in a car accident. That was what Soudoro had made them believe on his last visit. But before that, he'd come regularly to track me down. He'd threaten them, but sensed that they weren't lying when they said they didn't know where I was. Then he sent henchmen to check. Two months before I went up to see them, that monster had returned to Flumet for Blanche's identity papers. He must have first been to her place of birth to pick up a civil-status record. The little girl wasn't with him. He'd told my parents that, one morning, I'd returned to the circus, and a while later, I'd been killed on the road. That I was buried in the Ardennes . . . but he could no longer remember the exact name of the village."

I take her daughter's identity card out of my bag.

"Here, you can keep it."

Marie/Amélie stares at me for a moment, then indicates a case to me.

"Would you pass me my glasses, please?"

With shaky hands, she removes those she's wearing and puts on those I'm handing to her. She discovers the face of her daughter at twelve years old. She brings the photo closer to her eyes to study it, then kisses it. Her tears fall again. I notice some tissues on the bedside table and give her several. She wipes her face gently, as if caressing it.

Then, obsessively, she reads and rereads out loud, as if searching for some hidden meaning:

"'Préfecture of Savoie, identity card issued to French citizens, No. 98761, first name: Blanche, born on March 7, 1946, in Flumet, département of Savoie, domicile: Flumet, description: height: 1.43 meters, hair: chestnut brown, eyes: brown, nose: average, face shape: oval, complexion, distinguishing marks, fingerprints, signature of holder, in Chambéry, on January 3, 1958, the Préfet.' Did you see, she crossed out her surname . . . She crossed out her father's surname. Did you see, she didn't look like him. She never looked like him."

"Did you see your daughter again?"

"I heard her," she replies, in a murmur. "She spoke to me."

Exhausted, she places the ID card against her heart and closes her eyes. I realize that I've been in this room for more than two hours. I whisper in her ear: "I'll be back." She nods yes. And I repeat several times: "I'll be back, it's a promise. Promise."

Before going, I leave a note at reception for Éloïse. Along with my phone number.

*

Once outside, I apologize profusely to the driver, who has waited for me for two hours.

"Don't you worry," he says, "I listened to the radio."

He takes me to a phone store inside a mall, where someone under the age of twenty removes the chip from my phone in record time.

"It's dead, madame," he tells me, slipping the chip into a new "state of the art" (obviously) phone. "This is the slimmest smartphone in the world, yours was old hat, we're already at fourth gen."

"Right, thanks."

"Would you like insurance, in case you smash this one, too?"

A voice tells me I have seven messages:

Saturday, 11:10 P.M.
It's Pierre. I was a bit hard on you. I'm sorry. See you soon. Bye for now.

Message deleted.

Sunday, 3:23 P.M.
Agnès, it's Cornélia here. Just hoping for news. Nothing new in Paris, all's well at the house. I got a message from Nana. And you, how are you? Would love to hear the sound of your voice, really.

Message deleted.

Sunday, 11:12 P.M.
Hi, Mom, it's me. Just calling to send you hugs and kisses. Love you.

Message saved.

Monday, 8:40 A.M.
Hi Agnès, Nathalie here. Call me back with what you found out in Flumet, I'm dying to know. Just having coffee at the Petit Bar before heading to the paper. I'm with Hervé and Adèle, call us back, big kiss.

Message deleted.

Monday, 11:10 A.M.
Good morning, Madame Dugain. My name is Laurence Davis, and I work for the Beverly-Wood Festival. We met a few years ago, in LA. We'd like to do a retrospective of your movies and for you to be our guest of honor. And of course, some of your actors

would be welcome, too. Our festival takes place annually, in May. Do call me at this number to discuss further. Many thanks.

Message deleted.

Monday, 2:08 P.M.

Morning, Madame Dugain, it's Captain Rampin. Cyril Rampin. I've just received the burial permit for your aunt. You'll need to come by the Gueugnon gendarmerie. Call me back, thanks.

Message saved.

Monday, 3 P.M.

Hey, Agnès, it's Ilyas, where are you? I just got back to the hotel, and you're not here. Went to the doctor's, and he'd not seen you. Oh, shit, I've just realized, you're phoneless.

Message deleted.

Monday, 3:50 P.M.

Hey, Agnès, it's Ilyas again. What the hell are you up to?

Message deleted.

41

November 3, 2010

I live in the house across the street. I've made some soup with vegetables from the market. It's delicious. As Agnès got back during the night, I'm going to leave a pot of it outside her door, like last time. Since being here, she's stayed shut away in that house for hours, which isn't healthy. She should go out, walk. Knock on my door. Why doesn't she cross the road to come talk to me?

I was pleased the day before yesterday when I saw her leaving in the car with Ilyas. I've always liked that boy. He's a good guy. As a kid, he was shy, reserved. Never raised his voice. He was lovely-looking. Still is. I knew his parents well, they ran the grocery store.

My career was working at the Gueugnon town hall. In the public records office, from 1956 to 1996. It was me who kept the official records. Births, deaths, marriages, adoptions, family record books, family and individual civil status files. I know nearly everyone in Gueugnon.

Ilyas came with his father to register his little sister, Zeïa, who was born at home. Labor went so fast, her mother didn't have time to get to the maternity clinic. It was Dr. Pieri who delivered her.

On Monday evenings, on top of my work at the town hall, I volunteered to organize French classes for adults in a room lent by the municipality. Ilyas came with his parents. I'd always make him a chocolate cake to take home with him. I gave support classes to Algerians, Moroccans, Portuguese, Tunisians, Spaniards, and Poles during the 70s, 80s, and 90s. Later, in the 2000s, I taught a good many Thai women. Some employees at the Gueugnon factory opted to go off to a branch in Thailand, to train workers in Pattaya. Some of them didn't return alone. They fell in love over there and got married, which is why we have such a large Thai community in Gueugnon. That's the power of iron- and steel-industry towns. Parts of the world have migrated to the heart of Burgundy to live and put down roots here.

I loved my work, except for the days when people came to register a death. Over the years, that became the undertaker's unpleasant task, but at first, I was the one who received the bereaved families.

After the war, when women started having their babies in hospital, births in Gueugnon itself were rare, apart from the years 1968 to 1971, when there was a maternity clinic at the Château de la Fourrier. Then it closed. And women went elsewhere. I'll admit, I had my doubts about some births, when I saw what the father looked like . . .

I would also receive families who wanted to acquire a burial plot at the cemetery. It was quite amusing when, as they looked at the layout, they'd say: "No, not next to that family; we can't stand them. Not too exposed to the sun; not too much in the shade; not near the entrance, it's too noisy."

And I was the one who welcomed the soon-to-be married when they brought in their marriage files.

I'd often make a bet with myself on which one would leave first. Sometimes I won; sometimes I lost. Never trust appearances. I even found myself attending a ceremony at which the bride didn't turn up. As I watched the guests go their separate ways, I thought how truly rotten life can sometimes be.

I still teach French to adults. At the moment, I'm helping two wives of footballers, one Senegalese and one Nigerian. We have a lot of fun. The municipality still lends me a room. I'm seventy-two, rheumatism everywhere, but on Monday evenings, I cycle over there. Keeps me fit.

42

1961

Father Aubry never gives lengthy sermons. He prefers to express himself with a trowel in his hand. This priest-laborer divides his energy between building projects and sacerdotal duties. A stonemason and the son of an architect, he participates in the construction of social housing, assisted by other volunteers. He worked for a long time in Flacé, a neighborhood of Mâcon. Now he officiates in Gueugnon.

At catechism classes, Pierre Aubry delights the children with his anecdotes. His memories of building sites, of the war when he was taken prisoner and then consigned to forced labor. Thanks to him, more than a hundred houses now exist. They're built by their future inhabitants, who help each other, one house to the next.

To the children, this builder-priest, who's so close to ordinary families, is a fascinating and respectable grown-up. Unlike anyone else. He's even more fun than the playground. Between articles of faith, he asks his pupils to join in, encourages them to ask questions without clowning around, and to illustrate passages from the Bible with crayons he hands out, then gathers up again, storing them in cardboard boxes. And after the Our Father and the Hail Mary, he organizes dodgeball games in the courtyard adjoining the parish hall. No distinction between girls and boys, everyone equal in the two competing teams. With Father Aubry, speech is as free as a bird whose cage has finally been opened. The man is a ray of sunshine to everyone. If this is religion, then it's pretty great.

Among the pupils this year is Jean Septembre. The Father has been teaching him the catechism since he moved in at Mokhtar's and began playing the organ in the church every day after school, and on Sundays after the homily. Jean Septembre deeply troubles Father Aubry, although he's used to dealing with tricky, painful situations. He's the one who listens to parishioners in the confessional. Who takes in the suffering and often challenging daily life of his flock. He knows how to hear them. And sometimes, how to respond to them. But never has a case troubled him this much. Because there's something of the divine in this young boy. Because he really shouldn't be here; his place is elsewhere. Whenever Jean is silent, it feels to him like the triumph of the devil.

One Tuesday morning in 1961, he pushes open the door to Mokhtar's shoe-repair shop. There are two places where Father Aubry feels at ease: on the building sites, having a sandwich with the Portuguese workers, and at the Place des Forges café with Mokhtar, when the two of them put the world to rights over their third coffee.

Sitting behind the sewing machine, young Colette is easing a belt along under the needle. Mokhtar has a shoe clamped between his knees, into which he's hammering something. Gentle music plays on the radio and there's a smell of leather and glue. The June sun glints off the shelves and counter. The two stop working when they see the priest. Colette is the first to speak:

"You don't want Jean to play in the church anymore? Is his music bothering you?"

"How on earth could it bother me?" Father Aubry replies, almost offended. "I'd have to be an idiot or an atheist."

"It bothered Sénéchal."

"The marquess is impervious to beauty. The proof, he kills stags. No, the question is: what are we going to do for Jean?"

Colette turns to Mokhtar, who speaks:

"I'm not the boy's father. I can do nothing other than welcome him under my roof so that he can play under yours, in the church."

The priest looks from one to the other, then, with a mischievous twinkle in his eye, solemnly announces:

"This morning, when praying to Our Lord, I had an idea for financing his studies."

* * *

Cassette No. 12

COLETTE

Gueugnon's ironworks was modernizing, and the town would soon be the global capital of stainless steel! Can you imagine, Agnès? Our own little town, in the middle of France, was going to become important to the entire world! It saved Mokhtar's finances, and me at the same time. We were so busy with the shoes of all those people arriving to work here that we tripled our efforts and I became an employee, no longer an apprentice. I began paying Mokhtar for our room and board. The factory would soon take on almost four thousand workers, entering its golden age. That's how Father Aubry came up with his idea for Jean. The town needed extra accommodation. A new workers' neighborhood, financed by the factory, was in the process of being built. The Gagères neighborhood. Houses set close together in the lower part of the town. The rents would be modest. Our priest went to see the director at the Forges factory, whose name I forget, and made him a proposal: to organize a raffle in the region that would enable the factory and the church to sponsor a child prodigy. Apparently, the man nearly fell off his chair.

"A child prodigy in Gueugnon?"

"Monsieur," the priest was said to have replied, "if you attended Mass, you'd know all about it."

Everyone could buy a ticket, and the winner would get a house. Yes, a house. A lot of money had to be raised; Jean was still only young. He had years of study ahead of him.

It still exists, that house. Go and see it again one day, Agnès. And say thank you to it. It's on the road from Toulon-sur-Arroux, toward the Château des Presles. Do you remember it? We went there with Louis Berthéol.

She takes a break but doesn't stop recording. Which room is Colette in? What time is it? What's she wearing? These cassettes demand a lot from my imagination.

COLETTE

The factory needed to donate a plot of land and some building materials, and our priest, assisted by his skilled friends, would do the rest. Father Aubry went to a great deal of trouble. Stonemasons, road workers, electricians, roofers, plumbers. Everyone went along with him, starting with the factory. The building sprouted up within a few months. It's a very basic house. Typical of those built in the sixties. But with three bedrooms and a garage, all the same. I only saw the inside of it once. On the day the winners collected the keys . . . They were called Monsieur and Madame Été . . . Their son Antoine, whom I know well, still lives in that house.

She pauses the recording. I hear the click of the stop button. And then she resumes.

COLETTE

Father Aubry said that it had to be done fast. That Jean's musical studies couldn't wait any longer. He was worse than me. It was all he lived for at the time. Much later, I learned that the marchioness had confided in him. She was being closely watched by her husband, but she would contribute to the project. We were all obsessed with my Jean's talent. Except for the mother . . . Two weeks before the raffle began, the rumor had spread everywhere: there was a little genius among the residents of Gueugnon, the kid of a peasant, whose father had died . . . The population needed to rally around to send the little lad to study in Lyon. And above all, there was a house to be won.

On the Sunday before the big launch, which became the *event of the 1960s, the church in Gueugnon was overflowing in all directions. The square was teeming with people. From across the region, folks were there to hear the little lad, and doubtless to say an opportune prayer so they won the prize. A crazy amount of people. Even the mother was there, stoic, white as the robe of a girl taking her first communion. I greeted her; Danièle seized the opportunity to cry and I to get away and join Blaise. The marquess was sulking, but he was there. He strode past Blaise and me without glancing at us, stiff as a poker.*

I hear her laughing.

COLETTE

Madame de Sénéchal didn't dare let her joy show. Where she had failed, someone else might still succeed. Blaise held my hand all through Mass. When the first notes of Bach made the walls vibrate, I knew the pain was over, the injustice of a humble birth. We were going to win. My purpose on this earth would be fulfilled: your father would no longer be separated from his piano. Mokhtar remained outside the church, as usual, on his bench.

A few days later, the mayor, the director of the factory, and the priest launched the raffle in front of the public and the local press. Many families bought several tickets to increase their chances of winning the finest of prizes: a new house. You had to go to the town hall to purchase tickets. There was a safe at the reception desk. Every evening, it was emptied and the money put in the bank. It was still the old francs back then. A ticket cost ten thousand francs . . . That's barely a euro today. 6,757 tickets were sold. Oh, yes, I remember that number. I often dreamt of it at night: 6,757.

The factory printed the tickets. At first, a thousand were printed. And then it didn't stop. The raffle raised 67 million old francs. A fortune at the time. The factory management had the money deposited into a bank account to which no one had access. It was the financial director of the Forges who was responsible for funding board and lodging for seven years, until Jean came of age. Plus the cost of his clothing and train journeys. There was still some money left in 1968, when Jean had completed his studies with Monsieur Levitan. After a vote, it was agreed between the factory, church, and town hall that what remained would go to the Secours populaire *charity.*

A stop. Then the recording resumes.

COLETTE

The raffle draw took place on July 14, 1961, on the Place des Forges. For the occasion, the town hall team had set up a dais. Jean, standing between Father Aubry and the mayor, was searching for me in the crowd.

He didn't really understand what was happening. Jean was always in his world of music. That morning, I had primed him:

"The most important thing is to say 'thank you' clearly when the microphone is held out to you. 'Thank you to everyone for helping me. I will never forget what you have done for me; thanks to you, I will achieve my dream.' Repeat that, Jean, go on, repeat it until you know the words by heart."

"Thank you to everyone for helping me. I will never forget what you have done for me; thanks to you, I will achieve my dream."

A long silence.

COLETTE

It was Maître Duclos, the lawyer, who drew the ticket and announced the name of the winners. Monsieur and Madame Été, as I told you.

The landline phone in the house rings. I jump. It's the first time that's happened. Who is being rung? My aunt or me? Does the person at the other end of the line know that my aunt has died? I stand up, hesitant. It could be a wrong number. I check the time: 8:30 A.M. I stop the recording.

"Hello?"

The phone rings again four times. I answer it four times, but no one replies. I think I hear breathing down the line. Is it Marie Roman wanting to tell me something?

"Marie? Is that you?"

I think I hear "yes" whispered several times.

"Did Éloïse give you this number?"

Nothing more. There's a long silence, and the person hangs up. It rings again. I answer. I hear the same breathing.

"Hello?"

A barely audible sound. Creepy. Like someone struggling to breathe.

"Marie?"

Then I remember that, at the *Tous les soleils* care home, she's called Amélie.

"Sorry, Amélie? Is that you?"

And then it keeps happening, three more rings. Then hanging up.

An hour goes by in silence. I daren't leave the house. But I have to be at the gendarmerie at 11:00 A.M. I have an appointment with Captain Rampin to pick up the permit to bury Colette. Ilyas is going with me. Friendship is strange. The two of us are just as close as we were as children and teens, despite a twenty-year separation. A large gulf, during which I made a child and some movies, whereas he had a rough time of it. A really rough time. The assault he suffered damaged the man he became. As a child, Ilyas was joyful. As an adolescent, too. I can still see him on his moped, with his permanent smile and swarms of girls buzzing around him. He was joy itself. As the years went by, he was brought down by a series of ticking time bombs.

I'm almost certain that I left Éloïse Cardine my cellphone number, not the landline one. But now I'm not sure. Maybe I scribbled it down without thinking. I know it off by heart. I just can't remember. I end up phoning the switchboard of the retirement home to speak to Éloïse. If Marie/Amélie wants me, the young woman is bound to know about it. I'm passed from department to department, until I'm finally told that she's off today.

"May I speak to the resident Amélie Andrieux, please?"

"Hold the line."

After more than thirty unanswered rings, I finally hang up, disheartened.

As I leave the house, I discover another pot of soup on the doormat. I really must meet the neighbor across the road.

43

November 3, 2010

Captain Rampin hands me Colette's burial permit.

"Your aunt didn't have an infectious disease and didn't wear an appliance containing a battery. She hadn't declined organ donation. No sign of cancer or pregnancy. She died of a myocardial infarction, more commonly known as a heart attack, in her sleep. Blood flow to the heart was blocked and destroyed part of the cardiac muscle. Her heart wasn't strong enough to pump the blood to the rest of the body. Leading to a fatal cardiac insufficiency. You need to declare the death at the town hall of the place of death, the funeral parlor or mortuary . . . and at the appropriate town hall, wherever the burial will take place, if that isn't Gueugnon . . . Anyhow, here's the authorization to bury her remains. The mayor will need to . . . But . . . "

Cyril Rampin blanches as I stammer: "I'm so sorry, I just can't . . . I'm sorry . . . really . . . forgive me . . . Sorry."

I'm having the most horrendous fit of the giggles. I hide my face behind my hands, and the more I tell myself to calm down, the more the word "pregnancy" bounces back into my head, like a pinball on Ecstasy.

Beside me, Ilyas is speechless. I can feel his mortified eyes on me. I can't even raise my head. I haven't had a laughing fit like this since . . . since never. My belly's aching from it.

Impassive, the captain continues:

"Permission to bury should be distinguished from the death certificate and permission to close the coffin, which are supplied by the public records office of the municipality in which the death occurred."

Cyril Rampin hands me an umpteenth form, which I grab. What follows seems to last an eternity. It's Ilyas who does the talking, asks the questions, while I'm suffocating beside him. What needs to be done first? Who's responsible for returning my aunt? When? Will Colette remain in the funeral parlor in Gueugnon prior to being cremated? Are people embalmed before cremation? Are the last wishes Colette Septembre wrote on a bit of paper valid? What will happen to the person who's been buried instead of Colette for the past three years? When will the exhumation take place? Who will be present?

And me, sitting beside Ilyas and opposite the captain, I'm incapable of speaking. My body feels as stiff as it does light. What a strange feeling of elation a fit of laughter gives you. The more the two men talk among themselves, the harder I laugh. As if I were no longer part of their world, as if I were witnessing a scene that didn't concern me.

At one point, I hear the captain replying to Ilyas:

"These things can happen; it's a nervous reaction, look, it happens all the time at funerals."

And I realize that he's talking about me.

*

Dad died beside the sea at ten in the morning. Dad died in Cassis. It's so beautiful there, you couldn't pick a worse setting for dying. I'd have wanted him to go in winter, at the end of a concert, old and tired, in an ugly, gray, and drafty town. He closed his eyes on Sunday, June 21, 1987, the first day of summer, at the age of thirty-seven, in the wonderful light of the South.

The day of the *Fête de la Musique* took away one of its greatest advocates. It was 20 degrees in the shade of the café's terrace, where he was drinking tea and reading a music magazine. Mom, in a dreamy state, was holding his hand watching people go by. He let go of her hand amid a strange clatter. His head hit the cup, which smashed on the floor, he died seated, face-down on the table. He didn't even die at a piano.

A tourist who was a doctor tried to resuscitate him. In vain. The paramedics attempted the impossible, but my father hadn't been breathing for too long.

My parents had been playing Bach's preludes at the Marseille

Opera House for ten days, with the Grand Orchestre de Paris. The three of us were staying at a hotel on the little harbor of Cassis. I'd joined them for the weekend. They'd agreed to let me skip school the following Monday because my tenth-grade year was coming to an end. I didn't set foot in school again before the start of the autumn term.

I was still asleep when Mom showed up in my room. She sat on my bed and stroked my cheek. I opened my eyes to see her face bathed in tears; her big, light eyes had already changed, as if something had suddenly gone out in them. Their spark, no doubt. She never got it back. She said:

"Daddy's gone."

I grimaced, emerging from sleep in a bad mood.

"Gone?"

Since Mom was super sensitive and would weep at the sight of a wilted plant, I didn't understand at first. But she finally whispered, between sobs, gripping my hand:

"He's dead."

It takes time for certain words to reach and penetrate our brains. Sometimes a few seconds, sometimes a few minutes, sometimes years.

The previous day, they had dressed up for their last concert. They left the hotel clad in black in the late afternoon, left me on my own; I hadn't fancied coming with them, despite their insistence. I'd had enough of their classical music. In 1987, I was listening to "*Duel au soleil,*" "Blue Hotel," and "*T'en va pas*"—Don't Go. For a long time, I wondered if my father had gone because of that song I'd bawl out at the top of my voice in my messy room. Like a punishment, a sentence:

Daddy don't go
We can't live without you
Don't leave at the end of the night
Night, you scare me
Night, you never end
Like a thief
He left without me
No more trips to the flicks for us three.

Instead of the concert, I went to the cinema in Cassis to see *L'Été en pente douce*—Summer on a Gentle Slope. I loved it. Then I had a sundae with whipped cream beside the harbor and went back to the hotel. We had adjoining rooms. I still remember the numbers. 7 and 8. I was in number 7. Later, I thought that if I'd been in 8, Dad wouldn't have died. The number 7 would've protected him. Returning from their concert, they knocked on my door. I was watching the variety show *Champs-Élysées* on TV and kissed them distractedly, too engrossed in Michel Drucker's program, on which the singer Jean-Jacques Goldman was guest of honor.

Mom asked me if the movie was good, I replied with no more than a vague "yes." Dad asked if the music was good. I said "great" without the slightest idea. All I wanted was to be Pauline Lafont, the movie's star. I wanted to be blond, sweet, and desirable, when instead I had dark hair, was permanently exasperated, and as flat as a board for slicing *saucisson*. I'd paid no attention at all to the film's original soundtrack.

Dad sat beside me and watched the end of the program, seeming hypnotized by the images he was seeing. We didn't have a TV at home. My parents lived on another planet. The one of pop videos and shows like *Top 50* and *Enfants du rock* was unknown to them. Dad hobnobbed with Mozart, Bach, and Chopin. Not with Étienne Daho, Chris Izaak, Madonna, or Elsa. As he listened to Jean-Jacques Goldman, he smiled several times and repeated: "It's well-written."

I loved him from a distance. He was handsome, tall, slender, a dreamer. I loved him the way you love someone who's never really there. On the one hand, because he was often away, accompanied by Mom; on the other, because when he got back, he'd be working at his piano. I didn't understand why he played so doggedly, when the keyboard was merely an extension of himself.

"Because one can lose everything, darling."

"Lose everything?"

"One must work every day so as not to lose one's piano."

When Mom and I emerged from the hotel, there were crowds on the terraces, laughter, children, ice cream, and coffees on tables, the sea, the sun, and boats. On us, it was raining. Like on the old Snoopy poster I had as a child: "It always rains on our generation." A cloud releasing raindrops only on the dog, when all around him, it's sunny.

A decision had to be made: where would Dad rest for all eternity? In Gueugnon, close to his sister. It was obvious. The place that had enabled him to access a musical education. But he lived in Lyon. He'd done all his studies there, given his first concerts there. And if his friends and admirers wanted to visit his grave, it would be easier there than in Gueugnon. Mom had stopped speaking. I was as if dazzled by something that was preventing me from moving forward, from seeing more than a meter in front of me. I had to cling to an arm—any arm—to be able to walk. It was Alain Terzieff, director of the conservatoire in Lyon and Dad's best friend, who organized everything. He even took care of finding a site at La Guillotière Cemetery, and transporting the body from the funeral parlor in Cassis to the one in Lyon.

Colette took the TGV, accompanied by Louis Berthéol. A 40-minute train journey from the TGV station to the Lyon-Part-Dieu station. A car awaited them. Colette wanted to be present for the placing of the body in the coffin. I didn't recognize her at first. It was only when she was 20 centimeters away from me that I realized it was her. First, because she'd made an effort to dress up, and second, because she'd aged by ten years, maybe twenty. All her hair had turned white during the night of June 21 to 22, 1987.

It snowed on "Yesterday"
The evening they parted
Penny Lane is already far away now
But she'll never have white hair
It snowed on "Yesterday"
That year, even in summer
While picking those flowers
Lady Madonna trembled
But it wasn't from the cold.

During the ceremony, that song kept going round in my head. I didn't hear the eulogies, neither the priest's, nor Dad's friend Alain's. I didn't hear the music that those close to Dad played for him on the violin. I heard only that song by Marie Laforêt inside my head. Because of my aunt's white hair.

To bid farewell to Dad, the brother of "their" Colette Septembre, many people from Gueugnon were present. All silent, contemplative. *Thirty-seven is no age to die.*

They were there for Colette. Few people in Gueugnon remembered Dad. He was just the kid whose photo was displayed in the entrance to the town hall and the community center, the one who'd left when he was little to become a young prodigy they rarely saw on TV, and who would come back home from time to time to give a classical music concert that few people attended.

44

November 4, 2010

Paul, I have two questions to ask you. Can you get me the phone numbers of people who've called a landline number in Gueugnon, in Saône-et-Loire? And can you trace a certain Levgueni Soudkovski, known as Soudoro, for me?"

I spell out the first name and surname twice.

"I don't know his nationality. He'd have been born in 1928, a year before a woman, his wife, whom he left for dead . . . She's called Marie Roman. And was born in 1929 in Flumet, in Savoie. She's still alive, under legal protection. Soudkovski was sentenced to prison without remission for assaulting Marie. I don't know in which court. He was a fairground type. He ran a circus. So dates of birth and addresses can only be approximate."

"Are you researching for a new movie?" he finally asks.

Paul is a police captain at 36, Quai des Orfèvres, the HQ of the police force in Paris.

"No, I'm trying to understand the shadowy parts of my aunt's life."

"Your aunt?"

"Yes. She was a shoe-mender. And believe me, there are some seriously shady parts to her life . . . As to all lives, no doubt."

"So you'll make a movie about that?"

"No."

"Right. Doing okay otherwise?"

"Not too bad, and you?"

"Fine. The routine, with no routine, a cop's life in other words. I heard about your separation. So you've moved back to France?"

"Yes. I returned to Paris three years ago. With my daughter. And Pierre, too. But he lives with his new woman."

"..."

"Right now, I'm in Burgundy, in my aunt's old house. But when I get back, let's have a drink."

"Yeah. What's the number of the landline you want to trace the calls to?"

"03 85 85 65 93."

"You want incoming and outgoing calls?"

"If you can, yes. That would be great."

"How many months back do you want to go?"

"I don't know . . . six?"

"I'll see what I can find and get back to you. For the list of phone numbers, it'll be quick. For your circus guy, it's bound to take longer."

"Thanks, Paul."

"At your service, chief."

Paul has always called me "chief." I met him in the early 2000s, when I was working on a new movie, *Les Silences de Dieu*. The portrait of a misanthropic private detective who reluctantly finds himself working on an investigation into some serial killings. I had a few technical questions to ask. I needed to be precise on the sequence of events, the investigation, and the procedures to follow. Someone—can't remember who—said to me: "Go and see Paul Seran; he's really nice, and I think he's already done that for the director Bertrand Tavernier." A phone call later, I found myself in his office at 36, Quai des Orfèvres with a notebook in my hand and a bitter semblance of coffee in a pottery goblet bearing the Olympique de Marseille FC crest.

"So, what can I do for you?" he asked me. "What's your movie going to be about?"

Paul is short, bald, and looks older than his age. So much for the dishy, tanned, hunky cop in jeans they peddle in TV series. He has zero sex appeal and appears to pick his clothes from his grandads' cupboards. And yet he has always appealed to me. Maybe due to his voice. He could do voiceovers, his tone's so lovely. And to his eyes, at once intelligent, mischievous, and distinctive. Two marbles blue as lagoons.

I took a deep breath before outlining the story, and, God knows why, suddenly said:

"You're misbuttoned."

"Sorry?"

"'Shirtlopped,' if you prefer."

And I stared hard at his 70s-collared checked shirt.

"Questioning that went on forever. Didn't get time to go and change this morning, just a swift shower in the cloakroom."

He rebuttoned his shirt in front of me. I felt myself blushing. Why had I said such a thing to him? And what right did I have?

"Okay, now the error has been rectified, how can I help you?"

I gripped my ridiculous notebook and pencil, and dived in, stammering. I was so impressed to be in this legendary place, facing a great cop to whom I'd made an inappropriate remark, that my hands were clammy and shaky.

"I'm going to portray a man, a private detective, who lives off petty surveillance in cases of adultery and tricky divorces. His daily life is like some light comedy . . . Jealous husbands, deceived women, gold diggers, Dr. Bovarys."

"I don't think dear Dr. Bovary would've sought the help of a detective," he interrupted, mischievously.

I had to smile, stupidly, before continuing. Back then, I could be thrown by the smallest thing, doubt everything, but as soon as I started talking about my movies, my projects, nothing could stop me. I have no idea today how I could turn up on a film set like it was my sitting room, work with my technical team, draw up a schedule with my first assistant and continuity girl. Discuss things with my costume designer, my editor, my hairdresser, my production designer. How I could shout, several times a day, without questioning it: "Quiet! Roll! Action!"

Was I someone else when I had Pierre as a husband? And yet, the absolute necessity to direct movies came long before I met him. I must have been around ten when I knew it was what I wanted to do. I was at the Danton movie theater in Gueugnon with Ilyas, Adèle, and Hervé when it hit me. We'd seen a horror movie that had terrified me: *Amityville II: The Possession*. We should never have been allowed in to watch it, but Hervé had come up with some trick and we'd hidden until the movie started. During the screening, Ilyas kept saying in my ear: "It's all pretend, it's just a movie, it isn't true." That day, I knew I wanted to make movies that didn't terrify the audience, but did bring a kind of thrill when seated before a screen. Like the Sempé drawings I'd have liked to live in. Clothing flung on a beach and the head of a gleeful boy who's splashing about in the water; a huge building, snow falling, and at a window—just one, when there are plenty—a child who's watching the snowflakes and smiling. It was at that movie that horrified me that I decided to become a film director.

"How would you define the films of Agnès Dugain?" a journalist had asked Pierre during an interview a few years ago.

"They're light, with a social backdrop. They're satires. Intelligent without being didactic. And yet they don't just deal with the funny side of men and women. There's a kind of indulgence with her; she doesn't judge. Her gaze is tender, but not taken in."

This was said before he started only appearing in other people's movies.

I continued with the outline of my next film for the police captain, who was still staring at me:

"One day, a fourteen-year-old boy, Samy, walks into the detective's office. The kid explains to him that one of his friends, Martin, has disappeared and that, unlike everyone else, he doesn't believe at all that he's run away. Samy is sure something awful has happened to his pal, that he couldn't have just left on a whim. The detective sends him packing. He's not interested in kids' affairs. And on top of that, Samy has no money to pay him. The months go by. One morning, the detective discovers, in the news-in-brief column of his daily paper, that Samy himself had disappeared the day after he'd visited his office. Guilt pushes the man to investigate. That's when he learns that Samy lied to him. No child named Martin had been declared missing in the area. At this point, the detective latches on and starts prowling around the school to find out if Martin really exists . . . So I'll need your help, Captain Seran, to know how it all works between the national police, municipal police, and gendarmerie. The procedures with schools, who looks after what, do you have access to the same files, and if so, who has access to them, who registers complaints, who looks into them, at what stage do the police or gendarmerie intervene, why, etc., and in particular, what kind of relationship do you have with private detectives—do you ever collaborate with them?"

"I'm at your disposal, chief. How does it end, your story? And why's it called *Les Silences de Dieu*?"

"You'll find that out at the preview . . . "

I wrote the screenplay in a few months. I called Paul Seran often to ask him questions. Despite his very busy schedule, he always answered me or called me back within the hour. I met up with him a few more times at cafés. During editing, he phoned me several times to find out if I was happy with the result. He came to the Paris preview of the movie. I called him up onto the stage after the screening, to join the actors and me. Then I lost touch with him. We sent each other season's greetings every New Year. He wrote to me after seeing my last movie to tell me how much he liked it. And time went by. During which, my aunt died twice.

And now I have to organize her funeral. Have her cremated, scatter some of the ashes at the Jean-Laville stadium, and then take the urn to place it beside Dad and Mom in Lyon. A mountain to climb.

45

November 5, 2010

No one wakes up one morning thinking, Great, today I'm going to get sloshed and stuff my nostrils."

I don't know why our conversation has swerved to this. Ilyas and I are at the Creusot crematorium. Colette's "fully combustible" wooden coffin is just disappearing into a crematory furnace at 850°C. The undertaker told us to allow at least an hour-and-a-half for the body to be reduced to ashes, depending on the corpulence of the deceased. For my aunt, it shouldn't take very long.

With Ana's agreement, I decided not to hold any kind of ceremony at the crematorium, but rather to organize one at the Lyon cemetery for mid-November, when she'd be back from paradise, bronzed and beautiful, and a death notice would have appeared in the local papers. The undertaker I dealt with when choosing the coffin gave me the contact number of "the right person," who wouldn't mind bending the rules to collect a small quantity of the ashes to scatter at the Jean-Laville stadium, as Colette had wished. The official urn will remain at the crematorium until the Lyon ceremony and then be placed in the vault alongside Dad and Mom. And Colette's name will be engraved on the tombstone already decorated with a violin and a piano. Before, I wanted to be buried close to Pierre when "no longer here." As they say. Though I've already not really been here for three years. Most of me is numb. Some people never get over a breakup. That does exist. A few years ago, Ana was forever asking, "Mom, does *that* exist?", about everything. She had a visceral need to know the truth. Doubtless because of our jobs; her father and I both told stories that didn't really exist.

Yes, when I'm no longer here, I'll be close to them. Jean, Hannah, and Colette. Maybe an engraving of a movie camera will join the violin and piano of my parents. We'll be the four of us once again, like when we'd celebrate Christmas Eve at Georges Vezant's restaurant. Maybe a shoe or a football should be engraved in tribute to Colette. Which would she have preferred?

I wanted to hold onto the memory of her working in the shoe-repair shop, behind her old workbench stained with polish, oil, and dye. Of her expression when "her" team had just scored a goal, or when she saw Ana for the first time.

So, to say farewell to Colette, I asked the undertaker not to remove the sheet covering her before being put into the coffin. Before he sealed the casket, I whispered: "Thank you for the cassettes, thank you for your trust, I love you."

Ilyas and I are having a coffee from the machine in which all the drinks are sweet. Even the soups. The corridor where we're waiting for the ashes leads to an indoor "garden." Its trees are bare and the sky is leaden. The gray ugliness of the white tiling completes the dismal scene.

"Why is it that, one day, it works? What helped you quit drinking?"

"The look in the medics' eyes. Of course, every time Nathalie managed to get me hospitalized, when I couldn't stand upright anymore, having mixed hard liquor and meds for weeks, I'd be released the following morning. Whereas she'd hoped I'd be put into psychiatric care to protect me from myself. No emergency doctor made the decision to get me treatment. For years, they all considered me capable of making my own decisions, thought I was sufficiently aware to stop using. They'd drop me like a hot potato. I'd hoodwink them in no time at all, and they'd show me the exit. Nathalie would phone them, insult them, beg them, explain that I might die, but it wasn't their problem. When you first turn up at the emergency department, and you're young, cute as pie, you sense the nurses' compassion for you, but at thirty-five, you can see in their eyes that you've become the resident bum. At state-run hospitals, an alcoholic isn't considered a sick person, just a damned nuisance to be gotten rid of, pronto. At the Garches hospital, the guy in charge of the addiction department is called Valentin Avenir—you couldn't make it up. And I can tell you, with him, it's no joke. Him you can't hoodwink. He was forever saying that he saved no one. That I had to save myself, on my own. I was at rock-bottom when Nathalie broke open her piggy bank and managed to get me transferred over there. It's very expensive. She says it's the best investment she ever made. You never stop drinking to please others. If it's for others, it doesn't work. Over there, I realized that I had to stop for myself.

"The hardest thing about detox is going back home. You've regained a kind of health, have gotten your colors back, seen some shrinks, explained stuff to them, or not, depending on the look of the shrink and whether you trust them . . . When you're on drugs or alcohol, often both, you don't really trust anyone anymore, especially not yourself. But yeah, the hardest thing is going back home. Often, the first thing you do is go buy a bottle of hooch at the corner store, lowering your eyes at the till. When I got back from Garches, I bought Sprite and lemon juice. And here I am before you, sober and magnificent, waiting for your aunt's ashes in a place that makes one want to die. Isn't life grand?"

"The last time you saw Charpie—when was that?"

The "right person" interrupts us by handing me a small urn, as if passing me drugs or dynamite.

"Here you are."

I don't know what to say. *Here's a little bit of your aunt, here's a life, here, it's all over.*

"We're really nothing much,
And my friend the rose
Told me that this morning . . ." as Françoise Hardy sings.

I finally stammer my thanks, and we hit the road. Ilyas has borrowed a colleague's car. Didn't want to take the Méhari or Adèle's Citroën. In honor of Colette, we slide in a solo CD of Dad at the piano, playing "Air on the G String" from Bach's third orchestral suite in D major.

While Ilyas drives, I grip the urn with both hands and gaze at the road. Right then, the Los Angeles avenues I'd cruise up and down, with Ana in her carseat, come back to me. And then Ana getting bigger in my rearview mirror. The kilometers we racked up in that vast city. The light. We lived in a bubble, in Pacific Palisades, I had my home, my nest for Pierre and Ana, a huge office overlooking the sea for me. I did yoga, swam in our pool, had a healthy lifestyle and lots of money. A firm butt and abs. But I lost my joy and my husband there. And somewhere between Sunset Boulevard and Melrose Studios Hollywood, I also lost the desire to make movies. Everything was fake. I'd become my child's chauffeur. Everything was far away, and I insisted on driving her to school, to her dance class, to her piano lesson, to a birthday party. I didn't want Cornélia to be the one doing it. Piano-wise, I had one delivered to the house, along with a private teacher. Ana had already reached such a high level and was so passionate about it, I didn't hesitate. The rush hour comes back to me, the dread of traffic jams between 7 and 10 in the morning and 4 and 7 in the afternoon. In Los Angeles, you're supposed to eat well, breathe well, but only if you've got money; otherwise you're dead, you live in a car stuck in the middle of other cars.

The American dream . . . speaking English, improving your accent, watching tons of undubbed movies, talking with your agent twice a day to finally be fortunate enough to make a movie, everyone receiving you warmly, thinking you've hit the jackpot at every meeting, and then radio silence. What the hell were we doing over there? I can't remember which of us came out with: "What if we moved to Hollywood?" You can't even swim in the sea at Malibu Beach, only look at it.

Ilyas parks outside the house, on Rue des Fredins, and jolts me from my thoughts. Back to Gueugnon, exit Santa Monica.

On paper, it looks good to say you live in LA, particularly when you work in the movies, but what does a life lived on a red carpet measure up to?

"Want me to come inside with you?" Ilyas asks.

"No. Thanks for taking me over there."

I hug him.

"I'm going to keep listening to Colette, to her voice on the cassettes.

That way, it'll be like she's with me, sort of. Sometimes, there's half an hour of birdsong, particularly blackbirds, from her garden . . . Sometimes, fifteen minutes of a football match. As if she was recording the days, life. I'd like to have finished listening before the ceremony. I still have about ten days."

"Okay, call me if you need to, and I'll be straight here."

"Do you realize," I say, opening the car door, "that if Colette hadn't died twice, I probably never would've seen you again? Weird . . . "

"And I wouldn't have met Lina," he declares, with a grin.

"You're going to see her again?"

"I'm even going to marry her."

"Are you serious?"

"Of course I'm serious. It's about time I start living."

He watches me get out, clutching my urn. Before leaving, he lowers the passenger-side window.

"The last time I saw Charpie was in Cannes, last year."

He drives off, and I watch his car disappear at the end of the road, without moving.

*

Colette's voice floods the room once more. I'm lying on my inflatable mattress, eyes closed, having placed the urn containing "the little pile of her" outside the door to her room. I'll go to the stadium early tomorrow morning to avoid meeting anyone. She'll get up early for the last time. When I used to turn up at the shop or in the kitchen on a Sunday morning, it would be around 9 or 10 o'clock. I'd feel as if she'd already begun her day hours ago.

COLETTE

First, you should know that the summer of 1976 was very hot. There was no talk yet of global warming, and those who dared suggest it on TV were seen as totally mad. In the streets of Gueugnon, people were walking around bare-chested, or in swimsuits and tees. That really struck me.

At the end of my street, the shoe brand Eram had just opened a store, which wasn't good news at all for my business . . . If Mokhtar had seen that! It's around then that folks started giving up on decent pairs of shoes to put cheap rubbish on their feet. Rubbish that would be tossed when worn out rather than properly repaired. Anyhow, when those shoes had had it, they'd had it. There was nothing to save. And folks would head straight off to buy another pair, much to the despair of Madame Bresciani, owner of the proper shoe store. Do you remember, she'd always stare at folks' feet before greeting them, to check that what they were wearing had come from her store?

She laughs. A stifled laugh. She mutters something inaudible and then continues.

COLETTE

Fortunately, I still had the belts, bags, wallets, and dress shoes. For weddings, christenings, first communions, and funerals. And many men who wore quality. Men who worked in the offices at the Forges factory. Sales of laces, insoles, and polish, which supplemented my income, slowed down. Unbelievably, those crooked peddlers of cheap shoes sold all that stuff, too. They even stocked nylon pantyhose, can you imagine, Agnès? And waterproofing sprays! They'd even come up with a loyalty card! For four pairs purchased, 10 francs off the fifth pair!

I hear her drinking. My aunt only ever drank water—*water will be fine.* Never sodas, or beer, or wine. "What would you like to drink, Colette?"—"Water will be fine." Even at the stadium's refreshments stall. Defeat or victory, no bubbles. The only exception was Christmas Eve, because her brother would hand her a glass of champagne, which she'd never felt able to refuse. She'd take just one sip.

COLETTE

It was that year that I learned how to use a machine for duplicating keys. And thank goodness. Otherwise, I'd have had to lock up for the last time with my own key. It was your father who bought the machine for me. He was forever wanting to give me money, to the extent that our only arguments were about that.

She goes quiet. As she does whenever recalling her brother. And when she picks up her story, it's in a hushed voice, as if some of her strength had deserted her.

COLETTE
I found myself with a brand-new machine in my shop. A machine that took up the entire workbench. I'm sure Jean chose the most expensive one. The high-performance one. He had a touch of folie des grandeurs. *Probably due to his music.*

Silence.

COLETTE
It looked like a flying saucer. If Mokhtar had seen that . . . and what's more, it was orange. And heavy, really heavy! Always needed at least three men to shift it. And strong guys. Not pussycats. Along with my machine, I received an unimaginable stock of key blanks, and a board to hang them on and display them. All at once, my little shop became modern. New customers showed up. Customers in worn-out shoes came merely to get duplicate keys made. If Mokhtar had seen that . . . I hung on to that machine. Even when the technology changed, I kept my first machine. Someone from Chalon-sur-Saône delivered it to me, and the following day, a really nice man came to teach me how to use it. It wasn't difficult, it was like doing a tracing, except the machine did it for me. You just had to select the correct type of key, and then it did all the work. I simply had to watch it. And check at the end that it hadn't made a mistake. I'd press "on." And when it was finished, I'd press "off." It was in English. And that's how, in the middle of a heatwave, in the summer of '76, I started selling keys. When the man from Chalon-sur-Saône, who trained me, left the shop, another man came in. Their paths crossed.

She changes her voice.

COLETTE
"Good day, Madame Septembre, may I call you Colette?"

Silence.

Colette

Oh, how handsome he was. I've never seen anyone that handsome since! I grabbed onto my orange machine. I was proud of it, of owning modernity, but my legs wouldn't support me anymore.

A long silence.

Colette

He was getting back to football training the following day. He was in blue Bermuda shorts and a blue undershirt, with black espadrilles. His arms were slender and muscular. His dark skin glistened, because of the heat. I'd never looked at a footballer the way I looked at him. In him, I saw the man. Not the left winger. And his curls weren't hidden by his beanie anymore. He was sweating. We were all sweating. The heat was unbearable. It was hard to breathe. Anyone who hadn't gone away on vacation was either at the pool or in the Arroux. In its water holes, because the river itself had dried up. In my shop, an old fan was stirring the stifling air. I said yes. "Yes, call me Colette."

She changes her voice again, to sound like him.

Colette

"My name is Aimé."

Quick as a flash, I said:

"Aimé Chauvel. No. 11. Left winger."

It just burst out of my mouth. He smiled.

"Everyone says you're the best supporter. And you know more about football than anyone."

"Who's everyone?"

"The players, the superfans, the managers, the journalists, the vendors."

"Ah, well, that's quite a crowd . . . Are you liking it here, in our town?"

"Yes."

I asked him where he was living, when in fact I already knew. I'd seen him going in and out of the place. He told me that he was renting a small apartment above the Café Thillet, on Place des Forges. But that, if he stayed on, he might rent a house. But a house on one's own, at eighteen, wasn't a good idea. Then he added:

"Today's my birthday."

And again, I feigned surprise. I knew all the players' dates of birth. Their age is so important . . . A career is so short.

"Well, happy birthday, then . . . "

I gave him a pair of black laces, muttering:

"They always come in handy one day."

He took them, looking surprised.

"Thanks. Colette. Thanks."

After that, I asked him how I could help him. He held out a plastic bag containing a pair of worn-out brown leather loafers. The soles needed replacing. Inside and out. The leather feeding. And a few seams reinforcing. I again thought of Mokhtar; it was a repair job he would have liked.

"They belonged to my grandfather, we're the same shoe size. It's not urgent. They're to wear in the autumn, when we won't be dying from the heat so much."

As I held these winter shoes, I really wondered why he was bringing them to me on July 19. What was this tall young man doing in my shoe-repair shop? I was thinking of that when I said:

"Some people are very good attackers, others much better in defense . . . Football's collective, like life. Need to find your place. There aren't really any football stars, only players who are in the right place . . . and get on well together. As soon as there's cohesion, youth, desire, and players well-positioned by the manager, there's often a great team. If you put Pelé in the goal, he probably won't do that much. You, Aimé, you play as a left winger, fine. But in my opinion, and it's just my opinion, your great strength would be stopping the attackers from getting through. Your place is surely at the back. You should ask the coach . . . But you, you'd definitely be better for stopping the attacker from getting past the defender."

"You don't think I'm good?"

"Yes, I do. Very good. But I don't think you're in the right position."
"But I've always played left winger."
"Habits can be changed."
"You think?"
"Yes."
"What are you doing tonight?"

I had to hold on to my new machine again. Why was he asking me that question? Generally, in the evening, once I'd shut the shop, I'd have a light supper and then read, or cut out articles for my collection, or watch Maigret *on TV, or listen to Pierre Bellemare on the radio. Agnès, did you know that it was Pierre Bellemare who was behind the creation of the Paris Saint-Germain club?*

I hear her take a sip as if waiting for my reply. She worshipped Pierre Bellemare. I even suspected her of being a little in love with him.

COLETTE

But right then it was summer; the season was about to start again . . . I didn't have a single article to cut out. And in 1976, you were still too little to spend the vacation with me. Your parents would take you with them on tour. They must have had some kind of nanny . . . Since it was stiflingly hot, in the evening, after work, I'd eat tomatoes and melon in my little courtyard, in the shade, with my feet in a bowl of water, waiting for night to fall. Sometimes, Louis Berthéol would come and keep me company. But you know, my own company never bored me. I've never been a pain to myself.

Silence. I imagine her in the solitude of her house. In the solitude of her life, facing my teen cassette recorder.

COLETTE

"Why do you ask?" I said.
"You could come and eat at my place."
"Me?"
"Yes, you," he said, smiling.

I've never seen a more beautiful smile.
"But I . . . "
I couldn't find an excuse. So I said:
"Okay."

I press stop. I'm exhausted. Sorry, my dear aunt, to cut you off. Your unexpected words. Your enthusiasm, your life. I'm discovering your life through your own so lovely voice.

46

November 6, 2010

It had made Colette laugh. Or at least, she'd laughed as she told me about it: "Agnès, we're all contaminated. Like in Chernobyl, but less seriously . . . or at least, I think so. But can you believe it, Gueugnon's fitness trail is radioactive!"

I remember that trail, beside the stadium; I'd go jogging there with Ilyas. The Jean-Laville stadium was opened on July 14, 1939. Just before the war. What's totally insane is that it was right next to a factory that processed minerals, including uranium, in operation from 1955 to 1980. The land on which some stadium stands and the car park are built contains radioactive waste. Twelve hectares were contaminated, not to mention the river that flows between the former factory and the stadium. Since last year, work has been ongoing to bury the radioactive pollution in landfill sites, at the company Areva's expense.

"At the state's expense, more like," Nathalie often retorts, when they get her started on the subject at the paper. "In other words, at the taxpayer's expense!" But that's not what mattered to my aunt. For her, radioactive or not, it was at that stadium, sitting in one of those stands, that she'd experienced, and doubtless lived, the most intense moments of her life. "Of course," she'd said to Louis Berthéol, when I was around ten, "there's my brother's music, too, but when Gueugnon are playing, I tremble like a leaf." Slightly exasperated, I'd asked her:

"Why do you tremble like a leaf?"

She'd seemed surprised at my joining in the conversation; I never asked her any questions. And she'd answered me:

"It's like a great big bonfire on Midsummer Night. Have you ever seen a big bonfire?"

I'd nodded my head to end the exchange, because at ten, the game was to speak to her as little as possible.

"It's like that, but right through the body," she'd added, flatly, as if saying, "Pass me the salt."

I'd nodded again while turning my back on her and thinking: *Shit, as well as being a pain with a smelly house, she's nuts.*

I'm alone in the dark, holding my urn and heading for the stadium. I've seen this in movies, but never in real life. It's drizzling, but there's no wind. Where am I going to scatter these ashes? Where would have a meaning for her?

I'm about to listen to what comes next on the recording concerning Aimé. I'd slipped the cassette into a Walkman. A real one. With auto reverse. Like the ones we had as teenagers. It's Hervé who left it on the doormat at the Fredins house. With this note: "Now you can listen to your aunt's cassettes while you walk. Big kiss. Hervé."

To bolster myself and to hear her, I press play. Her voice in my ears, the vastness of the stadium, plunged in darkness, surrounding me. Is Colette's ghost accompanying me? Is it dancing around me? Dad, Mom, Blaise, Mokhtar, Blanche?

COLETTE

I saw Aimé's smile again at seven that very evening. It must have still been around 40 degrees outside. And I didn't know the first thing. At thirty, I didn't know how to dress, didn't know what kind of gift to bring. I'd phoned Jean, but he knew even less than me when it came to the done thing, so he put your mother on to me. "It's Colette, she has a question."

Hannah had asked me:

"How many people will be there?"

I hadn't thought of that. But yes, how many people would be at his place? Just the two of us, or with other people? It was Aimé's birthday. Of course he must have organized a party.

"It's always good to bring a bottle," Hannah had advised me. "A bottle of wine or champagne. And for the gift, if he's eighteen, choose a record at Madame Bedin's store. A single or an LP. Or then two singles. It depends how much you want to spend."

"But which record?" I asked, in a panic.

"Tell Madame Bedin to give you the biggest hits of the year."

"Okay."

Madame Bedin owned the finest store in Gueugnon. She sold decorative items, and at the back, records. Entire shelves of records, including all those made by Dad and Mom. They were all there, on the highest shelf.

COLETTE

"And what should I wear?"

"Go to Causard, Monsieur Soussand will know."

"How do you know he's called Monsieur Soussand? And Madame Bedin? Why do you know her, Hannah?"

She was laughing as she replied:

"Because we've been going to them every Christmas Eve since I married your brother."

"Oh, yes. True. Thanks, Hannah."

She laughed some more. She did laugh, your mom. She often laughed. About nothing, about everything. I loved her dearly, you know. Jean loved her. He loved her in his own way, from his own world, but he loved her . . . I didn't go to Monsieur Soussand's. I found a dress. An old dress, but since I've never gained a kilo since the age of eighteen, maybe even sixteen or seventeen, it still fitted me. It was a summer dress that Blaise had given me. It buttoned down the front. I wouldn't buy a dress. I wasn't going to a wedding, for goodness' sake! On the other hand, Madame Bedin suggested I get "Daddy Cool" *by Boney M. and* "Dancing Queen" *by the group ABBA. Never heard of them. But she said she knew the tastes of the young people who bought their music from her, "and most importantly, Mademoiselle Septembre, if the boy already has them, tell him I'm happy to exchange them."*

She thought I was going to a child's birthday. Not that of an eighteen-year-old footballer. I don't know why, but I also bought a "poubelle de table"*—a kind of ceramic table-tidy pot with a lid. Madame Bedin asked if I'd like it gift-wrapped, or if it was for me, and* *not daring to say it was for "the boy," I said it was for me. And then wrapped it myself.*

Silence.

COLETTE

He was alone, Agnès. I was expecting to find the whole FCG team there to celebrate his birthday . . . the coach, some players, his family. Right away, I said:

"How many are you expecting?"

"Just you," he replied, seeming blasé. As if it were a minor detail.

"I'm going to heat up a can of something . . . but I did go to the pâtisserie. And I bought some champagne . . . I picked it randomly, I never drink."

"Me neither," I said. "Water will be fine."

"Fine? Come on, I'm eighteen today! I've come of age, I'm an adult . . ."

His big dark eyes looked deep into mine, and I must have babbled:

"Sure, of course, if that's what you'd like."

"I'm pleased that you came, Colette."

He said that to me as if singing it . . . he was joyful, light-hearted. On the pitch, he was the complete opposite. Like all great players, the slightest move was a matter of life or death. He was tall. I know, I've already said that. But he was a giant. And me, a tiny little thing compared with him. If I'd hugged him, my head would have rested at the level of his chest, of his heart.

I remember Aimé Chauvel. I came across him one day when shopping at Ilyas's parents' store. As usual, I'd handed over the list jotted down by my aunt on a scrap of paper. Aimé had walked in. I'd say he was around thirty, and I was a teenager. It's true that he was particularly handsome. I blushed when he greeted me, because he knew my name.

COLETTE

He opened a cupboard, took out some peanuts, which he poured into a Banania-branded bowl, and two empty mustard glasses for the champagne, apologizing that they were the only glasses he owned.

"But if you like, I'll go down to the Café Thillet to ask for some proper ones!"

On one of the glasses, there was a picture of Popeye, pipe in mouth. Before asking me to sit down in front of a coffee table, he opened another cupboard to show me a can of ravioli, a can of cassoulet, and a can of couscous, stored beside the cutlery.

"Which would you prefer? Or shall we choose later?"

"Sure," I murmured.

As you can imagine, I wasn't remotely hungry . . . And it must have been some 40 degrees in his place. I regretted wearing that dress, which stuck to my skin. I still had the records and the poubelle de table *in my hands. He opened the bottle and shrieked gleefully because half the contents ended up on the floor amid the dreadful din of the cork exploding a lightbulb. I helped him to mop it all up with toilet paper; he didn't own a tea towel or washcloth. He'd leave his dishes to dry beside the sink. His laundry was washed and his two-room apartment cleaned once a week by the owners of the café below. It was included in the rent.*

We replaced the lightbulb. The sun was still searing the walls. I suggested that we open all the windows to create some drafts; it would still be warm for one or two hours, but then, naturally, the air would cool down. As I was saying this, I thought to myself that, in any case, in two hours' time, I'd be back home and that . . .

I stop the cassette. Am I dreaming, or did someone just brush against my shoulder? Behind me, a shadow. I let out a cry of terror. The person who touched me jumps backward, too, just as startled.

"Don't be afraid! I scared you, oh, I'm so sorry!"

I recognize his voice in the darkness.

"For God's sake, Louis!!! Where were you? Are you finally going to explain everything to me?! And anyhow, now's not the time to just reappear like that, here! At six in the morning at the stadium! Jeez!"

"Forgive me, Agnès . . . I'm just back from Lyon, and I recognized Ilyas's yellow jeep in the car park as I was passing the stadium . . . It seemed strange."

"It seemed strange? Tell me, Louis, don't you think everything's been strange this past fortnight? Hmm?! Doesn't *everything* seem strange?!"

And the dam bursts. As they say. I start crying, letting out every tear in my body. As they also say. "Every tear in my body." It was Mom who used that expression. Louis remains at a distance, too nervous to come any closer.

"Where were you?"

He hesitates to reply, shifts from one foot to the other.

"I tried to find Blanche's father . . . But I lost track of him in Valence. And after that, I stopped off in Lyon to visit your parents' grave."

"Blanche's father? In Valence? Do you know his name?"

"His name at birth was Soudkovski . . . " he whispers, as if the man concerned could hear us. "Levgueni Soudkovski," he specifies.

I'm astounded.

"How do you know that?"

"I overheard a conversation between Colette and Blanche . . . once. Blanche was already living with your aunt, and I was repairing her washing machine for the umpteenth time, a pile of junk that never worked. They must have forgotten I was in the next room. 'Look!' Colette said to Blanche. 'Look! They're talking about him in this magazine!' Colette read the article out loud, and very clearly. It was in a magazine that a friend of hers had picked up in a waiting room—the *Nouveau Détective* of August 2003. I remember the cover, a photo of the actress Marie Trintignant, who'd recently been murdered. The whole of France was in a state of shock. When Colette discovered the article on Soudkovski, the magazine was about a year old."

"Do you think he's alive?"

"Yes."

"Why did you think you'd find him in Valence?"

I hear him sniff.

"A year before Colette's death, I mean her real death, I decided to search for that man. I found a detective, a private one, in Mâcon. But that lead to nothing . . . apart from costing me an arm and a leg . . . And then . . . A woman has just been found in Valence. Probably murdered by her neighbor, a certain Viktor Socha. He was her lover. The police gave a photo of Socha to a newspaper. The private detective recognized him. The photo had been taken by the victim, with her smartphone . . . The notorious Socha wasn't Socha."

"What?"

"It was Soudkovski . . . He'd disappeared overnight, after his mistress was found dead."

My arms fall, the urn of ashes almost crashing to the floor, but I just manage to catch it.

"What's that?" Louis asks.

"It's Tata . . . I mean, my aunt. Part of her. A small part. A few ashes. The rest will be placed beside Dad and Mom in Lyon."

This time, it's Louis who bursts into tears. What a scene, the two of us in the cold, the dark, the drizzle, in the middle of the stadium, one beside the other. Me hugging the urn with the Walkman headphones around my neck. I never would've put such a scene into one of my movies . . . particularly as there's no light . . . And dawn is stubbornly refusing to break. I don't dare ask Louis to leave. And yet I'd like to be alone. I need to live this moment alone. All the same, I'm dying for him to tell me about the article, and Blanche. Especially Blanche. And to show me the photo of the old Soudoro.

"Are you going back home, Louis?"

"Yes."

"And will you stay this time?"

"Yes. For good."

"I'll do what I need to do, and then stop by for a coffee."

"Alright," he stammers, laying his hand on the urn. "I'll be expecting you."

He moves off, but I shout after him:

"D'you think there's a place she'd have wanted to be, on the pitch?"

He stops for a moment, then I hear him walking back and intoning the names of teams, as if reliving a succession of matches in the dawn.

"Gueugnon's greatest victory, the one that took them to the Stade de France, was the League Cup quarter-final game, the Strasbourg-Gueugnon match . . . Our team won 20 on February 19, 2000 . . . Xavier Collin scored the winning goal, right there."

He points to one of the nets.

"I thought my Colette was about to kick the bucket. As usual, she didn't cheer. Nothing. *Nada*. Standing. Straight up. White as snow. Fists clenched. A glimmer of pride in her eyes. And her smile, which no one ever understood . . . She had two smiles, Colette, the one of sadness and the one of joy, but we never knew which one she was giving us . . . On April 3, we played against the Red Star FC . . . Not here. At another stadium. We went by bus, me, Colette, and every supporter we had back then. The score was 22. Penalty shootout time. You must put yourself in our place: imagine how our hearts were pounding. First shot, second shot, third shot, fourth shot . . . and each one stopped by our goalkeeper and the other goalkeeper. Final chance: our goalie, Richard Trivino, blocks the Red Star shot, and then that same Richard Trivino leaves his net, takes the last penalty shot, and the opposing goalie fails to stop the ball. And it goes smack into the top corner of the net! Gueugnon wins 9 to 8 . . . At this feat, when we realized that we'd made the final, Colette let out a cry. A strange cry. Like an animal caught in a trap. A sharp sound. And then nothing. Again standing straight up, fists clenched. Not even white anymore; translucent, she was."

I hug the urn tight like I never hugged Colette in real life. In the flesh, in one of her floaty dresses.

"Otherwise, there's the first time," Louis whispers.

"The first time?"

"The first time she came here, to the stadium, to watch a match, the day she became wedded to the ball, as it were . . . See you later."

And he disappears into the darkness. Might footballs, those from certain victories, have a soul?

47

The first time Colette attended a football match, it was a Sunday afternoon, October 7, 1956. The weather was dull, the fine rain sporadic, the pitch slippery. There were eight hundred and twenty spectators, including her, Blaise, and the marquess. Colette and Blaise were in fifth grade. She'd been a bit scared of going, scared or not that keen. It would just be boys with their fathers there. Entire families of them.

In Gueugnon, football was already the most important thing. Everyone talked about it, but for Colette, it wasn't her world. Television sets were for the rich, and her parents weren't interested in sports. But the team's scores were discussed everywhere, as keenly the weather forecast.

The school playground was only just starting to be mixed, but not the classes. Girls and boys stayed apart, eyeing each other warily. Even though they were allowed to, Colette and Blaise didn't speak to each other during recess, or when inside the school.

Blaise had begged Colette to come with him to the stadium. The marquess would be far away from them, and there'd be peanuts and a soda at half-time! An orange fizzy drink like she'd never tasted before. A thing to make you want to keep going to matches forever.

"But are you sure girls are allowed in?"

"For goodness' sake, Colette, what world are you living in?"

"How should I dress?"

"Same as for school. But wrap up warm. It can be cold in the stands."

The father and mother had agreed to it. As far back as she could remember, Colette had been close to Blaise, and Blaise to Colette. They'd taken their first steps together. Her in clumpy little shoes, him in fine slippers. Later, to meet up with her, he'd pull on a pair of hunting boots that had belonged to the marquess as a child. It had always surprised Blaise that his father could have ever been a child, he who seemed more adult than other adults. Wearing his boots gave Blaise a strange feeling. Would he become like him? Cold and curt?

At the end of the path that separated the entrance to the château and the main body of the farm, Blaise and Colette would always end up coming across each other. The property towered over their smallholding. The two of them were bound to see each other every day. Blaise had never known a girl to do such arduous work. He had watched the men bent over the earth, plowing, carrying heavy loads, but never someone his age. From time to time, he would help her, on the quiet, to pick the potatoes or milk the ewes, so she'd have time to play a little.

At around six years old, Blaise had taught her to swim breaststroke in the lake beside the forest. And later, to keep her balance on a bicycle. As for Colette, she'd taught him how to care for tadpoles in a basin before returning them to a pond once they were starting to develop; to recognize boletuses, ceps, and chanterelles; to differentiate tits from goldfinches; and to detect the smell of lindens, beeches, and oaks.

For his seventh birthday, by way of a gift, Colette had put a lamb into his arms so he could feel the warmth of purity. The little creature had fallen asleep against him. He'd sworn that it had been his best birthday ever. Until Robin Septembre died, she'd done the same thing many times.

In the morning, they would go to school together. Either in the car with the marchioness, or by bike. At first, Colette would set off on foot, but the marchioness would pull up on the roadside so she could take her place beside Blaise in the back seat. Later on, Jean would join them, too.

Colette and Blaise were good pupils. They had understood that, to have peace, you had to bring home good grades. Particularly Blaise. For Colette, that wasn't the issue. Her parents couldn't care less about her report card. But the marquess would never have allowed his son to frequent a bad pupil. That was the price she had to pay.

Blaise knew that he would pursue his studies to the highest level to become an important person. Important in what way? He didn't know.

Very early on, he'd confided his secret to Colette, an unhappy secret that had grown within him the older he had become, and that would condemn him if ever his parents, and the rest of the world, found out about it.

Colette had pretended to be surprised, but she'd always known that Blaise liked boys. Such an attraction for the same sex wasn't rare among animals. She couldn't understand why he saw his difference as a sickness, something shameful. She trusted what nature and animals taught her more than what people said. To make him feel better, she'd tried to find a secret to admit to him, but in vain. She could have made one up, but Blaise didn't deserve a lie.

Blaise actually loathed football, but he was obsessed with a player three years older than him who served drinks and sandwiches at the refreshments stall on match nights.

"Don't leave me to go on my own, I need you!" he had implored. "My father scares everyone, and Mom and football, well . . . "

Colette had ended up just saying, "Okay, fine."

The match was Gueugnon versus Fontainebleau. A home match at the Jean-Laville stadium.

Colette had been surprised to discover that there were some girls and their mothers in the stands, entire families. She'd found the pitch enormous, even bigger than the pastures she'd take the animals to graze on. She'd even wondered whether the pitch's grass would be good for the sheep to eat.

There was a smell of food in the air. A startling mix of savory and sweet. A bit like at the fun fair, but a more meaty aroma.

"It's the sausages . . . " Blaise had explained.

He was wearing a navy-blue coat and new shoes. From time to time, he would blow on his big hands to warm them up, while also leaning forward to glimpse the refreshments stall, as it couldn't be seen from their seats. Blaise resembled his mother. The same fineness of features, same blondness, and eyes of an imperial green. He had always been huge. It was the only thing he had in common with his genitor. A few meters away from them, the marquess was surrounded by other men. For the first time, Colette saw him smile.

So this was football: it made stern people cheery. The singing in the stands, the joy, the laughter, the upbeat mood. This crowd that gathered in celebration had captured her heart.

When the two teams appeared, she'd been galvanized by the roaring of the fans all around her. Such jubilation was unknown to her. It had given her goose bumps. Her pulse had quickened. She'd touched the inside of her wrists: under the skin, it was pounding. Blaise had explained a few basic rules of the game to her, but the main point was to score goals. Like in the school playground when the kids were playing football and the goal area was just sweaters rolled up on the ground.

To score goals and avoid letting any in. And you had to encourage the players, too. The others would shout: "*Allez!*" as soon as a player's feet touched the ball. Even the marquess. Especially the marquess. So, the only place where men allowed themselves to be emotional was a stadium.

For the first twenty minutes, Gueugnon had been dominated by Fontainebleau, whose goalie had to wait until the twenty-first minute to see any action. Gueugnon's had already had to deflect three really fierce shots, at the twelfth, thirteenth, and sixteenth minute. And each time, stifled sighs and cries of relief had swept around the stands. Some bad words, too. Here, that wasn't forbidden. "Corner," some spectators had repeated several times. *What does "corner" mean?* Colette had wondered, without daring to ask out loud. Too busy waiting for half-time, Blaise was barely watching the players.

At the thirty-third minute, after another save by Gueugnon's goalkeeper, who was starting to be seen as a hero, a lucky devil, or a miracle worker, the *Forgerons* had turned the tide by scoring a goal. A header. When the ball hit the net, the air trembled. And everyone rose to their feet as one. Even the marquess. Especially the marquess, who, once again, had roared even louder than the rest. Some were shaking pennants, others banners. And so she had done like them; she'd stood up and applauded. Without daring to cheer, even though she really wanted to. In the north stand, some supporters were banging on sheet metal. It made an infernal din. She'd found out later that that stand, covered in metal panels, had received a battering for every single goal scored.

When the referee blew the half-time whistle, she felt a twinge of disappointment. She'd have liked the game to go on. Blaise took her hand and led her to the refreshments stall, leaving his father behind with the others. Everyone in the stands seemed to have decided to meet at the same place. The goal had electrified men, women, and children alike. She could hear the hope in everything they said. They'd been scared at the start, but now Gueugnon was on top; they just had to score again after half-time, and it would be in the bag.

Standing in line, the closer they got to the stall, the hotter and clammier Blaise's hand became in hers. He'd finally gone up to the guy serving to order two toasted sandwiches and two orange sodas. While fumbling in his pocket for the money, he'd stammered to the boy:

"You're well? When are you playing next?"

He'd replied:

"Wednesday, against Saint-Marcel, at the new-town stadium," and then handed him two bottles and two burning-hot sandwiches.

"Thanks. See you."

Blaise had about-turned as if he'd seen the devil, and they'd elbowed their way back to their seats.

"What's his name?" Colette whispered in Blaise's ear.

"Alain," Blaise whispered back, still overcome after exchanging three words with the young man.

"Well, Alain has put way too much yellow in our sandwiches. It tickles."

They'd giggled, enjoying the combination of orangeade, warm bread, and sausages smeared with mustard.

The match had restarted. Colette felt instantly happy. Not thanks to Blaise's company or the magical drink, but because she'd just become infatuated with what was taking place between the players, there in the cold, before her very eyes, amid the general jubilation.

As if football had wanted to seduce her, to set this burgeoning love in stone, the *Forgerons* team scored a second goal at the forty-seventh minute. And on that day, Colette had learned what clearing from the halfway line, long-balling, passing, burying the ball at the back of the net, fate, luck, and leaving it to God all meant.

48

November 6, 2010

It's eight in the morning when I push open the gate to Louis Berthéol's house. He lives halfway down Rue Saint-Pierre, about two hundred meters from the shoe-repair shop. A damp chill creeps into every pore of my skin. The sky is low, as if caught in ice. But day has finally broken. I know this house off by heart. Nothing has changed. Planters, an arbor close to a bike shed, a little stone windmill that Louis made for his daughter, with sails that still turn, a garden shed that's repainted every year. It's all meticulously maintained.

When I was a child, Louis's wife scared me because of her thinness. She was unwell and often bedridden. Louis had a bowl of candies in the hall and a daughter older than me who fascinated me. She was pursuing higher studies, smelled nice, was tall, elegant, and, most importantly, had a fiancé. To me, succeeding in life meant being betrothed to a prince charming. My God.

On Rue Saint-Pierre, most of the houses are identical, and often adjoining. For a long time, they belonged to the factory, which then sold them to private buyers in the 90s. I've always known Louis to live here. I believe his parents were already here when he was born.

I knock, he shouts to come in. The floor of the corridor is damp and smells of a eucalyptus-scented cleaning product. I can see he's just been doing some housework. The chairs are upended on the table in the dining room, which is plunged in darkness. Sitting at the kitchen table, Louis is drinking coffee. Before him, the *Journal de Saône-et-Loire* is open at the sports page. Unable to resist, I flick the switch, and the ceiling lamp warms the room with its yellow light. On the walls, a clock and two wedding photos. His own, and his daughter's, thirty years later.

Her prince charming has seriously aged. I smile inside. *Have you seen what yours looks like, Agnès? And it didn't stop him from clearing off, either.* I smile inside again. Colette died again, so thanks to her, I can smile inside again.

"Help yourself," Louis says, pointing at the coffee pot.

I hate cat's-piss coffee. I'm too used to espressos.

"Louis, the house Colette lived in on Rue des Fredins, I think I'd like to buy it from you."

"What for?"

"I don't know."

"There'll be work needed, if you want to modernize."

"I don't intend to modernize. I like it as it is, in its original state."

"But a girl like you could buy herself a château around here."

"I don't want a château, I want a house."

"It's worth peanuts . . . "

"Then I'll buy it from you with peanuts."

He shrugs his shoulders, as if to say, "do whatever makes you happy."

"Talking of a house, do you know the people living in the one from Dad's raffle?"

"Antoine Été. Used to be a doctor. Worked in the emergency department at Chalon hospital. Now he repairs old cars. Particularly those like Ilyas's. There are at least ten of them in his garden. White ones, blue ones, orange ones. Looks like a field of flowers. He bought a meadow from a farmer to keep them on. It's pretty to look at . . . "

"You mean Méharis?"

"Yes."

"That's funny, they're my favorite cars . . . Dad loved them, too. He'd be pleased to know that the raffle house is harboring plenty of them."

"Where did you put the ashes then?"

"A bit all over. Particularly around the left winger," I say, having no idea where he's to be found on a pitch, except to the left, maybe.

"The left winger?"

"Aimé Chauvel."

"Why are you bringing up Aimé?"

"And you, why are you blushing, Louis?"

He shrugs again, as if to say, "what nonsense."

"Do you plan to have music at the Lyon ceremony?" he asks, changing the subject.

"Haven't thought about that yet. Probably a recording of a sonata played by Dad."

He looks at me for a long time. He seems sad and tired. He strokes the newspaper with his fingertips. I can see that he's searching for his words, but I've plenty of time. I pour myself a cup of cat's piss.

"Have you listened to the cassettes?" he finally musters.

"Not all of them. Not yet. And you, Louis, did you listen to a few?"

He seems shocked by my question.

"No. I never would've taken that liberty. Those cassettes, they were for you. It was becoming an obsession at the end."

"An obsession?"

"It was all Colette thought about. When I'd drop by to see her, she was always sitting in front of that machine, recording herself."

"Why didn't you call me? Why didn't you tell me she was alive?"

"You were living in America. And also, after Blanche's death, Colette made me swear to silence, on my daughter's life. She said that as long as you knew nothing, you risked nothing. And me, it annoyed me that that guy, that Soudkovski, was calling the shots."

"I met Blanche's mother three days ago. She lives in a retirement home in Sallanches, under a false identity."

"She's alive?" he asks, flabbergasted.

"Yes."

"How did you find her?"

"It's a long story . . . But it started with an ID card hidden at Colette's, under the TV console."

"What ID card?"

"Blanche Soudkovski's, born March 7, 1946, in Flumet. I gave it to Marie. That's what she's called. Marie Roman."

"Marie . . . Blanche . . . Colette never knew that I'd phoned a private detective. She'd have bawled me out, called me reckless."

He opens an envelope that's on the table and hands me an article with a photo of a man in a gray coat, pulling a grocery cart behind him. Stooped, short, white hair.

"How can this little old man still terrorize everyone?"

"That," Louis replies, "I'd sure like to know . . . The perfect neighbor. Discreet, never a sound. Shopping in the morning, and then no one would see him again for the rest of the day. Until the day when the poor woman who took this photo from her window was found dead. Her name was Mathilde Pinson. The fact that he disappeared just after the murder roused suspicions. Particularly since he'd stripped his house, a rented one, of all his belongings. Gone without leaving a forwarding address . . . According to the investigation, the victim was his companion."

"How old was she?"

"Younger than him. Sixty-three. The poor woman."

"He did time in prison after leaving Blanche's mother for dead. I have a cop friend in Paris who's looking into him right now. I should tell him about Valence . . . Why was Blanche so scared of him? Do you think he would've harmed his daughter?"

"She never spoke to me about it. It was just understood, that terror."

"Did you keep the article from *Nouveau Détective*?"

"I have it in my head . . . Once I'd finished repairing 'that darned thing,' as I called Colette's washing machine," he continues, with a faint smile, "I managed to go to the bathroom with the magazine, which they'd hidden in the drawer of the kitchen table. I knew it was destined for the trash, just as soon as they'd burned it or ripped it up. Colette had gone back down to the shoe-repair shop, and Blanche was in her room. It was a miracle it was still there, in the drawer. I swiped it and went and locked myself in, like a thief. If Colette had caught me red-handed, she might never have spoken to me again. I swear my hands were shaking, but I had to know. Put yourself in my shoes! I looked through the magazine and found the headline Colette had read out loud: "Suspect on the run." The beginning of the article was horrendous. Soudkovski had laid into his companion, who wanted to leave him. There was a mugshot of him, one of those photos taken by police when a suspect gets nabbed. That one must have been a bit dated. The guy had escaped after assaulting her; he was wanted by the police. The article said he'd already been in trouble with the law for aggravated assaults, and had spent time in jail."

"You're telling me that after he got out of jail, he started up again?"

"Yes."

"And ended up killing."

"Yes. The article said that the victim, originally from Marseille, had miraculously survived. But he'd messed her up so badly that it would take years for her to live normally again."

He closes his eyes.

"Do you remember anything else, Louis?"

"No. I put the magazine back in the drawer and left without further ado. He'd eluded the police, he was wanted, so, from that day on, I was constantly scared for the two of them. I'd patrol outside the shoe-repair shop . . . at all hours. It was 2004, just before summer. I wanted to go to the gendarmerie to report that Colette and her friend were probably in danger, but since Blanche was hiding at Colette's, she clearly didn't trust the police."

"What was Blanche like?"

"Kind. Discreet. The spitting image of your aunt, but at the same time, totally different. One sensed that they hadn't lived the same life, the same story, and whereas Colette had always merged into her surroundings, for Blanche, even if she'd wanted to, that wouldn't have been possible . . ."

He glanced at his wedding photo as if apologizing to his better half.

"When I saw Blanche for the first time, she must have been around sixty . . . I didn't lift a finger, but to you, I can admit it: I'd have loved to have her in my bed. I'd have loved to kiss her. We're not supposed to say such things anymore, but if I could have slept with her . . . I'd have been the happiest of men."

The conversation is taking a more than unexpected turn. Louis, a retired baker, whose *pains au chocolat* we'd buy at four in the morning after a night at Tacot's, who, in his checked shirt, under his wedding photo, is now making a confession to me that I really wasn't expecting.

"You fell in love with her?"

He stares at me, stunned. Then answers, quick as a flash:

"Impossible not to fall in love with her. Impossible. She was too beautiful, too womanly, too everything. The entire world would have fallen in love with her. Even a stone, or a pathetic little pebble in a stream."

"But . . . do you think the feeling was mutual?"

"Of course not. Once she was in Gueugnon, you could sense that she just wanted peace. Not an affair with an old fart like me. Colette and Blanche were great friends. It was beautiful to see."

"I'd love to have a photo of the two of them, one beside the other . . ."

"Ah, well, I don't think such a thing exists."

"But did they ever go out? Do things outside the house?"

"Not to my knowledge."

"It's completely insane. Do you think they ever passed themselves off as each other?"

"I don't think so. Don't know."

"When did you find out about Blanche? I mean, that Colette was hiding her?"

"After the League Cup."

"You mean Gueugnon's victory at the Stade de France?"

"Yes."

"You mean in 2000?"

"Yes."

"When Colette disappeared for several days?"

"Yes."

"She was with Blanche?"

"Yes. That's when she came back with her."

"Blanche lived in Gueugnon for seven years?!"

"Yes. Seven years."

49

November 6, 2010

"Hello?"

"It stinks, your story."

"Hi, Paul. Hold on, I'm in the car."

I turn onto Place des Forges and park any old how. I'll be meeting Ilyas when he leaves work at midday. He started at four this morning. He suggested lunch at the Monge, before he goes home to hit the sack.

"All good, chief?" Paul asks.

"All good. I'm listening."

"Your guy, your circus man, he's wanted."

"I just found that out. Because of a woman he killed in Valence. And another he assaulted in Marseille."

"And that's not all. Forgery and the use of forgeries. Assuming another person's identity for years. Viktor Socha, a man who mysteriously disappeared from one day to the next. He was never found. Soudkovski took his place. Moved into his home, appropriated his ID papers, credit card, check book, bank account, social-security number, war veteran's pension. And then promptly moved to avoid arousing suspicion in the neighborhood. A wily guy . . . He was in jail from 2000 to 2002. He'd been sentenced to five years for aggravated violence to his ex-wife, but was released after two years for good behavior."

"Do you know where he was tried?"

"At the court in Annecy, in 2000. After that he went to Fresnes. Served his time there. Never caused any trouble. Waltzed out in 2002. We lose track of him in Marseille, in 2003. It's not yet known whether he knew Viktor Socha, a former traveling man like him. We presume he met with him again, Socha put him up, and Soudkovski bumped him off to take his place. Searches are underway of the house Socha lived in at the time, and of the garden."

"Where?"

"In Urmatt, near Strasbourg. The fellow was single, childless. No close family. A misfit who'd fought in Algeria. A godsend to Soudkovski."

"Do you know anything else about Soudkovski?"

"I read his prison file this morning. He apparently quit his circus work in 1970. Then did lots of casual jobs, stock clerk and the like, notably in the Lyon area. He has just one daughter and has never stopped searching for her."

My blood freezes. I'm struggling to breathe. It's happening again. I can feel myself going, like at the town hall in Flumet. I cut the call. *For God's sake*, I manage to think, *what's happening to me?* I'm roused by the ringing of my phone. Paul must think I hung up on him. I finally answer, with difficulty, after the third call. I manage to say:

"How d'you know that?"

"How do I know what?"

"About his daughter. That he's searching for her."

"Are you okay? You're sure?"

"I got heatstroke."

"You get heatstroke in November, do you?"

I don't answer. And Paul doesn't dwell on it.

"A fellow inmate, at Fresnes, who talked. And yet Soudkovski is a smart one. Not the sort to confide in anyone or pour out his feelings. But according to the inmate, he mentioned his daughter often, played the distraught father; supposedly, she'd betrayed him."

I'm incapable of uttering a word. My mouth's dry and there's a lump in my throat. I finally whisper to Paul that his daughter is the woman who died. The one buried instead of my aunt in Gueugnon cemetery.

"This really does stink. I'm going to come down to your neck of the woods to get to the bottom of this. Will you be there much longer?"

"About a fortnight. Then I'm off to Lyon for my aunt's funeral, where I'll be reunited with Ana, back from Mauritius. She's over there with her father and . . . "

He pauses awhile before saying:

"I'm in Urmatt. I'm waiting to see what the searches at Socha's turn up, and then I'll come to you. Who's in charge of the situation in Gueu . . . how d'you say it again?"

"Gueugnon. Captain Rampin at the gendarmerie, Cyril Rampin."

"You must tell me everything you know, all you've discovered since getting there. This sicko can't be allowed to remain at large."

"There's still something I don't get, Paul; this murderer must be over eighty, how can he still pose a danger to others?"

"Hatred and madness are ageless, chief."

*

"You don't look too happy . . . "

Ilyas is sitting close to the window. Nathalie is beside him. A delicious aroma wafts around the large, luminous restaurant. I'm happy to be back with them, and kiss them before taking my seat.

"Sorry, I'm late."

"Are you kidding? I was just telling Nat how I met Lina. And I wanted Nat to be here because . . . I have something to tell you . . . But you first. Why are you looking so pasty?"

I take a deep breath and smile so I don't burst into tears, and paradoxically, I am happy, and I don't know why. I wouldn't want to be anywhere else but in this restaurant in Gueugnon with them. Not even with Pierre, not even in America, or wherever. I want to be here, now, to understand what made my aunt protect a woman to the point of self-denial. And after this lunch, to return to Colette's voice and hear how Aimé Chauvel's birthday ended. How could I ever thank my aunt for leaving me such a gift, her confessions on tape? She who was so reserved.

"Well, I started the day by scattering Colette's ashes at the Jean-Laville stadium, at around six in the morning . . . It was freezing . . . Then I went to see Louis Berthéol, who's back now, alleluia! And who told me some really interesting stuff . . . And finally, I've just been talking on the phone to my pal who's a police captain at 36, Quai des Orfèvres, like in the movies, except he's coming here because the father of Blanche, the woman who's been lying in the cemetery instead of Colette for three years, is a crazy murdering bastard who's wanted by every police force in France!"

"That's totally insane!" Nathalie exclaims.

Ilyas remains speechless.

The waitress with the long braid, who rolls her eyes at the smallest request, puts the menu on the table.

"Would you folks like an aperitif?"

"A vodka, no ice, please."

Our eyes darting to Ilyas make him burst out laughing.

"I'm kidding! A Schweppes, please."

The waitress almost faints; she doesn't have that.

"An Ice Tea, then."

She jots it down, stressing that she'll see if she has any.

"Water will be fine," I say, as a nod to Colette.

"Sparkling or flat?"

"Flat. Bottled, not in a carafe," Nathalie specifies.

"I'm hungry," I say. "In fact, I'm dying of hunger."

"I'm starving, too," Ilyas says, amused.

"What did you want to tell me, Ilyas?"

*

Ilyas's parents never knew he was an addict. Or pretended not to know. He always tore himself apart secretly. In the evening, at night, in the dark, on the weekend, with the shutters closed. His mother would say of her son: "He has a delicate stomach, he's a sensitive child." And his father: "He's a good boy. He's decent. He didn't leave Gueugnon so he could look after us." When they sold their grocery store, his parents remained in their house, where they'd lived since arriving in France in 1964. Ilyas has an older sister, Fatiha, and a younger sister, Zeïa. The former is an airline pilot, the latter a lawyer. They're the pride of their family, in both France and Algeria. Brilliant studies thanks to scholarships, while Ilyas struggled to move up a grade, hated school, never did a stroke of work. The girls always had their noses in books, Ilyas a football at his feet, until he quit the game. "What a mistake, son," the coach had lamented. "What a mistake you're making; you could go really far, have a pro's career." "No, coach, I can't go anywhere. Look at me properly; I can't move anymore." Ilyas would sing snatches of the Alain Bashung song to anyone listening, especially himself: "My circuits are fucked / And something's been tripped [. . .] The frozen heart's still deaf / To the ice-cream vendor's cries."

His career he found at the factory, working on various lines. Not the same kind of lines as his big sister. For her, it was Paris-New York, for him, stainless-steel coils. At sixteen, he was already sharing a two-room apartment so he could booze in peace after work.

Fatiha got married. When he became an uncle, he was beyond thrilled. But soon after Sohan's birth, Ilyas become obsessed almost to the point of insanity. Of not being able to sleep anymore. He started by regularly calling his sister for news of the little one, then plagued her with questions: "Who've you got minding him? Who is this nanny? Is she married? Does she have sons? How old? You trust her? Who is she? He's never alone, hey? You're sure? Is he well? Nothing abnormal? You keep watch? What?! All alone at a birthday party?! But who's at this birthday party?! You're being reckless!" Until the day she hung up on him. Because she didn't know, couldn't understand. No one could. Ilyas never spoke of his abuse to his sisters, or to his parents. For a long time, Nathalie was the only one to know, to share the secret.

Last year, Nathalie dragged Ilyas on vacation. "Come on, come! We're off to Nice! We'll live the good life!" They rented a studio in the old town with a sea view. And spent their days devouring pizzas and *pans bagnats*, buying sunglasses, losing them, and lavender and postcards for no one, and then swimming. The perfect cliché. Total bliss. For the first time, Ilyas felt carefree. Nathalie's skin reddened, Ilyas's darkened. The girls ogled Ilyas, and Nathalie ogled the girls ogling Ilyas.

Sometimes, our brains don't make the right connections, that's just how it is. It can happen to all of us to go to a town and forget that someone lives there. A childhood friend, a pal from high school, a former colleague, a cousin, an uncle, a pedophile.

On July 7, 2009, they went to a screening in Cannes, at the Palais des Festivals, of *La Tournée des grands espaces*, a homage to Alain Bashung, Ilyas's favorite singer. Nathalie had managed to get tickets up at the front. Ilyas could have wept: "You really are like a sister to me." They were walking on air as they left and lingered on Cannes's terraces, going from decafs to ice creams to glasses of water to songs. All of *Fantaisie militaire*, Ilyas's favorite album, got covered.

It was while humming "*La nuit je mens*" that Ilyas saw him. At first, his eyes were drawn to a shadow, then to someone. That's what happens before comprehension dawns. Among the passersby, a bearing, a profile that stands out. Then Ilyas realized that *he* was there. That it was *him*, about sixty meters away. He was alone. Strolling along the Croisette. Tall, lean, nose in the air. Not the sort to look at his feet, no, more like a guy just walking home, a normal guy whose smart pace, under the streetlamps, is steady, serene. Him, he'd always survived, he'd never known the psychiatric hospital, fear in the belly, failure slung over the shoulder, and all the rest. Him, he retires to Cannes, on the Riviera, without anyone noticing . . . A statute of limitations. Limitations. A period of time passed when, according to the law, justice can no longer be sought.

When Nathalie saw Ilyas's face, followed his eyes, clocked the man, she exclaimed:

"He lives in Cannes!"

She didn't know him, but had strained her eyes enough studying the few photos still to be found of him on the net at the time. Later, she'd ruffled so many feathers asking questions about him that any trace of his time in Gueugnon had been erased. Not a doubt now. He'd aged, but it was him.

Nathalie saw Ilyas's face disintegrate before her. The look in his eyes, between terror, disbelief, and helplessness. After that day in the changing rooms, Ilyas had seen him around. At a distance. At the stadium, at matches, on Rue de la Liberté, at the Intermarché. After that day in the changing rooms, Charpie would occasionally greet him politely, and Ilyas would reply just as politely, "Morning, monsieur."

"Shall we follow him?" Nathalie suggested.

And since Ilyas remained mute, she asked again:

"Ilyas, d'you want us to follow him?"

"What for?"

"I don't know. You don't want to speak to him?"

"What for?"

"For him to apologize to you . . . I don't know."

"Apologize . . . " he repeated, wild-eyed.

They exchanged a glance and jumped up at the same time. Within seconds, they found themselves behind him. Nathalie grabbed Ilyas's hand. Ilyas gripped her hand hard. They looked like two lovebirds on the Croisette at midnight in July, ambling side by side without a care in the world, when in fact they were tense and nervous as never before. A few people were still walking back and forth, but the streets were starting to empty.

"Where d'you think he might be coming from at this hour?" Ilyas asked.

"Dinner with friends, maybe."

"I don't think he'd have many friends."

"He had quite a few in Gueugnon."

After about ten minutes, Ilyas let go of Nathalie's hand and darted toward him. He grabbed his arm.

"Sorry, monsieur, before, you had a little dog. Where is it, your dog?"

Charpie turned toward Ilyas, looked at him the way one looks at an individual, an Arab what's more, who fires questions you at midnight. Ilyas could feel his legs giving way, but he held strong, saying:

"Never forget one thing: in your world, I must look like a hoodlum, but in mine, you're a criminal."

The man turned white. And, unexpectedly, he freed himself from Ilyas's hold by punching him on the shoulder, an unbelievably violent blow, before running off as fast as he could. The impact knocked Ilyas backward.

Nathalie started screaming in the direction of the runaway:

"You dickhead! Dickhead!"

Passersby called out to them:

"Are you okay? What on earth happened?"

Someone asked Nathalie if the man had stolen something from them. She replied, sobbing:

"Lives, monsieur, that man stole lives."

"Would you like me to call the police, mademoiselle?"

"No, it's fine, thank you, monsieur."

He and Nathalie helped Ilyas get up; he was still in shock, but nothing was broken.

"Just a bit sore all over," he said.

"D'you want us to try to catch up with him?" Nathalie asked.

"No. You saw, he must be at least seventy-five, but did you see how strong he is? Can you imagine twenty-five years ago? What chance did we have?"

And he dissolved into tears in Nathalie's arms. They remained like that for several minutes, before returning to their car and driving back to Nice.

Nathalie suggested to Ilyas that they return the following day to find him. He said no.

"What for? I told him what I wanted to tell him. Now, if I see him, I kill him. And then what? I end my days in jail because of a bastard who destroyed me? He'll burn in hell, and he knows it. D'you think he recognized me?"

"Yes. In any case, he knew what you were talking about. His reaction, that was a confession."

"Nat, how many do you think there were?"

"How many what?"

"Victims."

"And after that?"

"After that we continued our vacation in Nice, never setting foot in Cannes again. I went back there on my own, after Charpie's death."

"You never wanted to take the law into your own hands, Ilyas?"

I say that a bit too loudly. The diners at the table nearby, a couple, well, I think they're a couple, both turn in my direction at the same time. Ilyas smiles as he answers me. Just then, I remember what Louis said to me about my aunt's two smiles. It's exactly the same with Ilyas.

"Wanting to kill someone, that's one thing. Killing, that's quite another. I'm not a murderer, Agnès . . . Right, dear friends, I'm off to bed, I'm beat. I start at four tomorrow morning. What will you both do this afternoon?"

"I'm going straight to the paper. I have three articles due."

"And I'm going home to listen to the rest of a recording. About a birthday dinner between Aimé Chauvel and Colette, above the Café Thillet."

"A birthday dinner!" Nathalie exclaims.

This time, she's the one who's spoken too loudly and seems to have disturbed our neighbors.

"Yes. In 1976."

"D'you think they had a love affair, your aunt and him? Whose birthday was it?" Nathalie asks.

"Aimé's. His eighteenth. I don't yet know whether he opened a can of ravioli, or cassoulet, or couscous, or whether they had a love affair . . . I can't wait to find out."

"If I were you," Ilyas says, "I'd make a movie out of these recordings. Out of this whole story."

"Maybe I'll write a novel."

"A novel? Is that similar to making a movie?" he wonders out loud.

Already standing, he kisses me. I answer him because I want to keep him here:

"Making a movie means writing for characters, real or fictional, with light, images, words, and feelings . . . "

"So true," Nathalie jumps in. "And when a novel's extraordinary, it has light, images, words, and feelings. And the characters become real because we grow attached to them."

"I'm happy I found the two of you again. I love you both."

"We love you, too," they respond in unison.

"By the way, I might be buying the Fredins house."

"Why?"

"To come back often."

50

I rewound cassette No. 20 back by a few minutes. The one about Aimé's birthday, purely for the pleasure.

COLETTE

[. . .] The sun was still searing the walls. I suggested that we open all the windows, to create some drafts; it would still be warm for one or two hours, but then, naturally, the air would get cooler. As I was saying this, I thought to myself that, in any case, in two hours' time, I'd be back home and that I couldn't remain alone with this young man. There was something abnormal about it. Why hadn't he invited friends his own age? He didn't give me the chance to ask, picking up the wrapped presents I'd placed on the table.

"Are these for me?"

"Yes."

"That's so kind."

Today I'm sixty-one and am supposed to be dead. So I'm really not interested in what people think of me, in what's good or bad. As Aimé opened his presents, he expressed himself like a kid:

"Wow, ABBA, they're fab . . . Hey, Boney M., brill to dance to. Oh, this thing's pretty, what is it? A vase with a lid?"

I had never been so happy. Because of his presence. It was as if everything smelled good, was pleasing, by his side. His face, his eyes, his hair, his hands, his white tee shirt, his massive legs, his dark skin.

Silence.

COLETTE

Happiness exists in different places and at different levels in a life. My life is simple. I've spent it here, repairing shoes and duplicating keys.

Unlike Jean and you, I haven't moved away. When your father left to pursue his studies in Lyon at David Levitan's place, I was happy. When I heard his first recording of Chopin on a vinyl record, I was happy. When I repaired my first pair of shoes unaided and realized that I could make a living with my hands, I was happy. When I took you and Ana into my arms for the first time, I was happy. When I saw your first movie, I was happy. When I saw the sea, I was happy. But never was I as happy as on that July 19, 1976. He may not have had a cloth to dry the dishes, but he did own a brand-new stereo system. Loads of records, LPs, were piled on the floor. I didn't know the artists on the sleeves. I only knew your father's music and the French songs played on the radio. He put the ABBA single on the turntable, and I discovered "Dancing Queen." It was fab.

I told Aimé that my brother, Jean Septembre, was a great musician. He said:

"I know."

"Really?"

"I know his story. Your story."

"Who told you about it?"

"I asked around."

I didn't have a chance to respond before he took my hand, stood close to me, placed his other hand on my hip, and we danced. That closeness. I immediately thought of Blaise. The only boy I'd danced with in my life. "So that we've practiced, just in case," Blaise would say.

I felt like crying, but I also felt joy. Sadness tried to get the upper hand but didn't succeed, because that moment resembled no other moment I'd lived through. The light, the heat, his presence, the music, the champagne. What's beautiful is, and will always be, what's strongest.

Silence.

COLETTE

I'd never had fun, apart from at football matches, but never with someone. I never went to dances. I was too shy. I was never courted. I didn't have any friends. Blanche was far away when I was sixteen, then twenty, then forty, fifty. There was actually a young man, a customer around my age. Mokhtar would say that he found any excuse to come to the shop. That he was getting the whole neighborhood's shoes repaired just to hand me another pair in the hope of receiving a smile. (She laughs.) *"Look, m'dear, he never brings the same size, he's raiding the cupboards of his entire family!" I didn't fancy him. Mokhtar would encourage me to go out, see people, but I preferred to stay on my own. After Blaise and Jean had left, it's true that I was very much alone.*

She drinks a few sips of water then continues with her story.

COLETTE

The rhythm of "Dancing Queen" is slow, but we were bathed in sweat. We finished the contents of our mustard glasses, the champagne tickling my nose. I started to cough, and Aimé to laugh. He put the ABBA record on again, and at the end of the second dance, I began to feel kind of uneasy. I suddenly had doubts. What if he'd made a bet with someone? And if so, what kind of bet? To get the old maid into bed? To kiss the shoe-mender for a laugh? Why was I alone at his place? Why was he making me dance? Drink champagne? But by the third dance, my uneasiness had disappeared. There was such simplicity and gentleness about Aimé. He was pure. He had the soul of a child and the physique of an adult. He looked older than his age. And for the first time in my life, I decided to make the most of something. That had never happened to me. To take, to help myself. I don't know how many times he replayed that song. Maybe twenty. Maybe more. By the end, we knew it by heart, without understanding a word of it. Aimé said: "All I get is 'dancing queen.'" We babbled on about this and that. He'd just passed his baccalauréat and started at the Forges factory. He worked in the morning and trained in the afternoon. That's what it was like then; the players were semi-professional. Viewed scathingly by those who were jealous. They were often called show-offs and good-for-nothings. Rich and cushy. "There are those who work, and there are footballers."

He ended up going to the kitchen to heat up the can of ravioli in an orange saucepan. The same orange as my key machine. Aimé took pleasure wherever it was to be found, no matter what he was doing. He was light-hearted. He carried on singing while putting out two mismatched plates and cutlery. I went into his bedroom. I opened several drawers and finally found what I was looking for, a tee shirt. I took off my clinging dress and pulled on the tee, which reached my knees. I went into his tiny bathroom, as tiny as mine in Rue Pasteur . . . Do you remember, Agnès, how you'd moan about my hip bath? You hated that house. Anyhow. I'm losing my thread. When I saw my reflection in the mirror, it was a shock. I'd never worn an item of men's clothing before, let alone a tee shirt. My clothes exasperated you, too. You thought I dressed like an old woman. Once—you must have been about twelve—I heard you tell Ilyas, "My aunt dresses like she lives in the last century! Like she was born a hundred and fifty years ago. Why'd anyone do everything to look ugly? Gets on my nerves." It isn't that I didn't want to be looked at, Agnès; I couldn't be. As I've already told you, I wanted to melt into the background. It was cowardly, convenient. And then, despite my clothes, my appearance, my hairstyle that never was one—well, Aimé did see me.

She leaves a long silence. What is she thinking about? Why is she telling me all this? What an unexpected confession. What trust she places in me. Guilt grips me. Thank goodness I made up for it over the years. Thank goodness that, as I grew up, got older, I considered her differently. Looked at her differently.

COLETTE
That evening, at Aimé's, seeing myself in the mirror, I don't know whether it was the champagne, the music, Aimé's heartbeat against my ear, but I'd gotten younger. I looked even younger than the day I'd set off to do my apprenticeship with Mokhtar. I splashed my face and nape with water. At the time, I still had shoulder-length hair. I had gathered it up with a barrette to go to Aimé's. I let it down.

She stops talking. Nothing but silence now. How frustrating. She let her hair down, and after that? I can hear her in her kitchen, the sound of plates. Then, after about twenty minutes, she's talking to an animal. Probably a cat visiting her garden. She finally returns to the vicinity of the recorder—does she realize that she hasn't switched the recording off?

Colette

Aimé lives in Gueugnon. I'd love for you to meet him, Agnès. I always hoped the two of you would meet.

End of the recording. I leave the tape still turning. Virgin tape. And I cry like a child whose parents have just left her with the teacher on the first day of school.

51

1961

"All that money, all that money . . . " Georgette ruminates, hand against cheek.

She doesn't so much wipe away her tears as slap them down. Why is she thinking about that now, at the hospital? She was among the crowd watching the raffle draw last July. Danièle was whining. She'd just spotted a candy stand.

"Want some! Want some!" she bawled, tugging on Georgette's skirt.

"Later, I said. You'll get some later."

Should've seen Gueugnon. Like a cattle market on Place des Forges! And a platform for Jean and the mayor, like for a President of the Republic! A crowd, what a crowd . . . And beside them the priest, who was in on it . . . who acted like a cockerel . . . who'd set the whole thing up . . . a house to be won . . . that was all they needed. The Septembre family being noticed, spoken about, gossiped about . . . this was the last straw. Her name would be in big letters in the paper, and for ages. Her name turned into a massive lottery to send the kid to Lyon! A collection, like they were beggars! They who did no harm to no one, what had they done to deserve this?

Georgette was sure, it was the marchioness pulling the strings of this whole mess, this disaster. Couldn't have happened otherwise. Revenge on her for telling the marquess about the trip to Lyon. The priest was under Eugénie de Sénéchal's heel. To the extent that the family even had its own pew in the church.

When she heard Jean saying into the mic, "Thank you to everyone for helping me. I will never forget what you have done for me; thanks to you, I will achieve my dream," Georgette went slightly mad. She saw everyone turning around to look at her, just her. The kid's mother. Not the mayor, not the director, not the priest, not Jean. The crowd was staring only at her. Once again, the shame. She let out a cry that no one heard because of the clapping. No one heard that guttural cry except Danièle, who, fearing her mother, jerked away from her, and fell on her ass.

What's stayed with her from that event, it isn't the name of the winner of the house, or Colette looking at her with disgust, or even Jean kissing the marchioness like she was his mom . . . What's stayed with her is a figure: 67 million. It's the director who'd proudly announced it: the raffle raised 67 million. Her son had become rich as if by magic. From one day to the next. How was that possible?

She's still ruminating when Colette turns up at the emergency department to see her sister. It was Blaise who called her at the shoe-repair shop to let her know: "Danièle is at the hospital. My mother says it's serious."

"What's wrong with her?" Colette asks Georgette. "What are the doctors saying?"

"Meningitis, so they think. But not for sure. It's puzzling, so they say. The fever, it went up and up . . . And the littl'un, she couldn't take it," she replies, slapping down a new tear on her cheek.

Colette observes Danièle, who is sound asleep. Her breathing seems rapid. Her closed eyelids keep flickering.

"If she dies, I'm going, too. I'm ashamed as it is . . . All that money for Jean. The Good Lord don't love me. The Good Lord hates me. Going to take her from me, he is."

Colette is shocked. The mother is mixing everything up. Jean, Danièle, the raffle, the illness. Colette can't stand her anymore, ever since she denounced the marchioness.

"What on earth are you talking about?" she retorts, louder than she'd meant to. "That money isn't for Jean; it's to pay for his board and lodging, and his studies. That money doesn't belong to him!"

"You'll bury us both in Curdin, on the Route des Bois."

"Danièle isn't going to die . . . Don't say things like that right beside her. She can hear us . . . "

"I sense she's going to die. Anyhow, she's three. What d'you think she can hear?"

"Stop it!"

"You're speaking bad to me. You've always spoken bad to me."

Colette doesn't respond. She approaches Danièle to kiss her forehead. How many times has she kissed her since she was born? Once? Twice? They'd always remained at a distance. She must have bottle-fed Jean a thousand times, but never held Danièle in her arms. She's burning hot. Colette breaks down the moment she lightly touches her sister's hair. She cries her eyes out, holding the little hand. She looks at the sleeping child, seriously ill, and realizes that she'd had more empathy when a lamb was about to have its throat cut.

She feels nothing, feels like she's light years away from this little girl. But all the same, it's a child. Innocent and fragile. Colette likes nothing about her. Is that because she's jealous of the love the mother shows her?

She tells herself that she's just like her mother: unfeeling toward some people. She's devastated. Her tears fall even faster. The mother continues to slap her own down in silence. Suddenly, Danièle's little hand moves inside Colette's. She's just waking up. She recognizes her sister, and Colette feels like she's a monster.

"You were sick, but it's over now, you're going to get better."

The mother rushes over to the little girl, who whimpers when she sees her. Already, Georgette has forgotten the presence of her eldest daughter and turns her back on her. Nurses come by, and a doctor declares that Danièle's life doesn't seem to be in danger anymore, but they'll keep her there for a few days, for observation. Colette leaves without saying goodbye to anyone.

Two hours later, she shares a frugal supper with Mokhtar, in his kitchen. It's with her apprenticeship master that she finds the warmth of home.

After the meal, Colette tells him what happened at the hospital, and says she'll go to the château the following Sunday to visit her sister, once she's back home, to try to build a bond. And that she'd take the chance to pay her respects to the marchioness, who's done so much for Jean.

*

Meanwhile, in Lyon, Jean is feeling lonely. Desperately lonely. He daren't admit it to anyone. He isn't very happy at the Levitans', despite all that people have done for him. And then there are the eyes of the priest and Colette that weigh down on him, follow him. Eyes full of confidence, a confidence that he's losing day by day. It's unthinkable that he should complain or disappoint them. But how austere his daily existence is. Sad and solitary. He likes nothing about the apartment he shares with the couple. Neither its smell, nor its yellowing tones. He likes even less the stuffed carp served on the Sabbath. David and Élia Levitan speak Yiddish between themselves, a language derived from German. But it's very rare for them to express themselves out loud. Élia is almost silent. She seems so much older than her husband, one might think that it's a mother and son living under the same roof. No children to make a racket. A few family photos on the walls, but Jean daren't ask any questions. Here, they don't say good morning, good evening, good night, how are you? Looks are exchanged in silence. Like in some place of worship or a library, while barely breathing.

David Levitan only expresses himself to teach him music. And Jean is hating his apprenticeship. He feels as if he's gradually losing his piano while working on it with this new, supposedly extraordinary teacher. And barely is the piano lid closed before a veil of silence settles on every room. Reaching even under the icy sheets of his bedroom. For two months now, cold weather has descended on the city of Lyon, and the apartment feels more like Siberia.

Jean walks to school. David Levitan scrutinizes his grades like a doctor would the ECG of a dying patient. He'd better not get less than 15 out of 20; the conservatoire only takes on good pupils.

When he comes back at the end of the day, Jean practices with his teacher. Only fingering technique. For hours and hours. Fingering develops according to the size of the hands, and more specifically, the span, the distance between the fingers. Levitan makes him work on each of his fingers, favoring exercises that help Jean to memorize the keyboard, with shifts from five notes to five notes, always played by the same hand.

"Later," he hectors Jean, "you will work on the distance between the thumb and the index finger. We have plenty of time! Only daily exercises will enable you to relax your hands and acquire the suppleness of the wrists necessary for you to play . . . the agility, independence, and strength of each of your fingers. And once you are finally comfortable, we will work on your two weakest fingers. Only them. With practice and the passing years, you will memorize the intervals and distances instinctively. You will use only the correct positions, and will almost never look at the directions on the score."

Why stop looking at the score, Jean wonders. What's the point of that? Levitan makes him work as if he were a competitor, not a performer. Hence his despair. He doesn't understand what he's doing there, and has doubts. In Gueugnon, they listened to him, they admired him. Now, he's living in a refrigerator of feelings, an antechamber of life, having fought to get there. He wants to feel the thrill again, so, when he can't bear to work on his wretched fingering anymore, he finally voices this:

"Professor, I want to feel the thrill."

To which Levitan replies, screwing up his eyes—because he never smiles—that before feeling the thrill, you have to learn to detach yourself. To levitate. And the thrill will then be all the more intense. This makes no sense to the young pianist.

The three of them dine at around 9 o'clock. The only sound in the room is the clinking of the cutlery. Jean is allowed a drop of red wine, which he dislikes, but it helps him to sleep. Then Élia disappears to her room, David settles into an armchair to read, and Jean takes refuge in his own room. Before, to fall asleep, he loved to go through scores, but according to his teacher, doing that before sitting at the piano is like learning to write before knowing how to speak . . . "Read novels instead; that will do far more for your sensitivity as a concert pianist." And Levitan locked all his scores in a drawer. "I'll return them to you later. You can help yourself from the bookcase in the sitting room. There's plenty of choice. But take good care of the books."

Jean wishes he could confide in someone. He's suffocating with boredom and loneliness. All that effort, that relentless struggle, just to end up here. At 3, Rue Joseph-de-Maistre, where he'll have to remain for seven years, if he succeeds in getting into the conservatoire in four years' time.

This seems impossible to him. He sees those years as a mountain that can't be climbed. What to do? Run away? Disappear? Resign himself? Who can he turn to, confide in?

His mother? Unthinkable. His sister? Unimaginable. Blaise, of course. Jean writes to tell him of his distress, begging him not to tell anyone. It's a secret. His childhood friend replies that next Sunday, he'll come and visit him. He's known the Levitans forever; David and Élia are close friends of the marchioness.

How is that possible? How can this austere couple be close to Éugénie de Sénéchal, who's so sunny, so sweet? But then, she did marry the most rigid, most unpleasant person in the world. How strange life is and people are.

52

Le Journal de Saône-et-Loire*, October 25, 2010*

"Mystery in Gueugnon: who is buried in the cemetery? The funeral of Colette Septembre took place in Gueugnon on August 13, 2007, and was attended by many friends and members of the Football Club, of which she was an ardent supporter.

"The sister of the celebrated pianist Jean Septembre, and the aunt of Agnès Dugain, the no less celebrated film director, Colette Septembre was herself very well known in the foundry town for having run the shoe-repair shop on Rue Pasteur from 1960 to 2007.

"No one has forgotten the kindness, discretion, and professionalism of this charming cobbler. And yet this apparently straightforward woman took a heavy secret with her. But did she take it in 2007, or two days ago? Because the lifeless body of a woman, found by the gendarmerie on Tuesday morning in the lower part of town, could be that of . . . Colette Septembre. She is said to have died in her sleep during the night of October 21-22. The gendarmerie is working to identify the body. If it is established that it is indeed Madame Septembre, an exhumation will then be requested to identify the remains that have been buried in the cemetery, under her name, for the past three years.

"But in that case, why would Colette Septembre have lived in anonymity since 2007, without ever giving a sign of life to her loved ones?

"We will keep you informed as the investigation progresses."

Nathalie Grandjean

*

October 31, 2010

He had read and reread the article. Ten times. Maybe more. Checked the date it had appeared. And studied the photo down below, which dated from 2003. The men posing side by side in their football kit. And then this woman at the end of the row, beside them. In black trousers and a black sweater. Hair tied back. The complete opposite of *her*. Always in colorful garb, a feisty look in her eyes, hair tumbling down. As far as he could recall, she didn't tie it back. And yet, that face seemed to be hers. But could it be her, so strangely rigged out? Her, a shoe-mender? No. A supporter? Impossible. And anyhow, she'd not spent her whole life in that hole. Dead, his daughter? Impossible. He'd have sensed it. Missing, yes. Hiding, probably. Dead, no.

It was while wrapping bottles of Burgundy in newspaper that he'd come across the article. Never read the papers, he didn't, except *Paris-Turf*. He always feared coming across his own mug. He'd kicked up a stink about having to do something so dumb. What the hell was the point of wrapping up bottles?

"To protect them!" Mathilde had snapped back.

"And how'll some newspaper protect a bottle?"

Damned waste of time. She was starting to get his goat, that woman.

"You use three sheets per bottle, and then you put them in the cellar."

He'd not gone on about it, just got on with it. After all, she was making a stew that smelled good, and he'd never eaten as well as since knowing her. He who'd nearly died of hunger. One, two, three sheets. Thirty-odd bottles. One, two, three. At the nineteenth bottle, one sheet, page 12. Top left. It was the word "Gueugnon" that had first jumped out at him. Had stopped him in his tracks. He knew the place. He'd been there a long time ago. He'd been to so many places in his life, but that name, he remembered it. Gueugnon sounded like "*guenon,*" a female monkey or a hag. That had made him laugh. "Cemetery. Mystery. Anonymity." A coincidence? He had to think about it. Gueugnon, Gueugnon . . . No particular image came back to him. Was the kid already born when he'd gone there? And that photo of the "dead woman" under the article. That face haunted him, kept going around in his head.

All his life, he'd operated on intuition. And right then, he'd sensed that he must get himself over there. Ask some questions to figure it out. Nothing was stopping him from doing so. He'd been called Viktor Socha since 2004. And would be called that until the day he died. He'd changed physically, aged, the young Soudkovski didn't exist anymore. The last snaps of him taken by the cops, or the hacks at the trial, went back ten years.

He'd finished wrapping the bottles, putting the article aside. He'd spent long minutes scrutinizing that picture of the dead woman beside the footballers. He'd found other photos and other articles on the internet. Archives of the *Journal de Saône-et-Loire* in which her brother, the pianist, was often mentioned. The spitting image of her. But it wasn't *her*. Of that he was sure. Thinking about it again, not only was Blanche already born when he went to that hole, but he'd also returned to it. Could she have made friends with someone? And what about him? Had he bedded and knocked up some woman?

Sparse memories came back to him; he'd slept with women who'd offered themselves, others he'd forced. But the towns were jumbled up in his old, sick mind. All the main squares his big top went up on looked alike. He needed to understand. So he'd decided. He switched off the computer and asked Mathilde to lend him her car. He had to go somewhere, just there and back. It was urgent. A day, two at most.

She was laying the table and, turning to him, not missing a beat, had replied:

"Fine, but I'm coming with you."

"Out of the question. It's a personal matter. None of your business."

He'd met Mathilde when he'd arrived in Valence. At first, he'd paid no attention to this neighbor. Then he'd been wary of her. He couldn't fathom how he could've taken her fancy. What did she want from him? Too intrusive, too plump, too blond for his liking. A bad dye-job on a chatterbox. But in the end, she'd looked after him so well, he'd given in to her advances. Every day a quiche, a slice of cake, some boeuf bourguignon, or a gratin dauphinois on a plate, left on his window ledge. After the umpteenth invitation declined or postponed, he'd finally crossed the road to have an aperitif at her place, and had lingered there. He hadn't needed to make any effort to seduce her, never had with anyone; he seemed to suit her just as he was. A quiet old dog with skin ravaged by work and the clink. But despite his age, he was fit. His toned, muscular body worked like a well-oiled and -maintained old machine. It was his head that was on the blink. Admittedly, he'd spent years searching for his wife and his daughter. Enough to drive you mad. *Where were those two bitches? Blanche, just like her mother, had ended up bugging off . . . A wicked pair. Mother and daughter, vanished.*

Mathilde owned a computer. He'd learned how to use one in prison. She'd logged him on as "Viktor," and he'd spent a good deal of time surfing. The net was handy for finding someone, doing research. That contraption could poke around in every corner of France and Navarre. He'd flagged two names in his alerts: Marie Madeleine Roman and Blanche Soudkovski. But nothing had turned up. As if the two women had never existed. Or then they weren't the right women. He'd found numerous other Marie Romans, as well as some articles on his trial in Annecy. Nothing more.

He knew he'd put his ex-wife in a wheelchair, and that she was living under a false name. It had been drummed into him enough in court. The officially appointed lawyer who'd defended him in Annecy, before he was locked up, had warned him: "Madame Roman won't be present at the trial and lives under an assumed name." And advised him, to his great irritation: "Don't even think of looking for her; that would be the very worst idea." Of course, as soon as he'd left prison, he'd done exactly that. But nothing. Not a trace of her. He'd contacted hospitals, hospices, sanatoriums, nursing homes of all kinds, had pretended to be a close relative, sometimes even a doctor, had never been disheartened. He'd combed Savoie, Haute-Savoie, and the neighboring *départements*. He was sure that "whore" hadn't quit her native region.

Why, oh why, hadn't he bumped her off? At least then he'd have done time for something. As for Blanche, she'd betrayed him, denounced him. His revenge would be dire. On both of them. When he thought about it, and he never stopped thinking about it, he could feel the hatred taking him over, his muscles tensing, his skin burning, as he imagined how he'd make them suffer. Conjured up the most macabre scenarios. And after that, he'd do himself in, too. He was old; all he lived for now was to find them and die with them.

For four years now, he'd been bedding Mathilde Pinson. Each living in their own homes, though. Never at his place, always at hers, three nights a week, he'd cross the road. They had their own little routine; he'd tinker around, surf the net, do bodybuilding and limbering-up exercises in the garage, bet on the races, read his *Turf*. She, retired from the civil service, would watch her serials, do the cooking and the crosswords in the magazines he'd buy her. He'd flick through them first, in case there was mention of any of his "business" in those rags. He was totally paranoid, like all fugitives. Even when Mathilde went to the doctor's, he'd accompany her to be sure she wouldn't come across some compromising article in the waiting room. He'd never been mentioned on the TV. He'd laid into his victims, but since they hadn't died, he didn't interest the media. After that business in Marseille, when he'd made a mess of the last "slut," he'd had a narrow escape. And then, salvation . . . In 2004, he'd met up with that old bastard Socha again and had lain low at his place. A "traveling man," like him. He'd lived with him for a few weeks, the time it took to figure out where his papers were kept and the codes for his bank account, and then got rid of him. Child's play. It was the first time he'd killed one of his kind in cold blood. Before, it had been during brawls, and he couldn't remember a thing. Now he had no choice; it was too good an opportunity. Carbon monoxide poisoning. He'd added a hefty dose of sleeping meds to his soup, dragged him into the garage, started the car, sealed all outlets. *Bye, old brother, see you in Hell.*

He had promptly moved away. Burned the car and license plates. No one had been surprised at Socha's departure; he was a bastard the neighbors couldn't stand. The kind who poisoned cats and trapped foxes. Soudkovski had made a fresh start by changing his identity. How easy it had been to slip into another man's clothes! A blessing, that good old Viktor. Luckiest he'd ever been. He even received his war-veteran's pension, when he'd never set foot in Algeria! It was Mathilde who filled in his forms, tax returns, and all that baloney. She'd have done anything for her dear Viktor.

Seemingly, he was enjoying some peaceful days. But there was his daughter. And he'd never sleep easy until he'd gotten hold of her. He knew that there'd be one day unlike all the rest. He'd always known it. Dead or alive, he'd flush her out. And this might be his chance.

But Mathilde, hands on hips, was eyeing him strangely and repeating, for the third time, that if he wanted her car, she'd be going with him. He'd never laid a hand on her. Not even a slap. Clearly, there was a first time for everything. But it was others who behaved badly, disappointed, betrayed. Not him.

"You want me to give you a good hiding? Is that what you're after?"

"If you touch me, I'll call the cops and tell them everything."

"Tell them what?" he'd asked, clenching his jaws and fists.

"That you never did Algeria. And that you're a compulsive liar . . . Do you know what a search history is?"

". . ."

"I can just go onto the computer after you and see where you've been ferreting about. Your ass ain't clean, my poor Viktor. Well, so-called Viktor . . . If you go, I'll never see you again. And that I couldn't bear . . . So I'm coming with you, and that's that."

Mathilde had taken off her apron and added:

"Sit and eat. A stew doesn't wait . . . It's simmered enough."

Normally, he'd have swiftly bled her to death. Without a thought. A cut below the throat. Like with lambs, pigs, young rabbits. He'd have drained her without the slightest scruple. Never had time for scruples. Had to save his skin. Since birth, he was like a pack dog, the one that bites hardest to get by. But he had sat down; he was hungry. And mainly, there was one question obsessing him. And he'd get an answer before leaving.

"Where d'you get those newspapers for wrapping the bottles? They're not the ones I usually buy."

Mathilde had smiled. Flashed her yellow teeth, which she brushed daily, in vain, with Émail Diamant whitening toothpaste. Her double chin was quivering, her podgy fingers had turned pink. *A little pig in a flowery dress.*

"Old mother Pons brought them over for me from Cluny, yesterday. Along with some cheese puffs and boxes to store my bottles in."

"Old mother Pons?"

"You know, the bric-a-brac dealer!"

Of course. The store at the corner with the jumble of crap. Junk displayed in a window and sold for a fortune because the items were more than fifty years old. People over forty were only good for the scrapheap, but somehow, those items went up in value the older they got.

While gobbling up his stew, he was thinking that he could put the body somewhere cold for forty-eight hours. While he drove there and back. The cellar would do nicely. Or the freezer. After that, he'd see. He'd never felt pity. For anyone.

He'd lost his mother at the age of four. She'd been snatched away from him. All he had left was the memory of her milky smell, her warmth, her gentleness. Her face and her smile leaning over him. And suddenly, her death, like a curse. A great black hole, people around him weeping. For him, it was a never-ending fall, something frozen in his veins. The feeling of being permanently in pain. The long, muffled sleep of his infancy. A raving mad father. Life under the big top, animal training and the whip since he'd first opened his eyes to the world. And fucking shit it was, that world. After the death of his mother, he'd never known the gentleness of a caress. He couldn't have tolerated anyone lightly stroking his skin. Even Mathilde wasn't allowed to touch him. He'd tumble her or get sucked off, then fall into a light sleep. Never a deep one. Deep sleep was for the rich, not for him. For him, human flesh was decay and fear. Like that of animals and the deformed, which he rated equally, good for nothing but exploiting or devouring.

Nothing and no one would stop him from finding his daughter. Maybe it was a red herring, this business of a cemetery and some woman dying twice, a woman who looked like Blanche, but it had to be checked. Straight after this meal.

53

November 7, 2010

He was in Gueugnon on November 1. We're even sure that he came inside here."

"Here?"

I catch Paul's arm.

"This house."

I hold onto him to keep from falling. I'm not thinking anymore; I'm scared. Paul says nothing. He seems concerned. He's just turned up at Rue des Fredins.

"Paul, are you joking with me?"

"Frankly, chief, do I look like I'm joking? Why do you think I'm here? For your lovely eyes?"

"Here, in this house?"

"Yes. And we're going to look for fingerprints."

"What day would he have come?"

"November 1."

"When Ilyas and I went off to Flumet."

"He'd have gone to the cemetery in the morning. Rampin had two officers posted at the entrance to watch over Colette Septembre's grave, and one of them remembers catching sight of an old man at the wheel of a green Renault Twingo, with 26 on its license plate, doing a hasty U-turn as if the devil were after him. He thought it must be because his vehicle inspection wasn't up to date. Except the Twingo probably belonged to Soudkovski's last victim, Mathilde Pinson."

"He's searching for Blanche."

Paul agrees with a grimace.

"There's something else," he adds, as if walking on eggshells.

"What?"

"He used the landline phone here to call his own cellphone. To log the number. He'd been using a prepaid phone for ages, and we were able to trace it thanks to that call. We've just found out that he'd top up his minutes at the *tabac* on his street, in Valence."

"Jeez, this is turning into a nightmare! Where is he, Paul? Where is Soudkovski?!"

"No idea. After coming to your place, well, your aunt's, we're sure he went back to Valence. After that, we lose track of him. He's used to melting into the crowd. He could be very far away, or just nearby. And today he's an old man. No one's wary of an old man. No one looks at old people . . . You're going to have to concentrate. We'll search each room to be sure he didn't take anything."

". . ."

"I'll be staying here until the exhumation," Paul adds.

"The exhumation?"

"I've just requested it from the state prosecutor. It's urgent."

"Blanche?"

"Yes. The body must be protected. I think he'd be capable of desecrating her grave."

Once again, that heat surging up my body. My strength suddenly deserts me. My sight blurs, knives pierce my skull, I try to speak, but nothing comes out of my mouth; a black veil descends, a hideous panic that crushes my ribcage, and then nothing.

I must have lost consciousness for a few seconds; I reopen my eyes on a Paul who's more incredulous than panicked.

"Are you okay? Does it happen often, you fainting like that?"

"At the moment, yes."

"What've you got?"

"I don't know. Too many emotions probably," I reply, with what little humor remains to me.

I stand up. Nothing broken, no pain anywhere. I walk a few steps in the small sitting room. I open the suitcase to check the number of cassettes inside it. All there, it seems. Anyhow, I'd taken it with me to Flumet. When I look up, I see Paul staring at me in a strange way. I manage to guess what he's thinking.

"You think I'm pregnant?"

He instantly blushes, embarrassed.

"Encephalogram of my love life: beyond flatlining. And for eons."

We leave it at that. And do the tour of the house. Nothing seems to have disappeared. In the sitting room I live in, my suitcase of clothes hasn't been rummaged through; I'd know if it had. In the bathroom and kitchen, everything seems to be in its place. He'd hardly have stolen two old mustard glasses or four painkillers. I check in Colette's room that her few belongings are still in the cupboard. In the sewing-machine room, the FCG collection is still there, too. As are the funeral plaques.

"The box of photos?"

I start to panic and search everywhere for it. And yet I'm sure I put it away carefully with the collection.

"What box of photos, Agnès?"

"A pink box . . . It's a shoebox covered in pink paper. Colette kept pictures of me in it. Since I was a baby."

The thought of that individual stealing my photos paralyzes me.

"If he came into the house, it's because he was looking for Blanche . . . Why would he have taken your photos?"

Paul takes my hand, looking vexed.

"He's the obsessed type . . . Those that nothing can stop. There's no logic in his head."

"But why did he steal my photos? And also, how did he find out Colette's last address?"

"He must have followed you."

Part II

1

HANNAH RUBEN

A screenplay by Agnès Dugain Septembre

Scene 1

Lyon, 1942. Large, bourgeois apartment. Parquet floor, molded ceiling. Vast dining-cum-sitting room, walls flooded with July light from big windows. German officers moving a black grand piano on a dolly. They are shouting loudly, sweating, seem at once excited, nervous, in a hurry.

Some take down paintings, others carry off crockery, two canteens of silver cutlery, a hanukkiah (nine-branched candelabrum used by Jews during celebration of Hanukkah), two Gallé lamps, a mirror.

Note: shoot close-ups of the family photos. Parents, two children, a baby.

Scene 2

Bedroom. Close-up on man's fingers rummaging in drawers as, laughing too loudly, he pulls out lingerie, lipsticks, and Caron powder compacts. This shot must evoke a rape. Other SS men are ransacking the hidden compartment of a wardrobe. They steal all the jewelry (details to be discussed with props person) and silverware, including a baby cup with the name Hannah engraved on it.

Scene 3

Same apartment building. Full shot of exterior. Then to the

floor below the one in the previous scene, where the Gravoin family live.

At the same time, baby Hannah, two months old, the only one to have escaped the arrest of which her parents and older brother and sister have just fallen victim on the floor above, is in the arms of an old lady who is singing a popular song ("Insensiblement") to her in a hushed voice:

Imperceptibly, you slipped into my life,
Imperceptibly, you settled in my heart,
I found better than a friend in you,
better than a sister,
We form a harmony,
The major chord.

Beside her, Éléonore Gravoin, a woman of around thirty, fine features, anxious, listens to the steps of the officers above her head; she removes a chain bracelet, on which we can read the name "Hannah," from the sleeping baby's wrist, and replaces it with one on which we can read the name "Marthe."

Cross-fade.

1952

Ten years later, the little girl wears two bracelets on her wrist, on which we can read "Hannah" and "Marthe." Éléonore, the woman who was praying in the preceding scene, is now forty, and the old lady who was singing lies dead, lit by candles. Several people are gathered around the bed she lies on. Including young Hannah, holding a violin. She starts to play the tune of the song "Insensiblement" for her deceased grandmother. The little girl is distraught with grief. She plays brilliantly.

Cross-fade.

1962

Hannah is twenty and still wears her two bracelets around her wrist. She's standing in front of a splendid cake. Friends of her age, three girls, two boys, are playing "Happy Birthday" to her on the violin. Éléonore and her adoptive father, Benjamin, are close to her. Éléonore says to her:

"Make a wish, my darling."

Hannah closes her eyes and blows out the candles. Everyone applauds her. She's a pretty young woman with light brown braids, radiant and shy. It's clear she's very moved.

Hannah: "My dear parents, my dear friends, it's twenty years now since the war stole my other parents, my brother, and my sister from me. And when I say 'stole,' I'm understating it. They were torn away from me to be exterminated. I still have a few photos thanks to Mom [she looks deeply into Éléonore's eyes] and sometimes dream of them. They come to see me while I'm sleeping, talk to me, and look at me from where they are, as if wanting to reassure me. I can't help thinking about them today. They didn't have my good fortune. To live, to be loved and protected by my heaven-sent family. Dad, Mom, I've never referred to you as my adoptive parents, but as my 'other parents.' If my biological mother hadn't entrusted me to my other mom the day before the roundup, I wouldn't be blowing out these twenty candles today. I also think warmly of my dear grandmother. [She raises her arm to show her wrist.] I thank Marthe, who saved Hannah from the claws of anti-Semitic insanity. I will keep these two bracelets around my wrist so that I never forget. And now, time to party! I raise my glass to those I love and will always love. To my conservatoire friends, and may life be beautiful!"

Everyone applauds her, shouts in unison: "Happy Birthday!" Her conservatoire friends play a joyful, lively waltz on the violin. Everyone starts dancing.

November 8, 2010

My phone rings; I answer because it's Ilyas.

"What's up, Ilyas?"

"Your voice sounds weird. What are you doing?"

"I'm rereading some notes."

"Ah. What notes?"

"I've started writing a screenplay on my mother's story."

"What fucking great news!"

"They're just notes, nothing definite."

"Shame."

"This whole business, what I'm going through right now, makes me feel like exploring Hannah Ruben's life."

"I didn't know her name."

"She was the sole survivor of a roundup. She was hidden by a Catholic family, who ended up adopting her . . . Her family never returned."

"D'you know what became of them?"

"We have the number of the convoy for Auschwitz. My grandmother, grandfather, aunt, and uncle were exterminated."

"You've never told me that."

"Mom didn't talk about it. So I didn't talk about it."

"You're Jewish, Agnès?"

"It's passed down through the mother. So, yes, I'm Jewish. Dad would attend Mass whenever he came back to Gueugnon, in memory of Father Aubry. The truth is, they were both believers, but nonpracticing. I've never set foot in a synagogue."

"You should make a movie about it."

"Ilyas, I don't want to make movies anymore . . . I've booked a table for 7:00 P.M. I want you all to meet Paul."

"Where's he sleeping?"

"At the Monge, where else would he be sleeping? It's the only hotel."

"Why isn't he sleeping with you?"

"Paul isn't my lover! He's a cop I consulted a few times for technical advice, and . . . "

"Yeah . . . Lina will be there," he interrupts me.

"Lina?"

"Flumet, the girl at the town hall; I'm in love, I want to marry her."

I burst out laughing.

"Don't laugh. I feel sure about this. We're going to get married; like I said, I have no more time to lose."

"Ilyas, you met her last week."

"So what?"

"So, why get married?"

"Because I'm a romantic."

"One can be a romantic and not get married."

"I don't think so."

"Are you serious? So, you're actually a stuffy old conservative."

"Ha, ha, ha. See you later . . . Agnès?"

"Yes?"

"You should make a movie about it."

He hangs up.

*

Paul sat next to Adèle, Hervé next to Lina, who sat close to Ilyas, they're holding hands under the table, and Nathalie and I sat facing the five of them. As I pulled back my chair, I thought of my first movie, *Le Banquet des anciens*. Of the position we choose around a table. Or that the hosts choose for us. I've always hated seating plans. They evoke something unpleasant, something that's scratchy, like a nasty woolen collar. Others decide for you, treat you like children. Who will get the best seat? People are sorted by category, not affinity. Is the guest five-star? Four-star? Or just three-star?

In Corsica, after the *Banquet des anciens* shoot and our wedding, I went with Pierre to a glitzy dinner party, a gathering of TV stars and famous actors on vacation. Pierre and I were separated as soon as we arrived, and I found myself at the children's table, between two little girls and a charming teenaged boy. The hosts hadn't known what to do with me, the young courtesan or fan accompanying that *tremendous actor*, Pierre Dugain. No one had said a word to me. No one knew that we'd just gotten married. I drank lots of champagne to ease my awkwardness. And ended up playing Uno with the children.

A few months later—my film had been released and was an instant hit—I came across the woman who had hosted the dinner and banished me to the end of the table with the little ones. She didn't remember me at all. A blank page. I said nothing, of course. She heaped praise on my work, at great length, and ended her monologue by inviting me to dinner at hers, in Paris, with a few "hand-picked" friends. We were at a film festival, I can't recall which one now. I politely replied that I didn't have my planner on me so I'd call her.

Paul informed us, despite it being confidential, that Blanche's exhumation will take place on November 25. So, ten days after Colette's funeral. I'm swimming in cemeteries right now. Paul says he won't be eating. He still has a lot of work to do, he tells us. He's friendly to everyone, shows interest in Adèle's job, asking her numerous questions about her daily life as a visiting nurse: "What time do you start, how many people a day; you must face some tough situations . . ."

He revealed to us that Soudkovski had probably come to Gueugnon after coming across Nathalie's article, which was widely picked up. He must have been intrigued by the story . . . and mainly by the photo alongside the article. Otherwise, why would he have set foot here again? Nathalie is appalled, feels really bad. He reassures her. She's not to blame. There's no controlling a man's madness. Paul doesn't mention the fact that the madman broke into my place, or that he stole the box of photos, because he doesn't know whether I've told them about it. And I'd been sure not to. I have no excuse. Not locking the door is hopelessly stupid, particularly since the house was Colette's refuge. If she hid there for three years, it's because she felt safe there. And then I turn up and leave the place open to all and sundry. Paul tells us that the cemetery in Gueugnon will be closely watched until the exhumation, because Soudkovski's notoriety has sky-rocketed since the murder of Mathilde Pinson. He's also the prime suspect of the apparent murder of Viktor Socha, whose body was discovered in his garden; the autopsy is underway. The police aren't informing the press at the moment. All that he's told us must remain between us, around this table:

"The murder of Mathilde Pinson has been alluded to, but without further detail. Soudkovski mustn't know that he's wanted behind Socha's identity. And once he's sure that it's his daughter lying in the cemetery, intuition tells me that he'll do himself in."

My friends are flabbergasted. Of all of them, Adèle seems most disturbed. She's turned deathly pale. She finally asks if I'm in any danger. Paul shakes his head, reassures her. The obsession is focused on Marie Roman, who lives under a false identity, and Blanche Soudkovski.

2

Cassette No. 53

Colette

1969. It started with a beauty spot on the neck. When he'd put on his shirt, the collar would rub against it, bothering him. Why do we call them "beauty spots" when they're skin lesions? That I'll never be able to understand. Personally, I hate them. "I've got lots, m'dear. Runs in the family," he'd grunt when I told him to see a doctor.

I kept an eye on that thing on his neck, which I ended up finding ugly, as it turned increasingly red. And then the thing got bigger, while Mokhtar was getting thinner. He was really handsome, Mokhtar. There was a nobility to him. He stood tall, proud of his craft. He had fine values, never spoke ill of anyone, but he wasn't taken in; he would often aim a twinkling glance at me, as if to say . . . amusing things without uttering a word. Especially when a difficult or disdainful customer would toss coins onto the counter after collecting a pair of shoes. He was discreet and approached life with simple elegance. When I think that he took Jean into his home and broke his piggy bank to do so, when he'd been saving for years to "make the trip" home. What generosity! But he was more stubborn than an ass.

"Why on earth would I go to a doctor to show him a spot?"

For months, he dabbed his wretched mole with some kind of embrocation.

"It disinfects, works for everything."

Finally, reluctantly, he did go to the doctor, but far too late. Eventually, it was itching him so much that I left him no choice. For the first time since being at his shop. I made the appointment and then accompanied him, to be sure he went. Even in the waiting room, I felt uneasy. He was pretending to read a magazine, but I sensed his anxiety. He'd never have admitted it. Men, they never get scared.

Labori, Dr. Pieri's predecessor, wasn't at all happy when he saw the size and shape of the melanoma. He'd allowed me to enter his office. I was sitting in front of the desk, they were in the adjacent room. I didn't see the doctor's expression, but I heard his silence. A very long silence. And his voice, far too solemn: "We're going to get that removed immediately, Monsieur Bayram; I'm calling the hospital." When they came to sit down, Mokhtar looked away. He'd understood. I always used to fill in his checks, and he'd sign them. I struggled to fill in that check; my hand was shaking, and the tears I was trying to hold back were stopping me from seeing what I was writing.

At the time, Jean had left for his piano, and I already knew that, once an artist is immersed in their passion, you lose them. I'd had no more news from Blaise; all I had left was Mokhtar, my pillar, my sun, my mentor, my life. I can say it today, my true father.

Three days after this consultation, they operated on him, but it was too late; ganglions in the throat had already been affected. The cancer had spread. They suggested taking the bull by the horns, with drastic treatment to target the metastases, to which he replied: "Do I look like a bull?" He turned everything down. And continued to work every day as if nothing had changed. If I just mentioned his cancer, he'd clam up. At first, he knocked back aspirins to kill his pain; I'd go get them from the drugstore. Then other pills, much stronger ones. He grew weaker, but kept working. This went on for nine months, from the operation to the last day. Every morning, I'd find him at his workbench, we'd have a bite at around noon, he'd have his nap on the ottoman, listen to the radio and, during the news, still curse in his language anytime a politician spoke.

In the evening, I'd make our supper. He'd give me instructions for "when he'd no longer be here." He asked me to note everything down. Which I did in an exercise book. Right until the end, he continued to come to matches with me and to join Father Aubry every morning for his coffee.

And then one morning, he didn't get up. He didn't open the shop. I had spare keys for his place; I'd never used them. A first customer arrived and found the door closed. Believe it or not, it was the son of the shop's owner, who'd just moved in nearby, on Rue Saint-Pierre. A boy my age. He had a white plastic bag in his hand with a pair of black boots sticking out of it. We were both twenty-three. I called no one. I sat on the first step of the stairs up to Mokhtar's house, and I wept. The boy came and sat beside me. He had a friendly face, and seemed so kind, with his big blue eyes. I instantly trusted him.

"What's your name?"

"Louis."

"You're not scared of the dead?"

He looked terrified.

". . ."

"Please come with me, Louis . . . "

He followed me, but at a distance. I struggled to open the door. I was shaking even more than the day I'd filled in that check. Louis stayed behind me. I asked him to wait for me on the landing. I went inside on my own . . . I saw a load of medication on Mokhtar's bedside table. I believe he ended his life, or perhaps increased the dose of his painkillers to stop the suffering, and his good heart, his big heart, gave up on him. My king had passed away.

She doesn't stop the recording, but allows long minutes to go by before saying anything else. She doesn't make a sound. She must have stayed there, close to the recorder, without speaking, without moving.

COLETTE

When I came back out, I took refuge in Louis's arms. On the day I lost Mokhtar, I met Louis Berthéol. I didn't know it yet, but on the day I thought I'd lost everything, I didn't lose everything.

I borrowed some money from the marchioness to send Mokhtar's body home to his family. I wanted him to rest with his brother, close to his loved ones. I paid her back over ten years, to the last centime in 1979. Jean never knew about that. No one ever knew about that. This is the first time I'm telling someone.

What came next, you know. I took over the rental of the house and shop. I moved into Mokhtar's, that place you didn't like . . . The look on your face whenever you'd visit . . .

She stifles a laugh.

COLETTE

. . . and I kept his shoe-repair shop going until 2007. I kept his memory alive. And after me, Louis, who inherited the shop from his parents, continued to rent it to shoe-menders.

Mokhtar's family buried him in Tunis, in the Jellaz cemetery. In 1986, his sister sent me a photograph of the grave, with all the members of the family around it. You'll find it on the last page of my collection—in the book for the 1981-1982 season, and also in the exercise book in which I wrote his instructions for when he'd no longer be here.

Please, Agnès, when I join Jean and Hannah again, have "Colette Septembre Bayram" engraved on our tombstone.

*

List of things to do when Mokhtar will no longer be here:

I'm pretending to write. I'm pretending to write.

3

November 9, 2010

She pretended to write when Mokhtar was dictating his last wishes to her. We'll never know what they were."

"That's because she was dreading his death. Writing them down would have turned a nightmare she refused to confront into reality. That doesn't surprise me of her. Nothing coming from her surprises me."

"And yet she made people think she herself was dead, for three years . . . "

"The day before her 'burial,' she phoned me at home. She knew I was alone. She said: 'Aimé, it's me. I'm not dead. Don't tell anyone I'm not dead, absolutely no one.' I think she repeated 'no one' at least ten times. And she added, 'I love you, you know. I'm taking you with me for eternity,' before hanging up. She was scared. I could hear that she was scared. So I said nothing. After that, I never heard another word from her. Enough to drive me crazy. I thought maybe I'd dreamed that phone call . . . or that it had been a hoax. That what I'd taken to be her scared voice simply wasn't Colette's, but that of someone who wanted to harm the two of us. Until she was discovered, fifteen days ago. When I think that she was living two hundred meters away from my place . . . And not a sign."

"Her funeral is next week, in Lyon. She wanted to be cremated and rejoin my parents. The details will be in the death-notice columns tomorrow. But I wanted to tell you about it before."

Aimé Chauvel doesn't respond. Observes me. His hair is white. His features have thickened. He seems immensely sad. Hard as I try, I can't find his beautiful face again. His imposing presence in the football photos.

"Aimé, sorry for asking you this question so . . . abruptly, but . . . what was the nature of your relationship?"

He smiles sadly before answering:

"I loved her."

We're walking side by side, wrapped up in our coats, around the Jean-Laville stadium. There's not a soul here. Except maybe Colette's, close to us. I'd phoned him and suggested that we meet here, far from the town center, where nosy people might have wondered what we were doing together, him the former footballer and me the film director.

"Colette talked about you a lot . . . She was very proud of your work. She loved your movies. When they were on at the Danton, she'd go to every screening. The evening ones and the Sunday afternoon ones. When one of your movies was showing, I was sure to see her. So I would go, too."

He barely manages to say these last words, overcome with emotion. We both are. I knew that she saw my movies, but didn't know that she went to every screening. She didn't talk to me about them. Never passed comment.

We continue to stroll along without saying anything. I venture to take his arm. His sorrow pierces me. Our sorrows combine to comfort us.

"I loved her. I always loved her. I was a crazy pup when I met her. She was already thoughtful. I could never have chatted her up. I didn't know that I loved her, that wanting to be with the same person all the time, that was being in love. I was programmed to be with the prettiest girl in Gueugnon. Not the shoe-mender who was twelve years older than me . . . And anyhow, you didn't chat Colette Septembre up, you became a footballer so she'd be interested in you. You tried to be good on the pitch. I'd never have had the career I had if Colette hadn't existed."

He pauses a long while. Blows into his hands, and finally asks me:

"You're living in her last house, on Rue des Fredins?"

"Yes."

"I saw your Méhari parked outside. Are you alone there?"

"Yes."

"Did you find her FCG collection?"

"Yes, she kept it."

"Could we go there? I mean, the two of us, now?"

"Of course."

We get into our separate cars. He follows me and parks behind me, outside the house. Once we're in the garden, and just about to go into the house, Aimé suddenly stops.

"Is it true that she died in her bed?"

"Yes. In her sleep."

"Is the door closed?"

"The door? Of her bedroom? Yes."

Relieved, he follows close behind me. Walks around the rooms. Remains rooted to the spot outside her bedroom. In the sewing-machine room, I show him the Formica cupboard containing her collection, classified by year. With tears in his eyes, he lightly strokes the brown-paper covers.

"Do you have coffee?" he asks me, as if ordering a pick-me-up or liqueur.

"I bought a small machine to make espresso; Tata only had an old coffeepot, with filters and all that."

"You called her Tata?"

"Never. I called her Colette. And when talking about her, I'd say 'Aunt Colette' . . . I'd forgotten that. You've just reminded me."

We settle on the sofa in the sitting room. He clocks my inflatable mattress in the middle of the room, and the old suitcase flat on the floor.

"I'm camping here . . . I'm going to find it hard to leave. I'll confess something to you, Aimé. A strange confession, but . . . I've never felt as good as I have here. It's a moment in time that'll be over after the funeral, and that I'll never forget. Seen from the outside, it's hardly uplifting. But in life, well, in my life, it is."

I go to open the suitcase and show him all the numbered cassettes.

"On recording No. 20, Colette talks about your eighteenth. About your birthday supper in the studio apartment you lived in, above the Café Thillet."

He doesn't respond. Hasn't taken his coat off. As if ready to leave. To rush out of here. He holds his cup still at the edge of his mouth. He's present and absent; I sense that he's tormented by the situation and by his memories, by this house, by Colette's silences. His eyes encourage me to continue. They're brimming with questions.

"She left me cassettes on which she talks about her life. A kind of testament or testimony. Did you know about this recorder?"

Since he can't seem to answer, I continue:

"It belonged to me. I forgot it at her house. I don't know why, but one fine day, she decided to record herself so as to talk to me . . . "

"One evening, I arrived at Colette's and heard her talking. I thought she was with Blanche . . . But I guess she must've been with you . . . in her thoughts."

"Was that a long time ago?"

"About five years. Once I was married, I always came to visit her on foot, when it was dark. Never during the day. People talk too much here. It's all they've got to do. Talk, and more than anything, they '*pident.*'"

"They . . . what?"

"They're on the lookout. '*Pider.*' It's a slang word the old folks here use, and it suits them down to the ground."

"You never lost touch, you and Colette?"

"At one point, I was bitterly resentful of her. Over a business about keys. But I ended up coming back . . . I always met up with Colette late at night. Even after Blanche came along."

He picks up the fob he'd placed on the coffee table.

"I always had a spare key. I've kept it."

He's just admitted to me that he'd meet up with Colette in the middle of the night. So there's no doubt about it, he and she were lovers. I'm dying to ask him if he was already visiting her when I was here on vacation. But honestly, how could I have ever believed, imagined, that my sweet little aunt was "receiving" a man in her bedroom? A married man! How could I have been so blind and deaf to the signs, the sounds, the scents? To the scarf or two glasses forgotten on the table? Me, a film director, for whom daily life is all about visual and sensory observation!

Aimé finishes his coffee, notices my preoccupation, unfolds himself to his full 1.88-meter height, and goes over to the suitcase. He kneels to look at the cassettes, one by one, and finally seizes one, which he hands to me.

"Could I listen to it, please?"

I don't have the heart to refuse. I lift the cover of the recorder and slip the cassette in. Colette's voice transfixes him. From the very first words. A few seconds go by before, clutching his chest, he asks me to stop it. I pause the recording. He leaves the room, reeling. I hear him running the tap in the bathroom. He returns, red-eyed. Sits back on the sofa.

"Okay, I'm ready. We can continue."

He closes his eyes, and I let the recording play on.

COLETTE

That evening, at Aimé's, seeing myself in the mirror, I don't know whether it was the champagne, the music, Aimé's heartbeat against my ear, but I'd gotten younger. I looked even younger than the day I'd set off to do my apprenticeship with Mokhtar. I splashed my face and nape with water. At the time, I still had shoulder-length hair. I had gathered it up with a barrette to go to Aimé's. I let it down.

After these words, Colette stops talking for ten minutes. Aimé opens his eyes and takes advantage of the silence to stand up. He's extremely pale. It takes him a moment to find his words:

"I'll come back later, Agnès, or tomorrow. Anyhow, I'll be back. I'm very happy to have met you."

He disappears into the corridor. I hear the front door closing behind him. In the street, the sound of his car's engine moving off. In the room, his woody scent lingers. I know he won't come back.

4

Colette

Preferences just can't be explained. It's like love—why him, and not him? Why her, and not her? I forced myself for years to go and see my sister Danièle. I didn't want Danièle. I never had wanted her. It was because of her that I had to stop going to school. And when I think about that today, I realize how awful that was for her.

After being in hospital, she quit sniveling over nothing. She became—not interesting, definitely not—but approachable. And when she'd see me turn up, she seemed pleased. We at least ended up smiling at each other.

I did the same back and forth as before, but without Blaise. Shoe-repair shop, château, château, shoe-repair shop. He'd given me his bike behind the marquess's back; where he was going, he wouldn't need it anymore. Those two wheels, like a treasure to me, that of freedom. I could move all around Gueugnon, and thereabouts.

I tried everything with my sister: teaching her to swim; how to care for Bijou, my horse, by then enjoying a peaceful retirement between stable and meadow thanks to Blaise and, mainly, to the marchioness; and all about mushrooms, trees, books, sewing. Nothing that I liked interested her. And yet I persisted!

"Danièle, I'll read you a story."

She'd say, "Okay," sit beside me, never on my knees, listen to me for two or three minutes, and then run off and disappear into her mother's skirts.

When she was little, Danièle always had a cloth in her hand to polish the coppers. She loved doing that. As she grew older, she became passionate about hunting and started accompanying the marquess's henchmen. In short, my little sister liked housework and hunting.

"What would you like to do, Danièle?"

"Nothing."

"Shall we go for a walk?"

"Nothing."

I'd end up laughing about it. Nervously. The older she got, the more she looked like the father . . . and looking like him was no gift.

Silence.

COLETTE

How nasty I am. I listen to myself and find that I'm nasty. You must think that your aunt was jealous, and nasty to her sister.

Silence.

COLETTE

Jean would write one letter a week to Georgette, which I would read out to her on arrival, after her Sunday-lunch service. Always the same deadly boring words: "Hello Mom, I'm well, I eat well, I sleep well, I work well, my school is beside the apartment, Lyon is an interesting city, with love to you and my little sister." Occasionally, he'd say what he'd eaten at a particular meal, or describe one of the rooms in the apartment. Without ever mentioning the piano or his lessons. As if that were taboo or forbidden.

How did Georgette feel? She'd stiffen as soon as I read the first words. I'd try to make it sound interesting, but it was a slog and a half, as young people say now.

Silence.

COLETTE

Georgette wouldn't open the envelopes from Jean. She'd slip them into a drawer and wait until I came, though she wasn't illiterate. Lack of interest? Shame? Modesty? Perhaps all three at once.

Silence.

COLETTE

Blaise wrote to me a lot at first. A lot. I put his letters into one of my FCG collection books, the 1977-1978 season one, I think . . . In 2007, when I had to leave my home in a rush, I hid all the important papers in my collection. You should look inside all of those books. Shake them to see what falls out of their pages. And when they finally establish a museum in Gueugnon, telling the story of the glorious ones, you can give them my collection. In the meantime, take great care of it.

*

November 25, 1961

My dear Colette,

*I feel alone. I have dark thoughts. At boarding school, I share a room with three others. I hate this lack of privacy. They spend their time ogling naked women in magazines. I pretend to laugh and enjoy it. I've learned to emulate the behavior of the biggest brawler here, a certain Jean-Claude. In this place, the insult of choice is "*fag,*" all day long. I know it's paradoxical, but I hate boys. I'd have liked to be normal, Colette; we could have gotten married and had children. If you'd wanted me.*

And you, how are you doing? How's Mokhtar? Father Aubry? Your last letter delighted me. Reading your words delights me. Tell me all about Gueugnon, the people, the gossip. I'll be back for Christmas. I promised Mom. She's increasingly unhappy with my father. I think she'll end up leaving, even though the Sénéchals never divorce.

I went to see your brother last Sunday. Had lunch with him at the Levitans'. Élia and David don't say much. They've always been that way. Once they've asked you three questions, making a supreme effort, they clam up. They live in their thoughts. Jean finds this difficult. And I understand that; he has to put up with the silence of his hosts. But so his fate has decreed. He's still so young. Us, too, Colette, we're young. How sad it is to realize that childhood is short. That we're fifteen and already expected to be and live like adults. You didn't have a happy childhood, but I hope you'll hold on to some good memories, because you deserve them. Back to Jean—I know it's him who interests you—after lunch, we went for a walk along the Rhône. He has a hard time believing it right now, but I explained to him that David Levitan is one of the best piano teachers in the world, that each teacher has their own method, and he must trust him. I hope I convinced him. Jean would like the training to go faster than the music, but that's impossible, considering the level of excellence he's aiming for. He must learn to take his time.

Next, my dear Colette, I took him to an ice-cream parlor, to tuck into a splendid peach Melba. You should've seen his eyes! And I told him Élia's and David's story. Which, for a long time, my mother was the only one to know. After the war, Mom moved to Lyon to help the Red Cross. To record the deported who were returning from the camps, find their families, get their apartments back if they owned them, rehouse them, offer them the support they needed. That's how she met the couple. Your brother needed to know the truth. The reason for their silence.

David and Élia met when very young, at the Conservatoire, and married in 1937. They were arrested in 1942, in Lyon. Élia was pregnant. They were sent to the Pithiviers camp for a few weeks, where she caught typhus. She suffered a miscarriage in the goods train deporting them to Auschwitz. This tragedy probably saved her life, since no one wanted pregnant women, old people, or children taking up space in the death camps.

When the doors of their wagon were opened, Élia escaped and begged the first armed SS man she saw to finish her off. The officer broke her nose. David intervened and received the same treatment. Then they were put in quarantine, David with the men, Élia with the women. They weren't exterminated because they were musicians. David was allowed into the officers' mess as a pianist. And Élia into the women's orchestra, which played for the Nazis, the guards, and a few inmates. This orchestra brought together Poles, Hungarians, Belgians, Ukrainians, Greeks . . . Élia was the only opera singer. She'd be asked for any song, and she'd sing it. She became the "music box" of hell. She lived in better conditions than the others, and eased the nightmarish daily existence of the women in the bunkhouses.

In 1944, she was moved to Bergen-Belsen. She had no idea where her husband was. During that death march, some women asked her to sing, and she did. Élia Levitan's songs were an unimaginably powerful support. They allowed her to resist. And to be treated less ruthlessly by her torturers. Who killed women, but not nightingales. That would have brought bad luck on an already dire situation.

There were 60,000 survivors when the British liberated the camp in 1945, and Élia was among them. When she arrived in Lyon, she didn't know whether David was alive. It was Mom who looked after her, in a building lent to the Red Cross by the French authorities, a building where one could get medical care, a wash, clothes, some sleep. All while trying to find one's family. But David was her only family. Élia would only eat when my mother fed her. She'd keep repeating: "I didn't die in 1942, but now that I'm free to die, let me go, Eugénie." Mom became particularly attached to her. I don't know how many days passed before David was, in turn, brought back to Lyon. My mother witnessed their reunion. Élia didn't recognize her husband. He'd aged thirty years in three, and lost almost forty kilos. The authorities returned their apartment to them, which had been requisitioned by the Vichy police, and David returned to the piano, particularly to teaching. As for Élia, she never sang again.

Now that Jean knows about his hosts' past, I hope he'll better understand and accept their silence.

I can hear the others coming back. I must hide this letter quickly. Seal it in an envelope. If someone comes across it, I'm dead.

Write to me soon.

I love you,

Blaise.

*

I know the story of Élia and David Levitan. My father told it to me. And for a long time, my mother wondered whether her parents, her brother and sister, might have encountered them in 1942, after they were arrested. But she never dared to ask the couple. Or show any photos. Before dying, she admitted to me that she'd feared their answers. Feared learning that they'd been tortured or killed in front of each other. When you have a nightmare, you have it alone. In the camps, the nightmare was collective. Mom was never under any illusion about her loved ones. When they got out of the train, Rafael and Agnès each had a child in their arms, and her father was fifty-five years old.

Dad and I were both at home. I must have been four or five. It's one of my earliest memories. He was crying while playing the piano when I came out of my room. When he saw me, he stopped playing and said:

"Every time Élia really looked at me, she'd think of the child she'd lost. If you knew how relieved I was when Blaise told me about them, about her. As if he'd lifted a dark veil shrouding the couple. I was eleven, and no one talked about the concentration camps. It wasn't until the series *Holocauste* was on TV, in the late seventies, that I first saw the images. Ten years after the liberation of the camps, there was Alain Resnais's documentary, *Nuit et brouillard—Night and Fog*—but I only saw it much later."

He burst into tears.

"I've almost never suffered as much as today."

He'd just heard that Élia had died in hospital following a pulmonary embolism. Why do I remember his words so precisely? What did I understand about what he'd told me? A child lost, a concentration camp, Alain Resnais, the Holocaust, almost never suffered as much. Why "almost," Dad? When was it, the last time you'd suffered? Where you addressing me? Someone else? A ghost or a memory?

Today, I realize that the only person who really looked after my father as a child was Colette. My aunt. Loving each other is also lying to each other. When he was studying in Lyon, every time Dad would phone her at Mokhtar's, he'd tell her that his hosts were warm, whimsical, and took him all over the place. To concerts, the theater, the cinema. But Élia only ventured out onto the street for her medical appointments. It was David who did the shopping, and he never took his pupil anywhere.

5

Gueugnon—Lyon

Agnès Septembre, *her niece,*
Ana Dugain, *her great-niece,*
Jean Septembre *(†), her brother, Danièle* Septembre *(†), her sister, Hannah* Septembre *(†), née* Ruben, *her sister-in-law,*
Louis Berthéol *and Blaise de* Sénéchal *(†), her friends,*
Mokhtar Bayram *(†),*
and the Football Club de Gueugnon,
have the sad duty to inform you of the death of

Madame Colette Septembre Bayram
née Septembre

on October 21, 2010, at the age of sixty-four.

Her public funeral will take place at La Guillotière Cemetery, Lyon, at 2:30 p.m. *on November 15.*

According to her wishes, Colette was cremated. Her ashes will be placed in the family vault.

Condolence book at ceremony.

This notice in lieu of invitation.

*

November 10, 2010

It's almost only dead people now. Just Ana left to have children. To replace birth certificates with death notices. Ana and hope.

There it is. One day you have to choose the right words, the right formula. I really hesitated over naming Georgette and Robin, but I believe Colette would have hated for them to appear on her death notice.

Paul knocks and comes into the house. He closes the door quickly behind him. He smells of winter, of log fires. His bomber jacket is covered in raindrops. Before even greeting me, he says, urgently:

"We've just received the list of people who contacted Colette on her landline over the past six months. Four individuals have been identified."

Four people knew that Colette Septembre was alive. But who? Apart from the good doctor Pieri and Louis Berthéol?

I think of Soudkovski. He didn't know that Blanche was lying in the cemetery when he entered here. What did he do in this house, apart from stealing my photos and calling his cell phone from the landline to log its number?

"We picked up three different sets of fingerprints on the telephone. Your aunt's and Soudkovski's. We need to confirm that the third set is definitely yours."

"You want my fingerprints?"

"Yes."

"Paul, we're living in a detective novel."

"I live in a detective novel every day, Agnès."

As he hands me the list of numbers, Paul asks me to move into the hotel for a while. I look at the list; a single number dominates: Louis Berthéol's. They'd call each other several times a day. Every day. Jacques Pieri rarely phoned; he'd drop by.

Soudkovski rang his cell phone on November 1 at 11:00 P.M. And he called here on the morning of November 3. Those repeated calls I got, they were him. It was him breathing heavily.

"Whose is the fourth number?"

"We haven't had time to check yet," Paul tells me.

"Hold on, I'm going to do it."

"No! I have to call first! You're not supposed to have this list. It's confidential."

"But Paul, this is about my aunt, who's just left me the story of her life on cassette tapes."

"If I were a good cop, I'd seize those cassettes of yours. But I'm terrible with you. A real rookie . . . When Soudkovski phoned you, do you remember what you said to him?"

"I'd gotten in late the night before. It must have been eight in the morning. I thought that it was Marie Roman and Éloïse Cardine, calling me from the retirement home. That maybe they'd forgotten to tell me something."

"Did you say their names?"

"Not their full names. But their first names. I must have said: 'Marie, or Éloïse, or Amélie, is that you?' I think I heard a 'yes' murmured in a breath. D'you think I did something really dumb? That I put them in danger?"

I sense that Paul is hiding something from me.

"Soudkovski might have been spotted in Sallanches, prowling around the establishment where Marie Roman resided."

By the time his words have reached my brain and I've registered them, all I can get out is:

"Why 'resided'?"

Paul's face changes before he quietly says:

"She's passed away."

I can imagine the scene perfectly, for a few seconds, but I feel as if the nightmare is going on forever in my mind. Soudkovski manages to get into the retirement home, walks up the stairs, with one or more knives in his pocket, enters Marie's room. She sees him, recognizes him, is terrified, paralyzed, can't shout for help, and he murders her cold-bloodedly after torturing her. Because of me.

When I open my eyes, I'm lying in an ambulance heading for the emergency department at the Paray-le-Monial hospital. Paul is holding my hand and immediately reassures me:

"Marie Roman died naturally."

I can close my eyes again.

I come around in a consulting room. A young doctor asks me a load of questions. And looks perplexed at my answers. Particularly when I tell him about a woman buried in another woman's grave. And when I finally say that a murderer entered my house, he grips his pen a bit tighter and starts to look at me as if I were delirious. And yet my vital signs are good, my blood pressure normal. And tests prove that I haven't ingested any illicit substance.

Once all my major organs have been examined, I'm allowed to leave. The doctor's conclusion: I've been debilitated by a traumatic personal situation. He prescribes me a mild antidepressant, which I won't take, and advises me to rest. *I've been resting for three years now. It's about time that stops.*

Paul is waiting for me at reception. "I'm not pregnant. I've been debilitated by a traumatic personal situation . . . Since when have you known that Marie Roman is dead?"

"I was told on my way to your place."

I immediately call *Tous les soleils* to speak to Éloïse Cardine, and am finally put through. I don't recognize her flat voice.

"Hello, Agnès. Amélie died in her sleep last night. It was me who found her this morning. Her face looked peaceful. Her sister's here. You know, the lady you met at the Flumet cemetery."

"Yes, I know . . . You're sure that . . . "

"That what?"

"No, nothing. Thanks, Éloïse."

She tells me that my visit had set Amélie's mind at rest. She was relieved to know that her daughter was safe with my aunt. She pressed Blanche's ID card to her heart and showed her photo to all the staff.

Before hanging up, I ask her to let me know the date and location of the funeral.

"Well," I say to Paul, "it's sure becoming suspicious, all these people dying in their sleep, don't you think? My aunt, Marie, Blanche three years ago. Normally, one dies of an illness, of old age, after an accident, a fall, a heart attack, an embolism, from a gunshot, suicide, a ruptured aneurysm, suffocation, drowning, due to a virus, in a fire . . . Around me, the women all die in their sleep. It's enough to make a person scared stiff of falling asleep."

"D'you want to stop off at the drugstore?"

"What for? To keep from dying in my sleep?"

"To get the meds the doc prescribed you at the hospital."

"No, thanks. Drop me off at my place, and I'll drive to the hotel in the Méhari."

"I'll wait outside while you pack your things."

"It's fine, Paul. I'm not going to get myself murdered."

"Soudkovski's cellphone pinged yesterday in Mâcon."

"I thought he was in Sallanches."

"The day before yesterday. Yesterday, his cellphone pinged in Mâcon. Which is good for us. He has no idea that we've traced his cellphone. We're a step ahead of him. His big mistake was phoning himself from your house. There's always a moment when the suspect does something dumb. You just have to wait."

*

It's midnight. It was back on October 22 that I last checked in here. In barely three weeks, my life has changed. The suitcase full of cassettes lies at the foot of my bed. And the recorder is on my bedside table. I've been given room 7. A lucky number. "Double-lock your door." "Yes, Paul. I'll double-lock my door."

That's what I did when Pierre left three years ago, and I've every intention of throwing everything wide open again. The future's going to need reinventing so that it's crazy again. So the dead can bear me aloft. I can't wait to hug Ana tight.

She'll be joining me on November 15, in the morning, along with Cornélia and her father, at the cemetery. There's a café next to it, *Les Passantes*. "The Passersby," a poetic name for a cemetery café. We'll meet there before the ceremony.

I wonder how many people will gather around the Septembre-Ruben grave. I wonder how I'll feel seeing Pierre again. I wonder how I'll feel seeing Pierre alongside Ilyas, Adèle, Hervé, Paul, Louis, and the others. Sounds like that movie—*Vincent, François, Paul et les autres*—by Claude Sautet. His titles certainly have a way of infiltrating my life. After the burial, which won't really be one as it's ashes, I'll go straight back to Paris. And then Ana will go back to school.

I hear the sound of footsteps out in the corridor, the floorboards creaking. Someone with a light step. It's normal to get back to hit the sack at midnight. In a hotel, there are comings and goings all night. *Double-lock your door.* Unlike the others, I'm not scared of Soudkovski, and I don't know why. I know, I sense that he'll do me no harm. Why am I sure of this? What are my body and brain trying to tell me? Why am I zonking out, when it's never happened to me before? Why am I not scared of that raving-mad maniac? Blanche and Marie spent their lives running away from him.

If it is him who's behind my door, best to know about it. I half-open it without making a sound, and I see Adèle going into Paul's room. But to do what? Change a dressing for him? Give him an injection? Take a blood sample? Stitch him up? I go straight back to bed to mull over the days ahead of me.

6

Adèle. Out of the group of four, she was the one who didn't talk. Who agreed to everything. The one who followed without asking any questions. The one who smelled of honeysuckle, and still does. The one who hasn't changed. The pretty, discreet one. The good pupil. The daughter of storekeepers, who'd go swimming in the ocean with her parents as a child. And who returns to the same spot with her daughters, since they were born, for the first three weeks of August. Saint-Palais-sur-Mer, on the Côte de Beauté. The Atlantic. Stocked up with syringes, dressings, and sample tubes, she's with her first patients in the back of beyond by 6 A.M., and if all goes well, she's home again at 8 P.M. She only gets Sunday to rest. When it's not her turn on duty. These days, she does speak a little, to say that the dead mustn't be disturbed or "each to their own evening."

In 1986, Colette gave me a camcorder. It became our main pastime. Ilyas, Adèle, and I would write flimsy stories, while Hervé set up the lighting, namely two weak spotlights salvaged from a former boutique. We'd improvise playlets about daily life, or made-up TV news bulletins, and spend our days filming ourselves, watching each other, starting over, giggling. It was the best fun. And almost always took place in Adèle's parents' beautiful, spacious house. Hervé, Ilyas, and I loved putting on makeup, whereas Adèle liked to stay in the background. Over time, I started to call the shots, to direct them. Adèle hated acting; she'd happily do anything, as long as she didn't have to speak.

Broadly, every scene revolved around a pretty, silent girl who would observe the exchanges between two funny but dim guys. She merely pouted or rolled her eyes. We'd recreate "sets" in Adèle's room. Or in the corridor on the first floor. We'd filch her mother's makeup. And before going home, we'd pour liters of makeup remover onto cotton balls. I would never have gone back to my aunt's wearing makeup. Not because she would have told me off, she never did, but out of respect for her. I would've hated for my parents to think that Colette let me do any old thing.

A year later, my father died. And took with him the summer I was fifteen. We stopped playing with the camcorder, skipped a stage, and went clubbing. At Tacot's, near Gueugnon. Adèle's parents would drive us there, and then collect us at two in the morning. Not a minute later, or we were punished and grounded. The funniest part was that they would hold out breathalyzers we each had to puff into. "Each to their own breathalyzer," Ilyas would quip. Which triggered some memorable fits of the giggles, and never, in two years, did Adèle's parents drop the testing rule. But once we came of age, we were spared it.

I don't know what became of my camcorder, our cassettes, our sketches, our goofing around with songs—"Billie Jean," "Sweet Dreams," "Too Shy," "*Mise au point*"—that bonded us together. Impossible to remember. Did I leave all that in Gueugnon? In Lyon, at Mom's? In the room I rented a few years later?

I'd never thought of all that again. It's just taken a sleepless night. I can't drop off so I'm thinking about my camcorder and Adèle. My childhood friend so long forgotten, too.

I don't know her daughters, who are three or four years older than Ana. I do remember having sent her colorful little undershirts and flowers when they were born. I saw a photo of the father of her children on Facebook, a former basketball player, I believe.

Yes, it's all coming back to me: Adèle played basketball, Ilyas football, and Hervé rugby. Now I remember. During vacations, we'd meet up after they finished practice, outside the gym. I'd wait for them, feeling like I had nothing to do. Occasionally, I'd whack a few balls against the wall of the tennis court, next to the gym.

Adèle and Paul are sleeping together in the next room. She didn't leave. And the name of a particular town I spotted on the GPS history in her Citroën keeps going around in my brain. When I'd entered my own destination, I hadn't paid it much attention.

Adèle uses that car, that sleeps in her garage, for vacations or to take her daughters to Dijon. Day to day, she uses a tiny car to whiz around the streets of Gueugnon and nearby.

That evening two days ago, after Paul had left the restaurant, we lingered around the table to chat. Nathalie asked Lina a few questions. Adèle, as usual, remained silent. I thought she was unsettled by the whole Soudkovski business. But if unsettled, it was more likely that Paul had just made an impression on her. I'm not sure why, but Charpie intruded on our conversation. Clearly, Ilyas had already told Lina about him because she didn't seem surprised. "He's part of my DNA, against my will." When I asked Ilyas if hearing of his death had been a relief, he told me that, for him, he'd already been dead a long time.

"But I battle every day against the monster he gifted me."

"He won't harm anyone anymore," Adèle pointed out.

Ilyas waved this aside and announced to us that he'd asked Lina to marry him. She smiled and told us she'd said yes. We applauded the pair of them. Nathalie asked where they intended to live. Sallanches? Gueugnon? Elsewhere? They couldn't answer. They'd see.

Personally, having always thought it really dumb to marry when you barely know each other, I shed a little tear. There are some couples, lovers, souls who just seem obvious together. I see Pierre and me again, in Giverny. We obviously weren't as well matched as all that.

I close my eyes, but sleep still eludes me. I open them again, and the GPS history is suddenly projected onto the ceiling of my room. My hypermnesia is in overdrive:

DIJON
GUEUGNON
DIJON
SAINT-PALAIS-SUR-MER
GUEUGNON
CANNES
GUEUGNON
DIJON
GUEUGNON
DIJON

7

November 11, 2010

I didn't die in my sleep; I did worse. I dreamed of Pierre. I was even making love with him. I open my eyes in my hotel room. All my bedrooms are hotel rooms since he left. The sheets are cold, the walls unknown. I'm mortified, and feel like I've taken a huge leap backward in just a few hours. *Get out of my life, Pierre Dugain.* I have to accept it. He'll never be part of me again, beyond Ana, but he'll be part of certain nights. Disjointed nights.

In 2007, everything went very fast. When Pierre announced he was leaving me, I didn't want to stay in the States. I hired a woman attorney—a killer—recommended by a French actress friend who'd lived in LA for years. And I asked her to inform Pierre of my decision to return to France with our daughter. He phoned me:

"You're sending me lawyers' letters now? We've reached that point?"

I replied:

"Get lost."

And I hung up. I might have added, "Go fuck yourself," but I'm not sure.

My aunt died on August 11. He told me he was leaving on September 1.

I moved back to Paris on January 1, 2008. *Happy new year and good health, particularly good health, that's the most important.* Needless to say, if I hadn't had Cornélia in my life, I'd have sunk straight to the bottom. She's the one who found the light-filled apartment in the Abbesses district, the beds, the sofa, a new piano for Ana, the crockery to put in the fitted kitchen, the scented diffusers . . . She's the one who resuscitated me every other week to go pick up Ana from school, have a quick junk-food snack before going home, organize sleepovers, watch a TV series with my daughter, accompany her to birthday parties, dance classes, the orthodontist, do one or two pieces of homework, "because, really, Mom, I'm begging you."

The usual humiliations ensued: Pierre and the other one on a magazine cover, making out in turquoise water; and even more nightmarish, Pierre and the other one outside their new apartment in the Marais district, in Paris. His hand under her sweater. I'd remain stuck for hours, just gazing at them on the glossy paper. Tear the magazine to pieces before throwing it away, and then go back down to the kiosk, blubbing, to buy another copy. And gape again at his hand under her sweater. "Pierre Dugain: a happy man. The beautiful American and our favorite actor. Out of love for him, she's sacrificing herself and moving to Paris." Three hundred square meters in the Marais's Saint-Paul with my husband, funny, witty, intelligent, sensual, famous. Some sacrifice! Life's a bitch.

Since I'm not an actress, and movie directors interest the tabloid press about as much as Art Deco does, I was spared the stolen photos of my haggard face, with its double chin due to my excess weight, doing my shopping in Abbesses and trying to articulate properly, before the greengrocers' astonished eyes: "A kilo of red apples for poisoning, please. Snow White's the other one. Me, I'm the mirror."

How do you get over a broken heart? Do you ever? And why get over it at all? I don't have the answer. But the worst of the worst, massacring my ego, was when they did their first TV program together. And not any old program. Not some general-knowledge quiz game to raise money for charity. No. The television news. Side by side, to promote the most recent movie by François Ozon, a director I'm mad about, as Pierre is well aware. Ozon had hired both of them because he'd discovered and adored her in my last movie—that I found out later, thank goodness—and had wanted to work with Pierre for a long time. She seemed like someone hard of hearing who could only read Pierre's lips. The cameraman kept doing close-ups of her, mute and sublime.

Someone knocks on my door. My life has turned into a light comedy. Doors are opened, doors are slammed, entrances are made through the door. Room-service breakfast? Not the hotel's style. Soudkovski here to murder me? Let's be done with it, once and for all. It's Adèle, in the same clothes as last night. Jeans, navy-blue sweater.

"Am I waking you?" she asks, looking embarrassed.

"No."

"I slept here," she murmurs.

"I know."

We smile at each other. She blushes and looks down. Like in the camcorder days.

"Want to have breakfast downstairs?"

I try to sound as casual as possible, but all I'm thinking about is the fact that she went to Cannes. It's all I can think of. I couldn't care less that she slept with Paul.

"Sure. Today, I'm doing the noon—10 P.M. shift."

Adèle orders a black coffee, I a triple espresso. Long-braid-down-her-back rolls her eyes.

"We don't do that."

"Then three coffees in three cups, side by side, please."

She leaves it at that, noticing that I'm not in the mood, and places a basket full of pastries on the table.

Adèle's cheeks are pale pink. Will I see my cheeks turn pink again one day?

"Tell me, Adèle, did you go to Cannes recently?"

"No, why?" she asks, biting into a croissant. "I've never been to the Midi. Maybe next year, my girls want to take me to Menton, for the lemon festival."

"And yet . . ."

I'm struggling to get to the point.

"And yet what?"

"The GPS in your Citroën lists Cannes."

"Oh, maybe. You know, I lend it to everyone."

"Really?"

I'm almost disappointed.

"To who?" I persist.

"My daughters' friends. Those with a license."

"I thought that . . . "

"That what, Agnès?"

"That you were mixed up in Charpie's disappearance."

She looks me deep in the eye, with her big eyes, smiling strangely.

"Are you investigating me?"

"Not at all. I couldn't sleep, and that detail came back to me. At night, everything becomes an obsession. I remembered having spotted the name of that city on your GPS history, and that's where Charpie was living when he died."

She tucks into her second croissant.

"I'm starving this morning, didn't have time for supper yesterday."

"Did you have a good night?" I venture, to ease the strained atmosphere.

"See, you are investigating me."

I burst out laughing. She takes a long swig of coffee and then orders a freshly squeezed orange juice.

"Did Nathalie and Ilyas tell you they saw him in Cannes, after they left the Palais des Festivals?"

I'm surprised she's gone back to Charpie. Maybe she wants to change the subject to avoid talking about Paul.

"Yes, they told me they followed him along the Croisette; it's crazy . . . he ran away and . . . "

Adèle cuts me short:

"I hope you don't hold it against me, about Paul."

"Why would I hold it against you?"

She bites her lip before continuing:

"You didn't have . . . have designs on him?"

I'm so taken aback by her question that tears come to my eyes. Adèle remains disconcerted. Her cheeks are turning crimson now. I admit to her that I'd love to have designs on someone. But it doesn't happen to me anymore. Any romantic interest I had in others has turned to ashes, like my poor aunt. She takes my hands and murmurs:

"Couldn't help it."

"Listen, Adèle, if you had a lovely night, that's great. And you owe nothing to anyone. After all, you said it yourself, 'each to their own evening.'"

Adèle's face abruptly falls.

"Are you okay, Adèle? If you've fallen in love with Paul, it's no big deal."

"I wanted to kill him."

Suddenly, I imagine Paul lying in the bed upstairs, killed with his service gun by my childhood friend, the one who didn't speak.

"Charpie," she whispers, bringing the cup to her lips.

8

Last year, when Ilyas and Nathalie got back from Nice, they came to see me at home. It was evening. It was late and I was watching TV, half-asleep, when they turned up, bronzed and beautiful, but distressed. The contrast between how well they looked and their solemn demeanor was striking. I thought something serious had happened . . . And it had: they'd seen Charpie. They seemed distraught. I sensed that Ilyas wanted to turn the page, and Nathalie respected his choice. Without understanding why, I found it all totally devastating. The fact that Charpie lived peacefully in the sun, with no questions ever asked, that felt like a profound injustice to me.

"In Gueugnon, we knew he'd been dismissed by the club and that he'd cleared off to the Midi pronto. A manager had caught him red-handed in the stadium's changing rooms, fondling a boy under the shower. I knew he was alive, I could have tracked him down before, but the fact that Ilyas and Nathalie were talking to me about it made it concrete. It existed.

"Personally, I never should've have married my daughters' father. My elementary-school sweetheart was called, still is called, Christophe Delannoy. He's the one I loved, and, sure, I know it's just kids' stuff, but there's no kid's love, there's just love. We'd promised to spend our lives together. I'd be a doctor, he'd be a footballer and sports commentator, and we'd have a three-story house like my parents', but better.

"He didn't get married, didn't have children or buy a house. Didn't pursue his studies. He was stuck in a rotten subsidiary school after seventh grade because school's mandatory, and once he turned sixteen, he was left to his own devices. He never took drugs, never drank, but he went crazy. Yes, there is such a thing as going crazy. Of course, you could find other terms: behavioral problems, bipolarity, depression, etc. Christophe wasn't born crazy. The person who destroyed his soul, I can swear to God, is Charpie. But that I found out and understood much later.

"He'd gone to Manosque with friends for a football training course; they must have been around ten years old. The course was overseen by Charpie. I don't know what he did to Christophe, but you hardly need to imagine to understand. When my little boyfriend returned, he wasn't himself anymore. He had set off on the bus on a Wednesday, all smiles, and the following Sunday, he was as if dead and buried. Of course, I didn't realize this immediately. Once he was back, I went over to his place as usual, and he was abnormally hyper. I thought it was joy, that he was happy to have played football with friends at a kind of holiday camp. We shut ourselves away in his room to chat, as usual. I wanted him to tell me all about it, but he told me nothing. He was stammering. I'd never heard him stammer before. I put it down to tiredness and overexcitement. I remember one thing very clearly. As if it were yesterday. He took out all his photo albums to show me pictures of him as a baby, and he kept repeating: "You see, that was before." How could I have understood what that 'before' meant? We stayed in his room all afternoon, looking through the albums.

"We really didn't get up to anything bad; we were ten-year-old babies. We'd kiss on the lips, we called it a 'peck.' Nothing more. Occasionally, we'd hold hands in the street, to be like grown-ups. Christophe was funny, gentle, and good-looking. But after Manosque, he started going through agitated periods, talking nonsense, he was no longer coherent, and then, all of a sudden, he'd become passive. He'd lie down and not move for hours. I saw the sadness in his eyes, a long and terrible sadness creeping in and taking hold, taking root. An endless descent to hell. I'd ask him what was wrong; he wouldn't answer. After a year, I told him that he'd changed. That he wasn't the same anymore. Even physically—he'd been so slim, but now he put on a lot of weight. As if he were on cortisone. I kept on at him so much, trying to find out what was wrong, that he finally threw me out, insulting me, calling me bourgeois, accusing me of thinking I was a star, that I was God's gift because I got good grades, of wanting to control everything in his life. That was devastating to me, too. There's nothing more terrible than losing someone without him dying, merely because he's absent from himself. And Christophe never came back. The kind Christophe. Who'd promised to have a fine future. When we moved up to junior high, he isolated himself from the others; he didn't have friends anymore, and he'd stopped playing football, when football had been his life. He'd taken up cycling, would disappear for hours, crossing the town like a madman on his two wheels. He became a laughingstock. The pupils started mocking him, calling him 'Toto'—dimwit. Toto here, Toto there. They laughed behind his back, and he became increasingly less coherent. Some teachers behaved like real assholes toward him, calling him moronic or ignorant; others were concerned and requested that he be examined by doctors. A psychological and psychiatric assessment was required. Christophe lived alone with his mother. She received a widow's pension. Everyone thought that he'd spiraled because of the accidental death of his father at the factory when he was five. That this event had made him vulnerable. I never believed that. He started to have spells in psychiatric hospitals; then he was declared disabled, though no one was able to define his illness. Schizophrenia was mentioned, hallucinatory and psychotic episodes linked to the loss of his father. One day, he threw himself off the third story, convinced he could fly away. He was saved by a neighbor's awning on a story below.

"After seventh grade, he went off to do the vocational certificate in woodworking. He must have lasted a few months. Today, at our age, he still lives at his mother's, and he's never worked.

"Life meant that I forgot our childhood promises. Like everyone else, I dropped him. Unloved him. I continued with my studies, went out, flirted, got married, had my daughters, a fascinating but demanding job. I still sometimes come across him when shopping or at the lab. We exchange a kiss in greeting; we have nothing to say to each other, but we do exchange a kiss. And come out with the same old 'nice weather today, isn't it freezing, your mother's well?' I stroke his shoulder and continue on my way.

"If he needs treatment or a blood test, he calls me. He doesn't want to deal with my colleagues. He comes to the office and waits for me like an obedient child. He sits down and doesn't budge. I find him behind the door. Each time, I have an irrepressible urge to cry, because it's such a waste. Ilyas pulled through. He had a hard time of it, but he pulled through. Whereas Christophe, he died in Manosque.

"He no longer resembles the beautiful boy of my childhood. He must weigh 90 kilos. He's bloated; he's had it. He doesn't seem unhappy. He smiles all the time, thanks to his medication. If, unfortunately, he stopped his treatment, it wouldn't be the same story. I think that, for now, he keeps going because he has his mother close to him. I'm convinced that when she goes, he'll follow.

"So, when Ilyas and Nathalie told me they'd seen Charpie, my heart missed a beat, everything came flooding back like a slap in the face, so I did some research. It's as if they'd brought up something buried inside me. I'm a nurse, it's not hard to find a postal address in a medical file, along with the social-security number. Within five minutes, I had the name of the street Charpie lived on. I waited until the weekend and then went there. I arrived on a Friday night. I'd booked a room in a hotel close to where he lived, the Belle Vue.

"It was peak season, the terraces, beach, and streets were packed. I got up very early on the Saturday morning. You won't believe me, but I'd never seen the Mediterranean. It took finding Christophe's abuser for me to see it. It was beautiful, that blue, unbelievable. But I couldn't see any beauty. I was in a bad way. I hadn't brought a swimsuit; I was in a different mode. I had no idea what I was going to do. I wanted to meet him, perhaps speak to him, slap him, or insult him. I didn't know. I did what they do in spy movies; I hid behind sunglasses and waited for him on the terrace of a café below his building.

"At midday, after four or five coffees and eighteen teas, I almost got back into my car. I really wondered what the hell I was doing there. The sun began to hit hard. I went to the edge of the sea to splash water on my nape. I zigzagged around towels, parasols, prone bodies, and I thought I might call him, find out his number to know whether he was at home and if it was worth waiting for him. I looked closely at the building he lived in. Five stories, two or three apartments per floor. White balconies and blue awnings. I thought of the one that had saved Christophe's life.

"On the first floor, a lady was watering her flowers. To her right, another was cleaning something, an object she was holding in her hand. On the third floor, to the left, a man was reading his paper on a deckchair. Still on the third, a couple was having lunch; on the fourth, a young girl was hanging washing on a line; on the top floor, a man was scanning the beach through binoculars glued to his eyes. I ended up dipping my ass in the water, in my undies, to observe the façade of the seafront building. Believe it or not, from noon to 1:30 P.M., the guy on the top floor didn't move, binoculars still stuck to his eyes. He intrigued me so much that I, too, didn't move. I got sunburned like never in my life. My forearms, my neck, and my cheeks got scorched without me feeling a thing. Was he waiting for someone? Admiring the boats? He reminded me of those big birds of prey that can remain with eyes riveted to a fixed spot before suddenly swooping down to the ground. All the other neighbors went inside, lowered their shutters, but not him. At around 1:30, he finally disappeared into his apartment. It wasn't Charpie I started to wait for, but the man with the binoculars. He reappeared at around 3:00 P.M. and went back to it. A statue with binoculars stuck to its face. He was wearing a red tee shirt and navy-blue Bermuda shorts. I thought, that can't be *him*. In Gueugnon, he was forever in beige overcoats and gray shirts and trousers. It was at around 5:00 P.M. that the fever hit me. I hurried into a pharmacy, red as a lobster. The pharmacist really bawled me out, recommending that I stop working for a few days, but I told him that was impossible because I was self-employed, and a nurse to boot! He sold me three tons of cream and other poultices, ordered me to go indoors immediately, and prescribed painkillers. He gave me the phone number of a doctor who'd visit me if the pain became too acute. 'Don't hesitate to go to the emergency department, depending on how things develop.'

"I went back to the hotel and to bed. And I slept like a log until the following morning. When I opened my eyes at 10 on the dot, my body was burning hot, my mouth dry, my eyes wet, and a hundred thousand percussion instruments were pounding inside my skull. It was Sunday, and I had to leave. The sky had turned gray, a dark gray that only let streaks of light through. The wind was buffeting the palm trees, and the temperature had plummeted by ten degrees. Unlike the previous day, the crowd had disappeared. I stuffed myself with painkillers and returned to the beach to see if binocular man was still up on the top floor. There were just two teenagers smoking cigarettes on the second-floor balcony.

"The beach was almost deserted. There were a few rash swimmers, but the sea was choppy and the red flag was up. All of a sudden, binocular man appeared on his balcony, but without his binoculars. He looked in my direction. He must have wondered why I was standing rooted on the beach, alone, in front of his building, looking up at the top floor. Was it Charpie? I was too far away to be sure, but it did look like him. In any case, this gray-haired man was staring at me from his apartment. It struck me right then that I hadn't seen him for a long time. That he was bound to have changed and I might not be able to recognize him. Surely close up. And me, had I changed? Was I far away enough for him not to recognize me? He used to come regularly to my parents' house for an aperitif, with others from the club.

"I felt so uncomfortable, I went back to the hotel. His building was large; it could be a coincidence, another resident, a voyeur obsessed with the sea, a fellow who was bored and filled his days as best he could.

"I went back to bed. Incapable of hitting the road, I begged the guy in reception to extend my stay. Considering the state I was in, and despite my room being booked for that very evening, he agreed, grumbling. I called my closest colleague to tell her that I was unwell and incapable of returning to work the following morning. And I stayed stuck in bed and shivering, thinking of the man on the top floor, of Christophe, of the time spent before and after Manosque, of Charpie, of Ilyas, of his resigned look when he'd come to see me with Nathalie the previous week. I ended up dropping off. My fever must have fallen during the night. When I woke at four in the morning, a storm had hit Italy and headed straight for the Mediterranean basin. Rain was hammering the windowpanes; the wind was wild.

"It was him who found me. He'd left an envelope addressed to me at reception. I imagine he went around all the hotels in the neighborhood. 'Hello, Adèle, I recognized you on the beach. What are you doing here? Why are you watching me? Last week, your little friends, this week, you. Call me, to be done with this, once and for all. R.' Along with his phone number. Just the first letter of his first name. As if he didn't want to leave any trace. So binocular man really was him. It made me feel deeply uncomfortable. What was he watching, all day long? Or rather, *whom*?

"I didn't call him. 'Your little friends.' Those three words sickened me. And what did 'to be done with this' mean? What he had done in Gueugnon, he surely must do it in Cannes. A predator remains a predator. Wherever he may be, even with gray hair. Men like that always find a job or voluntary work close to children.

"I decided that he must come down to do his shopping, go for a walk, have activities, so, starting at 7 in the morning that Monday, I posted myself at the foot of his building. Standing back a little, but so I could keep watch on the main entrance without being seen. He appeared in the lobby at 10:00 A.M. I waited until he was some distance away and then followed close behind him. The heat had returned. The sky cleared. A pure blue. In other circumstances, the city would doubtless have appealed to me. I was in a holiday world that wasn't mine. His bearing, his sprightly step, was unmistakable, chin up in the air; he seemed at ease with life, sure of himself. Just the same as when, as a child or teen, I'd had no idea what he was up to, because no one spoke of it. I'd found him cold, condescending. But not with my parents; as soon as he was dealing with adults, he'd instantly become warm.

"He walked as far as a medical lab, where he remained some twenty minutes. Was he there for a blood test? Next, he bought a newspaper, then a baguette, and turned back toward his apartment. Would it stop there? Would he go home and read his paper? Would I return to my car and my normal life without talking to him about Christophe, Manosque, and the others?

"Back at the hotel, I packed my bags, sobbing over my cowardice and stupidity. Why had I come? Who did I take myself for? Superwoman? And off I went.

"I got lost trying to get on the freeway, turning around in circles and cursing, and almost went past his building several times in the process. As if everything drew me back to that accursed place. The third time, I screamed with rage at myself. And suddenly, I spotted a panel indicating the way to a stadium. It was like an explosion inside my head. There was a stadium in the neighborhood. A strange coincidence or an irony of fate? The Hesperides, I believe. The car park was deserted, one door open. I passed a man in a hurry, who greeted me without asking what I was doing there. I branched off, went along corridors, looked at the photos of famous or unknown players, cups in display cabinets, pennants, locked changing rooms, I got back to the main artery, walked all the way around the stadium, thinking, and when I wanted to return to my car, I took the wrong corridor and found myself outside offices that, it being lunchtime, were empty. There, my heart skipped a beat, as they say. But my heart started racing when my eyes fell on that photo from the local paper. An article had been cut out and pinned onto a cork board in the middle of administrative papers, fliers, and the like. Charpie, all smiles, posing in the middle of a group of teenage boys. 'Wednesdays of Hope' was the headline. Friendly matches were being organized between professional footballers and teenagers with precarious backgrounds, and it was Charpie who coordinated the games.

"I looked, long and hard, into the eyes of the young boys posing around him for signs that maybe didn't exist. I sat on the floor, just to take it in. Then I snatched the article off the board and ripped it to pieces. Couldn't stop myself. As if doing that could erase years of unhappiness.

"And then I phoned him. He answered on the second ring. Neither warm nor cold. With the tone of someone responding to some administrative formality, when we knew each other. I needed time before seeing him. Wanted to wait until evening. Not in the light of day. As if I were scared of him. I told him that I could meet from eight onward, wherever suited him. He picked a bar on the Cap de la Croisette. A popular place, well known. Was he also scared of finding himself alone in front of me?

"I spent the afternoon wandering around a shopping mall, before parking close to the bar. I got there hours before the appointed time. And once again, I waited for him. But this time in my car. Behind the steering wheel. I wanted to be there first. I saw him arrive, look around for me, then sit down on the terrace.

"My hands were shaking, my heart pounding. He ordered a beer and looked out for me. For more than an hour. Night fell, and he kept glancing at his watch. Observed the people at tables around him, the passersby on the sidewalk. Uncomfortable. He knew why I'd arranged to see him. He knew what I would talk to him about. That much was obvious.

"I didn't get out of my car. I didn't confront him. I waited until he left the place. He walked as far as the harbor car park. I switched on the ignition and followed him, driving at walking pace. He sloped along the quayside in the dark. Seeing his shadow under the streetlamps, I saw Christophe again, his smile, the look in his eyes, lost somewhere between childhood and no-man's-land.

"When Charpie wanted to cross, I accelerated and drove straight at him, screaming. But I stopped when I reached him. He stared right at me. With his ice-cold reptilian eyes. And I, who dreamed of sending him flying into the water to avenge Christophe, I chickened out. It all happened so fast. I saw that he'd recognized me. I reversed and sped off.

"I kept driving until a gas station in Lyon, thinking of the cops who'd be waiting for me outside my home. If Charpie lodged a complaint against me . . . a complaint about what? A week later, I read in the paper that he'd been found in the sea off Cannes, a suspected drowning. And then nothing. Just silence. More silence. Had he committed suicide after my 'attempted murder'?

"I almost shouted who he'd been from the rooftops. But I'm the one who never speaks in public. I said nothing to Christophe, or to Ilyas. They don't know that I saw him. I kept quiet. Like I've always kept quiet."

9

November 11, 2010

"Hello?"

It's a male voice.

"Who is this?"

"Sorry?"

"Who are you?"

"It's you who called me, madame."

"You're on the list of people who regularly phoned my aunt, Colette Septembre, these last few years."

A silence.

"Are you Agnès? Agnès Septembre?"

Haven't been called that for ages. Agnès Dugain, it's like some soap or detergent brand name that I'm stuck with.

". . ."

"All my condolences. Come and see me; I'm at home. You know my house."

"Your house?"

"The raffle house."

Antoine Été has hands smeared in grease and black fingernails. His curly, salt-and-pepper hair is a mess. He's wearing worn-out jeans and a navy sweater with one out of three buttons missing. He smells good. I can't help it, before even greeting him, I ask him the name of his cologne. It's such an incongruous question, he just mumbles a vague "Dior."

He's more interested in my car than in me, and does a full tour of my Méhari.

"Is it Ilyas's?"

"You know Ilyas?"

He smiles kindly. His smile lights up his face. His eyes are deepest black.

"Yes. He's a friend. I'm the one who sold it to him. Come on in, we'll have a coffee."

*

1964

Jean goes into the house. Father Aubry, Colette, and Blaise wait for him outside. Monsieur and Madame Été are delighted to show him the furnished interior of the raffle house. Jean smiles politely, because it's to this building that he owes his future. He doesn't pretend to marvel at the brand-new furniture, because he's never known how to do such a thing. While he's shown one room after another, he thinks of his scores. Between him and the world, there are the scores.

Jean has come home from Lyon to spend Christmas with Colette, and to visit his mother and the Marchioness de Sénéchal.

It's the first time he's back in Gueugnon since leaving to live with the Levitans. He hides his hands in his pockets so the others don't notice that his fingers are moving, impatiently. He answers yes or no to the questions he's asked about his studies, and the competition to enter the conservatoire.

It's been two months now since David Levitan reopened that drawer.

"You're ready," his teacher told him, handing him his precious scores.

David Levitan was right. In every way. Never had Jean felt so free at the piano. Like a bird that had been caged for several years to fine-tune its wings. Wings that would carry him to a height he never suspected he could reach. Almost touching the stars. He feels it in the depths of his soul, his flesh, his blood. Never had a piano taken him on such journeys.

He suddenly realizes that he's benefited from the most extraordinary of apprenticeships. Almost mystical.

"You're not normal, professor, you're a piece of God."

David screws up his eyes, without smiling.

"Do you believe in God, Jean?"

"I believe in my sister, in Liszt, Shubert, Chopin, Mozart, and Bach. And mostly, I believe in you. So I must believe in God a little."

"Believe mostly in work, in effort. God is there when man doesn't lose heart."

But the price to pay is heavy, sometimes unbearable, his daily existence so very cold. Loveless. Never a hand to caress him or shake his own hand, never an embrace. Never a kiss, a bit of encouragement, a kind word. Never an admiring glance. Only Élia's, full of tears, that he sometimes catches directed at him. Barely three words in a day. And the inflexible rigor of David, who lets nothing go, watches his slightest movements, refuses him the right to be sick, or to complain, or to bring back a grade lower than 15.

Meanwhile, Jean thinks of Colette; it's because of her that he's not been back for three years. Because of the guilt that wracks him for having abandoned her to hard, manual work while he's privileged. The guilt of feeling forlorn at the Levitans', of daring to feel sorry for himself in silence, when he's where he should be. That all this strife is just to enable him to access the beauty of his art, while Colette handles worn-out shoes.

On one of her visits, when walking her back to the station, he'd told her that as soon as he could live off his music, he'd bring her over, and she'd be able to resume her studies. But he'd received a flat refusal:

"I like my work. I'm never leaving Gueugnon."

It was a fine day, and Jean had led her to the Parc de la Tête-d'Or to share some sandwiches. He'd claimed that the Levitans were away, so she wouldn't meet them. She'd have worried if she'd discovered their deadly dull interior, their oppressive solitude. She'd have realized that they lived on a desert island, and she'd have worried. Sitting on a bench, their talk had turned to their futures. Which were so different.

"You, you've got your piano; me, I've got you, my work, Mokhtar, and football. Enough to fill my life."

"In any case, you'll get married," Jean had objected.

"No," his sister had said, without any hesitation.

"But you'll have children!"

"You'll have them. Not me."

He hadn't felt he could ask her why she was so sure. And couldn't envisage his sister not doing like everyone else.

*

From the kitchen window, I look out at the meadow adjoining the house, and the twenty or so Méharis lined up like dolls. It's true that it looks like a field of flowers. There are white ones, green ones, orange ones, and those of various blues: navy, pastel, and cyan. They've all been restored and are shiny as new coins. Only an orange carcass, to one side, has been disemboweled, "on the operating table," its motor languishing on the ground.

"I imagine you know this house."

Antoine's voice interrupts my thoughts.

"I came with my aunt, as a child. Well, I think I did. I'm not that sure anymore. I've heard so much about it, I can't be sure of anything anymore. With Louis, Louis Berthéol, Colette's best friend, we'd sometimes go past it, but staying distant enough not to disturb your parents."

"I'll show you around if you'd—"

"Why were you talking to Colette on the phone? She was dead . . . supposedly."

"I looked after Blanche. Toward the end."

"Blanche?" I'm astonished.

"You know who Blanche is?"

"Now, yes . . . I know only too well."

"I read Nathalie's article on the 'second' death of Colette. You know, I'm so sorry."

". . ."

"Before repairing cars, I was a doctor. I quit. Changed occupation. I missed her heart. I got it wrong."

"Missed whose heart?"

"Blanche's."

He looks like a giant lost in a fifties kitchen with recent appliances. He washes his hands with *savon de Marseille* and switches on a machine that's "state of the art," as my ex-husband would say toward the end.

"Would you like sugar?"

"No thanks."

He pulls back two chairs and invites me to sit opposite him.

"You live alone?"

"Yes."

I'm ashamed to have asked that question just because the place is well-kept. As if a single man couldn't be clean and tidy. It's probably because, while he looks a mess, with his three-day beard and black fingernails, the inside of his house is spick and span. No photos on the walls. But a few Impressionist paintings of stunning beauty. Including two of the beach at Sainte-Andresse in Normandy. Nothing goes with anything in this place. I've never seen furniture so ill-matched with paintings, the sort you'd expect to find in a manor house or some other opulent interior.

"In 2004, I was an accident-and-emergency doctor in Chalon. One night, your aunt turned up. I'd always known her. Through my parents and the shoe-repair shop—we were customers. I grew up 'in Jean's house,' that of your father, the great pianist. I still have his records, vinyls. And . . . I'll show you later, a photo. Our families' destinies have always been linked thanks to that famous raffle. Anyhow, at the hospital, Colette asked to see me. She told me that she wasn't alone and wasn't there for herself, but I'd need to use her papers to treat the person with her, her social-security and health-insurance cards. At first, I refused. Then, when I saw Blanche sitting in the waiting room, I agreed."

"Why?"

"Because she was scared. It was as plain as the nose on your face. A doctor recognizes the look in the eyes of a victim. Later, she admitted to me that it wasn't a husband she was escaping from, but a father. She made me promise to say nothing. Anyhow. That night, I took care of her, as if she were Colette Septembre. Same for her prescriptions. In fact, to this day, I don't know Blanche's surname."

He waits for an answer that I don't give him. Hanging on his every word, I wait for him to continue. After all, I know nothing about him. I don't want to utter the name Soudkovski under this roof. Spatter the walls with the identity of a killer.

"On arrival at the hospital," he finally continues, "Blanche had pains in her chest, she was struggling to breathe, felt suffocated. I took it to be anxiety. I was sure she was having an acute anxiety attack. And that's when I missed her heart. In fact, yes, she really was having an anxiety attack, because she'd just seen a newspaper article about the man who was pursuing her. But she was also suffering from a cardiac malformation, which must have worsened with time. I made her have an ECG, but I should also have requested a sonagram of her heart. On the ECG, nothing abnormal, her heartbeats were regular. I looked for a coronary and ruled out the risk of stroke, without thinking about an anomaly. If I'd had the sonagram done, the cardiologist would have seen the compression of the inferior vena cava."

He looks down, wipes or erases something invisible on the table. He seems deeply affected. It's me who breaks the silence:

"And you remained in contact with her?"

"With her and Colette. I'd visit them from time to time, at the shoe-repair shop, in the adjoining house. Stupidly, I'd listen to Blanche's heart, take her blood pressure, prescribe tranquillizers to Colette that were destined for Blanche. Imagine my shock when I heard that Colette had died in 2007. I immediately thought of Blanche. What would become of her? Who would take care of her? In Gueugnon, only one person was aware of her presence at Colette's: Louis Berthéol."

Aimé Chauvel was, too. But I don't bring that up. Aimé and Colette hadn't kept that secret all their lives for me to reveal it.

"I immediately phoned him. Louis didn't answer. Since Jacques Pieri had signed the death certificate, I called him. Jacques was obliged to admit the truth to me, since I already knew part of it. Colette's plan seemed totally insane to me. I asked Louis to take me to see her. When I saw the distressed state she was in, I didn't go any further. I thought she must have her reasons. Reasons that were none of my business. We all do the best we can."

"You saw her in Rue des Fredins?"

"Yes."

"How were they, together? Colette and Blanche, I mean."

"Very close. Like two adoring sisters. You know Colette lost a sister when she was young. Maybe Blanche replaced her a little."

"Colette's tragedy was that she never loved her younger sister."

"She loved Blanche, that was obvious. She took care of her. When she lost her, it was her end of the world. I honestly didn't think it would last a week, that assuming of an identity, thought someone would discover the truth. It lasted three years."

"Did she tell you why she was pretending to be dead?"

"No. She told me that the less I knew, the better."

I stand up, without thinking, and go to the tap for a glass of water. I can feel Antoine's eyes on my back. I wonder if men still find me pretty. Thirty-eight years old. Never in makeup. Never with styled hair. My mop, dreaded by Mom. How many liters of conditioner had she poured onto my head?

"Did you go see my aunt at the mortuary?"

"Yes. Everyone knows me over there. Folks in this town still call me 'doctor' when they come across me. I went to say goodbye to her."

"You phoned her often."

"I worried about her. Three years without making a sound, three years without existing. She would read, sew, garden. Louis would visit her. But still . . . Her solitude haunted me."

"What would you say to each other?"

"I'd fret about her health, her nutrition. I'd make sure she was eating her meals properly. Isolated people often eat poorly. And we'd talk about the news and football matches."

"Do you think she'd go out into Gueugnon?"

He takes a moment to answer:

"It's possible. Dead people don't get seen."

"Except that her appearance was more than recognizable."

"You're thinking of your aunt when she was alive. But after she died, maybe she wasn't noticed."

"Did she talk to you about me?"

"She worried. She wondered how you were doing after separating from your husband."

His phone rings. He answers immediately. I can hear that the caller is looking for a white Méhari with a blue top.

"I have two like that," Antoine says. "You can come by today, late afternoon, at the raffle house."

And he hangs up.

"Do people around here really call this place 'the raffle house'?"

"For the past fifty years . . . "

"It remained uninhabited for a long while, didn't it?"

"Yes, until I reappropriated its walls."

" . . . "

"On the day I asked to see Blanche's body, to examine it, Jacques Pieri came with me. She'd suffered a cardiac arrest. That was the day I realized that I'd missed her heart, and on top of that, I'd prescribed medication that had probably led to her death. If she'd had a family, they could have lodged a complaint against me. I admitted it to Colette, but she never held it against me."

"Is that the reason you quit medicine?"

"Among others. Out of cowardice, too, so I wouldn't have to wake up in the middle of the night because I'd gotten a diagnosis wrong. This place, it's great for my new occupation. If one of my cars breaks down, it isn't serious . . . And you? Are you working on a new movie?"

I wasn't expecting that question at all.

"No. Like you, I quit out of cowardice. And also, I lost my leading man. I, likewise, missed his heart."

He smiles an inscrutable smile.

"Would you like another coffee?"

"No thanks. It's strange, you didn't mention it to me . . . You're the only one not to have brought it up."

He looks at me, baffled.

"The physical resemblance between Blanche and Colette."

"It's true they looked alike, but that seems incidental to me."

"Might there be a cassette player in one of your Méharis?"

"Why d'you ask?"

"Because my aunt recorded herself on cassettes."

"And you want to listen to the cassettes in one of my cars?"

"I was just thinking about something."

"In my car, there's a cassette player."

"Which car?"

"Mine."

"Are you joking?"

"I rarely joke. I'm deadly dull."

I burst out laughing.

"That makes you laugh? I'm a sad old fogey. I don't own a single CD. Just vinyl. And I kept all my cassettes. Barbara, Brel, Brassens, Téléphone, Mylène Farmer, Mireille Mathieu, Richard Clayderman. All of them."

Another burst of laughter.

"You're the first person that I amuse so much. Usually, I'm pretty grim."

I don't believe him. There's nothing grim about him.

"And what type of car is it?"

"A Renault 5 Alpine Turbo."

" . . . "

"Double carburetor, 1983 chassis, two valves per cylinder."

He walks out of the room, leaving me stunned, and returns with a photograph, which he hands to me.

"On this photo, I'm inside my mother's stomach. You can keep it; I have a copy."

His parents are posing in front of the raffle house beside my father, who must be around fifteen, along with Colette, Blaise, and Father Aubry. There's snow all around them. They're all wearing coats. If you didn't know, you wouldn't notice Antoine's mother's baby bump.

"Our fathers, side by side . . . I believe that's the last time Jean came here."

"He looks sad."

"My parents told me he was studying in Lyon at the time."

"Yes, at the Levitans' . . . It was complicated."

"He looks like a child."

"I think Dad always looked like a child."

I turn over the photo. Handwritten on the back, it says: "The Septembres, a friend, Father Aubry, and us (expecting Antoine)—December 1964."

"I was born the following year."

"And me, seven years after you."

"My parents sold this house in 1993, and I bought it back in 2007."

"Why?"

"Because it's lucky."

"You're superstitious?"

"Not at all," he retorted, with a mischievous glint in his eye.

"I have to go. I've got a meeting with the police officer dealing with this whole affair."

"I'll see you at the funeral."

"Yes. When is it again?"

"November 15, according to the death notice," he tells me with a smile.

"What day will it be in four days' time?"

"Saturday. Apparently, it's the happiest day of the week."

"You think there are days that are happier than others?"

"Depends who one's with."

"See you on Saturday, then."

"See you Saturday."

10

November 11, 2010

I return to my room at the Monge. Paul is supposed to be coming to see me with news of Soudkovski. *Where are you, you old murderer? Where are you hiding?* Adèle must be at a patient's home. What's she up to there? Is she reassuring the patient? I wonder how she felt after telling me everything.

Since I'm just killing time in my room, incapable of writing, or returning to, the screenplay on my mother's story, I open the cassette suitcase and randomly slip one into the recorder. I haven't heard Colette's voice for several days now. We should all record ourselves for someone. To be a little bit eternal. I suppose making movies is the same thing; it's eternalizing. And me, I've stopped eternalizing.

Dad and Mom did it thanks to their musical recordings. Why is this family obsessed with holding back time? I've often been asked why I didn't choose to be a musician, like my parents. I've always answered, "to not do the same as them." I grew up beside two adults who lived between suitcases. I spent all my school vacations at Colette's. No, or few, close times for just the three of us. A father bent over his piano all blessed day long, a slender mother clinging to her bow, violin propped on shoulder. Parents that were beautiful but absent. I must have been about ten when I asked them:

"Why did you make me? Music is much more important to you than me."

Paralyzed by my question, they exchanged the looks of wild animals caught in the headlights of a car. Then Mom burst into tears and took me in her arms, whispering sorry to me several times. And Dad added:

"Every single time I play, it's for you. You're part of me, my dear daughter, and I love you. Far more than this instrument."

And they never signed me up for piano or violin lessons. As if I, the extension of them, wouldn't make any music. As if it were ruled out. Or decreed. That I was destined for something else. I took classes in ballet and drawing. Which today seems totally insane. They gave me this cassette recorder because they knew I liked popular music. Then, later, Colette gave me my camcorder, because very early on, I'd told her that I'd be reporting from all over the world.

Dad didn't get time to find out that I'd become a movie director. When Mom and Colette saw my first short, "*Au piano*," they seemed blown away. Colette laughed all through the screening. Like a little girl seeing a Walt Disney film for the first time. My mom whispered in my ear that she was proud of me, that I was extremely "*doutée.*" She made that slip of the tongue. Instead of saying "*douée*"—talented—she'd said "*doutée*"—doubted. She'd always whisper important things into my ear. She never spoke loudly. Except when Dad died.

COLETTE

It happened two years before you were born, Agnès. A stray bullet. She didn't have time to suffer. She died on the spot. What a strange expression. It's to reassure those left behind, the living. To say there was no suffering. No time even to catch your breath. A year after Mokhtar passed away, my little sister followed. Danièle was twelve years old. After that, my life stopped. I mean, a part of my life. The mother started to look at me for the first time, but not out of regret or remorse for not having loved me. No. She began to look at me like a thief. Like the one who should have died. The one who should have been there instead of her daughter, her other daughter, her true daughter, the adored one. My God! Not that one! The other one! You've got it wrong. An accident.

It was around then that the marchioness left the marquess. Abandoned Danièle's killer. And, unbelievably, the mother remained in his service, carried on preparing meals and polishing the parquet of the man who had killed Danièle "by accident." That's what she kept repeating: "It was an accident. An unfortunate accident. The poor man wasn't to blame." She'd say "the poor man," and I'd keep quiet. I'd pinch the inside of my arm so as not to retort that "the poor man" had been going around with a shotgun in his hand since forever. And what's worse, even after that fateful day, he didn't stop hunting. And it was the mother who continued to clean his boots and cook the game for him and his friends.

Danièle joined the father in the family tomb that was gifted by the Sénéchals, a fine tomb of black marble with a splendid angel to represent Danièle. They also paid for the funeral. Jean and Blaise held my hands while Father Aubry delivered his funerary homily. The mother could barely stand and never stopped crying. A veritable fountain. I didn't look at her; I heard her sobbing. It was the Sénéchals who supported her. The world upside down.

Earth was thrown onto the coffin. And after the funeral, the marchioness told us that she was going away, leaving Gueugnon, and that she wanted to give the Steinway to Jean. A temporary home needed to be found for it; she'd spoken to the director of the factory and the mayor about it. Until Jean had completed his studies, the piano would be placed in Gueugnon's community center.

I returned to the scene of the accident. "Snow White's glade." That's what Blaise and I called it. We'd go there to gaze at the clouds, and sometimes we'd come across a doe. That's where my sister's little body fell. Three hundred meters from where Sénéchal had aimed at, then attempted to shoot, a roebuck. The bullet grazed the creature's ear, but continued on its trajectory. The marquess shot at it again and, this time, didn't miss. A bullet between the eyes. It was after the hunt that the marquess and two of his companions noticed the absence of the child.

She'd sneaked off to have a pee, slipping into the forest, which she knew like the back of her hand. She'd crouched down, and then that was it. She'd received that first bullet to the back of her head. She rose up to the kingdom of Heaven, as Father Aubry claimed. Her little body was discovered at around 7 P.M. *It was one of the dogs that found it. The marchioness undertook to break the news to the mother. I always thought that Georgette was in love with the marquess, and that that was what kept her going after Danièle's death. Knowing that she'd be living by his side, that she'd see him every day, breathe his presence within the walls of the building she looked after. With which she was associated, particularly after Eugénie de Sénéchal's departure. And that the marquess, being penitent, would speak to her even more kindly. I don't think I'm wrong. She became the mistress of the château, her, the peasant destined to be wed to a man of low station. A tragic fate made her go up in status. After the marchioness left, Sénéchal hired a maid-of-all-work to relieve the mother. Relieve her of what? Of the grief he had caused?*

In this Septembre family, there were always two clans: the father, the mother, and Danièle on one side; Jean and me on the other. That's why we'll never rest together. Even after life. I can't bear the thought of being back with the mother anywhere at all. And I'm so sorry about my little sister. To her, I was how Georgette was to me: unfeeling. And I never got over it. I never wanted to marry or have a child because of that. Because of me. Of my lack of feeling somewhere I can't control. How can I have loved you so much, Ana and you? Jean and Hannah? Mokhtar and Blanche? Blaise, Aimé, and Louis? And remained ice-cold toward my sister? Can you imagine if I'd had a child and hadn't loved it? No. That's too much grief, too much misery.

One day, Dad took me to the little cemetery where Danièle, Robin, and Georgette are buried. I didn't understand what he was doing in front of the grave of these unknown people with our name. I remember the angel on the black tombstone that Colette talks about. I was at the age when nothing really interested me. I dragged my boredom between the graves, picked up overturned pots of flowers. It was at that time that I was forever sulking and rolling my eyes as soon as my parents spoke to me. Dad had told me that, as a child, he had lost a little sister. I'd asked him where exactly he had lost her, and he'd explained to me that "lost" meant "died." That it was a long time ago and he hadn't known her well. I'd asked him if it had made him sad anyway, and he'd replied: "Of course, a little girl passing away, that's always sad."

Why "passing away"? Why was he suddenly telling me this? Like with Hannah's family. That drama Mom had come from, the miraculous survivor, it was like a cloud darkening the room when we dared to mention it. Was that the reason Mom fled from everyday life?

I encountered "the mother," my paternal grandmother, a few times in the hospice of sorts that she lived in and I hated going to. The place scared me; it smelled bad. Her fat legs were bandaged, and she never smiled, looked at us sternly. "Kiss your grandmother," my parents kept telling me. And I'd hold my breath; I found her prickly. I've forgotten her death. How is that possible? I have no memory of it whatsoever.

On the other hand, I do remember Dad telling me, as a teen, that Colette had been hospitalized due to grief. The grief of having lost her mother. I didn't go stay with her for the February break. They sent me to ski school, where I was miserable as hell. It was then that I discovered how much I hated winter sports, and realized how great Gueugnon really was—I could do as I liked, and best of all, there was Hervé, Adèle, and Ilyas. At Easter, I was back with Colette. I didn't ask her a single question about her grief. I observed her on the sly. Still as badly dressed as ever, she'd neither lost nor gained any weight, didn't cry. She smiled at me and worked away as usual. I thought that Dad had lied to me, that he'd come up with an excuse to send me skiing.

Paul knocks on my door. He looks annoyed.

"Are you okay?"

He looks at me strangely. Does he know that I know about his night with Adèle?

"Something's not right, Agnès."

I stare at him, unable to respond that nothing had been "right" since we'd discovered that Colette didn't die in 2007.

"I think there's been a lab error."

"What lab?"

"The one analyzing the fingerprints on your aunt's landline phone . . ."

" . . . "

"There are your prints, those of Madame Septembre, and those of Soudkovski."

"And?"

"The analysis needs to be done again."

"Why?"

"There's been a screw-up somewhere."

11

November 15, 2010

I never called you Tata. It wouldn't have entered our minds, neither yours nor mine. I believe that when someone dies, one of their joys should always be honored at their funeral. Ana, you were one of Colette's joys. Your birth represented a new world for her, a world of light. It was a small life, but huge. After all her dead, the ghosts that surrounded her, life, your life, reasserted itself. She looked at you shyly; you enchanted her. Then you got older, and you made her laugh. You called her Coco. No one had ever called her that except her brother Jean, when little. She gave you slightly old-fashioned presents, because Colette never quite understood the rules of the game, apart from those of football. China dolls covered in lace, outdated clothes you never wore, scents and makeup she found at the Gueugnon market, colors that didn't suit you. She built up collections of encyclopedias for you, including the one on birds of the world, which took up a lot of space in your room and got very dusty because you rarely opened them, but which you treasured. You loved seeing your great-aunt, staying in her shoe-repair shop for hours to watch her work. And above all, above all, I'm sure that it was for her, and no one else, that you took up the piano. I'll never forget the look in her eyes when you let go of her hand to go sit at the Steinway, in the community center, and play the opening bars of the *Toccata*. You were five-and-a-half. You didn't play for us; you played for Colette. 'Listen, Coco!' Her joy when she discovered that you were already talented. So, yes, Ana, you were one of Colette's great joys, one of her sparkling lights.

"Now, I must talk about her. About her alone. I never understood a thing about football, but for my aunt, it held no secrets. She would say: 'You see football superstars all over the place. For me, superstars don't exist. It's just a superlative. In the entire history of football, I can name ten super-players, if that. When you look at the past of the players they talk about on TV, most often, they've spent their entire careers in just one place. If they'd gone off somewhere else, would they have enjoyed the same careers? Would they have been as impressive? Not necessarily. Many shone at one club and got completely lost at another. I could give you plenty of examples.' That's what Colette would say, but sadly, I never asked her for any examples. I'd leave her to soliloquize in her kitchen.

"Once, just once, I asked her, as if it were a reproach: 'But what is it you like so much about football?' She replied: 'Across the world, any kid can play it. It's a sport of the people, and I love that. I love that, Agnès.'

"It's November 15, 2010, and according to her last wishes, her ashes will be placed beside my parents, Hannah and Jean.

"We'll now listen to a recording of Jean Septembre playing Liszt's *Piano Concerto No. 1 in E flat major*, with the Orchestre Philharmonique de Paris. It was one of her favorite recordings. We'll let her return to her loved ones surrounded by music. And I'd ask Gueugnon supporters, and all of us, to applaud her, remembering the goals the *Forgerons* scored—and will score—that so thrilled her."

I slip my speech into my handbag.

"That's what I'm going to read. If I ad-lib, I'll fall apart. Having it written down is like clinging to a handrail. I usually loathe people who unfold a piece of paper; it's my worst fear, even. It removes all spontaneity, but right now, I no longer have the strength to go for it. D'you understand?"

". . ."

"On top of that, there'll be Pierre."

". . ."

"Without you, I don't think I'd be going."

". . ."

"You're not saying anything?"

"You'd have gone for your daughter. And for Colette."

"That's true. But Louis could've done it perfectly well instead of me."

"Of course he couldn't. Louis isn't you."

"Have you ever been married?"

"No, but I have a twenty-year-old son."

"I didn't see any photos at your place."

"They're in my bedroom. Don't feel like putting my son's smile on display in my sitting room. Particularly since most people who come into my house are there to buy or sell a car."

Antoine has smartened up for the funeral. He looks elegant and sober. He even has clean fingernails. I don't know how, but he's tidied up his hair. Makes me think of that Dalida song: "I tidied up my hair. Put a bit more black on my eyes . . . That made him laugh." I haven't put any black on my eyes. Because I know I'm going to cry. Because I feel like dying. Because I'm 78 kilometers from Lyon, it was written on a road sign, "Lyon 80," about two minutes ago, and since his Renault 5 Alpine Turbo goes at 150km/h, and I'm rubbish at math, we're probably 78km from the cemetery. I'm thinking about any old thing to avoid, at all costs, thinking about Pierre, who will be there.

The urn containing Colette's ashes is on the back seat, to the right; Antoine secured it with the safety belt, wrapping it around several times to protect it. So, her hearse will be a Renault 5 Alpine.

Antoine Été is my fellow traveler for today because I asked him to drive "us" there. Ilyas arrived at the station early this morning because he was in Flumet, at Lina's. Adèle, Hervé, Nathalie, and others I don't know are coming on a shuttle service. Paul left with Louis. He's had the Lyon cemetery, and the Gueugnon one, closely watched, in case Soudkovski were to make an appearance. I thought of Antoine Été because he's called Antoine Été, and you won't find a lovelier name. Someone I don't know and who lives in the raffle house. How great are people who don't know us, whom we haven't yet disappointed, or driven mad, or betrayed, and who drive a sensible car thinking about something else. Actually, I wonder what he's thinking about. I don't wait long to find out:

"When was the last time you saw your ex-husband?"

"In 2007, in Los Angeles."

12

Music has always been predominant in the story that connected me to the cinema and to life. For a long time, I was "the musicians' daughter." My favorite film is *Amadeus*, directed by Milos Forman. I was twelve when it was released. I saw it with my aunt, at the Danton, in Gueugnon. That's the only time we went there together. Feels weird that the only movie I saw with her should be my favorite one. No other movie since has managed to usurp it. In my heart, it's the absolute masterpiece. The love of my life.

I have no other image of my aunt at the Danton except for that day, when the shop must've been closed, making it a Sunday afternoon. Only the stands at the stadium seemed to lure her beyond the town center. At the time, *La Boum—The Party*—was the only movie for me, so the first time I saw *Amadeus*, I just thought it quite good and well-acted. Colette emerged from it drained, vacant. She was deeply moved. She just murmured: "Ending up in a pauper's grave so young, how sad is that." And then, by the following night, the movie had seeped into me; I saw it again in my mind. I projected it onto the ceiling of my bedroom, Mozart, his laughter, his impertinence, his pain, his genius, the *Requiem*, the lighting, the costumes, the scenery, the madness, the priest who hears Salieri's revelations, powerlessly. And the music, THAT music. And the sequence shot at the end inside the asylum . . .

I returned to the Danton the next day, to see it again with Ilyas, Adèle, and Hervé, who fell asleep. Ilyas was in his Michael Jackson phase, so Mozart, not really his thing, and he told me the film had freaked him out. I think Adèle liked it. And me, I remained glued to my seat. In fact, a part of me has remained on that seat in the Danton. Since then, I don't know how many times I've rewatched the movie, but I know the shots and dialogues off by heart. I've rediscovered it several times a year, for the past twenty-six years, with the same thrill, the same excitement, the same enthrallment. Pierre gave me the extended version two months before leaving me. It allowed me to discover what Milos Forman had cut during editing, just before the film's release—my greatest lesson in moviemaking.

Toujours la même chanson—always the same song, always the same old story—is the title of my last feature film. The last by an unhappy famous director, cheated on by her actor husband, a pitiful cliché. Predictable. The last movie. The end of a love story. And yet it's my most assured movie about love. And the one people most talk to me about. Maybe because it's the last one. "It was your biggest box-office success worldwide, Agnès!" my dear producers and friends, Samuel and Victor, keep telling me. It's a love story, and maybe that's why it's been such a global hit. Because the public wants to see love stories in cinemas, theaters, literature, museums. I wrote it in 2005, directed it in early 2006, and it was released in September that same year. The only one of my films shot entirely in a studio and in the States. And in which the plot unfolds entirely in New York, from 1966 to 2006.

Of course, I wrote it for Pierre. A splendid French-American hero who, every time he hears this one song, sees his life turned upside down. I hired a child and a teenager who resembled him to play the part. And created a suit tailor-made for him. We used real and digital "makeup" so he looked younger for when he was twenty in the movie.

His character, Zachary, is seven when he hears the song on the radio for the first time. It's 1966, and his mother is listening to a musical program in the kitchen while her son celebrates his birthday in the room next door with his friends. That very evening, she vanishes. But her coat, handbag, and other belongings are in the hall. Has she disappeared? Run away? Been abducted? No one knows. They search for her high and low, but she's vanished into thin air.

At around twelve years old, Zachary hears the song again in a fast-food joint, but pays no attention to it. He only has eyes for Michelle, who is five years older than him, but it's instantaneous. An extraordinary case of love at first sight. He would only see her again eight years later, when he'd hear the song for the third time, at a party. This time, the tune and the lyrics call out to him, trouble him. The song is like a memory and a premonition. And at that very moment, he recognizes Michelle, who really sticks out, dressed like Audrey Hepburn in *Breakfast at Tiffany's*. When Zachary gets up the courage to ask her why she's dressed like that, she tells him that it's in case she comes across her ex. To make sure he has regrets. Zachary is terribly disappointed.

"You love him that much?"

"Absolutely not. But I like to provoke regret in others."

I still don't know how I managed to convince Jennifer Coolidge to take on the role of Michelle as an adult. That kind of close encounter of the third kind is what I miss today. To the extent of dreaming about it at night. Seeing an actress transform each gesture and each word into a masterpiece. So naturally.

We see Zachary get older. He and Michelle separate, get back together when he hears his song. The penultimate time he hears it is the day of his wedding. Among the guests is Michelle, who smiles sadly at him, alongside her husband. The last time he hears it, he's in a movie theater. He rushes out of the auditorium. Finds himself on a sidewalk, distraught. A woman bumps into him. She apologizes. He doesn't respond. She looks like his mother, who had disappeared forty years previously. Dream or reality?

The song is called "That's All Right (Mama)." Like some magic spell. As if the sky, or life, or some unknown force were addressing him, and him alone. No matter who's singing it: Arthur Crudup, who wrote it, Elvis Presley, The Beatles, Rod Stewart, Johnny Hallyday, Paul McCartney, Tyler Hilton, or an unknown female singer.

Well, that's all right, mama
That's all right for you
That's all right, mama, just anyway you do.

And then *she* arrived for the shoot. My continuity girl let me know that Audrey Tudor was there. I joined her in the makeup trailer; she smelled of jasmine. She smiled at me, so sweet. Everyone found her sweet. She had, still has, something of Audrey Hepburn about her, at Hepburn's splendid best. I know no other version of Audrey Hepburn. She'd worked on her part. A lot. She was ready.

We selected her outfit together. A down-market black sheath dress. She was playing a bar singer who earns her living from one week to the next. I'd given her different interpretations of the song, by Elvis, Arthur Crudup, and Rod Stewart, that I really love. I'd said to her: "Do a mix, but choose the one you like best."

On set, she started to sing. A bewitching voice, deep and jazzy, that can soar up to the highest notes with ease. She was magnetic. I thought to myself, we're going to shoot a fantastic scene with this girl. We set up our two cameras.

In that scene, Zachary was supposed to be forty-five, around Pierre's actual age, so no need for makeup. The version of him at that age: irresistible. He had to enter the club a bit tipsy, order a drink at the bar, pay no attention to the singer, until she sang "That's All Right."

Close-up on Zachary. As soon as he hears the first few notes, he turns to the young woman, shocked, then angry. He goes up to her. "Who asked you to sing that? Do we know each other? Is this a sick joke?" In the background, the soundtrack keeps playing. The singer is terrified. Ashamed, he apologizes to her and leaves. Cut.

We stopped for lunch. I kept to myself, stretched out on the club set, thinking about how I was going to shoot the kiss between Zachary and the singer. When shooting resumed, I didn't see whether Pierre and Audrey had come back together. Later, I wondered what they'd talked about during that lunch break. They were with the others, not alone together.

Zachary returns to the club the following day, closely shaven this time and holding a bouquet. He waits for her to leave the stage to give her the roses and apologize again. The singer recognizes him and thanks him, but is wary of him. "Since I was young, every time I hear that song, my life is . . . That's why I reacted . . . like an asshole," he promptly tells her. She stares at him.

"'That's All Right'?"

"Yes," he admits, like a child.

"Thanks for the flowers."

She disappears around the back, bouquet in hand, then reappears and sings "That's All Right," watched by a mesmerized Zachary. At the end, he claps. She, standing in front of the mic, doesn't move. Zachary continues clapping as he approaches. He puts his arms around her and kisses her. A real Hollywood kiss. Then he leaves the club.

He'll never see her again in the movie, but in real life, he will.

13

November 15, 2010

"I loved your last movie," Antoine Été tells me, staring at the road ahead.

We're stationary in the Fourvière tunnel, around ten kilometers from La Guillotière Cemetery. Stuck in a traffic jam. The urn still attached with the safety belt, like a good child.

"Me, not so much."

"Why's that?"

"Because after the shoot, I lost my footing and my husband. And then I moved. But mainly, I regret."

". . ."

"My daughter suffered, seeing me in such a pitiful state . . . "

"You regret what?"

"Having been unhappy."

"But that's not your fault. We can't decide to be happy or unhappy."

"Yes, we can. Why did I cling to Pierre? To the hope of Pierre? It hurt Ana too much. She's sensitive. When she'd get back home after a weekend with him, she must've sensed that it was her father I was waiting for behind the door, not her . . . She must've felt powerless confronted with my sadness. And I was a coward. I could have carried on making movies, but I was scared of messing up. When I'd never messed up. My movies all did well. There'll always be one flop, well, not necessarily a flop, but a movie that's a bit shaky, or less what the public expects, that's just par for the course; but me, I preferred to hide behind my broken heart rather than face up to what came next."

"Broken hearts are a convenient excuse sometimes."

"Are you still on good terms with the mother of your son?"

"More or less. After the ceremony, I'll drop in on them. My son lives in Lyon, at his mother's. And you? Still heading for Paris later?"

"Yes, with Ana and Cornélia."

"Cornélia?"

"The lady that looks after me."

"Ah, you have a nanny?"

He manages to make me smile.

"You could put it like that . . . "

"Is it okay to arrive late at a funeral? Considering that we have Colette with us . . . "

I pull a cassette of Coldplay out of the player and slip in the one I've had in my pocket since we left the Monge. Antoine watches me without saying a thing.

The sound of rain falling on the glass roof of the shoe-repair shop. Colette probably recorded the thunder and downpour on a summer day. Antoine and I remain silent, listening religiously to what this storm is telling us. Then Colette's voice rings out in the car.

COLETTE

It was raining cats and dogs when we arrived at the Stade de France. My ticket was so sodden, I couldn't get it validated at the gate. It was unreadable. A supporter helped me, Bernadette she's called. A good person . . . So kind. We've done some trips, the two of us. Football is what gave us a chance to get out of Gueugnon. Once we were inside, I sat down, gazed at the pitch, the crowd; it was huge. There were journalists with mics everywhere.

And I waited. Our players walked out. And we, in the Forgerons stands, we cheered them.

You know what happened next, Agnès. You saw it on TV. I can't explain the nerves, the joy, the bond between players and supporters, each in their place, the perfect coach, the yearning. The ball went into the net twice. By the time it had sunk in that we'd scored two goals, the referee blew the final whistle. We made history. We'll forever be the second-division club that won the League Cup in 2000. When I was a little lass and people would talk to me about the year 2000, I'd imagine flying saucers, doors that would open and speak on their own, lights all over the place, weird things in the sky and on our plates . . . but never that we'd win that cup at the Stade de France against Paris-Saint Germain!

She starts to laugh. Antoine stares at me, moved by her voice. It's as if she were close to us, hidden in the urn as if in a magic lamp.

COLETTE
Everyone lingered in the stadium for a long time before leaving. Even me, I sang as if I'd drunk some wine! Me, your aunt, I sang the chants of the ultras!

She starts to sing, softly:
If there's only you left,
And you still have faith,
Never forget to sing
For your colors,
For your pride,
Gueugnonnais allez, allez, allez!
If you're proud of your colors
Let's sing this chant together,
Gueugnonnais, la, la, la!

As she chuckles again, with her breathy, restrained little laugh, Antoine and I are overcome with emotion.

COLETTE
And then I saw her. She was waiting for me outside the stadium. There were thousands of us, how did she find me? In whom, in what should we believe? In the survival instinct? In God? In chance? I've never believed in chance; it doesn't exist. But there she was. She'd seen a program on TV in which the goalkeeper of PSG had said, a week before the match, that Gueugnon would be hammered by his team. Gueugnon. Hearing that name was like a blow to the stomach. They broadcast the date and location. She thought that I was bound to be there, if I was alive. She didn't think that it would have been easier to catch a train and come directly to my place for refuge, or to phone me. I'm in the

directory. No. When she heard the name of the town, she saw it as a sign. An answer. Life had put years between us, but there she was, wrapped in a red coat, a dog in her arms, a garbage bag in one hand, in the middle of the crowd jostling to leave the stadium. I recognized her immediately. But I was in a weird state, as if I'd drunk some wine, and I thought it was a mirage. I hadn't seen Blanche for such a long time. She was fifty-four, her, the young girl, my childhood friend. The last time I'd seen her, she was twenty-six. And yet it really was her, and it was me she was waiting for. I know that others have often gotten the two of us confused, but for me, it wasn't my reflection that I was seeing, no—it was Blanche.

Silence.

COLETTE

It's not my style to take people into my arms. Not my style at all. And yet, that evening, I hugged her so tight. She was as slight as me. A little thing. She was trembling and said to me: "I had to see you before disappearing forever."

"So they saw each other again at twenty-six."

"We're here, Agnès."

I look up, and facing me is the gate to the cemetery.

14

October 31, 2010

His mistress hadn't suffered. Didn't know what had hit her. To avoid bloodshed, he'd dealt her a mortal blow to the back of the head, shortly after the stew. He'd waited until she'd cleared up in the kitchen, and the sideboard and sink were wiped clean. A spotless interior is never suspicious. Even once Luminol is applied. One well-aimed strike with the baseball bat that Mathilde kept as a souvenir of her trip to America as a teenager. She'd become infatuated with a player, a certain Tim Hathaway, who'd given her the bat signed with a black felt-tip pen. When this memory came back to her, she'd have tears in her eyes. But the bat had still ended up on a shelf in the basement, beside the pots of jam.

He'd dragged the body down to the freezer in that basement. Mathilde was heavy. She'd picked a chest freezer at Darty, a top-opening one. Handy. He'd hoisted her up and dumped her on top of the boxes of ice-cream bars and containers of frozen food, then closed the lid. *Blanche was close by, within reach.*

He'd get back to Valence in two days' time to empty the house, before anyone noticed Mathilde's disappearance. What made things easier with her was that she had no children. Married once, long divorced.

He'd arrived in Gueugnon in the late afternoon. It was almost dark. He'd parked in front of cemetery gate. It was locked. He'd jumped over it. Still quite agile after the circus, an athlete's physique plus those daily exercises. He'd walked up and down the paths for several hours, flashlight in hand, but its light was fading because the batteries were dying. Just as he was thinking he'd have to come back the next day, he'd spotted it: Colette Septembre's grave.

And he'd immediately understood. It had to be Blanche who was lying under it. The article he'd read was telling the truth. Suddenly, every blade tattooed on his skin had plunged into his flesh. He'd had to sit down on the ground.

She was dead. Otherwise, who would've placed that pair of shoes instead of a plaque on the tombstone? They were his daughter's. The ones she always wore around the time she'd vanished. Or then it was a trap to deceive him. But even he didn't believe that.

He would come back the following day to dig up the body. He had to touch her one last time. Even dead, even decomposed, he had to kill her with his own hands. He'd vowed he would, ever since she'd squealed to the cops about him. He got back in the Twingo, stopped on Place de l'Église for a takeaway pizza. He ate it in the car near a derelict warehouse and then conked out, totally drained. She was dead.

The following morning, in a hypermarket, he'd bought a manual hoist to remove the tombstone, and some snacks. Then he'd returned to the cemetery. He knew he couldn't do a thing in broad daylight, but he wanted to see those shoes again. And that's when he was stopped in his tracks: the cemetery was crawling with people. *Fucking All Saints' Day.* And two cops were posted at the gates. Had someone clocked him last night? He made a quick escape, cursing all the way, and parked on Place de l'Église. He needed to think. Just his luck, turning up on All Saints weekend! He looked out. An urge to hit someone. Anyone, randomly, to let off steam. Old age hadn't subdued his impulses in the slightest.

People had come out of the church, after Mass, and he'd looked at them without seeing them. Thinking about what he had to do. And that's when she appeared, a few meters away. She was heading into the café opposite the church, with some others. But he'd looked only at her. In her black coat, with her hair messily tied back. Her face, her expression. She'd flapped something away in front of her eyes, some dust, or maybe an idea.

An unknown feeling. Warmth and light had penetrated him like arrows shot at point-blank range. An internal explosion like he'd never experienced before.

Soudkovski knew he had a heart of stone. He'd never loved anyone. Starting with himself. Devoid of empathy, he lived in the shadows, in the darkness of his soul. He had no memory of crying since the death of his mother. What's the point of crying when your mother's not there to wipe away your tears? No memory of ever having roared with laughter. Happiness was unfamiliar to him, joy a mystery that had never crossed his path. He'd experienced pleasure, occasionally, when ejaculating. The previous day, with the near certainty of his daughter's death, he'd felt only bitterness, and regret at not having snatched her from life himself. Because she'd left him, abandoned him, thrown him to the wolves. And all just to die young. He'd disowned her, viscerally, and built up a boundless hatred toward her.

But when he'd caught sight of that woman on the sidewalk opposite, something unknown had seized him, caused a chink in his armor. Everything had risen to the surface, like a sewer backing up.

Clutching the wheel, he'd waited for her to reappear. Same feeling when she came out of the café. As if his skin was melting. Wax in contact with a flame. She'd gotten into an old car, deep in thought. He'd followed her for five minutes, keeping his distance. She'd parked on a residential street. Half an hour later, with a traveling bag over her shoulder, she'd stood waiting on the sidewalk, and then, pulling up alongside her, a guy had come to pick her up. She'd suddenly turned and gone back inside. He'd thought, *she's not leaving anymore.* But she'd come back out, carrying an old suitcase.

He'd decided to wait for darkness. He'd cogitated, ruminated, the way others read, watch TV, go for a stroll, listen to music when they have some spare time. Who was this woman? What was her name? He'd understood why she had that effect on him, but not how he could feel "that." Soudkovski didn't wear armor; he *was* armor. And yet he felt like crying as he watched her disappear at the end of the street. Inconceivable. Particularly for a man like him. He'd soon have the answer.

At 8 P.M., not a soul remained on that street. Most of the shutters were closed. He'd slipped into the garden. Tossed a few small stones at the windows to be sure there was no one inside to react. He'd been ready to force the lock, but the woman hadn't bolted the front door. He entered the house, flashlight in hand. Went into every room. No mail addressed to the owners. He'd breathed in the smell of the clothes in the wardrobe of the only bedroom. Apart from a green-and-black coat, just old folks' garb.

He'd been surprised to discover an inflatable mattress in the middle of the sitting room, blankets thrown over it. A few things scattered on the floor. Two pairs of trousers, a sweater. A screenplay by Agnès Septembre, *Hannah Ruben*, annotated. She'd crossed out Dugain. Why? Agnès Dugain.

The article by Nathalie Grandjean mentioned that woman, Colette Septembre's niece. The pianist's daughter, who made movies. It was her.

He must be in Colette Septembre's hideout. He put the pieces back together in his mind. Hence that *France Football* mag and those notebooks full of cuttings. So he'd gone into all the rooms again, searching meticulously, but not a trace of Blanche. That's when he'd come across a box of photos. The movie woman at every age.

He'd never set foot in a movie theater. Why on earth would he sit in front of a screen to watch some character's made-up life? Cinema was the main rival of the circus. Whereas movie theaters were expanding, circuses were shrinking, big tops diminishing, disappearing. They even came up with circuses without animals because, supposedly, the animals were miserable. Any old nonsense. Animals existed to serve men.

Why had she moved in here? At her aunt's? What did she know about Blanche? Where had she gone? Why hadn't she locked the door? Was someone due to turn up? He'd knelt down on the mattress and sniffed the pillowcase. And that feeling had returned, even more violently, more intense. A familiar perfume, the smell of an exhumed memory. How was that possible? His emotions had been consumed by the flames of his four-year-old self.

He stayed in the house for a long time, studying the photos, inspecting the drawers, the wardrobe, the collections, the cupboards, the garbage can, which contained an empty whiskey bottle. Did Agnès have a man in her life? He had to see her again. Hear the sound of her voice. He'd search for her on the net later. If she made movies, he'd find pictures of her. Before leaving, he'd phoned himself to log the number of the landline. Then he'd tied a scarf belonging to Agnès around his neck. Never, in all his life, had he done such a thing. An impulsive act that had instantly unsettled him. He couldn't bring himself to leave the box of photos behind.

He drove off, immediately leaving town to return to Valence. He'd come back in a few days' time to dig up Blanche's body, and to figure out who this Agnès Dugain really was, and where she came from. Once he'd cleared out Mathilde's house, before her body was found in the freezer.

15

November 15, 2010

Antoine Été parks just beyond the cemetery gate. I retrieve the cassette and slip it into my pocket. It's over. In an hour, Colette will be back with my parents, and life will get back to normal. All I have left now is this urn, and soon I'll have nothing but memories and her voice. She'll be dead forever.

He's the first person I see when I look up. I recognize him from behind, from a distance. I've filmed, observed, devoured, loved him so much. Why has he arrived before me? He's stepped aside to talk on the phone. A few meters away, Cornélia and Ana are holding hands outside the café, *Les Passantes*. I just want to rush over to my daughter and hug her, but first, I plant a kiss on Antoine's cheek.

"I'll never forget what you've just done for me, or your Renault 5 Alpine."

His collar smells of cologne.

"And you," he replies, laconically, "don't forget that your things are in my trunk."

My bag of clothes and the suitcase of cassettes I want to take back to Paris. My hands are shaking so much, I can't untie the safety belt from around the urn. Antoine notices and moves me aside to do it for me, whispering in my ear: "It's going to be fine, you're a queen, don't forget that, either." I haven't had such comforting words whispered to me since time began.

A man in a dark suit, friendly, introducing himself as the funeral director, has come to take the urn from me. He reminds me that we've exchanged a few words over the phone. He's the master of ceremonies. From then on, I experience all that takes place as if I'm outside my body. Ana, tanned, smiling, hugs me. I breathe in her neck to give myself strength.

"Mom, who's that guy?"

"Which guy?"

"Him, with his weird car! You just arrived with him. It's obvious you're into each other."

"Not at all, he's an acquaintance from Gueugnon. The raffle house, I'll tell you about it."

"I know about the raffle house, Mom, it's the one that paid for Grandfather's studies, but what's that got to do with it?"

She looks at me strangely, with an intrigued and mischievous smile. Cornélia, true to form, after kissing me, goes further:

"Met someone?"

"As I said, he's just an acquaintance . . . and . . . "

Pierre walks up to us, hands deep in the pockets of a navy coat. Same color as the one he wore the day he waited for me outside the Maison de la Presse in Lyon. The day he'd asked me my age. He's even more tanned than our daughter and plants a kiss on my forehead. Didn't Judas kiss Jesus that way to single him out to the Romans? I notice a line between his eyebrows, a mark that didn't exist *in my time*. He's changed his cologne. Before, he wore Eau d'Hadrien. I loved that fragrance. I'd given it to him. His eyes pierce me. I still love him. And hate him because I'm still crazy about him. Because I realize that here, now, in front of this cemetery, if he said to me, "Shall we head off?," I'd follow him without a second thought.

My friends arrive, and I feel less vulnerable. Ilyas, Adèle, Hervé, Nathalie, Dr. Pieri, Louis, and Paul, who seems to be on high alert. There must be plain-clothed lookouts dotted around. Antoine joins them. My personal bodyguard.

Three minibuses from Gueugnon park, and supporters file out, and players, club members, former customers. I recognize some of them. Several generations side by side. Aimé Chauvel is among them, deathly pale. My aunt's secret love gives me a hug. "She'd gotten us used to her death, but it's still a sad day."

Are these the same people who were there in 2007, when Colette died for the first time? In a flash, everyone's at the counter of the bar to order coffees. It's kisses all around, which would please Colette: a pre-match atmosphere, when serious fans meet up, talk rankings, remember the good old days, when the team was in the first division and "their" Colette could predict the number of goals. Where did she hide her crystal ball? And that's how I learn that she'd won at the football pools several times and donated money to the animal refuge in Gueugnon.

We're around a hundred, walking up the path toward my parents' grave. The funeral director leads the way, holding the urn. In front of the tomb, a sound system has been set up, along with a mic. The FCG has had a football carved out of black and white marble. Louis, a plaque with the inscription, "To my friend." Two more plaques, from people I can't identify. A white heart that I guess must be Aimé's. And finally, ours, "To our aunt and great-aunt, forever in our hearts." I squeeze Ana's hand a bit tighter. The speech I've prepared is going to be hard to get out. If Pierre wasn't here, it would be different. I realize yet again how painful it is to be alone. To no longer have "*une nuit sur son épaule*"—a night resting on his shoulder—as Véronique Sanson sings.

The master of ceremonies starts to speak:

"We are gathered here today to say a final farewell to Colette Septembre Bayram. She will rest close to her brother, Jean Septembre, and her sister-in-law, Hannah Ruben. Her niece and great-niece will pay a final homage to her. And to accompany his sister Colette with music, we will listen to the late Jean Septembre playing a piano concerto by Franz Liszt."

I didn't know that Ana would be saying something. She lets go of my hand and walks over to the mic. I can sense Pierre behind my back, Louis to my right, and beside him, Cornélia, who's keeping watch. My daughter is in jeans, black sneakers, and a white, belted coat. She's alarmingly beautiful, increasingly resembles my father. She's put a touch of makeup on her big green eyes. Her crystal-clear voice cleaves through the crowd gathered around us:

"My Coco, I adored spending time with you in your shoe-repair shop; it was like something out of a children's book. All those keys, I'd imagine they opened secret chests. And the shoes all lined up, one pair beside another . . . You'd say to me: 'Can you imagine the number of steps there are inside my shop?' You'd give me tins of polish as if they were paints, and I'd smear the polish on my fingers and create rainbows on big pads of paper. Occasionally, you took me to the football, but it was you I'd watch, not the match. Those matches were more interesting in your eyes than on the pitch. I found you beautiful and shy. I loved you; it's thanks to you that I play the piano, because of all my grandfather's records that we listened to together. I didn't see you that much, didn't know you that well, but you don't have to see people a lot to know you love them and that they're important. What counts is their presence when they're there. Not the number of times you see them. And when I'd arrive at your house with my parents, you were instantly there. With me. We were together. Thank you, my Coco."

Ana returns to me. I squeeze her hand; she's shaking. The master of ceremonies beckons me over. My legs are about to give way. I get a grip, ordering myself to do this. If my daughter managed it, I can, too. Even if it's just for them, Ana and Colette.

"I never called you Tata. It wouldn't have entered our minds, neither yours nor mine. I think that's how the speech I wrote for you begins. It's right here, in my bag. But I'm not going to read it to you right now. I'll come back later. The most important thing today is the farewell we're all bidding you, it's the presence of your friends, here, now. We covered some ground, my dear Colette. And I would like to thank you. Thanks to your second death, you brought me back to life. One day, I'll explain this to you; I'll come and tell you everything when it's just the two of us. Colette, whenever I picture my father, I see you, sitting close to him and his piano, a frail figure in a coat that's too big, your little handbag propped on your knees, listening to him play, religiously. My father's shadow, that's you, Colette. But you weren't just a shadow, you were: You."

16

Blanche

By the time I was three, I could already balance on a ball and circle the arena. Somersaults, forward flips, backflips, juggling . . . I learned to balance on a wire when I was five. I loved being a tightrope walker. And I continued to practice all my life. As if another circus was waiting for me. In my next life, I want to join the Cirque du Soleil. That's my dream. Loving to read, that came later. I accepted being a recluse because I read. Otherwise, I'd have died. In our country, there are municipal libraries in every town. Even in villages. A national treasure. Colette, when you showed me the one in Gueugnon that first time, I couldn't believe it. Nestled like that, inside a château.

Silence.

Blanche

From the sixties onward, Soudoro started to get spooked, became increasingly nervous. Exhibiting "freaks" was punishable by prison, and our circus was on file for illegal working conditions. That's how the authorities referred to the exploitation of vulnerable people . . . We were forever having to turn up in new towns, unknown towns, where we hadn't yet been found out. No more school for me. Soudoro threw in the towel in 1970. He sold the big top to an Italian family, along with Fabrizio, Nestor, and our divine creature, Noé.

Silence.

Blanche

We parted forever on a sidewalk. I was twenty-four, and my only true family, the one I'd loved, stood there before me. A very small man, a giant in tears, cradling Noé in his arms. All three of them unbelievably gentle and sensitive. They promised to keep in touch with me. But how can you keep in touch with someone who has no address?

Soudoro and I moved to a first apartment in Lyon, then to a second, a third, a fourth, like fugitives. For those first few years, we moved constantly. We finally settled down in the town center. My room adjoined his. He insisted on hearing me come and go.

He got me work at a cabaret, the Cabaret des Oiseaux, *in the second arrondissement. The owners, Arielle and Sam, had known Soudoro for a long time. I was always close to Arielle, but always wary of Sam. If my genitor had assigned me to them, it was so he could be kept informed of my every move and deed. The cabaret offered dinner with a show. I worked in reception, sold cigarettes, did a little waitressing. No more acrobatics, but I still got to wear sequined dresses like the ones I'd always loved. The team was young and had been trained at circus schools. Compared with them, I'd just come off the street. It was with them that I kept up my training. To maintain my athletic body. Protect that one place of inner freedom. These artistes formed a family I became attached to, but never as much as to Natalia, Fabrizio, and Nestor.*

I'm going to attempt to summarize thirty years of life in a few words. It's not that hard when every day is identical. Soudoro would do odd jobs here and there, and we lived like a couple who don't share the same bed. I never mentioned the thought of leaving; I wasn't allowed to leave him. An implicit ban. I belonged to him. Meeting a boy and getting married was unthinkable. He took my entire wages and would accompany me to the stores, the supermarket, the doctor, would wait for me at the checkout or in the waiting room, pockets stuffed with banknotes. Never a checkbook or a credit card in our drawers. I had no privacy whatsoever. He never touched me or beat me. But I always knew that if I left, he would find me and kill me. Sometimes he'd come to fetch me after work. Just like that, no warning. To show me just how much control he had over me.

In 1980, he finally agreed to buy me a TV, but kept a close eye on which programs I watched. In case they put any ideas into my head. What ideas? He must have thought I knew nothing about love. Poor fool. He never said I love you to me, or spoke to me, or kissed me. I never said I love you to him, or spoke to him, or kissed him. People who don't talk to each other, they exist everywhere. And I think they exist in great numbers.

I had friends, casual lovers; the cabaret was a godsend. But there was no waking up, or tomorrows, wrapped in unknown arms. I made out that I was a girl who refused to get attached, when I was simply a prisoner. I made love very fast, too fast, between the end of my shift and whenever I had to be home. I was against the clock. I did fall in love once. Once, but forever. An impossible love. What else could it be with a sword of Damocles hanging over me?

Silence.

BLANCHE

Soudoro was a manipulator. For my twenty-fifth birthday, he gave me the present I was dreaming of: a dog. Véra. A little spaniel-dachshund mix bitch. That day, he knew I'd never attempt to run away. He'd mind her when I went off to work. But I'd walk her before going to the cabaret, and on my return, Véra would be waiting for me at the door. I'd take her out, and then we'd fall asleep together.

Every month, Soudoro would be away from the nineteenth to the twenty-third. He'd disappear with Véra. I screamed, cried, begged him, but he never left her with me. When they got back, she didn't appear to have been mistreated or ill-fed. And I always wondered where she was when he went away. Where did he go? I never found a single train or bus ticket in his pockets. No clue. His regular absences went on for three years. One day, he just stopped going, without the slightest explanation.

I remained a prisoner for thirty years. The bars of my prison had been patiently assembled from my birth onward. Thanks to his only daughter, Soudoro had treated himself to a servant and a regular income. I thought of killing him. Often. Pushing him down the stairs. Poisoning him. Suffocating him. But I never dared. I was far too scared of the reprisals if I didn't pull it off. And I'm not the murdering kind.

We continued not to talk to each other. I aged before his eyes. He aged before mine. I never left the Cabaret des Oiseaux. *In time, I became responsible for bookings and the till. Unbelievable as it might seem, I swear on your life, Colette, I never got a centime, and was never declared. Sam would give my wages directly to Soudoro, under the impression that everything was deposited into an account of mine in Russia, my father's native land. And when Arielle asked me questions, I played along. I was my jailer's accomplice.*

When Véra died of old age in my arms, Soudoro promptly came home with a new dog. A young Jack Russell. He was intuitive, and sensed he was going to lose me. I was completely lost, devastated, even wanted to end it all. My work, my life. Véra was irreplaceable. And yet, little by little, I succumbed to the pup's loving eyes and his energy. I named him Lancelot. He's the only knight to have saved my life. Those two dogs, they're all I've ever owned. Otherwise, I've possessed nothing other than your friendship, Colette.

17

November 15, 2010

Cornélia did it on purpose. Obviously. She's intelligent, so she did it on purpose. I feel like killing her, but since I'm exhausted, I'll spare her. For now. She booked four first-class seats on the TGV. I'm opposite Ana. Cornélia is beside me, and Pierre opposite her. How dare she put us together? Pierre with us. We're speeding toward Paris, it's 5:30 P.M., and Colette has returned to my parents for all eternity. I'd slid the suitcase of cassettes under my seat.

Ana is chatting to me about everything and nothing. About Colette, the shoe-repair shop, her vacation, Blanche's exhumation, asks if I'll be there, about the boat she saw dolphins from, and the ocean. She adds that, at the hotel, there was a grand piano and she played it every day, the manager allowed her to, though it was usually forbidden. Reserved for the musicians in the evening. I try to concentrate on listening to her, answering her questions, but I'm fighting an urge to turn my head slightly to observe Pierre, who hasn't taken off his coat. Always seems about to leave.

A passenger comes to ask for his autograph. He's welcoming, courteous, and smiling, thanks her when she admits to loving him in all his movies, especially *Le Banquet des anciens* and *La Fenêtre*. He replies: "That's lucky, the director's right there," indicating me. I sense a slight annoyance in his voice. A fake niceness all of sudden. No doubt he's often dragged back to me. The passenger smiles at me nicely. "Oh, bravo Madame Dugain, I adore your movies! Are you working on a new one with your husband?" She clearly doesn't read the gossip press. I can feel myself blushing and hear myself stammering: "I'm finishing a screenplay." Enthusiastically, Ana jumps in: "My parents are separated. But Mom's still working on a new movie." Pierre and I smile inanely at the passenger, not knowing what else to say.

When she leaves with her two autographs, Pierre turns to me.

"You're working on something?"

I brazenly lie, replying without batting an eyelid:

"Yes, I'm sewing up *Hannah Ruben*."

I can tell by his expression that he's intrigued.

"You're doing a movie on your mother's story?"

"Yes."

"Hey, Mom, that's great! Could I have a small part?"

"If you'd like to, darling, I'll write something in for you."

"Could I be a pianist?"

"Yes. Lovely idea."

"Your speech for Colette was splendid," Pierre says, taking hold of her hand.

Is he trying to change the subject? Ana looks happy. She thinks I'm back on the creative track. I gaze at her, and the words come out of their own accord. I can't help myself. I'd prefer to be alone to tell her this, but words you've held back for too long sometimes escape without your being able to stop them. Emotions can't be schooled.

"I'm so sorry, sweetheart."

Ana frowns. I love it when she does that; she looks even more like my father.

"I'm sorry for the harm I did you."

"But, Mom?"

"I let myself be swamped by grief, and you suffered because of me. It won't happen again. Our life's going to change."

"Well I like our life, Mom. I don't want it to change . . . And anyhow, everyone's allowed to suffer. Only, you did look a bit iffy these past few years. But now, look, now you've got a guy and you're preparing working on a movie."

Thank goodness I'm sitting down. I feel a mix of shame and bafflement. Pierre stares at me, sneeringly.

"You've met someone? That's good."

His patronizing tone, as if handing out stars, profoundly annoys me. And to cap it off, he adds:

"Which actor is it? Do I know him?"

I burst out laughing and snap back:

"No thank you, I've had a bellyful of actors. My friend's a doctor."

Second lie. I can sense Cornélia looking at Ana, who's looking at Cornélia. They're satisfied. Smiling at each other. The traitors. If they only knew. And then Pierre digs deeper:

"What's his specialty?"

"Méharis."

The look on his face. It's so funny. If I wasn't returning from a funeral, it would probably be one of the finest moments of my life. He really does look bothered. Why? Because I'm working on a movie without him? Or because a new man has taken his place? A place he left vacant and so very cold. He says nothing more, pretends to read *Le Parisien*, bought at the station kiosk. He's on the political pages. He loathes politics. "Nicolas Sarkozy's new government proposed by François Fillon." I can see the reflection of the headlines in his glasses. Tinted lenses so as not to be recognized. What a dork! Yes, I'm thinking what a dork about Pierre Dugain, who was my king. My life. My love. The guy I'd have followed out of the funeral, earlier on, if he'd asked me to. So life can boil down to so little, then? Our children aside, people are just potential dorks in the making . . . "*Avec le temps / Avec le temps, va, tout s'en va*," as Léo Ferré sang. With time, well, everything fades away.

He must be thinking that the movie I'm working on can't work because it won't feature him. And that I owe him all my success. I'm sure he's convinced of that. Personally, I gloated when I heard the box-office figures for *his* last film. A resounding flop. What's more, the other one was in it. Let's be honest. In any line of work, when we part ways with an associate, we don't wish them the best. We can say good luck, loud and clear, but it's bullshit, as Ana would say.

"Mom, what's your first memory with Colette?"

Ana jolts me from my thoughts. Pierre is still pretending to read. Cornélia is dozing. I try to remember, think hard about it.

"I don't have a precise memory. It's more the smell of leather and shoe polish. And I have an image of Colette approaching me on Rue Jean Jaurès, in Gueugnon. I'm pleased to see her again. My parents must surely be close by, but I have no memory of that. Colette has just turned up from I don't know where. And I'm happy to be back with her on that sidewalk. I was very little then."

"Did you listen to her cassettes?"

"Not all of them."

"Could I listen to them with you?"

"Yes. You'll see, Blanche speaks, too. There are silences, rainfall, birdsong. Colette recorded everything."

"That would make a wizard movie, too."

"As you say, a wizard movie . . . "

"Are we seeing the new *Harry Potter* tonight, Mom?"

"If you like."

"You're not too bushed?"

"No. On the contrary. It'll take my mind off things."

"It's previewing at Studio 28. And then we'll go eat at Villa des Abbesses?"

"Sure."

"Cornélia, will you come with us?"

"I can't tonight."

"Got a date?"

"Ana," I say, "that's her business."

"No. Cornélia's business is my business. Dad, will you come with us?"

Has my daughter lost her mind?

"Where?"

Pierre promptly closes his newspaper.

"To see the latest *Harry Potter*. Audrey's not in Paris. You're not going to stay alone. You don't mind, Mom?"

Pierre looks at me. Is he waiting for my consent? I don't know what he's waiting for.

"Sounds like a good idea."

I feel like dying. My daughter and Cornélia are conspiring, and I don't know what they're after. I'm in a right fix. What am I going to do with that screenplay? Work for months on it? I never envisaged making a movie about my mother's story and her meeting with my father. I'm logging their memories. I've only ever made mood movies, and although I have been inspired by observations, local news stories, first-hand accounts, I've never written about my own family.

Pierre stands up to go to the bar car and asks us what we'd like to drink. What does one drink when returning from a funeral? After lying? In a speeding train with one's ex sitting opposite? And when one risks spending the evening with him?

"A bourbon, no ice, please."

"Aged 300 years?" he retorts, quick as a flash.

"That'll be perfect, thanks."

And we burst into laughter. Like before. We laughed all the time. We were always on the same wavelength. But that was before.

"Water will be fine, thanks."

"Okay."

Ana wants to go with him. So does Cornélia. I find myself alone. I watch the three of them disappear. Like before. Like when we lived in LA and they'd go off to do some shopping to let me write in peace.

Ana will be disappointed if she discovers that I lied about the screenplay. I'm light years away from entering the fray again. And yet, I can't help it, I start wondering who could play the part of Mom. She was so pretty, so slender. A slight sternness behind her beautiful green eyes. But scratch a little, and you realized that she was funny. I can't remember who said: "Don't shake me. I'm full of tears." With Mom, it was the opposite. It was her devastating humor that you'd hear. She was feminine, sophisticated. Magnificent hands, light skin, a small, straight nose. Finely drawn lips. I always felt as if I were one-and-a-half times bigger than my mother, through my height and my mop of hair, my fleshy lips, my dark eyes, and those same old sneakers on my feet, when she was forever in heels. Mom wasn't tactile. Gentle and kind, but not cuddly. Before my father's death, she'd give me a kiss on the cheek as if I were a friend. Afterward, she became far more affectionate. Me, I touch the people I love, as if my hands had a visceral need to connect me to them. And I think I smothered Ana with kisses. Still today, I can't be close to her without kissing or caressing her. My daughter is like me. I passed my sensory lovesickness on to her. Suddenly, a memory comes back to me. A question that I had asked: "Why does Dad always look sad?" My mother had given me this totally unexpected answer: "It isn't sadness, it's melancholy. Colette will tell you about it, one day. When and how, I don't know, but she'll tell you." Ana, Cornélia, and Pierre return, laughing, arms laden with drinks, cakes, and chips. And now, what am I going to do?

18

HANNAH RUBEN

(Contd.)

1942
Scene 3a

The Germans have gone. Éléonore Gravoin cautiously goes up to the next floor and through the half-open door of the apartment. She has to be quick. A neighbor might see her. The Rubens' home has been ransacked. Éléonore holds back her tears. She salvages what she can of family photos, framed portraits, some smashed, then hurries back down to her apartment.

1942
Scene 4a

The building's concierge, Madame Gauthier, moves new residents into the Rubens' apartment. Wary, the Gravoin family rocks the baby, who is passed from one pair of arms to another, so that no one can hear her. The father, Benjamin, the grandmother, and Éléonore reassure the little one with their eyes, while humming songs.

Scene 4b

Éléonore passes the new residents on the stairs. She greets them nervously.

Scene 4c

Éléonore goes into her apartment. The grandmother is playing with Hannah and has piled up building blocks on the floor.

*

Éléonore: I just met the Thénardiers on the stairs.

The grandmother: They'll be smiling on the other side of their faces soon.

Éléonore (*indicating little Hannah with her eyes*): Mom, where are her parents?

The grandmother (*under her breath*): In hell.

Éléonore: They say they're working in camps.

The grandmother: Cruel men are often compared to animals. They're said to behave like beasts. Never would any animal equal certain men when it comes to barbarity.

Just then, the pile of building blocks collapses. Éléonore and the grandmother put on a cheery front for Hannah. "Whoops a daisy!" they cry in unison at the beaming baby.

July 1943

It's a fine day. The Gravoins have opened their windows to let the sunshine in. Hannah is about to turn one and is starting to toddle across the apartment, laughing. Éléonore gently asks her to make less noise.

Benjamin: I'm sick of asking her to whisper and play hide-and-seek. I'm taking her to the park!

Panic-stricken, Éléonore begs her husband not to. The grandmother starts to weep, moaning: "Mother of God, they'll arrest him! They'll take her away from us!" But the father insists, they won't arrest them, he has the new papers for the little one. And who would arrest a child accompanied by her daddy, a doctor and a Catholic who saves lives every day at the Grange-Blanche Hospital?

Éléonore: I'm coming with you.

The three of them go down the stairs, the little girl in Benjamin's arms. And as they pass the concierge's lodge, Benjamin calls out to her.

Benjamin: Good day, Madame Gauthier, let me introduce you to my brother's daughter. Her mommy's unwell and can't look after her for the moment.

Éléonore: She's called Marthe. Marthe Gravoin. Give Madame Gauthier a smile, Marthe.

The concierge: I thought I'd heard children's voices coming from your place.

Busy distributing letters into mailboxes, she pays no attention to them.

The concierge: I hope her mother gets better soon.

Benjamin: So do we. Thanks. Have a good day!

The concierge: Have a good day, doctor.

They go out into the street, relieved.

Benjamin: Here we are, darling, this is Lyon. You'll see, it's a pretty city, and best of all, there's the Rhône, where people go swimming. We were in the unoccupied zone for a long time, but that's over now. There's a war on. There are nasty men who don't look nasty. And nasty women who don't look nasty. There are valiant folks who resist. Wars end up dying their own death. They suffocate. In the meantime, because everything is dangerous, we're going to be very careful. We're going to pretend to be obedient.

The little girl smiles. Not understanding a word of what Benjamin is telling her, but delighted to discover the outside world, having been deprived of it since she was born.

Scene 5a

December 8, 1943—Festival of Lights day in Lyon

Despite the war and the severe recession, the people of Lyon have placed candles and tapers on their windowsills to honor the Virgin Mary.

On a small square, Éléonore Gravoin is playing the violin for passersby, accompanied by an accordionist. They're playing a Mozart sonata, the K. 304 one, originally composed for piano and violin. Among the spectators are Benjamin, carrying Hannah, and the grandmother. Around a hundred anonymous people are listening to them play, including a few Germans in uniform. Everyone seems to be deeply moved by the music, notably little Hannah.

Scene 6
Spring 1945

Hannah, nearly three, is alone when she goes into the room where Éléonore usually practices the violin. The child takes the instrument out of its case, places it on her knees and tries to get sounds out of it with the bow.

Scene 7
Summer 1945

Every day, Éléonore and Benjamin go to the Red Cross in the hope of hearing some news about the Ruben family. They check the lists and the photographs of those who have survived. They leave none the wiser. Are the two children still alive and safe with host families?

Scene 7a

Exterior shot of street, Lyon
The Gravoin couple walk side by side.

Éléonore (*to Benjamin)*: I've never been so unhappy. If they're dead, Hannah will never see her parents again, or her brother and sister. And if they do return, we'll have to part from her.

Benjamin: We've always known that.

Éléonore: But there's a world of difference between knowing it and living it.

1946

Hannah, four years old, starts having violin lessons with a teacher. That same year, the Gravoins retrieve the Rubens' apartment, requisitioned by the Germans, so that it can be returned to Hannah.

NB: Hannah will never go back there. When she comes of age, she'll sell it.

1947

Rafael, Agnès, Sasha, and Myriam Ruben are declared deceased by the administration. Benjamin and Éléonore follow procedures to adopt Hannah. She will always keep her birth surname, Ruben.

Scene 8
1952
Interior shot of apartment
Hannah, ten years old, looks at the portraits of her parents, her brother, and her sister. We recognize the photographs that Éléonore saved after the Germans ransacked the Rubens' apartment.

Note for props team: Use the real photos.

*

19

November 16, 2010

I kept those photos. Ana asked me for them, to hang up in her bedroom on Rue des Abbesses. There's a photo taken on Rafael's and Agnès's wedding day, one of Sasha holding his little sister Myriam in his arms, and one of the two children, aged around eight and four. And finally, a snap of Hannah as a newborn, sleeping in her mother's arms. They were deported a few months later.

I don't know why or how Agnès sensed she had to entrust her youngest to her neighbors and friends. Why not all three of her children? Why not have tried to escape all together? Did she think she wouldn't be able to care for a baby in those "labor" camps? But how would that have been possible for the two older children?

I gaze at our ancestors on the walls of the room, looking for likenesses. They're our martyred ghosts. They belong to the collective memory. Ana calls them "our guardian angels." Their first names and surnames are engraved on the wall of the Mémorial de la Shoah in Paris. They were part of convoy No. 42. The one that left Drancy on November 6, 1942, at 8:55 A.M. Upon their arrival at Auschwitz, on November 8, 145 men were selected for forced labor and tattooed with the numbers 74021 to 74165; and 82 women with the numbers 23963 to 24044. There were 1,000 deportees in that convoy, of which 217 were children. A total of 639 were killed on arrival, in the gas chambers. Neither Agnès nor Rafael were tattooed. They were among the 639 Jews gassed, along with their two children. I imagine that Agnès died with her children. I often pray that little Sasha didn't die with his father, among the men, but rather with his mother. I don't know why, but I want him to have passed away with his mother holding his hand. I'll never know. From this convoy, four people survived. Only men.

I don't remember seeing these photos in the apartment in Lyon when I was a child. I don't know where they were. But they appeared in Mom's bedroom after Dad's death. When I did see them, I understood who they were. Was it Dad who'd refused to see them? I doubt it; he was in his own world. Did Mom not want to put them on display? Had she hidden them from him? From us? When I asked her why she had called me Agnès, she said it was the name of her mother, who died during the war. Without saying anything more. Much later, she told me about the Shoah. And we studied it at school. When the history teacher asked us if any of us had a member of their family who had been deported to or returned from the camps, I didn't raise my hand, leaving my grandparents and their children under a bell jar of silence. When I got home, I felt terribly ashamed of having said nothing. Of having exterminated them a second time. Still today, I'm ashamed of having been ashamed to raise my hand.

My daughter has started to read my screenplay. She said that if I make a movie about them, they'll exist forever. I replied that the screenplay would exist forever if someone made the movie of it. But that wouldn't be me. If I must speak about them, I'll write a novel.

In the world of the living, it was Colette who occupied all the space. On Mom's side, my uncle and aunt were deported. And on my father's side, little Danièle died very young. Colette got the title of only aunt without wanting it. I think of her, now laid to rest in Lyon.

No news from Paul since the funeral. So, no news of Soudkovski.

A text message from Antoine Été: "Home safe?"

Reply: "Yes, thanks."

A call from Ilyas:

"That's it, we've set the date for the wedding! It'll be next June. Nathalie will be my witness, would you be happy to be Lina's?"

"I barely know her, she must have a best friend, or a godmother, or someone."

"She says that if it's you, it'll bring us luck."

"Seriously, Ilyas, do I look anything like a lucky charm?"

"I suppose you must. Right, so that's okay? You'll be my wife's witness?"

"Okay."

Ana goes back to school tomorrow; she's off visiting a friend. Yesterday evening, the preview of *Harry Potter* was booked out at Studio 28. Instead, the two of us went to have supper at Villa des Abbesses, while Pierre came up with an excuse to go straight back home. A Lyon-Paris train journey in such close proximity to me must have been enough for him for the next ten years. I'll see him again when Ana's thirty and marries a prince, not too charming, I hope. Just a prince will be enough.

20

November 2, 2010

Soudkovski had reached Valence at around one in the morning. He'd stopped at a service station near Mâcon to withdraw 700 euros with Mathilde's bank card, since he knew the PIN. He needed to have cash so he couldn't be traced. And he'd kept to the authorized weekly amount so the machine didn't swallow the card. He'd withdraw the same sum the following Monday, then destroy the card. He'd use Socha's card to get his war veteran's pension each month. Paranoid as he was, it seemed unthinkable to him to use it in any way other than to withdraw nearly all of his pension. He left 100 euros in Socha's current account to cover the monthly electricity bills. That was all. The rest he pocketed.

Not a soul at Mathilde's house. So, no one had reported her missing. When he'd left, he hadn't closed the shutters, to avoid attracting the neighbors' attention, had left a night light on. He parked her Twingo in its usual place.

Now he was back to clear out his own rental place. "Viktor Socha" was going to move again. Soudkovski didn't have much to collect, apart from clothes, shoes, a toolbox, dumbbells, and some admin papers. He'd thrown out all his newspapers. In barely an hour, he'd gathered what little he owned in the garage and washed his two-room abode with bleach, from floor to ceiling. It now looked like a sample apartment at a home expo.

He'd then walked to the car park at the station, and looked around at the vehicles there. Recent models were trickier to break into and start. Damned progress. He'd spotted a Honda with its back right door unlocked. A 1993 model. Forcing the Neiman steering lock and connecting the starter wires would be child's play. Admittedly, he'd stolen so many cars since he was a kid, and then abandoned them. Just as he'd abandoned Marie Roman at a brothel near Strasbourg. He'd have done better to kill her. And on top of that, it was because of her that he'd done time in prison and lost track of Blanche.

He'd returned to the apartment in the Honda to fill up the trunk and then hidden it in the garage. He had to leave before daybreak.

It must have been five in the morning when he'd slipped into Mathilde's house to delete the search history from her computer. All the research he'd done on Blanche and Marie Roman. No one must be able to trace a thing back to him—he'd disappeared off the radar since that Marseille business. No one had made the link between him and Viktor Socha.

But as soon as he'd sat down in front of the computer, he hadn't been able to resist typing in the name "Agnès Dugain." She'd appeared, all smiles, from the age of twenty up to today. In the street, on movie sets, directing actors he'd never heard of. On red carpets, in long black dresses, and always accompanied by the same man. It was definitely her. And once again, that strange warmth, that curious well-being he felt when he set eyes on her.

Soudkovski wasn't remotely cultured. He knew only the *Paris-Turf* newspaper, some DIY, limbering-up exercises, wheeling and dealing of all sorts, and prison. Computers had only served him for researching and investigating. Never learning. But he had felt a certain pride at the thought of her making movies. It meant she had the taste for entertainment. Directing movies and training animals both came down to seducing an audience. Her with a camera, him with a whip and food deprivation. By starving the animals, you could do what you wanted with them. They both had to control what was in front of them and use projectors to make the light dance. Like him, she belonged to the world of spectacle.

He'd retained the year she was born, 1972. And that she was the daughter of the pianist Jean Septembre and the violinist Hannah Ruben. That she was a screenplay writer and director and had won prizes all over the world for nearly fifteen years. That she had a daughter named Ana, born in Paris in 1995. That she'd been married to Pierre Dugain, and divorced since 2008. That she lived in Paris. That she hadn't made a movie since 2006. From that year onward, nothing more was mentioned. As if she'd died. He'd recalled the titles of her movies but hadn't seen any of them. Then he'd found himself on a link showing her ex-husband in the arms of a certain Audrey Tudor. He couldn't care less. Only Agnès interested him.

He had clicked on a video to hear the sound of her voice. It was filmed during the Cannes Film Festival in 1995, at which she was presenting *La Fenêtre*. She was pregnant. And filmed in close-up. She was wearing makeup and a red top with a low, rounded neckline, and was tanned. She was pretty. And younger than when he'd glimpsed her leaving the café. Soudkovski hadn't listened to a word of the interview, his eyes riveted on her lips, her smile, her nose, her eyes, the way she looked up when thinking, the tone of her voice when she answered, her nail-varnish- and jewelry-free hands. Totally captivated by this woman. A ghost that had returned to haunt him.

He had to go. It was almost 6:30 A.M. In haste, he'd deleted any traces of himself from the computer and left Mathilde's house without a backward glance. He'd thrown the duplicate keys into a crate full of trash. Then he'd connected the Honda's starter wires and hit the road for Lyon. There, he found a small hotel beside the Célestins car park. He'd only be staying there for a few nights, in order to think. And mainly, to understand. Agnès was born in 1972. He and Blanche were living together in Lyon at the time, he was sure of that. He'd sold the circus in 1970. That was the watershed in his life. In 1970. Dividing his grim existence in two. Before and after.

From his hotel room, he'd called the landline number of where Agnès lived in Gueugnon. It had rung for ages. Then she'd finally answered. He'd instantly hung up. And called again. Without saying a word, simply to hear her voice.

"Marie? Is that you?"

Marie. Marie. Marie. Marie. Marie. Marie. Marie. She'd said Marie. Agnès was in contact with Marie Roman. Something was becoming clearer. He didn't know what yet, but when she'd said her name, he'd realized that he was holding the cable linked to a detonator. He'd whispered "yes" under his breath.

"Did Éloïse give you this number?"

He'd hung up. Who was Éloïse? And then rung her again. She'd answered again. He'd breathed heavily into the receiver. So she'd keep talking, think someone was trying to tell her something. And it had worked:

"Hello? Marie? Sorry, Amélie? Is that you?"

He'd rung three more times, but Agnès hadn't said anything else. He'd placed his cellphone carefully on the bed, as if it still contained Agnès's words. Beside the box of photos. Now, all that remained was to piece the puzzle back together: Marie, Amélie. She'd changed her identity. The lawyer had warned him. So she must be called Amélie now. First point. Shame he hadn't managed to get her assumed surname. Second point, there was an Éloïse on the scene. Must be the person who looked after her. He'd condemned Marie to a wheelchair; she had to be in some institution. Of that, he'd been sure for years. When he'd beaten her "to death," she was living in Annecy. She couldn't have gone very far. That slut had never gone very far in her entire life. He'd forced her to spit out the information before laying into her. Sallanches. And her bitch of a sister lived in Flumet. He must look again at that list of establishments in Savoie and Haute-Savoie to find an Éloïse among the care staff. Éloïse wasn't a common name. And then phone them again, one by one. Prepare the perfect question so as not to arouse suspicion:

"Hello, it's the Annecy police here. I'm calling on behalf of Agnès Dugain. I'd like to speak to Éloïse, please."

If they replied, "Who?," hang up.

If they replied, "What name should I say?," have the name of an actual cop ready.

If they replied, "What is it concerning?," say: "The individual who was jailed for aggravated assault on one of your residents, Marie Roman. She now calls herself Amélie. Madame Dugain informed us that it's Éloïse who cares for her in your establishment, but she's forgotten her surname."

Add nothing more. Agnès was a well-known woman. If she was seen visiting a resident, they'd know who she was.

In the trunk of the Honda, he had that list of retirement homes and their phone numbers. All those he'd already contacted, in vain. He'd start over. Call them one after the other. And he'd find her in the end. He knew it. He'd known that by going to Gueugnon, after reading that Nathalie Grandjean's article, he'd unearth a clue. The start of something that would doubtless take him very far. His wretched instinct was unstoppable.

21

BLANCHE

Soudoro never spoke of his mother. Or of mine. We had in common the loss, at a young age, of what defines the foundations of a life. The smell of my mother, that was Natalia's smell; I found her beautiful, even if she did have an unfortunate face, as if squashed, and a long beard. She'd shave it often so it would grow back thick and bushy. She maintained it the way a gardener does his trees. Without this feature, she knew that Soudoro would have rejected her. Natalia smelled of spring, of lilac. Still today, whenever I smell that flower, it brings her back to me. She loved me like her own child. She patched up my cuts and scrapes, cuddled me, warmed me in her plump arms. When little, I was forever sitting in her lap. I was thirteen when Soudoro threw her out on the side of the road. Done on the quiet, at night, as usual. When I woke up, I paid no attention to her absence. That day, we kept driving until nightfall. At bedtime, she always came to kiss me. I asked Soudoro why the light wasn't on in Natalia's trailer. "She's sick as an old dog. Leave her in peace, she's sleeping." It took me two days to realize that she'd disappeared and her trailer had been emptied out. At first, Soudoro told me she'd cleared off. I didn't believe it. She'd never have left without me. Soudoro laughed in my face. "Of course she left without you, she found herself a man." I grew up convinced that no one wanted me. That I didn't deserve affection. Eleven years later, the year Soudoro sold the circus, Fabrizio admitted to me that Soudoro had gotten rid of Natalia, but he didn't know where or how. When I asked him why he hadn't told me before, he said he'd been too scared of reprisals. What had become of her? What had she been through, far away from us? Mockery, humiliation, without a doubt. But I was relieved to learn that she hadn't left me by choice. Not like my mother, who'd died after having abandoned me. A kind of divine retribution. As for Soudoro, he was hard because he'd suffered a lot as a child. Apparently, abused children nearly always defend their parents.

Time went by. There was much talk of the year 2000. And then, December 31, 1999, arrived. I woke up that morning with Lancelot sleeping beside me, thinking about how we were leaving the century behind. What would the next one be like? How much longer would I be living like this?

A very long silence. I can hear someone whispering to her, but can't make out the words. Colette is close by.

BLANCHE

I'd been working at the Cabaret des Oiseaux *for thirty years, had no salary, no social security number; officially, I didn't exist. I was under someone's control, like a child. But in 1999, I was fifty-three years old! Fifty-three! Everyone would say to me: "You don't look your age! You look like a young girl." Yes. An old young girl. Soudoro had left suddenly on December 30 and then returned during the night. Without taking Lancelot with him. He'd just discovered something, but what? I knew nothing about his wheeling and dealing.*

I got breakfast ready, then took the dog out. When I got back, I came face to face with him. He had a scratch on his cheek, but I paid no attention to it. I did some housework, and that's when I found them. His blood-stained trousers and sweater in the washing machine. I wondered who he'd killed. I really did wonder about that. And I took out the sweater to wash it by hand, but was then gripped by a strange feeling. An intuition. I stuffed it into a plastic bag without washing it, switched on the machine, then hung out the clean washing. End of story.

New Year's Eve arrived. The cabaret was fully booked. We were offering a special menu, a show with our usual artistes and some tightrope acrobats. They were the third generation of performers I rubbed shoulders with. Only youth, all around me. I loved my work. I felt I belonged. It was a bright interlude in my daily existence. And I like working in the evening.

That night, I earned 1,500 francs in tips, which I hid at the bottom of a bag of Lancelot's kibbles. The next day, I got up late. Soudoro had gone out for a walk. I switched the TV on and came across the local news bulletin for the Rhône-Alpes region. A festive report on that New Year's Eve, showing the fireworks and passersby embracing each other. A few days before, a storm had decimated hectares of forest in France. Images of joy and desolation in quick succession. But the famous Millennium Bug had been nipped in the bud. It was at the end of the bulletin that the news broke. A woman had been discovered in a serious condition in her home. She'd been beaten and stabbed several times. Her injuries were life-threatening. She was originally from Flumet and had been running from her husband for decades. He'd finally found her. The assault had taken place in the Annecy area. The individual was being pursued. "Her injuries were life-threatening." Those words kept going around in my head. And also "Flumet." The village my mother was born in.

It couldn't be a coincidence. No, it couldn't be, because I'd always known that Soudkovski was capable of killing the women who left him. I had the blood-stained sweater of the murderer, and that blood was doubtless my mother's. I knew that she was called Marie Roman. I began to shake like I'd never shaken before. My mother hadn't been dead. She'd gotten away. And he'd ended up slaughtering her.

Over the following weeks, using the cabaret phone, I rang the hospitals in Annecy, and finally found the department where the patient, Marie Roman, was in a coma. I said who I was: "I'm Blanche Soudkovski, Marie Roman's daughter." And I still remember the nurse's surprise: "I didn't know she had a daughter." I didn't reply: "I didn't know I had a mother." I hadn't been wrong; that blood was hers. And thus mine.

Four months went by. She was transferred elsewhere for her safety. I needed to go to the police. An investigation was underway, and I wanted to know where she was now. I almost asked Soudoro how my mother had died, but he was so sharp, he'd have realized that I knew something.

Four months went by without me changing my routine, even though I knew I was going to run away. Every morning, I'd watch him drink his coffee, repeating to myself that the man was a murderer. And then one day in April, the seventh, to be precise, I was cooking when I heard Benoît Duquesne talking about "small fry against big fish" on the national news. A small football team was going to face the biggest of them all. Gueugnon was playing PSG at the Stade de France. Gueugnon! I took it as a fateful sign. Heaven was offering me a helping hand. Colette. Colette Septembre. The match would be on April 22. I had fifteen days to prepare for my departure. And I made sure not to prepare anything at all.

On April 22, I hastily stuffed a dress, some trousers, the blood-stained sweater, my tips, and my old ID card into a garbage bag. I slipped on my coat and went down to walk Lancelot, holding a second garbage bag, as well. I left everything as it was in my room. Engrossed in reading his Paris-Turf *in the kitchen, Soudoro noticed nothing out of the ordinary. I left him without saying a word. I knew I'd never see him again. At least, I hoped not. Because, by leaving, I was signing my death warrant. I took a great many risks. I was convinced that Colette would be at the Stade de France. If she wasn't there, I was done for, but it was better to take that risk to save myself than to return to a murderer who would keep his gun trained on me until the day he died. Mad as it might seem, I cried a lot as I was leaving. The fear of the void. The fear of leaving one's torturer is overwhelming. I grew up under his eyes, with his smell, his voice. A whole life spent with him. Just toe the line, and you'll be fine. You breathe almost normally. That man never beat me. The threat and the fear were understood. Disobey just once, and your peace will be over. I'll never forget the stairs on each floor I had to walk down, although I flew down them every day. Or the streets to get to the station. The weather. The sky. The people. At Lyon-Part-Dieu, I boarded a train for Paris.*

On arrival, I knew the RER D train journey, Creil, by heart. At 9:00 P.M., I was outside the stadium. The match was underway. I waited in the rain, with my dog in my arms. A gentleman asked me if I needed any help, I said: "I'm waiting for someone." He replied: "The match has just started." I remember buying a hot dog for Lancelot. I remember the roar of the supporters. I saw nothing of the match, but I did hear it. I'll never forget their cheering as I waited for Colette. The stadium was massive, with multiple exits. I put my trust in life. For once, it would be kind to me, since Colette's team was inside this place. And I've often regretted that choice. Because by finding you again, Colette, I made you an accomplice. By finding you again, I imposed terror on you, my terror. I contaminated you with the worst of diseases, living under the threat of Soudkovski.

Ana and I have just listened to Blanche without a break, as if downing a drink in one. We barely breathed. End of the cassette. Silence. I glance at my watch: 11:00 P.M.!

"And do you know what they did next, Mom?" Ana asks me, super excited by the recordings.

I have to fill in the blanks. Answer her questions.

"I believe Colette disappeared for a few days, before reappearing at the shoe-repair shop. But I don't know where they went after that great match."

We warm up some lasagna and eat it straight from the dish, to get back to the recorder and cassettes as quickly as possible. No time to sit at the table. After just three forkfuls, Ana picks a new cassette from the ten we have yet to listen to, and slips it into the recorder. Since we've been back, we've been sticking Post-it notes on them, detailing who is speaking and on what subject. The first names, the surnames, the years. Ana is curious and very keen. We have the whole weekend to finish listening to them. Colette's voice allows us to stick the pieces of her life back together, but also the pieces of others' lives, including our own.

22

April 2000

Finding Blanche again at the Stade de France made Colette think of Father Aubry, her little brother playing the organ, the raffle house, Aimé, God, and the blue shoes that had brought Blanche to her. They walked side by side, with the little dog in front of them. It stopped raining. Two slender figures under the streetlights. They found a small hotel in Saint-Denis, but first they went to a store to buy something to eat and a bottle of champagne. When the assistant asked them which brand they wanted, they didn't know what to say. The last time Colette had bought any was for Aimé's eighteenth. So Blanche chose.

Before drinking from their plastic cups, Blanche dabbed a drop of champagne behind Colette's ear. "It brings good luck. The customers at the cabaret do it all the time." They had two victories to celebrate. Gueugnon's and Blanche's. She had finally run away. Then they settled Lancelot between them on the bed, and Blanche told my aunt everything. Right up to the blood-stained sweater at the bottom of the garbage bag. Colette listened to her breathlessly, eyes riveted to the ceiling and fingers buried in the dog's coat.

"And you, Colette, what have you been up to all these years? Twenty-eight years without seeing you, thinking of you day and night."

Colette took a deep breath before replying:

"The mother died five years before Jean did. I could tell you about plenty of things, plenty of people who brought me sorrow and joy. But the death of that woman unhinged me. I used to visit her at lunchtime, before reopening the shoe-repair shop, to bring her fruit, clean laundry, newspapers. She would look at me without saying a word. With hatred in her eyes. Reproaching me for not having died instead of my little sister, Danièle. It got worse with the passing years. At first, she'd followed Sénéchal to a clinic. A luxurious kind of hospice, because the marquess had lost his marbles. During the day, she'd go to his room to help him to eat, bawling out the nurses if they were late with his medication. That went on for a few years. They lived like a couple who retired in the evening to separate rooms. Then, when he died, the mother became entrenched in silence and her hatred of me, her hatred of everything. I suggested finding her a small apartment. "So you can come and poison me?" Those were her last words! Two months later, she threw herself from the sixth story. That jump, it was me that it killed. I couldn't even get out of bed, couldn't stop crying. Morbid thoughts filled my head. I wanted to end it all. Louis and my brother didn't know what to do anymore. The doctor put me in with the loonies, you know. They gave me injections and all that. My shop remained closed . . . Which shows that, when parents die, whether they were kind or nasty, gentle or violent, it's too hard a blow. My mother's death was the most hideous to hit me. Because, by committing suicide, she was trying to finish me off. Inflict the coup de grâce. She was determined that I wouldn't survive her. She could never bear me even breathing . . . And there was the guilt she made me carry when Danièle was killed. When it was actually the man she worshipped, whom she'd served right to the end like a slave, who had shot dead the only child she'd ever loved . . . That injustice, I was the one who paid for it . . . And then one day, the sun found its way back into my head. I rediscovered my love of eating, of listening to Jean's music, of attending matches."

Blanche took hold of Colette's hand and they finally fell asleep, side by side. Blanche dreamed of Soudoro, who was searching high and low for her, like a madman. Lancelot woke them on the Sunday morning. They took him out and then had breakfast in a café. "And what would the photocopies like?" the waiter quipped. His allusion to their resemblance passed them by. Blanche kept jumping at the slightest noise, found it hard to breathe.

The next day, they caught a train at Gare de Lyon. Colette had never traveled by metro. Blanche was quite used to it. They were like two sisters who had been separated at birth. Seemingly, one was resourceful, the other more fearful. As soon as they arrived in Annecy, Blanche went to the police station. Colette waited for her, with Lancelot, beside the lake. Seeing it for the first time, she thought the sea must look similar. It was a fine day, the spring sun warmed the streets and was reflected on the water. Colette had been away from Gueugnon since Saturday, no one knew where she was.

At the front desk, Blanche gave her name and said she'd come about an assault. That she had proof. She was received by an Inspector Perret, an affable man. Blanche handed him the plastic bag, explaining that the blood on the sweater was doubtless that of Marie Roman, her mother, assaulted on December 30, 1999, in Annecy, by Levgueni Soudkovski, who resided at 54, Avenue du Maréchal-de-Saxe, in Lyon 3, fourth floor, door on the left. When the inspector asked how to contact her, she replied:

"I'll call you. From today, I no longer exist. That man is my genitor and he'll search everywhere for me, to do the same to me as he did to my mother."

"We can place you under protection, madame."

"No one can protect me from him."

"You should trust the police."

"I trust no one. Except Colette."

"Who is Colette?"

"My only friend."

Blanche asked the inspector to take her to wherever her mother was secretly hospitalized. She needed to see her once before leaving.

"I'm nearly fifty-four, and I have no memory of her. Levgueni Soudkovski always claimed that she was dead. He separated us when I was two years old."

The inspector promised he'd look into it and gave her a 9:00 A.M. appointment at the police station the following day.

Blanche returned to Colette. They ate a sandwich beside the lake.

"Can you swim?"

"Yes, Blaise taught me."

"The tall boy who always stuck up for you at school!"

They slept in a small bed-and-breakfast outside the town center. Colette tasted a *fondue savoyarde* for the first time. A two-day interlude that felt unreal, blissful. Blanche would be coming home with her. They would never be apart again. We often say of a person we like that we could go on vacation with them. Affinities can't be explained. During those two days in Annecy, Colette decided that she would go on vacation with Blanche, above the shoe-repair shop, and for a very long time.

23

November 9, 2010

She knows he's there, that he's found her. She senses his presence, senses that he's coming, that he's climbing floor by floor, that he's closing in on her like a beast that has picked up the scent of prey it has never stopped hunting. She knows he'll end up pushing open the door. For the first time, she's not afraid of him. She's leaving. By the time he sets foot in this room, she'll already be far away. Where he won't be able to torment her anymore. Neither in this life, nor in the next. Marie Roman falls asleep, the picture of her daughter in her hands.

Marie would have liked Agnès to visit again. She'd have liked to tell her that, after laying low in the stockroom of the bookstore, she'd left Sallanches in 1990 to settle in Talloires, in a small apartment complex. A few kilometers from the Lac d'Annecy. It was her sister who'd found the apartment for her, signing for it with her married name: Jeanne Mons. Marie was sixty-one and had never lowered her guard. For nine years, she'd kept her terror at bay, thinking, at every moment, of her daughter. Did she live in France? Had she had children? Married happily? Her sister had asked a gendarme friend to do some research on Blanche, but he couldn't find a single trace of her after the circus was sold in 1970. She seemed not to exist. No death record, social security number, postal address, or employer. The gendarme had suggested putting out a missing-person appeal, but Marie had been totally against it. If her daughter had managed to escape the monster's clutches, doing such a thing would risk putting her in danger.

Nine years of an almost normal life. A kind of exile, a respite from the anguish caused by fear. Apart from going shopping, she only went out with Jeanne, never alone. Occasionally, they would go swimming in the lake, and for Marie, those days were the loveliest of her life.

Until that October 3, 1999, when, without realizing it, she'd crossed paths with Viktor Socha on a sidewalk in Talloires. They had met several times, forty years earlier. How could she possibly have recognized this ugly little man? He, on the other hand, had noticed the way she walked. Something about how she held her head that was familiar to him. He loathed old people, dreaded old age. And yet that particular woman had drawn his attention. Viktor Socha was illiterate but had an abnormally good memory for faces, with an exceptional awareness of detail and direction. She had aged, but not changed. Same bearing, same figure, same face.

In another life, he would have done anything to have her, but she was an untouchable beauty because she was married to a madman, a real one. Never had Socha known a man more violent than Soudkovski. That brute was afraid of nothing. And then one day, his wife had disappeared. In the traveling-circus world, people thought Soudkovski had killed her, but then they found out that he was searching for her. And continued searching for decades. Finding her became an obsession, and a significant reward was offered to anyone who brought him information.

She was called Marie. Socha was sure of that. She was called Marie like the Holy Virgin his mother prayed to every night, back in Warsaw. So, without thinking, he'd called out, like a plea, though not in her direction, as if calling someone else: "Marie!"

And she had looked back. Before hurriedly setting off again. Socha had followed her at a distance and mentally logged her address: a white, four-story residence beside a bakery with a yellow façade and a public garden with an umbrella pine at least ten meters tall.

He hadn't thought twice about it. He knew that, by informing Soudkovski, he was signing this woman's death warrant. He hadn't felt the slightest pity. On the contrary, she'd never even looked at him back then, as if he were transparent. And now he held her fate in his hands.

The worst of it is that Socha should never have been in Talloires. The previous day, a guy from Urmatt had offered him five hundred francs to deliver a dozen desks, from a former school, to the Père-Bise Inn: "It's a good deal. Eight hundred kilometers there and back. We'll go via Basel. The guy supposed to come with me is sick. We'll take turns at the wheel."

Back in Alsace, it had taken Socha weeks to get hold of Soudkovski, who didn't own a phone. In late December, the boss of a scrapyard in Bron had finally given the message to Soudkovski in person: Viktor Socha was looking for him, it was urgent. Soudkovski had called him, and then gone to check the information he'd given him. It was three in the afternoon when he found himself outside her place. No point forcing any locks or climbing up balconies at nightfall. He'd just ring the doorbell. Without a spyhole to check, Marie had simply opened the door. Several seconds of silence had ensued, while he blocked the door with his foot and she struggled to breathe. White as a sheet, she'd half-opened her mouth but had been incapable of calling for help. When he left the apartment half an hour later, he was sure he'd killed her.

At the first stab of the knife, she'd finally screamed, thinking of her daughter. A desperate scream, before collapsing. It was thanks to that cry that a neighbor had called the police and Marie had been saved in time.

So long, Levgueni, you really always wanted me dead because I never loved you.

Before dying, Marie remembers hearing Blanche's voice from the depths of her coma: "It's me, Blanche. I know he did this to you. I've reported him to the police. Don't worry about me, I have a friend. I'm going to live with her. We're saved, Mommy." She'd said "Mommy." Marie remembers hearing another voice, too. Of a woman who was with Blanche.

I knew my daughter was protected by someone. I just didn't know who.

Marie Roman is dead when Soudkovski opens the door to her room in the *Tous les soleils* rest home. It's four in the morning. She lies lifeless, with their daughter's identity card in her hands. He doesn't take it. Why would he? It's incriminating evidence.

Now, he thinks, all that's left for me to do is breathe in Agnès's skin and then go.

24

Colette

Blaise disappeared between 1965 and 1969. He bolted from Lyon without telling anyone. He'd sent me a card to wish me a happy 1965, and seven days later, he vanished. I read and reread that card, searching his words, scrawled with a fountain pen, for any hint or clue: "My dear Colette, may this new year bring you joys and happinesses." Joys and happinesses plural. That was it.

On January 7, the headmaster of his boarding school phoned his mother to inform her of his absence. Blaise had emptied the cupboards in his room and left. He'd said nothing to the other boarders.

I still don't know today what kind of relationship I've had with God, but I certainly lit plenty of candles in the church in Gueugnon then, praying that no harm would come to him. And then there's that angel, at the back on the left, that looks like him. I'd talk to it. I'd beg it to protect Blaise.

I switch off the recording. Ana jumps, surprised at my interrupting her great-aunt.

"I've seen that sculpture. The angel has the face of a young boy. A bit like Michelangelo's *David* . . . Have you ever seen a photo of Blaise?"

"No, I don't think so," she says, frowning.

I go and fetch the snap that Antoine Été gave me, of Blaise, my father, and Antoine's parents in front of the raffle house, to show her.

"That's him, there."

"Classy! Did you know him?"

"No. I know that Colette visited him on the day he died. But everything was secret. Whenever she spoke of him to Eugénie de Sénéchal, Blaise's mother, she'd whisper down the phone. There was a photo of him in her room, on her bedside table."

"Oh yes, I remember! When I was little, I asked Colette if he was her husband. She replied that she'd never been married. So I asked her why not. She gave me a strange answer, kind of, you don't need to be married to love . . . "

"It's insane, all the mysteries she left us with."

"Well, I really like it. There aren't many people who leave cassettes and mysteries before dying. It means that Coco, she wasn't like other people."

"That's for sure. Shall we carry on?"

Ana nods, sucking Ice Tea through a straw. I press play.

COLETTE

One morning in 1969, May 6 to be precise, he was waiting for me outside the shoe-repair shop. Blaise hadn't wanted to come inside, despite Mokhtar's insistence; he kept saying: "I'll wait for her out here, the sun's shining, I want to make the most of it." I didn't recognize him when I first saw him, sitting there on one of the big stone planters in his Prince of Wales check suit and green shirt, eyes closed, face turned up to the sky. Blaise had "grown up." I couldn't say a thing; we didn't belong to the same world anymore. I knew that before, but right then, it really hit me. He stood up, smiling, and handed me a book.

"The first edition, it's for you, my Colette."

My Colette. I was still the first one, the important one, the friend. I looked at the cover. L'Éternité, a novel, Blaise de Sénéchal.

"You've written a book?" I asked, stupidly, when I'd spent our childhood predicting to him that he'd write dozens of them.

"Yes."

He spoke to me as if we'd seen each other the previous day. He looked tired. Damaged. Aged. And yet he was only twenty-three. Once I was sure it was really him, with his first novel in my hand, I hugged him. He smelled different, a whiff of the attic, a mix of polish, wood, and dust. He handed me an envelope.

"Read it when I'm gone."

Mokhtar came out of the shop to give me the day off, so I could make the most of my friend being there. But Blaise said there was no need, he was leaving right away. He'd only come to bring me his book, he was expected back in Paris. I remember thinking, so, he lives in Paris. He kissed me on the lips, shook Mokhtar's hand, then disappeared around the corner of the street. I screamed his name, and he came back.

"You're going, just like that? You're leaving me all alone?"

Even during matches, I'd never shouted so loud. He smiled sadly at me, planted another kiss on my lips, and murmured:

"Blaise is dead."

Shocked, I said nothing. I was turned to jelly.

"Take the day off, m'dear, really," Mokhtar insisted sadly, when he was never sad.

Mokhtar, how I miss him.

"Make yourself comfortable up there, in my place, and read all that."

He indicated the envelope and the book in my hands. I hesitated, because he was already ill and weak, but seeing the insistence in his eyes, I obeyed.

Colette can be heard taking a letter out of its envelope and unfolding it.

COLETTE

May 1, 1969

My dear Colette, my dear Mom,

I've missed both of you, terribly. I apologize to you. In Lyon, I met a man who ran a jazz club in Paris. A guy who was so attractive, I didn't hesitate when he suggested that I come with him. I saw him as the best luck I'd ever had. What a mistake . . . Luck is depending on no one. I moved into his place and played the piano at his club. I soon became disillusioned. But I was ashamed of having left like a thief in the night, of having abandoned you both. I was very young, and it took me some time to escape from his clutches. Fortunately, one of the club's musicians took me under her wing. She put me up. I started to write L'Éternité. *A story I've carried with me since the day you placed a lamb in my arms, my Colette. It took me three years to write it. This love story, it's you who inspired it, you and the feelings I have for you. There's probably nothing worse for a boy than to love a girl knowing that he'll never be able to commit to her.*

In this novel, I imagined our life, year after year, if I'd been able to make love to you, marry you, wake up and fall asleep beside you. Give you children. I imagined how we'd have grown up and grown old together. What our daily life would have been like, where we'd have lived, in which town, which street, which house, the color of the curtains. The faces of our children, their names, their school, their godfathers and godmothers, their likes and dislikes. I dreamed of our dinners, our Christmases, our vacations with Jean, and of how two childhood friends reinvent their love, day after day, for decades. Writing allowed me to feel what I was incapable of living.

When I'd finished my manuscript, I sent it to a dozen or so editors. Only one responded. And my prayers were answered. I dedicated this novel to the two of you, Colette and Mom, because you are, and always will be, the two feminine figures who saved my childhood. Yes, you saved my childhood, and I will never forget it. Know that you are both in my heart, I love you.

Your devoted,
Blaise

COLETTE

I didn't read L'Éternité, *Agnès . . . When I saw, on the first page, "To Colette S. and to my mother," I closed it again. Only Aimé ever talked to me about it, because I allowed him to do so. I wanted to know if Blaise had kept my first name, but the heroine is called Tess, like the Thomas Hardy novel. I wouldn't let Aimé read me any excerpts . . . I think that if I had read it then, it would have felt like open heart surgery without anesthetic. I saw Blaise again a year later, when Danièle was killed by his father, the father he feared. Blaise and Jean were the ones holding my hands at the cemetery. Blaise phoned me and wrote to me after Mokhtar's death. But when my sister died, he came back in person. He slept at mine, refusing to go to the château, to "the scene of the crime." He never went back there again. That was the last night we spent together. Him on the ottoman, me in my room. He left the day after the funeral. I saw him again when Jean received his first prize at the conservatoire. And then years later . . . It's strange how Blaise filled in my childhood, like those books you colored in as a child, Agnès. Do you remember? I'd buy them at the* tabac. *There were outlines on each page and you'd fill them in with your felt-tip pens. Blaise did the same, he filled me in with colors. He will always be the boy who slipped money into my pocket on the day of the empty suitcase, the day when the mother didn't watch me leave home to become Mokhtar's apprentice.*

Blaise remained in Paris. In the early seventies, with the money he'd earned from his novel, he got together with a dodgy guy to open a nightclub, on Rue Campagne-Première. One of those trendy places popular with actors, singers, TV types, and where quite a lot of drugs circulated . . . It was Jean and Louis who told me about it.

One day, I advised him to keep writing, and he replied:

"What for, Colette? Even you haven't read my book."

"I have, and what's more, it's very good."

He called me a liar. And he was right. And he shouted down the phone: "Very good, that's worse than anything!" before hanging up on me. I'd disappointed him. I hadn't been equal to our friendship. I did nothing to help him. For a long time, I thought that, had it been the other way around, he would have offered me a helping hand.

Colette stops speaking for a few minutes. Ana and I look at each other without saying anything.

COLETTE

Jean took me to Paris to see him in 1973. Blaise was just skin and bones. The three of us had lunch near his nightclub. He was nervous, smelled of alcohol. Pretended in every way. To listen to us, to reply to us. It was all fake. His joy at seeing us, his words. It was like he was just reciting a lesson. He rushed through lunch so it wouldn't last too long. It was that day I realized that a part of him had been dead for a long time. All that remained was his sadness. A survivor full of sadness. When I asked him if he'd met anyone, he said, "And you, Colette?" without answering my question.

25

November 19, 2010

It's the first time I'm entering the building. Usually, I drop Ana off outside and drive away. Code 1925B. I know that he lives on the top floor. That they live on the top floor. That the view is amazing. Ana told me. I get into the elevator. My heart is beating, nothing abnormal. I don't know if Pierre's home, but I know the other one isn't; she's filming in Spain. I haven't called, haven't announced my arrival. I reach the eighth floor, two doors on the landing. Their names on the one to the left. Ana, Audrey, Pierre. If I'd read those three names side by side just over a month ago, I'd have collapsed. Thank you, Colette.

I ring the doorbell. I hear steps. He opens the door. Looks furtively behind me. He realizes that I'm alone. He's in jeans and a black sweater.

"Come in."

Seeing a red coat and flowery scarf hanging on the peg stops me in my tracks. I even recoil. Why have I come up here, among their furniture, their decorations, their photos, their scents, their lights?

"It might be better if we go down to the café."

"Are you sure?"

"Yes."

"Okay."

He grabs a coat, and here I am, back in the corridor with him, opening the door to the elevator.

"All's well?" he asks.

"All's well. We finished listening to Colette's cassettes, Ana and I . . . We finished yesterday evening."

"And?"

"And . . . a life."

That's all I can think of saying in response. A life. Like the title of Maupassant's novel. *Une vie.*

We say nothing more until we're in the café. We haven't walked together for such a long time. Inside, we pick a corner with no one around. I order a stiff double espresso; he goes for an Americano. He stares at me, waiting for me to speak.

"I wanted to know, when you'd phone each other, you and Colette, what did you talk about?"

"She almost only talked about you. She'd ask me questions. She wanted to know how you were, what you were doing. To find out about your plans, if you were smiling, if you were looking well. She'd question me like a police inspector."

"Are you serious?"

"Yes."

"But I called her every week . . . She could have asked me those questions."

"She thought you lied to reassure her."

"That's the pot calling the kettle black! She spent her life hiding crazy things from us! To the extent of dying without dying."

He takes a while to respond. He's trying to find the right words:

"I think Colette knew something about you. Something she was afraid you'd discover."

"Stop it, Pierre, you're freaking me out."

"That's all I know."

I look hard at him, as if he were lying to me.

"I swear to you, Agnès."

"On Ana's life?"

He sighs.

"On Ana's life."

We stop talking. He strokes the table with his fingertips, then asks me if I'm well.

"I am well."

"I'm not filming anything before March. Until then, I'm going to make the most of Ana."

"Since she's spending the week at yours, I'll probably go back to Gueugnon."

"To see your boyfriend?"

I blush like a schoolgirl.

"I'd like to buy a house there."

"What for?"

He asked the question slightly aggressively. As if I were losing my mind.

"To live there for part of the year."

"But why?"

"Why not?"

"So it's serious, then," he says, mockingly.

"What's serious?"

"Your guy."

If he only knew how alone I am. If he only knew . . . I return to what interests me, what brought me here to Saint-Paul.

"What makes you think that Colette was afraid I would discover something about myself?"

"Intuition. She was beating around the bush . . . What's Agnès doing, where's Agnès going, who does she talk to . . . I don't think she liked us being so far away . . . She'd say it reassured her to hear me . . . I really liked Colette, you know."

"I know."

"Thinking back on it, it was as if she was scared for you. Particularly after your mother died. After Hannah's funeral, that's when it started."

"What started?"

"Before that, I'd phone her from time to time. After Hannah passed away, Colette would ask me for news every week."

"But why call her without telling me about it?"

"She asked me not to. She didn't want to worry you."

"But for God's sake, I had her on the phone every Tuesday. You must admit, it's weird."

He plucks an e-cigarette from his pocket. I can't help but stare, wide-eyed. He takes a big drag before saying:

"One day, she asked me something odd; she asked if our house had any security . . . I thought to myself, she's getting paranoid."

"Pierre, did you know that she wasn't dead in 2007?"

"Of course not . . . "

He seems sincere. I say nothing more. I have nothing more to say to him. I try to remember my conversations with Colette when I was living in LA. Pierre interrupts my thoughts.

"Something else to drink?"

"A small Vittel water, please."

He's on first-name terms with the waiter. I watch him raising his hand, calling out his name, saying hello back to two strangers who are smiling at him, so used is he to being in demand. He's handsome. So I'm doomed to finding him handsome to the end of my days.

"What are you looking at?" he asks.

"You. I'm looking at you. Ana doesn't look like us. She looks like my father."

He smiles.

"Did she tell you that she wants to go to the conservatoire, like him?"

"Of course. I'm not deaf yet, despite my great age. She spends hours at the piano, like Dad."

"How far have you gotten with your screenplay on your mother's story?"

"I'm almost done."

He looks at me with curiosity. Like when we were together and he was waiting for me to tell him about my next movie, in which he would have the star part.

"You're retracing Hannah's entire life?"

"Until she meets my father. What's really crazy about my parents is how they met."

"Who will get my part?"

I look down.

"No one."

". . ."

"Pierre, I won't be making that movie. Not that one, not any other one. I'm done with film."

". . ."

"I'm finishing the screenplay to turn it into a novel. It's the only form of expression I know right now. I'm going to learn to write like I learned to hold a camera. Once I've reached the end of the story, like the end of a journey, I'll turn each scene into a chapter, keeping the situations and the dialogues."

"You're going to become a novelist?"

"I'm going to try."

"You'll do it."

"I hope so."

"For sure."

"..."

"Is it because of me?"

"Because of you?"

"That you're done with film?"

"It's because of life. Of the time that's passed. I feel like writing, not returning to a movie set. I feel like traveling, working wherever, and writing allows that. My head's bursting with ideas."

I sense that he's troubled. Tears are welling up in his eyes. Which is rare. Pierre is a man who holds back his emotions, except in front of a camera when he's playing someone else. *Another man, another chance*, like that movie title.

"I have to tell you something," he whispers.

"..."

"But promise me not to talk to Ana about it. I want to do that myself."

"I promise."

I grip the banquette under my thighs with both hands.

"I'm going to be a father again. Audrey is pregnant."

26

HANNAH RUBEN

(Contd.)

1970

Hannah is twenty-eight when she receives a phone call from Jean. He is twenty.

"Are you Hannah Ruben?"

"Yes."

"Hello, my name is Jean Septembre."

She knows who Jean is. All the musicians know that Jean Septembre is an exceptional pianist, who left the Lyon conservatoire with the top prize two years ago.

"Why are you calling me?"

She's short of breath. She's hoping he's contacting her to create a piece of music. To do a piano-violin duet together. That he's heard of her, too.

"I'd like to meet you. I have something very important to give you. I can't talk to you about it over the phone."

"Where do you live?"

She hears an embarrassed laugh before he says:

"With Élia and David Levitan . . . Well, my teachers . . . I can't manage to leave them."

"So you're in Lyon."

"Yes . . . when I'm not playing. I'm a pianist."

"I know. Will you be in Lyon on Saturday or Sunday?"

"Monday. I'll be in Lyon on Monday."

"And I'll be away."

"Ah."

"I'm playing in Paris starting on Monday. Recording the *Brandenburgs* at the Studio Davout. I'll be in Paris all next week."

"You're a musician?"

She's cut to the quick. He doesn't know who she is. She hesitates, piqued, but finally says:

"Violinist."

"That's wonderful."

His response surprises her.

"I suggest we meet in Paris," he adds. "I'll wait for you at the exit of Studio Davout on Tuesday evening, if you're free."

"Fine."

And they hang up without agreeing on a time, without her asking why it's so important.

The following Tuesday, he's there when she leaves the studio at 7 o'clock. He's been waiting for three hours, sitting on a bench, numb with cold. Still as a statue, white as a snowflake. She recognizes him, whereas he has no idea what she looks like. She walks up to him.

"I'm Hannah Ruben."

She isn't what he'd expected. She's extremely pretty, he thinks, *extremely*. She has a sky-blue bow in her hair, which is spring-like even though it's winter, and carries her violin case in her right hand. She looks at him without smiling. Jean stands up; he's tall, and remains rooted there, staring at her in silence.

"Come," she directs him. "It's cold. There's a café on the corner of the street . . . Ah, actually, no, I'm hungry. Will you treat me to supper?"

"Yes."

And he adds:

"With pleasure. Forgive me, I'm not used to this. Away from my piano, I struggle with good manners. I've been looking for you for a year. You can't imagine how hard I've looked for you, Hannah Ruben."

The restaurant, on Rue Auguste-Chapuis, gradually fills

up. Having arrived early, they're served first. "This evening, it's as much sauerkraut and Riesling as you like," the manager announces.

Hannah wolfs down her meal. Jean wonders how such a slim woman can eat so much. It's as if she hasn't eaten for days.

"Forgive me," she finally says. "When I'm playing, I only eat in the evening. During the day, I prefer to work on an empty stomach. Why were you looking for me, Jean Septembre?"

And, as if scared of what he's going to say, she keeps talking. He can't get a word in edgeways. Jean has never dined tête-à-tête with a woman. Since she's already on her second glass of wine and must weigh 40 kilos, she's probably tipsy. That's the word Colette uses when talking about a player or supporter who's drunk too much after a match.

Hannah shows him the two name bracelets she wears on her wrist: Hannah and Marthe.

"I had them altered to fit me."

Hannah tells him that the second name had saved her life during the war. That she, too, had attended the Lyon conservatoire and had won second prize in her year, but longer ago than him since she's older than him, and that it's a shame they're only meeting now because she's getting married in a month's time. She'd hesitated before agreeing to meet because she's still in mourning for her adoptive parents, who were wonderful people.

"My father, Benjamin Gravoin, a doctor at the Grange-Blanche Hospital, and my mother, Éléonore Gravoin . . . She was a great violinist."

Jean concurs. Of course, he's heard recordings of her playing. Without drawing breath, Hannah explains that she's an orphan twice over. That her biological parents had died when deported, and her adoptive parents in a plane crash.

"You know, the Caravelle 'Béarn' No. 244, registration F-BOHB . . . The Air France flight 1611, Ajaccio-Nice-Côte d'Azur, on September 11, 1968, September 11," she repeats. "And yet the weather was great that day. They were returning from vacation. They'd decided to spend the night in Nice's Old

Town before heading up to Lyon. But half an hour after take-off, the pilot announced that a fire had started in the aircraft. That he needed to land ASAP . . . There were 95 people on board that wretched plane. An hour after the distress call, the debris was found scattered across the sea. They said it was due to a water-heater in the bathroom, or someone throwing a partially extinguished cigarette into a container . . . A fire that had spread. How could people as good as my parents have to suffer that? I can tell you, Jean, I'll never set foot inside a church or synagogue again. Never. Unless it's me who brings bad luck. My parents were exterminated twice in succession . . . Once in Auschwitz and once in the sky. Ten days after the crash, on September 21, to be precise, a journalist declared that the plane might have been struck by a missile during military exercises. An accident . . .

Hannah stops talking. She's mixing mustard into her cabbage. Jean is incapable of uttering a word. They remain silent in the hubbub that surrounds them. *How can I tell her what I've come here to tell her after what she's just told me?*, he thinks. He'd like to have a piano at hand so as to play what's on his mind. She's a musician, she'd understand a bit better than someone else. He can't tell her that it started a year ago. He was due to give a concert for the people of Gueugnon. A free concert to thank all the residents who'd taken part in the raffle.

That day, Jean had arrived at the community center in the early afternoon, with Colette. Returning to the piano of his childhood was deeply moving to him. A tuner was due to come from Autun at around three. Colette sat in a corner. Jean sat at the piano. He asked Colette what she'd like to hear, and she replied: "Any sonata by Chopin, please." He played "*Clair de lune*." Colette was in seventh heaven. He recalled what his teacher, David Levitan, would often say to him: "Be a musician unconditionally; don't start playing a piece if you're not at one with your piano." Just as he was thinking that, a key got stuck. Jean finished playing the sonata for his sister all the same. Pianos hate traveling. They transport us to sublime heights but can't stand moving, changing temperature. "Pianos are homebodies," David Levitan always said. This one can't have appreciated being moved from the château to the community center.

Jean unscrewed the end blocks to access the Steinway's skeleton. That's when he discovered that a piece of paper slipped under an F key was blocking it, when that had never happened before. It took Jean a while to make out the marks written in black ink. At first, he thought it might have been some game of Blaise's when he was little, or a note written by the tuner. And then he remembered that the piano had arrived at the château during the Occupation, in 1942, for a German officer, and had then been abandoned by the Nazis when they were routed. Eugénie de Sénéchal always said she had no idea where the grand piano had originally come from.

He showed the piece of paper to Colette. They went back to the shoe-repair shop. Colette placed it under the lamp and had a long look at it. In a notebook, she tried to copy out each mark, but bigger. Apart from the date, it made no sense to her:

אנחנו יוצאים ליעד לא ידוע. אם תמצא את המילה הזו זה אומר שאני 1942.
לא אחזור. הפסנתר הזה שייך לילדי נח ורפאל רובן.

Jean recognized Élia and David Levitan's mother tongue. Élia only read books in Hebrew, starting them at the end and reading from right to left on the page. As for David, he read in French and English. Who had written this note? The former owners of the instrument? An employee at the factory where it had been made?

"Where are fine pianos like that one made?" Colette asked.

"In Hamburg. For Europe, they all come from Hamburg."

That evening, Jean gave a concert lasting two hours. He'd chosen several pieces by Beethoven, Chopin, and Mozart. While playing, he forgot about the note he'd slipped into his wallet, left in the cloakroom.

But when he got back to Lyon and, at the table, said to the Levitans: "Actually, look what I found under a key of my childhood

Steinway . . ." his old teacher took the piece of paper, and Élia fetched her magnifying glass and translated what was written out loud:

"1942. We are leaving for an unknown destination. If you find this note, it means I won't be coming back . . . "

Élia stopped speaking for a few seconds, then continued:

"This piano belongs to the children of Agnès and Rafael Ruben."

A long silence followed. One of those silences Jean was now so familiar with, and to which he had become attached. He'd ended up feeling comfortable in the couple's silence. In their restrained reactions, their unspoken love, their deep and meaningful looks. But that evening, the silence was heavier than usual.

The note had been written by Rafael. That was discovered much later. How to find Rafael and Agnès? How to trace all the way back to them? This piano could come from France or a neighboring country. It was to Eugénie de Sénéchal that the Levitans turned to try to find the Rubens. But there were many people with that surname, even just in France. What nationality were they? If they were French, in which town did they live? Had they been deported? If so, where had they been arrested? It was in 1942 that the major roundups had taken place. What were the names of the children mentioned? How many children were involved? Were any members of this family still alive? Had one of them been saved? If so, where was that person?

With the help of the Red Cross lists, Eugénie found several hundred Rubens in France in the forties, now scattered all over Europe. A year of research, a year of false trails, a year of doubts, a year bent over lists of decimated families. Numbers, faces in photographs. And death convoys that left packed with people and from which no one returned. Too many Rubens to find Agnès or Rafael. Too many homonyms. Discouraged, Eugénie came up with the idea of making the piano talk. Why hadn't she thought of that before?

She phoned Colette to ask her to find the serial number. Probably inside, on the frame or under the soundboard. Colette called her back an hour later, out of breath: 289019! And that's how Eugénie finally discovered that the Steinway had been bought on Quai Romain-Rolland, in Lyon's fifth arrondissement, in 1937 by a certain Germaine Rouve. There was an address in the delivery records. Madame Rouve had sold the piano, two years after purchasing it, to a family also living in Lyon. She knew neither their name, nor their address, but she was certain that they lived in Lyon and were Jewish.

"What makes you think that, madame?" Eugénie asked her.

"The accent and the type," Germaine had replied.

"The type?"

"The type that's perfectly presentable, but very Jewish, if you see what I mean."

Eugénie didn't see, but she was so relieved to learn that the Steinway had remained in Lyon, she could have hugged the woman.

So, it was Rafael Ruben who had come to try out the piano. He had said it was a birthday present for his wife. Once he'd bought it, he'd organized its transport himself. Germaine Rouve remembered him indicating that he lived just a stone's throw away. This information enabled the marchioness to identify the family with ease on the list of deportations provided by the Red Cross. Agnès, Rafael, Sasha, and Myriam Ruben had been arrested by the Gestapo on October 16, 1942—so, four months before the great roundup on Rue Sainte-Catherine—under the orders of Klaus Barbie. Not one member of the Ruben family had returned. Only the youngest, a two-month-old baby, had been saved by a Righteous couple, Benjamin and Éléonore Gravoin. Neighbors and friends to whom Agnès had entrusted her baby. A year of research to identify and find Hannah Ruben, born August 15, 1942.

Eugénie had succeeded. Without realizing it, she had lived for decades alongside a piano stolen from innocent people. And that same instrument had revealed the talent of another kind of innocent, Jean. *Thank you, Rafael, thank you for having slipped that piece of paper under a key.*

Eugénie had sought Jean out one evening, after a concert, and handed him a notebook on which she'd written: "Hannah Ruben, born August 15, 1942, adopted in 1947 by the Gravoins." Along with an address and a phone number.

Jean had waited a few weeks before deciding to phone this Hannah. And now she was here, in front of him, in this packed place smelling of both cabbage and wine, looking him straight in the eye, waiting for him to decide to speak.

Jean, who has never drunk alcohol, pours himself a glass of Reisling to give an impression of composure. And can only muster a single sentence:

"The piano that saved my life, it's yours."

27

November 20, 2010

"On the day that Marie Roman gets buried, her daughter is being exhumed . . . Is that what you're telling me, Paul?"

"Friday, at 9:00 A.M."

"And Marie's funeral will take place on Friday at 3:00 P.M."

"Would you like to attend the exhumation of Blanche Soudkovski on Friday?"

"I'm allowed to?"

"Normally, no. But you are involved, since it's your aunt's grave, and you and your daughter are her only living relatives. I can get a special dispensation for you."

"But . . . let's agree that I won't stay for when you open the coffin."

"A coffin is never opened in the cemetery, except when it's to transfer ancient bones to the ossuary. The body will go straight to Dijon for identification. They have the DNA of her aunt Jeanne, and of Marie Roman and Soudkovski, her parents."

He's about to add something but stops himself, clearly swallowing his own words.

"Everything okay, Paul?"

He smiles at me sadly. He seems to have fallen out with his razor since he's been sleeping in Gueugnon. Unless it's Adèle who's been making his nights sleepless . . . He's looking haggard to me. We're in the dining room at the Monge hotel. I've only just arrived in Gueugnon. It's 11 A.M.; I cried all night and caught a train this morning. I wonder how Ana will react when Pierre tells her the news.

"As long as we haven't arrested Soudkovski, everything won't be okay. After going to Sallanches, he switched off his phone. But then his signal was picked up in Paris."

"In Paris?"

He nods.

"Whereabouts?"

"We don't know yet, not precisely."

"Can I go back to the Rue des Fredins house this evening?"

"I'd rather you sleep at the Monge for now. Are you staying long?"

"Seven days. I leave Sunday morning, to pick up Ana. She's at her father's this week . . . I'll be at the cemetery on Friday morning."

"You won't pass out?"

"I'll try not to."

"You do look a bit washed out, Agnès."

"I cried all night. Did me good."

". . ."

"Pierre Dugain's new young woman is pregnant."

". . ."

"Don't look at me like that, Paul. I'm done mourning Pierre . . . which is what you say when you've stopped hoping someone will come back into your life, and only dream about them every other night. Having said that, I don't know how Ana's going to react."

"Is that why you cried?"

"Yes. I cried because I'm an only child. And because I'd have loved it if my parents had given me a brother or sister. I begged them. But no dice. They were taken up with their passion, their traveling. And Colette would've been landed with two brats during school vacations, instead of one . . . She didn't have the space, my poor Colette . . . "

I knock my cup over on the table. There's coffee everywhere. I go grab a sponge from behind the counter. The dining room is empty. I come here so often now, I behave as if I'm at home.

"Sorry, Paul," I say, sponging away. "Since I didn't want Ana to be alone, I wanted a second child with Pierre, and he always found some excuse. With the new woman, he found no excuse . . . Basically, what was wrong in our relationship was us."

Ilyas turns up. I can see he's come straight from work and hasn't slept. I'd sent him a message to join me here.

"I was on the night shift . . . At last, it's the weekend! Lina arrives this evening."

He greets Paul and kisses my hair.

"You smell good. Like chamomile . . . Been crying?"

"It's a peony shampoo . . . So, mister future groom, how's this wedding shaping up?"

"Well! I'm scared stiff. I'm happy, and I'm scared stiff."

"You're still in love?"

"I'll always be in love with Lina. I know it."

"Where will you live?"

"I think she's going to come and bury herself here . . . So she told me. She's already sent a CV to the town hall."

"She's going to leave her lovely mountains?"

"She's like you, she hates the mountains . . . Is it true you're going to buy the Fredins house?"

"If Ana's okay with it. I'm going to come and bury myself here with you, too. Every other week at first, and then we'll see."

"Lina received your civil-status papers . . . Thanks for being her witness. I was amazed to see that you were born in Gueugnon! I was convinced you were born in Lyon."

"My mother gave birth above the shoe-repair shop, at Colette's. There was barely half an hour between the first contractions and my birth. I was in a hurry to arrive."

"That's funny, my little sister was born at home, too. My mother didn't have time to get to the hospital, either . . . "

"It's because we were so impatient to see you, Zeïa and me."

Ilyas chuckles.

"Why were you crying?" he asks.

"Pierre Dugain is going to be a father again."

"Good riddance. You'll finally be able to move on."

I'm cut to the quick, like Mom, when Dad phoned her that first time and didn't even know she was a musician.

"I've already moved on, Ilyas."

"Not enough. Right, friends, I'm off to bed. Need to be in shape this evening. How long are you staying, Agnès?"

"A week."

"Shall we have a bite with the gang?"

"Yes. I'll be here at the Monge. Paul doesn't want me going back to Rue des Fredins until Soudkovski's been arrested."

"Jeez, ever since you turned up in Gueugnon, it's like being in a detective novel!"

"Are you saying that to Paul, or to me?"

"To both of you!"

*

I settle into room No. 1. Outside, it's cold and dry, just how I like it. I've asked reception to make me a sandwich, and I'll go walking for a few hours. I packed one of Colette's cassettes and Hervé's Walkman in my suitcase. I didn't bring any old cassette; I picked the one on which Ana has written, on a blue Post-it: "Aimé and Blanche."

I feel like listening to it again. Immersing myself in my aunt's voice again. I think it's my favorite cassette. The way one has a favorite movie, book, piece of music. I'm going to walk to the Château de Sénéchal listening to it. There are paths around the château where the countryside is splendid, even in the middle of winter.

To get there, I cross the river using the footbridge I loved during my vacations, then walk around the stadium and the animal refuge. Maybe on the way back, I'll stop to adopt a dog. Adopting, that's a plan. Adopting, that's a commitment. It's about time I looked elsewhere to see if I'm there.

COLETTE

It's October 19, 2010. This is my last cassette. None left after that.

Silence.

COLETTE

I'm a bit fed up with being falsely dead. I think I'd like to be back with my ghosts again. To look after Danièle, too. Teach her to read and to love trees. Do you think one makes up for lost time when one's really dead? Do you think there are trees and birds around when one's really dead?

She switches off the recording.

COLETTE

Agnès, you're about to be thirty-eight, that's so young. Just eight years older than me when I met Aimé. I wouldn't want you to do like me, wouldn't want you to miss out on something or someone. I imagine that you're not feeling great. I hope I'm wrong. Louis told me that you were living in Paris. That you'd returned to France with Ana the year of my death. I ask your forgiveness. I can't phone you. I'm scared of him. Of him hurting you. I hope that once you've listened to me, and listened to Blanche . . . I hope you'll understand that I had to protect her until she was in her coffin. Had to protect her coffin. Since Blanche has been buried instead of me, I've been living in a house you don't know.

Silence.

COLETTE

You know, at this house, I go out into the garden, I watch TV, I listen to the radio. Louis comes to see me, brings me sewing work, books from the library, and newspapers. What I miss most is not hearing you, Ana and you. When I was alive, we'd talk every Tuesday. On Tuesdays, when I'd first open my eyes, I'd think, this afternoon, Agnès will call. It was weird, with the time difference. For you it was morning, for me, late afternoon. You were having your breakfast with Pierre and Ana, and me, in the winter, I was warming up my soup. I never really liked you being so far away with a different time to mine.

Silence.

COLETTE

In a magazine, I saw a photo of Pierre with a girl, an actress. I recognized her, she was in your last movie. At first, it made me feel terrible for you and Ana. But then I thought, talk about scoring, him in swimming trunks with a kid. Betrayal is betrayal. We all have it within us. Me, I betrayed Aimé. I don't know if you'll already have met him when you listen to this cassette.

Her phone rings, she goes to answer it without switching off the recording: "Hello, Antoine. All's well, I'm recording a cassette for Agnès. Yes. The last one. None left after this one. Sure. That's kind. See you later." I hear her walking back to the recorder as if I was in the room and she was rejoining me to finish her tea.

COLETTE

Have you already listened to the one where I talk about Aimé's birthday? His eighteenth, ABBA, the champagne and ravioli. The heat that started to break around midnight, the windows wide open. Me in a tee shirt, not at all the same person anymore. They say, "The habit doesn't make the monk," but really? It's like the saying that shoemakers always wear the worst shoes. Childhood apart, I've never worn bad shoes. That evening, it was off with the dated party dress Blaise had given me, out with my usual oversized garb that was quick to iron, quick to pull on. I was dancing, pressed against a towering young man, I was dancing barefoot, hair untied, eyes closed, with a long tee covering my body. We danced all night without saying a word. When each record ended, Aimé would go to the turntable, randomly pick another one, and come back to me to carry on dancing. We swayed exactly the same, whether the music was slow or fast: very gently. One against the other. My small hand in his, his other hand on my back. When I went home, dawn was breaking. The birds were singing their heads off in the École Pasteur's chestnut trees. The following day was a Sunday. My phone rang at about ten in the morning, Aimé said to me: "Colette, I'm coming by to pick you up."

Ten minutes later, he was parked outside the shoe-repair shop at the wheel of a Citroën DS, lent to him by another footballer. I couldn't tell you where we went. We drove for a good hour, though he didn't yet have his license. We ate some fried fish at an open-air café beside the water and drank lemon sodas. Within twenty-four hours, I, at the age of thirty, did what I'd never done before in my life. Danced an entire night with a boy, and then lunched with him, just the two of us. Those twenty-four hours, I told myself that they'd be enough to fill my life with happy memories. That there was no point looking any further. What a mistake, Agnès. You know, I never feared the silences between Aimé and me. I never feared not knowing what to say to him. We always had something to tell each other. And we never dreaded silence. Everything was easy between us, except for me. I was simply an idiot and a coward. I felt ashamed about what people would think. Because of my age. But why the hell should we care about what people think? The thought of being with such a handsome and talented young man held me back. Me, I was the shoe-mender of Gueugnon, an old maid of thirty; him, he was a star, a splendid young man of eighteen. I was Victor Hugo's famous earthworm in love with a star in the sky. Anyhow, that's what I told myself. From the moment the coach put him in defense, he became the star of the club. And I wanted much better for him than me. I decided for him. I sowed a bad seed that finally germinated, asking fate to make Aimé meet someone, so we could break up. After a match, playing away, on a Sunday, during the vacation . . . But he was at my door every evening, like some stowaway. I was nasty . . . How nasty I was. Sometimes, I wouldn't even open the door. He'd leave, not understanding.

Her voice cracks. A long silence. I can't hear a thing, not even her breathing.

COLETTE

The answer walked into my shop late one Tuesday afternoon. An answer with the graceful features of a seventeen-year-old girl with golden locks. Isabelle's parents were old customers. Third generation since Mokhtar. Only top-quality shoes. The father an engineer, I believe, the mother with a good position in Mâcon. Something like a magistrate. I loved taking care of that family's shoes and handbags. Isabelle was, and still is, beautiful as anything, kind, gentle, sensitive. Her mother was never around, and, if I understood correctly, Isabelle didn't get on with her parents. She wanted out of the family home. It didn't seem to be just a whim. She seemed deadly serious. With tears in her eyes, she asked me, as she placed a pair of pumps on the counter, if I might know of someone who would rent her a studio, or even have her as a lodger. I immediately thought of Mokhtar's room in the courtyard; a bit of renovation and a lick of paint with Louis's help, and it could be just the thing . . . But I said nothing. As I was about to speak, something stopped me. The eyes of the mother, my mother, who had never looked at me. When your own mother doesn't love you, how can you not think that the world is full of people who are better than you?

I had an idea. Agnès, don't think this diabolical idea didn't wrench my heart and guts. Don't think I dialed the Thillets' number, with Isabelle's lovely eyes watching me, without pinching the inside of my arm to keep from crying. I'd thought of the empty studio opposite Aimé's apartment, on the same landing. He'd mentioned that a young player from the club was supposed to be moving in. I explained the girl's situation to Monsieur Thillet, the urgency, and I heard him reply: "Of course, Colette, if she comes with your recommendation." I hung up smiling, when my entire soul was actually screaming in pain, and told Isabelle that she'd have a furnished, low-priced studio, that it was all arranged, that it was Tuesday and she could move in that same day. She threw her arms around my neck, saying she'd never forget what I'd just done for her. Neither would I; I would never forget. I put Aimé's future wife right on his path, outside his door. Like when you chose Pierre's actress, you put her, without knowing it, on his landing. But me, Colette Septembre, I knew it. I threw Isabelle onto Aimé's landing the way one throws a bottle out to sea. It was stupid. Why do such a thing when I loved him?

An hour later, Isabelle was back at the shop with a traveling bag over her shoulder. "Sorry, Madame Septembre, I don't have the address." I gave it to her: 3, Place des Forges, right beside the café. Then handed her the key, adding: "Red door, first floor, anyhow, there's only one." She looked surprised that I had the key, then glanced at my orange machine and smiled. She must have thought I had copies of the entire town's keys. She set off, leaving the powdery smell of Anaïs Anaïs in her wake. I remember that smell clearly; you wore that perfume, Agnès. One evening, you were off to Tacot's, Ilyas was waiting for you in the hall, you were made up like a stolen truck and wearing perfume. I recognized it on you, it took me back years. I never forget smells or music. Their effect on me. Once Isabelle Émorine had gone, I sat down. I was reeling.

Aimé didn't speak to me for weeks. When I'd come across him after matches, he'd hang his head.

Silence.

COLETTE

*That particular evening, I knew he wasn't training. I knew he'd be at home. She tried the key, not knowing that I'd given her the one to Aimé's apartment. She came face to face with him and apologized. She stammered that she'd made a mistake and was looking for her studio. Aimé told her that it must be across the landing. They thought that maybe the same key opened both locks, but no. They went down to the café to ask the owners for the right key. And came back upstairs, side by side. Aimé watched Isabelle enter her studio. Before closing her door, Isabelle asked him: "Should I return your keys to Madame Septembre?" And that's when he understood. That evening, he slipped a note under my doormat. "If you want to get rid of me, at least do it properly"—he addressed me with the formal "*vous*" for a long time. Progressed to "*tu*" later.*

From living on the same landing, they became friends. "You wouldn't have a little butter, would you? I've run out of coffee. Sorry, but did you have a power cut, too? Yes. Come in, I have candles while we wait. Don't stay in the dark. Football going well? Scoring any goals? Come to a match, you'll see. Oh, right, you're doing your exams? I'll be careful with my music, then, make sure it's not too loud. A French teacher? Great. And you, do you have a girlfriend? It's a bit complicated. Oh really, why? Is she married? No, not even, but it's complicated. And you, do you have a boyfriend? Yes. Pretty as you are, makes sense. Same to you, but how old are you? Your age. I look older than you. Bye now, see you later. I've got girlfriends coming around on Saturday night, we'll try not to make too much noise. Don't worry, I'll be away, we're playing in Monaco . . ."

Aimé left in 1978. He was bought by a club where he was really miserable. Forever on the subs' bench. No cohesion in the team. He missed Gueugnon. He missed everything. His team, his life, me. He told me so. He asked me to marry him. I didn't say no, I did worse. I pretended not to hear and changed the subject. I was sure I was a passing fancy, that he was clinging because I was running away. I remained distant so he'd love elsewhere, have children elsewhere. He returned to the Gueugnon club in 1980, never to leave again. Isabelle had split with her boyfriend. You see, Agnès, she actually waited for him. During the week, she studied in Dijon, but every weekend she was back home, above the Café Thillet. And little by little, from one invitation to the next, from aperitifs to quick coffees together . . . As you know, I live a hundred meters from the church. That day the bells rang out for their wedding, I won't forget it. Even if illness took all my memory away, I would never forget the sound of those bells. I had won my loss.

Two years went by without Aimé and I seeing each other, apart from at matches. He'd greet me nicely. They moved to La Pépinière, a neighborhood five minutes away from my place, a lovely white three-story house beside other lovely white three-story houses. They had a first baby, Nadège, then another little girl, Edwige. Two pretty girls with dark hair, like their father, and with the fair skin and blue eyes of their mother. Isabelle came to the shop to introduce them to me. She was always so sweet to me.

She switches off the recording.

Colette

Nadège and Edwige got older and started bringing me their parents' shoes all on their own. There was barely a year between them, they were like twins. "Hello, Madame Septembre, here are daddy's shoes!" When I was holding one of Aimé's shoes, it was like I was hugging him. Like when I'd danced in his arms on the night of his eighteenth. I'd often return the shoes to Isabelle, who'd come to pay, and they always looked finer than the day her husband had bought them. In time, the Chauvels ended up doing what everyone else did, picking a pair of shoes each season from those brands attached to hypermarkets. The kind of footwear people donate after wearing, to buy a new pair. Spring, summer, autumn, winter.

Two years after Aimé's and Isabelle's wedding, the mother died, taking almost all of me away with her. Aimé heard from Louis that I'd been confined to a psychiatric hospital. He managed to visit me there because he knew a doctor at the clinic. They gave him ten minutes with me. When I opened my eyes, I thought I was hallucinating. There he was, so close to me. He was sad because I'd been strapped down; he removed my restraints. All I could think of was doing like the mother, throwing myself out the window. I was a danger to myself. First, he kissed the inside of my wrists. I couldn't say a word. I had no more words. I could see us from above in that room; my mind had risen from my body like a helium balloon, and I saw us both, him young, very young, and me old, very old. I could hear the mother whispering in my ear: "You'll shame me to the end, being infatuated with that kid."

He laid his head against my heart and said:

"I hear your heart, I love you, I will always love you."

I felt paralyzed by emotion. He added that I'd "knocked him out" the first time he'd seen me. When he'd asked the other players who I was, they'd said: "That's Colette Septembre, of course." As if it was obvious. He continued:

"The first time I saw you, I had to stop in my tracks. I stopped everything to look at you. Now I regret not having told you that before. I'd cross paths with you on purpose, but you, all you were thinking about was the football, and you were so reserved. I found you beautiful. One day, I said to the physio: 'Colette Septembre sure is beautiful.' At first, he seemed surprised; then, when he saw that I was serious, it made him laugh, as if my comment was weird. But me, you never made me laugh, Colette."

It's from that day onward that Aimé used the familiar "tu" *with me. He said:*

"Nothing and no one will ever stop me from seeing you again, especially not you, so get yourself out of here."

The ten minutes were up. He stood, kissed me on the lips; I felt like vomiting, screaming, tearing my skin off and gouging my eyes out, I hated myself so much. I felt disgusting. It took a few days for his words to block the massive destructive process instilled in me by the mother when Danièle died: he had spoken words of love to me. Words that finally slid under my skin as if to cleanse my blood. Like his scent, the smell of vetiver that my cotton nightdress had absorbed. I kept that nightdress close to me until my release.

I reopened my shoe-repair shop, finished the jobs I'd abandoned, found my customers again. For two months, I only saw Aimé at the stadium. One evening, he knocked on my door and came into my home as if he'd been doing so forever. We drank some tea, chatted about everything and nothing. He was wearing jeans and I was wearing a black pleated skirt. He took it off me. Like you, he hated my clothes; he'd whisper to me, smiling, that he preferred me without any. He came back often. I didn't wait for him. We didn't arrange to meet. We never talked about living together. Aimé loved Isabelle and his two daughters, and me, I loved my solitude. When it's your best friend, solitude is neither sad, nor endured, it's chosen. I'd say to Aimé: "I'm your love on the side." And he'd say: "No, you're my other love, my love, the other one." No one ever knew about it. I'd stake my shoe-mender's hand and Aimé's right foot on it. Louis may have suspected something. But even that's not for sure. Never could anyone have imagined that Colette Septembre and Aimé Chauvel were having an affair. No one could have imagined that I could be someone's lover. Even the imagination has its limits. I also think that's why, right to the end, I dressed badly. So that no one could see anything else of me, other than Colette Septembre, old maid, football fan, the one who repairs shoes and belts. The one who sells polish and laces and cuts spare keys.

She switches off the recording.

COLETTE

When I came home with Blanche in 2000, it had already been eighteen years since Aimé had taken off my black pleated skirt. Eighteen years of secret love. He was married to Isabelle, and I to independence. We were free of each other. He never came to mine without calling me first. I was slightly scared that he'd fall in love with Blanche. For the first two weeks after our return from Annecy, I didn't answer the phone. Aimé ended up coming to the shop with a pair of loafers from goodness knows where. They weren't even his size.

"Why did you disappear after the match? We looked everywhere for you!"

I closed the shop and asked him to follow me. I'd never done that before. He'd never entered my house in broad daylight before. Indeed, that's the only time it ever happened.

"I'm going to introduce you to someone. A person who is very

important to me. But you can't tell anyone about it. Only Louis knows. You'll be the only ones to know that I live with someone now."

His face fell. I realized that he thought I'd just gotten married, or something like that. He stopped in front of my door.

"I don't think I want to meet him."

He sat down on a step.

"I'm not ready, Colette."

"Her name is Blanche."

He stood up and followed me. He had his back to the light. He turned toward the sun. I remember it clearly because I thought to myself, he's just as handsome, the years haven't spoiled him, he's my beautiful love, and I'm lucky. I felt like hugging him. Of course, I didn't. I've always been scared of touching others, except for Jean when he was little. Him, I'd cuddle.

Blanche was in the kitchen. She was singing to herself as she made lunch. She looked up at us. Before greeting her, Aimé said:

"You have a sister, Colette?"

"No. We just look a bit alike. I've told you a lot about Blanche."

"Ah, it's you!"

Aimé knew who Blanche was. She came over and hugged him, saying:

"Delighted to meet you. You're well, I hope?"

She returned to her apple tart, and I to my work. Someone was waiting outside the door of the shop, Monsieur Berry, a customer I adored. He said to me:

"So, Madame Septembre, playing hooky, were we?"

Aimé was behind me; I replied that Monsieur Chauvel and I were celebrating Gueugnon's victory. That made him smile. The town still hadn't gotten over having won the League Cup. I said to Aimé:

"I'll give you a ticket for your loafers, they'll be ready next week."

So began seven years of cohabitation with Blanche. Seven years, that might seem like a long time. It's seven Christmases, and spring seven times around. I often felt as if I were living in a fairy tale. Hiding a princess pursued by a monster. I, who loved solitude more than anyone, was never bothered by Blanche's presence. She was independent, lighthearted, never made it feel as if she needed me all the time. And yet we shared sixty-two square meters. That's not very big. But Blanche made no noise or fuss. And she delighted in everything.

Anyone might think that Gueugnon is of no great interest. Anyone might say, what's there to do here? Anyone might say, it's an industrial town, it has no charm. Anyone. But Blanche wasn't just anyone. On the first day, she went into my little back courtyard and marveled at the presence of the tree. The only one. An old lime that didn't provide blossom for tea.

When Blanche arrived at my house with Lancelot and discovered my three-room place with one room just for her—yours, Agnès, which you hadn't slept in for ages—at the end of the corridor, with no one to keep watch over her nights, she was thrilled: "I have a room all to myself!" Like a little girl who doesn't have to share a room with her siblings anymore.

Whatever the weather, Blanche would sit at the back of the garden, look up at the sky, and always marvel at it.

If I had to sum up all those years spent together, I'd say that Blanche taught me to look at the beauty of a sprig of mimosa in a small blue vase. To dance to "Don't Stop . . . "—something or other—by Michael Jackson. To admire the artistry of a hand-painted flower on the porcelain plates in my dresser. To walk toward the sun, low over the river Arroux, to follow the shadow of people fishing, often women from Thailand in recent years. They would make little signs to us, without knowing who I was, who Blanche was, and they'd stroke Lancelot. And we felt comfortable with them. They were like Blanche; they came from elsewhere. When I was living alone, I didn't care what I ate. With Blanche, I discovered our favorite dishes. We shared our tastes. When Aimé would visit, he'd find us like two sisters who live under the same roof.

Blanche went out once a day. In the morning. She'd walk up the Digoin road to stroll around the hypermarket. That's what she called it, "the hypermarket." Over there, no one notices anyone. Not like in the grocery store, where she would have been asked questions. Apart from that, she lived hidden. She never came to the shoe-repair shop. We found out that her father had been arrested in Lyon ten days after our visit to Annecy. That he'd been tried and sentenced to five years in prison. Five years of freedom for her. Something opened up inside her. That's when she started going out in the morning. At first, to keep busy, she asked me to teach her my shoe-mending skills. Like asking me to teach her an entire life. Instead, I chose to tell her about Mokhtar, and she told me about the Cabaret des Oiseaux, *the artistes, and her lovers. In the evening, we'd talk for a long time, share what we were reading. The only place she pretended to be me was the municipal library. She'd borrow books under my name.*

In 2004, our daily life suddenly changed. We discovered that the monster had been released from prison in 2002. He had assaulted a woman in Marseille in 2003. A friend of mine had come across an article in a magazine. She didn't know that Blanche lived with me, but she did know who she was. She made the connection between my childhood friend, the circus girl, and the appalling Soudkovski in the article. That's when I saw a picture of that bastard for the first time. And it's also from then on that Blanche began to decline. She was scared. He'd been free as a bird for two years! Two years! Having imagined him behind bars, she now started to shake, to struggle to breathe. She'd felt fear all the time, for too long. Marie Roman's battered face and body, in the hospital, were imprinted on her mind. The mom who'd been stolen from her, in a coma because of him. The mother who would remain paralyzed. Proof of what that monster was capable of doing. Blanche was outraged by the treatment of killers. She'd shouted at the TV when Bertrand Cantat had been released four years after killing Marie Trintignant. She kept saying: "Four years! Four years of prison between his sentencing and his release on parole! No victim has the right to parole in a coffin!"

In 2004, I had to call Louis to take Blanche to the hospital. I thought she was going to die in my arms on the back seat of the car. I took her to Chalon because Antoine Été, the owner of the raffle house, was an emergency doctor there. I begged him to treat her under my name. Blanche was registered under her father's social security number; she would have left a trace of having been there. We had to think of everything. All the time. The bolts on the doors, the lights that had to be switched off, the curtains that had to be drawn after dark. Antoine was my last hope. He agreed. That raffle house brought only good fortune to our family, Agnès. Even its occupants. Antoine continued to care for Blanche. He would come to the house. He does know that I didn't die on August 11, 2007. He often phones me and drops by to see me. You have to meet him before you go back to Paris. If there's one thing I fear, it's that you'll never come back here once I'm truly gone.

She switches off the recording.

COLETTE

One evening, after supper, Blanche fell asleep forever. She was very tired. Three days before, she had lost her smile, her light. As if she had forgotten them somewhere. She went to lie down. I went to her room at around 10 o'clock to see how she was feeling. It was over. As I stroked her face, I promised her that no one would be coming after her anymore. She'd often told me she was terrified Soudkovski would hurt her even in her coffin, and that she would die after me. That's why I decided to die the same day she did. By disappearing, I was losing you and I was losing Ana. But Blanche would finally find peace. You two, you were both far away, you had your own lives. Our paths had separated to the extent of being in different time zones. I phoned the good Dr. Pieri, who agreed to sign my death certificate. When Louis called you, I was right beside him. He told you he would organize everything, that you didn't need to travel here. He kept repeating sentences that I'd prepared . . . I put ballet slippers on her, pink ones, so she would continue to dance where she was going. She'd kept up her exercises right to the end. When she'd get back from shopping and before making lunch, she'd push the kitchen table aside to stretch. I'd often abandon my shoes to come up and watch her for a minute. How beautiful she was, my little soul sister.

Once again, her voice cracks. She switches off the recording. That way Colette has of refusing to let me hear her sadness.

COLETTE

I chose a red dress for her last outfit. I tied ribbons in her hair, like when she walked on her tightrope. The funeral directors put her into her coffin in front of Louis, who was crying his eyes out as if it really was me. He was in love with Blanche; it was blatantly obvious. He'd blush like a schoolboy whenever he looked at her. Blanche attracted men. She had that thing . . . (she searches for the right word) . . . *magnetism. She had a seductive power that wasn't intentional, she had it just by moving, breathing, existing. Fortune favors the innocent.*

Two days after her funeral, I went up to the cemetery to place her blue shoes there. I went at lunchtime, when no one's around. How overwhelming it was, reading my own name and surname on a gravestone. It was August, people were either on vacation or dead. I often returned there to remove the pennants or notes intended for me. They're all in my cupboard with my FCG collection, I think you must have found them by now. I kept them for my final resting place, in Lyon. I would polish her blue shoes and then leave. I never came across anyone at the cemetery, as if it emptied from quarter past twelve to leave all the space to me. By 1 o'clock, I was already gone. For three years, I went out into the streets, not those in the town center, of course, but the residential ones in the lower neighborhood: Rue d'Amsterdam, Rue de Prague, Rue de Madrid, Rue de Lisbonne, Rue de Varsovie, Rue de Rome, Rue de Paris. It was like going around the world. Sometimes, I'd go as far as the river, where I used to swim with Blaise. No one ever paid any attention to me. I'd carry a shopping bag so I didn't look like I was just taking a walk. When you came to visit my grave, I know you asked Louis whom the blue shoes belonged to. They're the ones Blanche was wearing that night outside the Stade de France; she never let them get worn out. She loved them, said they symbolized her escape. During seven years of life with her, I bought clothes for Blanche, and she'd choose the complete opposite to me from the catalogues. Colorful dresses, scarves. All I kept of hers was a green and black coat, so I wouldn't be recognized. But who would recognize a dead woman? You see, Agnès, the habit can make another monk. Lancelot died in my arms in 2002. Thanks to Blanche, I knew the joy of having a dog, and because of her, I experienced what I dreaded: losing him. We buried him in his blanket, under the lime tree that didn't provide blossom for tea. Occasionally, Blanche would go and talk to him. Blanche used to talk to the stars, the birds, the bees, the sky. Blanche talked to the universe. I miss her. Those seven years with her went by like a dream. Like those luminous streaks you can see in the sky, clusters of stars. Despite the threat of her father, her nightmares, her panic attacks when she was sure she'd glimpsed him on the street from the window, we did laugh. We had fun like two women, two little girls, who hadn't had a mother, hadn't had a childhood. In the early 2000s, you came to spend several Christmas Eves in a row with me: Pierre, Ana, and you. Blanche would wait for me at the house while we went to dine at Vezant's . . . Even though Georges Vezant was no longer with us. Blanche would stay in your room as you were all arriving. You hadn't gone into it for a long time. You would have been really surprised if you'd opened the door; Blanche had covered the walls with flowery paper and painted the door, window frame, and baseboards pink. She could hear your voices. Then she'd watch us through the window, walking down the road. I knew that she was watching us and that it made her happy.

This time, I'm the one who pauses the cassette. And yet I've heard it several times. Each time, I imagine Blanche watching us. It's unbelievable, realizing how close to us she was, hiding in the shadows. I stop walking for a moment, take off my headphones, and sit on a large rock. The pale winter sun lights up the façade of the ancient Château de Sénéchal, bought by private individuals after the marquess's death. The edifice is still just as beautiful. Down below, the farm my grandparents lived in is derelict. Georgette's little house, adjoining the château, has become a charming residence. It has been nicely restored, and all the stonework cleaned. Red shutters frame the new windows. I imagine Colette and Blaise sneaking into the château to join Dad at the piano.

Eugénie de Sénéchal had Blaise buried at Père-Lachaise. She lives in a building right beside the cemetery and puts fresh flowers on her son's grave every week. I always call her to wish her a happy new year. How does she spend her time? I know she's very involved, as a volunteer, with Vestiaire—"changing room"—an emergency-aid group that helps migrants by supplying them with clothes, shoes, sleeping bags, hygiene products, notebooks, and human warmth.

COLETTE

When we'd get back at around eleven, we'd go up to the kitchen to find the presents I'd hidden before setting off. You'd all have an herbal tea, give me a hug, and then return to the hotel to sleep. Blanche would appear, and we'd celebrate Christmas Eve together. I wasn't hungry anymore. She'd say to me: "That doesn't matter, but tell me all about it." Blanche insisted on the details. She'd close her eyes as soon as I began to describe the evening, your words, our discussions, your plans, which menu you'd all chosen, starters, mains, wines, desserts. And while I was talking, she'd picture it all.

Long silence.

COLETTE
Sometimes, Blanche would play the "when he's dead" game. When he's dead, we'll go see the sea. When he's dead, we'll take the plane to visit Italy. When he's dead, we'll go back to Lac d'Annecy, we'll go watch a match at the Stade de France, admire the artists at the Cabaret des Oiseaux. I'll go out at any old time and I'll shout: "My name is Blanche Roman and I'm freeeee!" When he's dead, I'll use my mother's surname and bring her to live with me. When he's dead, I'll dance on the sidewalks. I'll find a job. I'll go window-shopping. I'll go sit on café terraces to get a tan and read my newspaper. I'll volunteer at the animal refuge so I can walk the dogs and stroke the cats. I'll appear on TV in one of those silly game shows. When he's dead, I'll have my own social security number and a mailbox attached to a blue gate, and behind that gate will be my house and it will be pink. When he's dead, I'll plant hydrangeas and trees in my garden. When he's dead, you'll be my neighbor and we'll eat together every day. I'll phone to come around for tea at 5 o'clock, like in England. And most importantly, Colette, when he's dead, we'll go see the dolphins.

End of the final cassette.

28

November 25, 2010

9:00 A.M. Gueugnon cemetery. There's just Paul, Cyril Rampin, two gravediggers, a stonemason, two funeral directors, a forensic pathologist, four gendarmes, and me. The cemetery is closed. I think to myself, Blanche and I are the only women here. "Exhumations are always done outside of opening hours, except in winter when the light doesn't allow it," Paul explained. He added that the forensic pathologist wasn't always present, but this case was serious enough for him to be there.

Helped by the gravediggers, the funeral directors remove the marble plaque, open the grave, and slide ropes down to the coffin to hoist it up. When it appears, I clench my fists in my pockets. Irrepressible emotion seizes me. I imagine Blanche in her sequined costume, a little girl, an artiste on tightrope and wire. I realize I have no photo of her, and think I might find one by going to poke around at the Cabaret des Oiseaux.

The small oak coffin is placed on the frozen ground. I was the one who'd chosen it, from LA, because many Steinways are made of oak. I'd passed that on to Louis. I must have thought that it would be less sad to rest surrounded by a wood that produces music. I ask Paul where the blue shoes have gone; he tells me they will join any potential evidence. He checks that the official seals have been affixed to the coffin. The two funeral directors then carry it to the hearse. The entire procedure didn't even take half an hour. I'm unhappy knowing that she's going to be disturbed. Once again. But this step is necessary; even Colette knew it. What she couldn't have imagined is that, despite the "when he's dead" game, Soudkovski is well and truly alive. I watch the dark vehicle and the cars of Paul, the gendarmes, and Captain Rampin disappearing at the end of the path.

I remain at the edge of the empty grave, rigid. I can't seem to move anymore. The stonemason removes the gravestone on which the name Colette Septembre is engraved in golden letters. This site will be vacant again from today. Blanche will never come back here. It's her Aunt Jeanne who will decide where her mortal remains will finally rest, for eternity. No doubt close to Marie, in Flumet. I wonder what Blanche would want. To be beside her mother or Colette? On my way back to the gate, I greet Father Aubry, who lies under a tombstone covered in seashells. As I'm walking down the hill, I come across Antoine Été at the wheel of the Renault. I'm happy to see him. He appears like a ray of light under a leaden sky.

"I came to collect you."

"That's kind."

"It's no problem. I just passed the hearse and the cowboys behind it."

"They're going to Dijon."

"Yes, I know, to the medicolegal institute. Are you okay?"

"I'm okay. What will they do to Blanche?"

"I'm no forensics expert, but I have attended that kind of procedure. Do you really want to know?"

"Yes. I get the feeling that, since the beginning of this whole business, something's being hidden from me. Even Paul seems to be lying."

"Paul's the police captain?"

"Yes, Paul Serran. I met him when I was working on *Les Silences de Dieu*. I never would've believed I'd end up dealing with him in real life . . . And now it seems like he's trying to hold back information . . . To protect me. He doesn't look at me the same way anymore. So yes, I want to know."

"Okay. Do you have anything planned for today?"

"No."

"Perfect."

Antoine takes the road that leads to the raffle house but doesn't stop there; he drives right out of Gueugnon. He turns up the car's heating system before speaking. As if the words he's about to say are going to chill me.

"At the medicolegal institute, a forensic pathologist will open the coffin in the presence of Paul Serran. Cyril Rampin and a cop from the criminal records office will probably be there, too. The police carrying out the inquiry will present the report to the magistrate in charge of the case. First, they'll take photos of the coffin, check again that the seals are still there. Then they'll open it and remove the remains. The only time I attended this procedure, the scientist took photos of the coffin, then of the body as found. When possible, they scan it to get a radiological record . . . It depends on the medicolegal institute, how well-equipped they are. The one in Dijon is next to a hospital. Her remains will probably be taken there very late tonight, or very early tomorrow morning, to see whether there are any fractures or other injuries. In any case, it will happen after, or before, patients start arriving. The examination depends on the state of the body. After three years, it will be more or less altered, depending on the method of interment and the treatment applied by the embalmer. Next, the pathologist will proceed with a traditional autopsy to be sure that Blanche died a natural death, and will take samples of fluids and tissues to establish her genetic profile. Her DNA will be tested in a lab to establish Blanche's genetic ID. That will then be compared with the DNA of those closest to her. They'll be looking for any family links. And mainly, they'll confirm that it really is her."

"That would be Jeanne, Marie Roman's sister. Marie Roman is Blanche's mother. She's being buried later today."

"What? Who's being buried later today?"

"Marie Roman, Blanche's mother . . . She's being buried today in Flumet."

Antoine seems dumbfounded and remains silent.

"They'll also compare Blanche's DNA with that of her father, Soudkovski."

"The madman?"

"Yes."

"Where is he now?"

"No idea. They're searching for him. He's killed twice. He tried to murder Marie Roman in 1999, leaving her confined to a wheelchair, and he terrorized Blanche her entire life. Even imagined that he could come and desecrate her grave."

A thought crosses my mind. I immediately ring Paul's number. He answers straight away.

"Paul, it's Agnès. Blanche is wearing a red dress and pink ballet shoes. Could you call me to confirm that?"

He says yes and hangs up. He's not alone, and I already know too much. A sign saying Toulon-sur-Arroux indicates the entrance to a village.

"Where are you taking me, Antoine?"

"To visit a house."

"You've become a real-estate agent?"

"Not yet. I feel like buying it, but I'd like your opinion."

"You're going to part with the raffle house?"

"No."

"You're going to own two houses?"

"Yes. One for the summer, and another for life."

"Because the summer isn't life?"

"Not really."

"I've had my fill of cemeteries, separations, women who fall pregnant . . . So I'd be delighted to visit your house!"

"After the visit, I'll take you to the Méridien."

"What's that?"

"It's a great restaurant in Toulon."

"What a nice idea . . . Antoine?"

"Yes."

"To leave death behind, once and for all: after they've done all that . . . what will become of Blanche?"

"Her body will be placed in a new coffin. And her next of kin will have to wait for instructions from the judge, who will or won't sign a burial permit, depending on the findings from the inquiry. The judge will contact those eligible and ask them where they would like her to be laid to rest."

"I wonder if Blanche was a believer. And I don't know, either, which denomination she might have been. Colette doesn't mention it on the cassettes."

Once we've driven through the little village, we go over a pretty bridge and along the river. Then we take a country road, with a fine oak forest on one side, and undulating meadows on the other. Antoine parks outside an ugly house, poorly constructed, as if cut in two. Modern to the left, old to the right. An unsuccessful marriage. I so want to laugh, I pinch my hand not to. Antoine seems so confident that I follow him, eyes down.

"You have the keys?"

"Yes, a friend gave them to me."

"Talking of keys, did you know that Colette and Aimé Chauvel loved each other?"

"No. But that's good news."

"Why?"

"It's always good news when people love each other."

"Just don't tell anyone."

"Promise."

He walks down the side of the house and unlocks a glass door. Once inside, I'm stunned by the beauty of the stone walls, the paintwork, the natural woodwork, the windows. It's all splendid, luminous. An industrial staircase leads up to the kitchen and the other floors. This house keeps its cards close to its chest. I fall instantly in love with it. Silently, we go from one room to another, like a couple of newlyweds exploring their future home. All the views of the countryside are breathtaking. I can't even imagine how glorious spring must be here. And yet there's no sea. Antoine says just one thing during our visit:

"There's a river about two hundred meters away. In summer, you can swim in it."

As we get back into the car, he whispers to me:

"So? Do I buy it?"

"Yes!"

*

"A novelist?"

"Perhaps. I'll give it a go."

"That's a fine plan."

At the Méridien, we're sipping our third coffee. The other customers have all left. Just two men, leaning on the bar, finishing their drinks. The two of us linger in the dining room, unable to tear ourselves away. At the end of service, the owner had told us: "No problem, we don't close in the afternoon."

"Have you already started writing?"

"I've written the screenplay of my parents' story, which I'm now turning into a novel. It's as if I were translating a foreign language, because the language of the screenplay isn't the same as that of literature. And you, Antoine? When will you go back to the hospital?"

"When I get sick, if I absolutely have to. Or to visit a friend."

"But I'm talking about your profession. Don't you miss treating people?"

"I miss the patients, but the anxiety of overlooking an ailment, no."

"Basically, you're a bit of a coward."

"Yes. Like you quitting movies with the excuse that the leading actor in your life had gone."

"That's true. We're as bad as each other. Here's to cowards!"

He raises his cup.

"To the good health of cowards!"

29

November 25, 2010

I'm at the Monge hotel, and Ana is sleeping, cuddled up to me. She and Cornélia surprised me. They came here by train without telling me. Cornélia is sleeping on the floor above. I breathe in the smell of my daughter's skin, her nape is warm, I can hear from her breathing that she's sound asleep. I plant light kisses on her hair, so as not to wake her.

When I was a child, I liked falling ill because Mom would sleep with me. And once my fever had passed, she'd return to my father. So I'd pretend to her that I was aching here, and there, so she'd stay close to me. I've often slept with Ana, even long before her father and I separated. They say that's a mistake, but the mistake would be not to make the most of her presence. My only child. Next year, she'll be going to high school, and she'll be spending the night at friends' houses, not with me anymore.

Ana fell out with her father when he told her that Audrey was pregnant. She told him that she never thought he could be that stupid. That she wouldn't be growing up with that child because she was practically old enough to be its mother, and he was old enough to be its grandfather, not its father. Pierre took it very badly. Ana left, slamming the door. He must have cursed me, thinking that she definitely took after me. It's always the mothers' fault.

Ana threw herself into my arms when she arrived at the Monge. I was in my room, eating my supper alone, when there was a knock on the door. I thought it was Adèle, coming to reveal who knows what about her nights with Paul or her trips to Cannes. When I saw my daughter, I couldn't stifle a delighted shriek. What a lovely surprise!

Everything will work out in the end. When Ana meets her little sister or brother, she'll fall madly in love. That's how life goes.

Ana asked me why I was staying at the hotel rather than in the house I kept on about, the one I wanted to buy and that she *so* wanted to see ("*Please*, Mom!"). I explained that it was because of Blanche's father, without giving any details so as not to scare her. But not giving any details to a teenager who asks umpteen questions a minute and won't give up until you answer with utmost precision is a losing battle. I ended up admitting about Soudkovski's crimes. It was me admitting them instead of him.

She opened the window in the room, leaned out, looked around the deserted Rue Jean-Jaurès, where only the store windows were lit up, and said to me:

"He's probably spying on us right now."

I tried to reassure her:

"No, the last time his cell-phone signal was picked up, he was in Paris."

"In Rue des Abbesses?!" she exclaimed.

"No," I lied, "in a distant suburb. And anyhow, I have nothing to do with Blanche. I think Paul's going over the top."

I check my phone, no message from Antoine. His last one was over two hours ago: "That was a lovely day, thanks for removing any doubt in my mind about the house, good night." And now here I am, reduced to the level of a silly girl, waiting for a guy to call.

I hear footsteps getting closer. My room is the last one, at the end of the corridor. The footsteps stop. Like in horror movies, I can make out a shadow under my door. It instantly reminds me of *Les Diaboliques*, Henri-Georges Clouzot's movie. Except I'm not in a movie, I'm in Gueugnon, hiding away "to be on the safe side." The person behind the door doesn't move. It must be one or two in the morning. I think of Cornélia upstairs but can't get a word out. Unless it's Paul returning, or Antoine, thinking I'm alone. But what if it's a ghost? Blanche's? I start to get palpitations. Did I lock the door properly? The young woman from reception brought up a *croque-monsieur* for Ana at around ten. I replay the scene in my mind. She knocked, entered, we exchanged a few words, and I looked for change in my bag to give her a tip, just as my phone rang with Antoine's message. Keen to read it, I didn't go close the door behind her, and Ana was already tucking in at a corner of the table. How is that possible? How can I have forgotten to lock the door? Someone pushes it open. Never would Paul, Cornélia, or Antoine enter my room without knocking. The light from the corridor shines on Ana's traveling bag, thrown on the floor. I glimpse the silhouette of a man against the light; he closes the door behind him. I hear him turning the key on the inside. The sound paralyzes me. I pretend to sleep, but I see him getting closer to the bed, then walking around it to get closer to me. He gives off a smell like damp earth after the rain. It's *him*. A cemetery smell. It's *him*. How did he get into the hotel? What does he want? What's he looking for? Does he think I know something he doesn't? I remain paralyzed, as if I've been made to take GHB, that drug that paralyzes victims and that I talk about in *Les Silences de Dieu*. I try raising my arms to touch Ana, but I'm incapable of moving. Incapable of calling for help. I'm locked in a diving-suit of ice. He leans toward me, sniffs my hair and neck like an animal would; I can feel his breath on me. I try to summon the strength to hurl myself at him, but my body isn't responding anymore. Am I actually dying, like the other women in my family? Am I the last one on the list?

A drop falls on my cheek. Then another one. As if it were starting to rain on me. I hear a car passing in the street, pick up the rap the driver's listening to, must be loud. It takes me a while to realize that the intruder is crying. He remains leaning over me for a long time, still with that smell of damp earth. My tears of terror mingle with his on my cheeks. I'm going to die because of his grief. Why? Why am I going to die because of his grief? My phone's ringtone shocks me out of my prostration.

I finally manage to scream:

"Why should I die because of his grief?!"

Panic-stricken, Ana switches on all the lamps. It's just the two of us in the room. But the presence of the intruder haunts me. I don't see my daughter's tense features as she stares at me in alarm. I don't hear her say:

"Mom, you had a nightmare."

I can't tell her that, no, *he* is in the room. *He* is hiding under the bed. I shout:

"Ana, run to the door! Quick! Go now! Go!"

She doesn't move. I rush to the door, which isn't locked anymore, open it, go back to grab Ana's hand, and drag her to Paul's room, screaming:

"Help!"

Paul appears in the doorway before I knock on his door, his phone pressed to his ear.

"Agnès, I've just called you and . . . "

The occupants of the neighboring rooms come out, astonished, some angry, others scared; one couple thinks there's a fire, and they all look at me as if I've taken leave of my senses.

"Paul! Why should I die because of Soudkovski's grief?"

" . . . "

"Paul! He's in my room! Under the bed! Go look under the bed! He's crying! He won't stop crying!"

I watch Paul go to check, to reassure me. He comes back out. "There's no one there, Agnès."

"Did you look in the cupboards?"

"There's no one in the cupboards, Agnès. You must've had a bad dream."

The three of us head back to my room. I apologize to all the guests in pajamas, nightdresses, or tee shirts, barefoot or in carpet slippers, gaping at me.

"I'm so sorry, I had a nightmare."

Paul has another look in the bathroom and around the room itself. The windows are closed. The cupboards, empty.

"And there's no one under the bed."

Ana is pale; I've scared her.

"Sorry, sweetheart. So sorry to have woken you both up," I say to Ana and Paul. "I'm so very sorry."

"I wasn't sleeping," he tells me, "I was phoning you."

"Oh yes, that's true . . . What did you want to say?"

"Blanche was holding a cassette."

30

Levgueni Soudkovski is born in 1928. His parents left their native Russia two years before the birth of their son, to settle in France. In 1927, his mother, trained by acrobats in Riga, Latvia, is taken on by the Circus Elliott. The highlight of the show is the final trapeze act, in which Levgueni's mother is the first woman to perform a double somersault and then be caught by her partner.

The father works as a delivery driver. When he's in towns the circus is coming to, he regularly slips away to paste up the posters, two meters by three, featuring his wife's beautiful face. It's his regular absences, when alone on the road, that sow doubts in his mind, instill jealousy. While he's away delivering, she's clinging to another man, to great applause. He could see the wonderment in the spectators' eyes only too clearly. What does she get up to when he isn't there?

A month before giving birth, she's still spinning through the air, her body compressed in a corset, and she's back on the trapeze when Levgueni is fifteen days old. The baby spends his days in the arms of his mother or in his carriage at the side of the ring. He's barely opened his eyes and is already seeing different landscapes rolling by and his mother flying in sparkly costumes. A little one breastfed on demand, smothered in kisses, rocked to the songs his mother hums to him. He's never heard to cry, except when his father flies into a terrible rage, even beating his wife. Levgueni takes his first steps in sawdust, watching his mother glide across the big top's sky. He stretches his arms up to her so she comes down to fetch him. When she leaps from the platform above the net, he imagines she's a bird. At three, he calls her "Mommy bride." Because she only ever wears white silk chiffon.

Whenever she's near him, his little hands grab her breast to drink his mother's milk, and he closes his eyes in bliss. Levgueni grows up with the sensual delight of an ethereal mother fragrant with the floral water she applies to her body every day. At three, he can juggle and keep his balance on a taut wire. Six months later, she teaches him acrobatics, and how to fling himself from one trapeze to another, having first lowered them to a meter from the ground. A dream life for a child. Aside from his brute of a father, who never even looks at him. A life attached to his mother's life. They breathe as one. On his fourth birthday, Levgueni achieves his first move above the net: a forward somersault. He sees in her eyes that she's amazed. Levgueni has just one dream: to fly with her.

But suddenly his life is turned upside down. His father hits too hard, and his mother, dazed and covered in bruises, must stay in bed. Levgueni lies beside her and remains there. Then his father gets into such a violent argument with the owners of the circus, he obliges his wife to leave them. They move to insalubrious two-room lodgings in Caluire-et-Cuire, a suburb of Lyon. No more landscapes rolling by, no more feeding the elephants, farewell to the music, the clowns, the smell of straw and dung.

His father now works at night, in the factory, and his mother is no longer allowed out on her own. He accompanies her everywhere, even to do the shopping, leaving the child alone and unprotected at home, standing at the door, breathlessly awaiting their return. He throws himself at his mother's legs when they arrive. She can't walk a step in those lodgings without him clinging to her.

To pass the time, they train together, doing lifting exercises in the tiny kitchen, banging into each other, bruising themselves, and collapsing in fits of laughter. But this phony happiness is fleeting. The child watches his beautiful, trapped bird of paradise fading away, being humiliated, falling silent. Obedient as a tamed animal, she doesn't try to escape, or can't find the door to her cage. Before, she'd give herself to the spectators; now Levgueni has her all to himself. Feelings jostle in his young mind. He senses that she's not happy anymore, but finds it reassuring to know that she's cloistered with him, dedicated to him alone. His father is never there. He gets up at eleven, loiters in the bar until three, comes home to eat and have a drunken nap, then grabs a bite and leaves for work. He only gets back at five in the morning.

To cheer up their dreary daily life, his mother makes up stories about the circus, about tightrope-walkers, trapeze artists, and acrobats, but loses none of her gentleness. One day, she promises him, they will put on some unbelievable shows. *And yet,* the little boy thinks, *leaving here would mean being separated again. She'd go back to the others and wouldn't be mine anymore. I wouldn't have her hands, her softness, her beauty, and her tummy all to myself anymore.* In the evening, Levgueni cuddles against his mother, curling up in the warmth and smell of her. In the middle of the night, she slips him into his own little bed. Then the father takes the place, still warm, of the child, who's not allowed into the marital bedroom when there are noises.

One morning, while the father is asleep beside her, the little one sneaks around the bed to slide under the sheets. His mother doesn't move. The child takes her hand and silently cries. He's thinking of the day before, of that second hot chocolate she'd refused to make him, and how he'd flown into a mad rage, rained punches on her, pummeled her legs, bottom, and back. Horrified, she'd just stared at him, then started to scream in Russian, when she only ever spoke to him in French. He hadn't understood all her words. Except that using violence is the worst thing you can do in life. He'd apologized: "Sorry, Mommy, sorry, Mommy," because she was crying a lot. It was the first time he saw her shed tears because of him. "Sorry, Mommy."

That morning, his mother's body is cold. He listens to his father's breathing, as he sleeps peacefully, but his mother has flown away. Her eyes are closed, with dark shadows under them, her face wan, almost blue, but not like the sky. A terrifying blue. Like frost. Like skin when it's cold. She'd left on her own. Without him. Because he was a naughty boy. There are brown marks around her neck. He will be the only one to notice them. When his father wakes up, he doesn't seem surprised at her death and looks at her with a vaguely annoyed expression. What on earth is he going do with her?

Levgueni thinks back to his mother's words: "You know, my love, when I met your father, he wasn't like that." Why does become "like that"? "When I met him, he was funny, kind, he sang all the time. We both ran away to be together, because my parents didn't want us to marry, they found him too immature."

The father dresses the dead woman in a turtleneck sweater and trousers before calling a doctor, who hurriedly designates it a medication-related death. The strangulation marks won't be mentioned on the death certificate. Levgueni is four-and-a-half when his life stops, and he's convinced that his mother has gone because of him. An unspeakable wrench. His soul gets lost under the pressure of an icy chill flooding through him like curare. They had shared a heart. She'd taken it with her. He hears a word he doesn't know, doesn't understand, "suicide." A neighbor mutters: "She could have thought of the little one, all the same."

The neighbors band together to provide a funeral worthy of the name for "the pretty lady on the fifth floor we hardly ever saw." The coffin is made of fir wood. When the lid is brought down on his mother's face, the child feels a kind of acid rain eating into his body, until he blacks out. He's just been torn apart with a knife, the way two things stuck together are separated. He is brought around by his father's slaps, to the alarm of the undertaker, known as the *croque-mort*.

"Father, why's he called a *croque-mort*?"—"Because he eats the dead, idiot."

There is no marble plaque or headstone. She's buried in a corner of the Caluire cemetery. Far from the other tombs, far from the other families whose portraits shine in the sun. Only a wreath of white fabric roses is placed against the wooden cross on which her name is carved: "Liouba Rozov, married name Soudkovski." The cross casts its shadow on the freshly turned soil. The child, who can't read, stands at the funeral without anyone holding his hand. At the end of the homily, of which he hasn't understood a word, one lady strokes his shoulder affectionately, and he pushes her away violently. "Poor little boy, it's grief." The father sniffs, but doesn't cry. *Poor man*.

Once they're back home, he switches the blows he'd inflict on his wife onto the child. Levgueni is almost relieved that this is his fate. Now, his mother won't hurt anymore, he'll take it on, all of it. *Sorry, Mommy*.

The father promptly sells his boy's skills to the owner of the Alcaraz et Frères Circus. Levgueni becomes one of the youngest tightropewalkers in France. He trains relentlessly on the parallel bars, morning to night. From 1934 to 1938, people come from afar to admire the young boy juggling and balancing on a ball, a wire, a horse. But he never smiles. And only turns around when he's called Soudoro. Levgueni Soudkovski, the child of Liouba Rozov, no longer exists.

War breaks out. The Alcaraz circus moves close to Albertville, joining a group of Romanies who work the land. They own a few plots and a fine farmyard. They all live off the black market, not performing anymore. At this farm, Levgueni learns to read and write thanks to "the old biddy." That's what they called a former governess who ran away with a fairground worker. She schools him every morning for seven years, but teaches him only French: reading, grammar, conjugations. No history or math lessons. During those war years, Levgueni does learn knife-throwing. First at a target, a meter away, then two, then three. He acquires perseverance and precision. After years of practicing, he decides to try it out with a human target. That would be Leïla, the granddaughter of "the old biddy," who trusts him. She's become infatuated with him. Levgueni aims all around her, while respecting the forty-centimeter safety margin. Together, they prepare an act that they hope to present when the war's over. They improve the spectacle by attaching Leïla to a rotating wheel. Leïla is three years older than him and is scared of nothing. After the knife, she wants to teach him love. He agrees, but imposes one condition: she's not allowed to touch him. She keeps her hands tied behind her back and gives him neither kisses nor caresses. At the start of their strange relationship, Leïla finds this amusing. She loves this wild and mysterious boy. But after several months, she ends up kissing his hair. He slaps her. "Do that again, and you'll die with a knife in your heart." Shocked at his violence, Leïla rejects him and dumps him on the spot: "We're not seeing each other anymore. Not with the knives, not in bed. It's over between us." He goes mad and gives her a thrashing. *You don't abandon Soudoro.*

At the end of the war, his father announces to him that he's the owner of the Alcaraz circus; he has the papers to prove it. How did he do that? Levgueni doesn't know. He's eighteen and meets Marie Roman. His father dies on January 20, 1946, the day General de Gaulle resigns from the government. A fatal fall from one of the big-top's masts. Levgueni doesn't get him buried in Caluire but, instead, thrown into a communal grave at Albertville's cemetery. *See you in Hell, you old murderer.*

In 1950, he has a white marble tomb erected for his mother. White, like the outfits she wore. He pays with banknotes. A fortune. He requests that her name, Liouba Rozov, be engraved in golden letters. When asked what he'd like to choose as an epitaph, he doesn't know what say. He's presented with several options, which he finds ludicrous. In the end, he writes his own, in Russian, so that no one can understand it. "To my trapezist mother, may she carry me away with her."

31

November 26, 2010

Ana gets to see the house on Rue des Fredins. We walked over from the Monge. She daren't tell me she finds it ugly, but I can hear her thinking it. She pretends to approve of the kitchen cupboards, whispering, "Nice," when she thinks the opposite, her face falling as the tour progresses. Four rooms in total. Then, in front of the closed door of the bedroom, she finally speaks her mind:

"I'm against it. Coco died here, inside that room you refuse to enter, Mom . . . So, personally, I refuse to let you buy this house. Find another one. Sure, you've spent two or three crazy weeks here, listening to the cassettes, and you met up with your bestest friends, and even the Été son, but now it's time to give this house back to Louis . . . This isn't your house; it's a place for dying in. I'm already about to have a sister or brother, so for pity's sake, when I come visit you here in the countryside, as much as I like it . . . I mean—if you were buying the shoe-repair shop, I'd get it, that really is Colette, we could do something with it. But not this place."

She looks at me imploringly, before adding:

"Know what? We'll go online and check out all the real-estate agencies. We'll find somewhere!"

I hear myself replying: "Okay." Ana looks at me in disbelief.

"You're not disappointed?"

"You're right. People should listen to their children more often."

"Their child."

I smile at her as I make for Colette's collection in the cupboard, wanting to take it back to Paris and read it. Until now, I've merely leafed through it, turning pages randomly, stopping at the photos of Aimé Chauvel.

"When do we get the cassette Blanche was holding?" Ana asks me.

"No idea. According to Paul, it will have been sent to the judge. It's going to take ages . . . "

"Does Paul think it's audible?"

"Yes. It was protected in plastic bags and wrapped in film. It would still have been intact in a hundred years."

"What a crazy story . . . "

"I can hardly believe it."

"What was your nightmare about last night, Mom? I'd never seen you like that . . . Even when Dad left."

I pull out the valve and deflate my mattress by walking on it. The air escapes with a strange, prolonged moan. Is it disappointed that I'm clearing off?

"Levgueni Soudkovski was close to me, in our room. He was breathing. I mean, he was breathing in the smell of my skin. I felt his breath on my neck. He smelled like damp earth. At first, I was petrified. I thought he was going to kill me, like he killed his mistress and Viktor Socha . . . But he was searching for someone through me. And his sadness was so profound, it radiated from him to me, and from me back to him . . . His tears were falling on me like raindrops. I could feel his distress, not his murderous insanity. When Paul phoned me, the ringtone woke me up . . . But I struggled to shake off all that suffering. I still find it hard to believe that he wasn't there."

"Mom, he's just been found. He was locked up for good last night."

"I know, but . . . he was there."

*

In front of the window of the real-estate agency on Rue Jean-Jaurès, we're studying what's on offer, the number of rooms, peering at the photos of gardens. Ana wants three bedrooms minimum. One for her, one for Cornélia, and one for me. I think again of the house I visited with Antoine. I'm just about to tell her that yesterday I found the ideal house, but my phone vibrates in my pocket.

"He's in a coma," Paul informs me, without greeting me.

He'd set off very early this morning, telling me that Soudkovski had just been located. That his phone's signal had pinged at the same place for several hours.

The call drops. I grab Ana's arm and whisper to her: "Soudkovski's in a coma." Ana, nose pressed to the window, turns around and stares at me, wide-eyed. Paul calls me back.

"Paul, are you sure it's him? He could've just put his phone and papers in someone else's jacket pocket."

"Agnès, it's him. He was found lying across his mother's grave."

"His mother?"

"Yes."

"Where?"

"At the cemetery in Caluire."

"Why's he in a coma?"

"Massive overdose of opioids."

"He committed suicide?"

"Must have. There's no sign of any struggle."

"Could he have been in Gueugnon last night?"

"His phone signal was first picked up in Caluire at around three in the morning."

*

His subconscious floats on an ocean of uncertainty. The sky. Above a big top. He flies over a village on the main square, the trailers are side by side. It's an evening when his father has gone far ahead, to put up more posters. He's in his mother's arms, she's relaxed, he's dozing. He hears the beating of her heart.

Voices and machine noises. He's neither cold nor hot. He's floating in a kind of torpor, a nice feeling. He's not hurting anywhere. He feels, breathes, hears, but he's outside of the world. It's the first time he's stopped. That he's not on his guard. He's at the mercy of others. Between life and death. He still has that smell of earth in his nostrils. The compost and humus that have covered his mother for seventy-eight years.

He wasn't expecting to remember the worst day of his life so precisely. He was expecting to find an ancient tomb, neglected, in this corner of the cemetery. The surname erased by the weather. Only the letter L or A of Liouba still legible. The beginning and the end. He'd forgotten having this splendid tomb erected. How could he have forgotten?

He can't tell the difference between day and night. At this moment in time, where he's to be found, he's neither a murderer nor a nice guy.

Just a child who could have done like his mother but who chose to do like his father.

*

"Mom, it's 10 A.M. on Saturday, November 26, and we've got nothing better to do!"

"Right, let's go."

We went into the real-estate agency and were offered three visits. As I leave each house, all I can think of is the one I saw yesterday with Antoine. I end up telling the young agent about it.

"Yes, I know exactly the property you mean. Restored houses like that are rare around here. I'm the one who brokered the sale a few years ago. I didn't know it was on the market again . . . If it's not indiscreet to ask, who made an offer on it?"

"Antoine Été."

The young lady starts to laugh.

"I think there's been a misunderstanding. Antoine Été is the owner. He could be the seller, but definitely not the buyer . . . In fact, I had no idea he wanted to part with it."

I phone Antoine on the spot. He answers cheerily.

"Antoine, I'm with Ana; we're visiting houses because the Rue des Fredins one is too small. And . . . Well. The one we visited yesterday belongs to you?"

Annoyed, I speak too loudly. Why make me believe it was for sale?

"Yes."

"You're selling it?"

"Yes."

"But I thought that . . . "

He doesn't let me finish my sentence, saying:

"I'll pick you up at the Monge at 1 o'clock and take you both over there to see it again."

*

Now everything's gone dark. Like the storage room he'd hide in, in Caluire, when his father came home blind drunk. He felt safe there. He can make out sounds, voices. Men talking about DNA. He also hears, "He's going under." Hears, then forgets. Occasionally, his eyelid is lifted up, and the light dazzles him. Within that artificial sun, he glimpses the silhouette of his mother, who swings forward, hanging onto her trapeze, lets go of it, spins around, and lands in firm hands: his hands. "I caught you, Mommy." He can remember these last few days. Before them, everything is blurred. Just sensations, impressions. Only one person is clear in his mind. Agnès. That stranger links him to his childhood love.

In Paris, he followed her for several days. On the last one, she went into an apartment building and then came out with a man. The actor in her films. He'd watched them all, her films. But they hadn't interested him since she wasn't in them. He prefers her interviews. They went to a brasserie to talk. He sat in a distant corner, to watch them without being noticed. Then Agnès left. She made her way to the metro. He followed her onto the train. Standing in the packed carriage, forehead pressed to the partition, hand gripping the handle, she started to cry. He was so close to her, he could have touched her. He'd have liked to pull back the collar of her coat to breathe in the smell of her skin, find "the" scent again. Minor miracle, at the Madeleine stop, he was jolted against her, his nose in her hair, which was gathered into a messy bun. He whispered, "Sorry," but Agnès didn't hear him. She didn't react. It seemed right to speak to her so casually. The passengers became annoyed, "Stop pushing!", but he'd have liked this moment to go on forever. Her barrette came undone and slipped down her collar. Just before it fell, he caught it in his cupped hand and clenched his fist over it. He glanced around him; no one was paying attention to anyone. They were all stressed, riled, silent, resigned. Agnès closed her eyes, forehead still stuck to the glass. As if asleep.

What was she thinking about? Why did she seem so sad? She looked like his mother when she lived cloistered in the Caluire lodgings.

He knew he'd never get another chance to be so close to her. He closed his eyes, too, until the Saint-Lazare stop, and didn't move anymore. This time, he was sure of it; it could no longer be a coincidence. Freshly picked verbena. Only his mother had that distinctive smell. Agnès's skin had the same aroma. Four minutes plunged into his memories, up close to the woman he'd never thought about again, for fear of being struck down dead. Then she turned around, said excuse me several times as she edged through the crowd, and got off the train. He remained standing, not moving, the barrette still clenched in his fist.

Later, when he returned to Rue des Abbesses, he could see a light on in her apartment. It was cold. He couldn't sleep in the street, so he slipped into the back courtyard of a restaurant opposite where she lived. The kitchen's extraction fan produced some warmth for a few hours. It was the cold that woke him at about five in the morning, and he found refuge in a bar on Rue Lepic. After a quick coffee, he'd returned to her building, only to see her getting into a taxi, alone. He lost her that morning.

*

Antoine is waiting for us on the sidewalk, all smiles, when we arrive at the Monge.

"Why did you tell me your house was for sale?"

"Because it is, but only to you two."

Ana and I exchange an alarmed look, before bursting into laughter.

*

It's 8:30 P.M. We make up a large, noisy table in the restaurant at the Monge. Ilyas, Lina, Hervé and his sixteen-year-old son, Nathalie and her other half, Adèle and her two daughters, Antoine, Ana, and me. Tonight, it's paella and rosé all around. Except for the children, who have instinctively gathered at one end of the table to talk in whispers and drink cans of Ice Tea. Our conversations jump from one subject to another, but "Soudkovski, Colette, Blanche, the wedding, the sound system, the DJ, the sugared almonds, not religious, have you chosen your dress, publishing the banns, the match result . . . " all keep coming back. Paul turns up, looking haggard.

"Soudkovski is in intensive care. He probably won't last the night."

His presence in my hotel room comes back to me. His tears, too. He was there. "He probably won't last the night." Blanche waited so long for those words. I'm just about to ask Paul if Soudkovski could have been in Gueugnon last night, but I see him take a chair and sit next to Adèle, after kissing her hair. This totally intimate gesture in front of everyone gives me the shivers and stops me from speaking. Nathalie, who seems less soppy than me, pulls out her Columbo notebook.

"Don't worry, I won't talk about it until you allow me to . . . But can I say that there was an audio cassette in Blanche's coffin? Have you listened to it? Who's speaking in the recording?"

Antoine keeps looking at me; I keep looking at Antoine. I'm going to buy his house.

In the late afternoon, I visited Louis Berthéol, while Ana had a bath listening to Lady Gaga on her mini speaker. To Louis, I admitted for the first time what I'm sensing. That I think I'm at the heart of this whole story. And that I have no one left to answer my questions. Neither my parents, nor Colette, nor Blanche.

"Rue des Fredins," he replied. "Opposite Colette's house, there's a lady. Cross the road and knock on her door. She'll have answers."

"The lady who leaves soups for me?"

"She may well make soup, too."

"What's her name?"

"Madame Aubert."

"I met a Monsieur Aubert at the café; he remembered Soudkovski and his daughter. He worked at the town hall and was called when an animal had escaped from the circus menagerie."

"This neighbor, she's Monsieur Aubert's daughter."

Here, everyone knows everyone.

"Did you know that Blanche was holding a cassette?"

"The day before the funeral, Colette handed me a blue plastic bag. It was overprotected, entirely wrapped in film. I thought it was a small radio to listen to music, but I didn't ask any questions. Colette asked me to slip this bag into the coffin. Colette might've seemed like a simple woman, but she wasn't. And more than anything, she was secretive. So secretive. Even with me."

After leaving Louis, I went straight to the neighbor's house, once again pushed open the gate, knocked, called out, but no one answered. It was dark and cold.

I'll go back there tomorrow morning, before heading back to Paris.

32

January 19, 1972

This evening, it's the birthday of one of the Cabaret des Oiseaux's customers. The premises have been privately hired for around a hundred guests. Blanche and two other hostesses had to come in earlier than usual to help get the place and the decorations ready, and supervise preparations: the artistes who would be performing, the cake, the surprises. Soudkovski went with her right up to the door, to be sure she wasn't lying. "Four o'clock, that's early."

Inside, someone is sitting at the old piano, placed center-stage for the occasion. He improvises on the *Goldberg Variations*. Blanche knows neither this music, nor the person at the keyboard. Standing with her back to the bar, she can't move. She has never heard music like it. "He has God in each finger," she whispers to a colleague, who doesn't know what she's talking about.

When the musician stands up, she's surprised at how young he looks. Don't you have to be old to play that way? The pianist sees her standing still in front of him, a few meters away, and heads straight toward her. He's huge. Suddenly, he stops and stares at her with his big, light eyes, with such intensity that she feels as if he's touching her. And Blanche allows herself to be examined without saying a word.

"You look like someone," he murmurs. "But without looking like her. What's your name?"

"Blanche."

"Blanche. 'White.' Lovely . . . A white note is worth two beats. Any idea where I could find a glass of water?"

Once he's drunk it, he returns to his keyboard and she to her work.

At six-thirty, the team gathers for a bite to eat before the guests arrive. The pianist stays with the group and sits beside Blanche as if he knew her, but says not a word to her. During the evening, she learns that he's called Jean and gives concerts all over the world. *All over the world,* Blanche thinks. *But then, what's he doing here, at this cabaret?*

The man celebrating his birthday, Alain Terzieff, is the director of the Lyon conservatoire, where this pianist had studied. Jean has a surprise for him.

It's me he's surprising. This thought keeps ringing in her head, endlessly.

When Alain Terzieff walks into the cabaret, all his friends are there. The party starts. Jean plays a polonaise on the piano to welcome Terzieff. Happy, he hugs him. Blanche is surprised by this show of affection. *These people are all so beautiful,* she thinks. *They don't belong to my world. They're free, they go where they like, make music, are poets. No one would ever give me such a present. I have no friends to celebrate me. My birthdays are just ordinary days. Before, when Natalia was around, she'd turn up in the morning with a lovely cake and candles for me. Every year, Soudoro would say, "Watch out, old girl, you'll burn your goatee with that nonsense." He was jealous of my love for her.*

There's an acrobatic display, a magician, balloons, a giant Bavarian-cream dessert. Blanche saves the fifty blown-out candles. She's been light-fingered since she was little, and marvels at the simplest thing. As those who lack everything do.

There are the presents: a seaside vacation, a golden fountain pen, books, a scarf, bottles of wine, an antique engraving. She watches this showering of gifts with delight and envy. Wonders what she'd like to receive as a gift, if she could, apart from being free.

A love as beautiful as the pianist.

Normally, Jean should have left with the others, after the party. Normally, Blanche should have hotfooted it home before *he* got up and noticed her absence in the room next to his. But *he* was away. Blanche and Jean were swept along by the same desire, at the same moment: the desire to disobey life. She waited for him. He knew she'd wait for him. She took his arm and told him that her time was limited. He thought she meant she was going to die. They walked past a club and went in. It was Jean who led her by the hand. And when the other musicians had left, they sat together at a piano; she laid her fingers over his and followed his movements. He played adagio, between sixty-six and seventy-six beats to the minute.

The moment she'd set eyes on him behind the cabaret's piano, Blanche had known that this night would be the most important of her life. An intuition that had preceded all the others. A night that would be like no other.

They parted at around seven in the morning. The apartment was silent. *He* and the dog, Véra, had been away since the previous day. *He* had left "money to eat" on the kitchen table. It was January 20.

When her genitor got back two days later, *he* suspected nothing. Neither that she had loved, nor that she'd spent the night with someone, nor that she would never forget.

That's how I imagine things went. That's how I would have filmed their meeting if I'd carried on making movies. I don't know how things unfolded. How they met. But they met and I was conceived. I am the daughter of Jean Septembre and Blanche Soudkovski. Hannah Ruben didn't carry me in her belly. Paul told me this yesterday, after the boozy paella evening. It was two in the morning. Everyone had gone off to bed. We were both on the first floor of the Monge, and I took advantage of this one-to-one to tell him that he'd changed. Didn't look me in the eye anymore. And this feeling of not being looked at anymore was awful. As if I'd done something wrong. I asked him if I'd upset him. And so Paul spoke, relieved to come clean:

"You know that, in the Fredins house, we found fingerprints on the phone. Yours, your aunt's, and Soudkovski's. Your DNA being from the same source as Colette Septembre's, that's normal. Uncles and aunts share about 25% of their genes with their nephews and nieces. But . . . "

"But?"

"Soudkovski's genetic markers are the same as yours."

*

I'm called Agnès, like my grandmother. Hannah Ruben is my mother. She's the one who slept close to me when I was feverish. I'm the one who held her hand when illness carried her off. It's also my hand that she held tight on the day of Dad's funeral. She entrusted her violin to me. Put on her pretty dress to come to our wedding. She was awkward, not knowing what to say or do on many occasions. Looked at me like a stranger when I was a teenager and slammed doors. She's the one I wanted to be like as a child, when she walked on stage, violin in hand.

She was the first person I showed my movies to. The one I'd ring in the evening to talk about my days: the day before, the day before that, that day, the following day . . . On official papers, I'm Agnès Septembre, daughter of Jean Septembre and Hannah Ruben. It may not be her blood that flows in my veins, but it's her universe. All my life, when I cried "Mom" instinctively, because I was scared of something, it was Hannah I called. She's the one I missed when Pierre left me. The one who was there the day Ana was born, and who was so touched at my baby being named after her.

"Agnès, all that you do is always full of grace," she said to me one day.

33

HANNAH RUBEN

(*Contd.*)

1970

They were among those who hadn't returned. The specters rarely spoken of. Those whose mortal remains would never be retrieved. Monuments would be erected, their names engraved, documentaries made, commemorations held. Visits to hell would be organized, as a reminder, but never again would anyone be able to reach out and touch them. "Where are your parents?" "Died in the war." A war that hadn't given back its dead. A war without graves. *Died in the war*. Almost a formality. And then they'd change the subject. Hannah never went into the details, even though she was full of questions. Myriam, Sasha, Rafael, and Agnès would forever be Hitler's ghosts among the millions of ghosts.

Hannah was there, in front of the piano. Jean and Colette were with her. Particularly Jean. Colette had hung back, standing in the doorway. Leaving them almost alone, side by side.

The piano. Material proof of their passage on this earth. Even more so than those few photos rescued at the last minute, after the Germans had raided and pillaged the apartment. Hannah dared neither move, nor touch the black wood.

Jean Septembre had arranged to meet her at the railway station a week after their initial meeting. They had traveled in silence. Hannah didn't know what to think about this resurrected piano, but she already knew what she thought about the pianist.

"Please, Jean, would you play it?" she'd asked, when she'd found herself facing the instrument.

Jean had agreed, first asking Hannah if she had a preference. She'd shaken her head.

The three of them were in the community center, where the imposing Steinway had pride of place. An incongruous beauty in that dated building. Colette was still hanging back. Hannah had also kept a certain distance, while Jean had chosen a Chopin sonata.

Hannah imagined Rafael and Agnès, in turn, at the keyboard. Her mother playing the piano, Rafael behind her, his hands on her shoulders, a kiss planted on her nape. Her brother and sister mischievously stroking the keys for fun. Waiting impatiently to be old enough to play it, too. Agnès must've played when she was pregnant with her. Hannah must've heard those notes from inside her belly. What remained of those moments? And she, Hannah, had chosen the violin, like her adoptive mother. She had inherited a different form of expression.

What was she going to do with this piano? This Steinway belonged to her, but didn't it belong even more to Jean and Colette Septembre? To this town, to its residents who had enabled their child prodigy to access his music tuition? To the living? What would her parents have wanted if they had returned? Would they have been delighted that their piano had changed the fate of a child? A child who had grown up and with whom Hannah had fallen instantly in love, over a plate of sauerkraut and a glass of Riesling. Oh, the irony of life.

On that day, Hannah was more deeply moved by Jean and Colette than by this unknown piano. It, too, represented one of Hitler's ghosts. The discreet love uniting the brother and sister made more of an impression on her, as did Colette's admiration for Jean when he played. He was undeniably her idol.

The three of them had lunch in a restaurant before she and Jean returned to Lyon. Sitting at a round table, not knowing what to say to each other. A brother and sister who were taciturn and shy. Each in their own world, but where the same silence reigned. Any words restrained. They didn't speak to say nothing. And their silences were never oppressive. They were comfortable, as relaxed as if beside a lake. Hannah was lost. Not knowing what to do with the piano, but wishing to link its fate to the Septembres.

In the train back to Lyon, she said just one thing: "I'm going to cancel my wedding." Without asking any questions, Jean looked straight at her with his big, light eyes and smiled at her the way a child smiles at life. At the luck he'd always had.

It was Hannah who made the first move, one evening in February 1971, after a concert. Chance had brought them together in Prague. They'd met under the astronomical clock. Under the calendar, the moon, and the sun. *Prague is perfect for kissing the man I love*, she thought. She waited until the clock sprang into action at 11:00 P.M. And they were so busy kissing at one second past eleven that they didn't see the Walk of the Apostles, those figures pursued around the dial by the skeleton of Death. After this languorous kiss, she suggested one last drink. Jean followed her. It may have been a last drink, but it was the first shared before many others.

In December 1971, Jean left the Levitans' home to move into the building opposite, on the third floor, with Hannah. From his new kitchen, he could see Élia Levitan dusting her sitting room. He'd gone from the apartment of his teacher to that of his future wife in a matter of seconds. There had been no transition between childhood and adulthood, just a road to cross. From then on, Hannah and Jean always had suitcases packed and ready, to set off again the following day.

In January 1972, Hannah wasn't able to attend the surprise birthday party for Alain Terzieff. She had been booked to be principal third violin in Vienna's great orchestra, an accolade. A six-month tour of performing at an increasingly frantic pace.

That past year, they'd met up wherever they could. After the birthday party, where Jean played for his friend, he admitted to Hannah that he'd spent the night with another woman. Jean didn't know how to lie. Hannah would have preferred that he did. But you can't change those you love. Or if you try, maybe you don't really love them. He never saw the unknown woman again. Like in the Cinderella story, she had disappeared without leaving a name or address, slipping away at the end of the street. He could have gone back to the cabaret, but he hadn't. For Hannah, out of fear, out of shyness. Hannah forgave Jean. And they never spoke of it again. Occasionally, when one of Jean's silences lasted too long, she wondered whether he was thinking of the girl from the cabaret.

The Steinway remained at the community center. A brass plaque in the entrance of the multipurpose hall, reads: "This Steinway was the piano on which Jean Septembre (1950–1987) learned to play. It was donated to the town of Gueugnon by the Ruben family, victims of the Nazi insanity."

34

November 28, 2010

I'm just emerging from the cinema when I discover I've received a voicemail from Paul. I try to watch, and sometime rewatch, movies in theaters. I've always loved an auditorium. Especially when it's the early screening. No popcorn-munching, rustling of candy wrappers, or the harsh light of a neighbor's smartphone. In the morning, there are few neighbors. I love the big screen, the trailers, and the ads. As the lights dim, my heart quickens.

I need to share the vision of film directors from around the world, whatever their age, their origins. To understand why they spent years preparing, writing, selling, clarifying, filming a story. You don't direct a great actor or actress, you "dose" them. I am, and always will be, in love with that dosing. Pierre is a Stradivarius of the profession. Mom loved it when I said that about my husband. It reminded her of the instrument she adored.

That morning, at Studio 28, they were celebrating the seventeenth anniversary of *The Piano*. Not the tenth or the twentieth. I asked the manager why the seventeenth. "Because it's a lucky number." How could luck resist Jane Campion? I'm thinking of her as I walk down Rue Tholozé, phone in hand, putting off listening to my cop friend's message. I think of Dad, who would have loved that film. Jane and Jean meet in my thoughts, it's cold, but the sun is brightening the neighborhood.

"You have a new message. Today, at 11:10 A.M.: "Hey, Agnès, it's Paul. Call me back, please, love for now . . . By the way, I'm back in Paris."

Last I heard, Soudkovski, who wasn't supposed to last the night, had already lasted two nights. I don't feel like calling Paul back. I'd rather linger for a few more minutes with Harvey Keitel and Holly Hunter on a beach in New Zealand. That's what movies are for.

I sit in the Villa des Abbesses restaurant for a quick coffee. I empty my cup before ringing his number. My heart is clenched like a fist. I don't think I want to know anything else. Colette's death threw me into a bottomless abyss. I talked to Ana. When she opened her eyes yesterday morning, I didn't draw the curtains, and in the half-light, I quietly said:

"Darling, Blanche is probably my biological mother."

A bottomless abyss. Ana wasn't ready to hear such cataclysmic news. She hugged me really tight. Without her asking me a thing, I added:

"My father and Blanche knew each other. And I had no idea."

On Rue de la Liberté, we bought some croissants and went into the Jade, the café opposite Gueugnon's town hall. I pictured my father walking into that building thirty-eight years ago to register my birth. Ana sat down in the street-facing room. She ordered a hot chocolate.

"It's so cool about Antoine's house. It really is your house, Mom."

And she continued without giving me time to reply:

"Mom, if you weren't my mother, would you tell me?"

"Darling, I conceived you, carried you, loved you. There was no intermediary between us."

"I know. I never doubted it."

"I have the feeling that Blanche entrusted me to Hannah to save me. To free me. To give me a life that would be different from hers . . . But Hannah will always be my mother and your grandmother."

"If I ever have a daughter, I'll call her Blanche. Like that, we'll have come full circle . . . "

I took her hands in mine, her beautiful pianist's hands, and we said nothing more for some minutes. Our respective ghosts were swirling around us.

"D'you think Coco knew?"

"Colette respected her brother's silence. Probably out of fear of Soudkovski . . . Him again . . . Always him . . . "

"Soudkovski, Scum-of-the-earth-i."

That amused me. Then Ana exclaimed:

"Shit, Mom, he's your grandfather!"

We stared at each other, goggle-eyed, before just laughing about it. What else could we do?

"A psychopath . . . That's all I needed," I finally said.

"Oh, *creepy . . .* "

"Colette sheltered Blanche for seven years. Their friendship went beyond anything we could imagine."

"But you, how does it make you feel, being hit with this bombshell?"

"Mom spoke so often to me about her adoptive parents, Benjamin and Éléonore. She adored them. She always said that blood ties don't make ties . . . When she talked about them, she was probably talking about us."

"Just look, Coco's real mother was a monster," Ana said.

"Yes, a monster. My aunt almost died because of it . . . Poor Colette. Thank goodness Mokhtar loved her like a father. You know, darling, a birth, it's wonderful. You're going to have a little brother or sister, and that's big and beautiful news. Believe me. I'd have loved not to be alone."

Ana first pulled a face, but finally came round.

We left the Jade. Ana took my arm. She hadn't done that for ages. We had three hours to kill before heading to the station. She wanted to come with me to Rue des Fredins, to meet "the neighbor across the street who makes soup and knows stuff." What stuff? Didn't I know enough? I think that's when I realized that I didn't want to piece the puzzle together anymore. I just wanted to put it away in a cupboard. It was others who wanted to know for me.

*

Madame Aubert was in her garden. She was pouring seeds into a small birdhouse hanging from a tree. It was the first time I was seeing her close up, rather than behind her window. With her short hair and pretty smile, she reminded me of the actress Josiane Balasko. Her simplicity and mischief-filled eyes did, too. Just then, I realized that her face wasn't unknown to me. She'd been a customer at the shoe-repair shop.

"Good morning, Agnès. Louis told me that you'd be coming to see me. Is this your daughter?"

"Yes, I'm Ana."

"Welcome, Ana. You look like your grandfather, two peas in a pod. Do you play the piano, like him?"

"Yes. I'm going to study at the conservatoire."

"Ah, that's great, my dear. Agnès, can I speak in front of your daughter?"

"Yes."

"Follow me. We're not staying out here, far too cold."

Her house was very like Louis's. Many houses and interiors look similar around here. Houses that have never been left. The same building contractors, same years of construction, mostly between 1950 and 1975, same windows, roofs, stucco, basements, furniture, fitted appliances, fabrics, curtains, wallpapers.

Like Louis, she made me a filter coffee. Ana had a bottle of orange juice. Madame Aubert drew up two chairs, placed a tin of Breton shortbread on the waxed tablecloth. A cliché: the waxed cloth, the tin, the sixties clock on the wall, children—doubtless adults by now—smiling beside the sea in frames, the pottery goblets, the sugar in another, smaller, tin.

Madame Aubert didn't wait for me to ask her anything, launching into a lengthy monologue that neither I, nor Ana, interrupted. You could have heard a fly go past when she paused to think, to be precise, though the flies are all dead at this time of year.

"I was born in Gueugnon during the war, in 1940. I was six years older than Colette. I got to know her when she started her apprenticeship with Mokhtar. My parents were customers of his. I was very fond of Colette. She was a kind person. I always knew she was great friends with the little circus girl. Blanche and Colette looked very alike. When they met at school in 1953, I was already in junior high. And when Blanche returned to the Pasteur school in 1956, I was a supervisor. I can still see them having lunch together on a bench in front of the school. They looked like twins. One day, my father went to help a lady because an animal had escaped from the circus. I got the fright of my life . . . I was involved with a member of the circus and we were in his trailer when I saw my father turn up, outside the big top. I thought he had come for me. To take me home.

"My sweetheart's name was Nestor. He was huge, and handsome as a god. We never did anything bad, he was always respectful toward me. He was fifteen years older than me, but I was madly in love with him. Sometimes, I regret having been such a good girl . . . I remember that particular morning like it was yesterday; we were saying our goodbyes. Nestor was going away, and I was weeping in his arms. We saw an altercation between Blanche's father and mine. I was shaking with fear. If my father had seen me, he'd have given me a hell of a hiding. Nestor's 2.1-meter height wouldn't have scared him. His underage daughter involved with an older man in the circus: it would have driven him crazy, my poor dad. That evening, he told me and my mother what he'd been through in the morning. The escaped animal, the screams of Madame Fernandez, at whose home the creature had taken refuge, the nasty piece of work who managed the circus, and his little girl, whom he'd felt sorry for. He repeated several times: 'Honestly, you can see in that little girl's eyes that she's not a little girl anymore, because her mother died.' Nestor had told me the kid's mother was called Marie Roman and she came from Flumet. 'Personally, I think she's hiding,' he'd added. 'There's no proof she's dead. She'd already run away once before. I knew her when Blanche was born. She traveled with us for two years, should've seen how unhappy she was with him. I've never seen a man be so nasty to his wife.'

"My father felt guilty that he hadn't been able to do anything for that child. And I couldn't admit to him what I knew. So I bought a postcard at the *tabac*. I picked a photo of Gueugnon's church, thinking that God might offer the little girl a helping hand. And I wrote in capital letters, with my left hand: 'The girl's mother is alive. She was born in Flumet and is called Marie Roman.' I addressed the card to my father and slipped it into the mailbox at the town hall. I did it so he'd try to find Marie Roman. But nothing happened. And Nestor and his circus never returned.

"Years later, I spoke to Colette about it, told her the whole story, including my infatuation with Nestor, whom she remembered. Blanche had told her that her mother was dead. The father must have lied to her. Colette had heard nothing more from her school friend, but she hadn't forgotten her. I didn't know the name Soudkovski for a long time. Nestor called him Soudoro. I'll admit, I waited for my handsome circus man for years. I dreamed for ages that he would come back to marry me. And then finally accepted that he wouldn't. Place de Gaulle remained as empty as my poor heart. I got married later in life to another man, and we had two beautiful children. Meanwhile, I, too, went to work at Gueugnon's town hall. In various departments. Now I'm retired. But I teach French voluntarily. And I'll never stop. I still have my father, but I lost my husband."

She stood up to go to the adjoining room, then returned triumphant with a bottle of port and two crystal glasses. Without asking me first, she poured one out for me. It was barely eleven in the morning and I had no desire whatsoever to drink. She looked me straight in the eye.

"And now I'm going to talk about the difficult stuff. About what concerns you, Agnès. This little glass of port won't go amiss. For either of us."

She matched action to words by downing a generous glassful. I sensed that Ana wanted to laugh, though she was hanging on Madame Aubert's every word.

"I'm going to start with Jean, who came to the town hall to register your birth on October 23, 1972. I remember everything about it. It was a Monday morning. Must have been 10 o'clock when he showed up. It was such a fine day, it could have been spring, and I'd opened the window in the office. Jean handed me your mother's and his identity papers, telling me: 'I'm the daddy of a little girl.' And he added: 'Hannah didn't have time to get to the hospital, the baby came so fast. She was born three weeks early.' Surprised, I asked who had helped bring the little girl into the world. With tears in his voice, he replied: 'My sister.'

"Colette? It hadn't been unusual for women to give birth at home, but since the sixties, it just didn't happen anymore. In 1972, there were only two births in Gueugnon, including yours. The other babies were born at the maternity clinic in Paray-le-Monial.

"'We came to spend a couple of days with Colette, and the little one arrived.' I didn't know that Jean's wife was pregnant. As for Colette, I saw her regularly, and she'd never mentioned it to me. It's true that she wasn't talkative—that's putting it mildly—but as soon as some event involved her brother or football, she'd become a bit chattier.

"I asked Jean if Hannah had seen a doctor. He replied that Dr. Labori had visited, and mother and child were doing well, but in his haste, the doctor had forgotten to fill in the delivery form. Colette would bring it to me that week. Jean looked overwhelmed. I naturally took his emotion to be that of a man becoming a father for the first time. I finalized the birth certificate, despite the missing form. You'll see, it's definitely my signature on it.

"Once the official papers were completed, I asked about your weight and size, just like that, instinctively. I saw that he had no idea. 'She's very small . . . But she's feeding well.' And when I congratulated him with a hug, he collapsed in my arms. We were alone in the department, and I thought what sensitive souls artists are. I made him a coffee, which he drank with a faraway look in his eyes, and then he left.

"I kept thinking about what he'd said to me, and started to have my doubts. You were born during the night of October 20. So, Friday into Saturday. And Jean had waited until Monday morning to register your birth. I called Dr. Labori to clear my mind. He was very close to Colette ever since he'd treated Mokhtar Bayram. Toward the end, he'd visit every day. His secretary told me that he was away. He'd been working elsewhere for a week. Why had Jean lied to me? What was this birth concealing that had made him sob in my arms?

"Seven days later, Colette came with the delivery form signed by Labori. As if it were he who'd delivered Hannah's baby. When I told her that she could have been a midwife, she begged me not to talk to anyone about it.

"To be honest, Agnès, at first I thought Colette was your mother, and due to some dark story, she'd entrusted you to her sister-in-law and brother. So I asked the question. Colette knew that I wouldn't let her go without an answer, and that I'd keep the secret. I know everything about everybody in this town, but no one knows anything about anybody that's come from me. Colette sat down; I felt sorry for her. She told me that on October 20, Jean had turned up at her place with two women. His wife and Blanche Soudkovski. At first, Colette had thought it was a surprise, they'd found her childhood friend! But their somber expressions made her think again. When Blanche took off her girdle, her pregnancy was obvious. Jean announced to his sister that he was the father of the child, with no explanation of how they'd met. Nothing. And since Jean was already with Hannah, Colette took Blanche to be a surrogate mother. Jean begged her to help Blanche bring this baby into the world. Colette refused at first, saying she didn't know what to do. Jean replied that she'd done it a hundred times, and promised that if there were any complications, he'd call a doctor on the spot. I can't recall Colette ever refusing her brother anything. As for Blanche, she saw Colette as her only friend, her salvation. The poor girl's time was limited; she had to be back in Lyon in three days' time, or Levgueni Soudkovski would kill her. Only three days to free this baby from a dire fate. Thanks to her girdle, the bastard hadn't noticed a thing. Colette then understood the situation. She said that not only had Hannah not appeared appalled or angry, but she'd even held Blanche's hand when labor started, offering her gentle and reassuring support. They ate late that night, and Blanche admitted to them that she lived like a recluse, despite having a job. And, in Colette's small kitchen, it was decided that the secret of this birth must never be revealed, so that the child might live in peace. Colette and Blanche slept in the same bed. What did Blanche confide to her about her liaison with Jean? I don't know and never dared ask the question. When someone shares a secret with you, be silent.

"Blanche's pregnancy was at full term. The poor thing had been downing liters of raspberry-leaf tea since the previous day to open her cervix, having heard that it would accelerate the birth. Was it thanks to this grandmother's remedy, or because, with Colette by her side, she'd felt secure and lowered her guard? At around one in the morning, her waters broke. And it was indeed Colette Septembre who helped bring you into the world . . . Hannah cut the umbilical cord. They discovered the sex of the baby together. All three of them.

"Blanche breastfed you during her two days of reprieve. And your two mothers watched over you, side by side. You all slept together, snuggled up close. You're a child of love, Agnès. No doubt about that."

I drained my glass of port. Ana wept in my arms. Why did I have to learn the circumstances of my birth at this stranger's house and with my daughter present? There was a reason for it. Colette helped bring me into the world . . .

Not a mention of the "event" in the recordings left for me by my aunt. Why? Out of fear that someone other than me would get hold of them? What had they whispered to me during those two days? Had they rocked me in turn? Sung lullabies to me? I closed my eyes. Placed my two fists on the waxed tablecloth and imagined my mothers leaning over me. My father and his sister entering and then leaving the room to leave those two women in peace with their newborn. Which of the two chose my name? And my dear Colette who had never been a mom, how did she experience this upheaval? I can't imagine their parting. When Blanche had to leave, did she ever return? Did she ask after me? Ask my parents or Colette? My mother or my father? When we visited my aunt years later, and Blanche would hear my voice and my daughter's voice, how did she feel? When she found out about me on TV or through my movies, what did she think? *That's my daughter* or *that's Agnès*? And when she learned of my father's death through the media, did she call Colette or Hannah? The more answers we get, the more questions we have.

Cécile Aubert drags me from my thoughts by continuing with her story:

"Then, in 2004, I'm in a waiting room, leafing through an old magazine, and his name jumps out at me. Soudkovski! He's wanted by the police in Marseille! I rushed to warn Colette. She went white when she saw the article. She thought he was in prison. She immediately closed her shop to go home. That's when I realized that she was still in touch with her childhood friend. And that she was afraid for you. I didn't know they were living together. I realized it three years later. Imagine my grief when I heard that Colette had died. And my astonishment when I saw Louis Berthéol coming every day to the house opposite the one I'd moved into. I never crossed the road to question

Colette; I saw her going out, I recognized her, I didn't call out to her. I let her live her death in peace. I knew it was a strange situation. Indeed, I never would've talked to you about it, either, if that old bastard hadn't been in a coma . . . If Blanche's father had known you existed, he'd have done the same as with the others, locked you up or killed you. Thanks to the silence of your father, Colette, Hannah, and Blanche, you grew up as a free woman . . . As did your daughter."

"Did Colette tell you what happened when Blanche had to leave me?"

This question is the only one I asked.

"Colette wasn't there for that. The three of them left in a car, with you in a Moses basket. Colette told me that, in the space of forty-eight hours, she'd gone from everything to nothing. To emptiness. Sitting in front of me, like a pitiful little thing, she came to the end of her extraordinary story. I felt so sorry for her that, from then on, I often dropped by to see her. And I watched you growing up. You certainly stayed with Colette a good deal. With your friends. Including my little Ilyas, of whom I'm so fond."

When I stood up, my legs could barely support me. Cécile Aubert kissed us both warmly. I asked whether, by any chance, she had a photo of Blanche, even as a child, since she'd known Nestor. But no. I also asked why she'd only crossed the road to leave soup on my doormat, rather than to talk to me. She replied that she would never have told me this story if I hadn't questioned her. Ana took my arm again.

We went back to the hotel to pack our bags. From time to time, we broke the silence by throwing out words or snatches of sentences to each other. I thought of Alain Souchon's song, "*Chanter, c'est lancer des balles*"—Singing is like throwing balls: "D'you think Jean and Blanche loved each other?—it's a bit weird, having a thing with a girl who looks like his sister—according to Louis, they had a different aura—d'you think it lasted a long time between them?—all the same, Colette—my health record with Labori's signature—we should bump the old man off, all of this is his fault—it all happened in Lyon—go to the Cabaret des Oiseaux—Marie Roman—he abandoned Natalia like a dog—the bearded lady, she brought her up—you'd sing '*Le Temps qui court*' to me—I weighed 2.4 kilos and measured 42 centimeters—come on, we'll go to the hospital and switch him off, like in *House*—why didn't Nestor come back?—d'you think, if Scum-of-the-earth-i hadn't existed, Jean would have preferred to stay with Blanche rather than Hannah?—a murderer—Cécile Aubert, maybe she loved her husband—will you be okay, Mom, you're sure?—I'll be okay, they're dead, my origins are resting in peace under the earth—are you in love with Antoine?—I almost want to reply to you: thank goodness."

35

November 28, 2010

Instead of phoning Paul, I've decided to go straight to Quai des Orfèvres. Whenever I enter this fabled police HQ, I think of the actor Louis Jouvet in the movie *Quai des Orfèvres* . . . who probably never set foot in the place. I'm asked to wait for Paul's return, and they leave me in his office. All over the walls, toll-free phone numbers. Domestic violence, addiction, the effects of cannabis, sexual assault. Magic numbers to ring to solve the unspeakable. I think of Ilyas, and of Charpie's other victims. How many were there? If, at the time, Ilyas had been able to ring such a magical phone number, would it have changed how things went? Would Charpie have been tried in court? And if so, how many years in jail would he have gotten? But you don't dial a phone number when you're seven years old. That particular phone weighs a ton. When you're seven, you don't say that a man in authority hurt you; you're ashamed, you feel dirty, because you didn't do anything to stop him from doing it. You're too afraid to cry in your mother's arms, and you keep quiet. We all know some victims, and we all know some predators. We shake their hands, ask how they're doing. The silence that surrounds the torturers and their prey is breathtaking.

The phone on Paul's desk rings, making me jump. I'm dying to answer it. Is it the hospital in Caluire? Is one of the world's torturers dead? Or is the person trying to reach Paul the magistrate working to establish Blanche's identity?

"You're here?" he says, surprised, when he turns up behind me.

This time, I haven't come to ask him questions for a movie, but so that he can tell me about my story. I question him on Soudkovski. Is he still alive? Paul says yes. I check that he can't fake being in a coma, that he can't escape.

"He's in a deep coma."

I tell him, in broad strokes, what I learned about my birth directly from the former municipal employee, Cécile Aubert.

"That corroborates your DNA."

"Yes, it corroborates . . . Did you listen to the cassette found in the coffin?"

He nods and unlocks a drawer.

"Here. This is a copy of it."

I look at him in astonishment.

"There were two cassettes," he tells me. "The first dates from 1985, when you were given your recorder. And the other is more recent. I've numbered them 1 and 2."

"Are you allowed to give them to me?"

"They're copies. And no, I'm not allowed to. But since they concern you, I'm infringing the law. For you, Agnès, it won't be the first time."

I daren't take them.

"They're yours."

*

JEAN

One, two, three. I think it's working. Yes, it's working. Before wrapping it, Hannah asked me to put in some batteries and check the recorder. I'm hiding in my sister's room. I can hear Hannah, Agnès, and Colette chatting in the kitchen. This evening, we'll be celebrating Christmas Eve. Our daughter's thirteenth Christmas. This evening, Hannah and I will give her a cassette recorder. It's the present she hoped for. I'm alone. Sitting on the bed. Where you gave birth to our Agnès. I've been alone, separated from you, since the night you gave birth to her. I'm a man, alone from you, who's testing our daughter's toy. And I won't erase this recording. I won't listen to it again, either. I can see that it seems to be working; a red light is indicating that my voice has been captured on the tape. I'll entrust this to Colette later, so she can give it to you one day, if she ever finds you. I always thought you'd come back. To Colette, to me, or to Agnès. Hannah told me she'd sent you pictures of Agnès, in care of the Lyon post office. I always wondered how you managed to collect the envelopes, since you have no ID card. You don't exist because of him, but you exist so much for those who love you. I often thought about how I could set you free. I even thought about paying a fortune to have him killed, because I'm a coward and don't have the soul of a murderer. But I didn't have the courage, because of Agnès, Hannah, and Colette. The person who hires a hit always ends up being traced, and I can't imagine being separated from them. I realize what I'm saying to you; I really am too stupid. You'll listen to my stupidity. I don't know what I mean to you, who I am beyond a one-night encounter that left its imprint for eternity through Agnès. An idiot who wasn't able to protect you. Since Agnès's birth, I play for her. I play for all of you, for you, Hannah, and Colette. Especially when I have Bach under my fingers. Bach automatically brings me back to you all. I've always included my sister in our story. What would've happened without her? It's funny, when I saw you, that first time, I thought you were her, and gradually, as the evening unfolded, as if on a magic carpet, you became completely remote from Colette. Appearance is nothing; what counts is movement. Exactly like a symphony. I'm alone from you in Colette's room, and I wonder what I'd say to you if you were here, close to me. "Thank you. I missed you. I will miss you. My heart is broken." It really is possible to love two women with the same intensity. It is, believe me. I could tell myself that I don't know you, that I only knew you for a few hours. Except that an hour can contain the entire world. We came to know each other to make Agnès. Our past, our present, our future belongs to her.

When I arrived at the Levitans' with our ten-day-old daughter in my arms, a miracle took place. I remember that, during our night together, I told you about David and Élia Levitan, about their deportation, about him and about his piano, about her and her voice that fell silent upon their return. Never again was Élia heard to sing. The nightingale of Auschwitz was dead. Well, that day, she was alone and silent in the kitchen, which stank of cabbage as usual. I walked into the apartment saying, "It's me." I still had the keys; I kept them even after they died. When she saw me with the baby in my arms, she stared wide-eyed and murmured something in Yiddish. We remained facing each other for a few seconds, and then, without leaving her any choice, I held out my little one for her to take her. "Meet my daughter. She's called Agnès. My darling, meet Élia, my friend."

She didn't ask me any questions, though she knew that Hannah had never been pregnant. She pulled a chair toward her, sat down with Agnès in her arms. David was away. It was just the three of us. Agnès was sleeping, her little fists clenched. She was wearing a pretty woolen coat. Dressed all in white, like on the day of a christening. I left the two of them to get acquainted, and sat at the piano. I played the opening bars of Mozart's Concerto No. 23.

After a few minutes, I heard voices. Was it the neighbors? Or sounds coming from the street? I stopped playing.

The kitchen.

Élia, usually as silent as the stuffed carp she'd serve us every Saturday, was singing for my daughter. I hid behind the door and saw Agnès, her eyes wide open, listening religiously to this stranger with the angelic voice who was rocking her. "Barcarolle" from Offenbach's Tales of Hoffmann. *What struck me the most was Élia's voice. It didn't sound like her. A host of elated birds in the throat. The figure of a doddery old admiral. A staggering dichotomy.*

That morning of November 1, 1972, the Day of the Dead, I witnessed the resurrection of Élia Levitan, who had died in Poland. I remained hidden. Like I am at this moment in Colette's room. I didn't want to interrupt their exchange. I thought of you then, a bit more than usual. I have no idea how many years I'll live, no idea if I'll see you again someday. I've never been back to the Cabaret des Oiseaux. I even avoid the neighborhood. It's strange to dream of it and fear it at the same time. Coming across you. What would become of us if, unfortunately or happily, we ran into each other? Of our night together, your symphony will remain with me for all eternity. When I told you about my childhood and you realized that I was the brother of Colette, the little girl at school who looked like you, the one who brought you things to eat, you held my face between your hands and repeated to me, "the little brother she loved so much." And your hands were as gentle as the first sunshine in spring. I closed my eyes, I remember, I closed my eyes, and you, you kept your hands on me. And I kissed you. I'd never kissed anyone first. You were my first move. I opened my eyes and saw yours, so deep. Something within you was in retreat. Instinctively, I knew that all that we were experiencing would be ephemeral. That you wouldn't stay. That I'd already lost you before I met you.

Someone knocks on the door and walks in. I recognize Hannah's voice:

"Are you coming, Jean?"
"I'm coming."
"Is it okay, it works?"
"It works."
"What are you doing?"
"Nothing. I'm coming."

End of the recording.

36

November 29, 2010

We all experience pretty much the same things in life. Of course, there are the surprises, the blows dealt by fate, good luck and bad luck, affluence and poverty, conflicts, religions, but in short, we're all pretty much destined to experience the same things. Building relationships with our parents, our brothers, our sisters, our friends, our neighbors. Learning from books when we're children, the pictures, poetry, history and geography, times tables, the conjugation of the verbs *être* and *avoir*; swimming, pedaling, meeting, choosing, working, traveling, trying to build a life with someone; having children; caring for our elders if they become dependent one day; trying to find a certain balance; not growing up thinking only about our looks; sharing and listening as best we can; helping each other; enjoying things; calling ourselves stupid occasionally, naïve often, smiling at and encouraging ourselves all the same. Dancing, above all.

I love Alain Souchon's song "*Foule sentimentale.*" It sums it all up. Funny how Souchon keeps reappearing in my life at the moment. He's my reference for the present.

Anyhow.

We're all destined to experience pretty much the same things; it's what makes us human. We all have more or less the same plans, the same dreams. But there's one sentence I never would've thought I'd hear in my entire life: "Agnès, since you're Soudkovski's only living relative, the Caluire medical team would like your permission before switching him off."

I agreed, but on two conditions: seeing him, and Paul coming with me. A drive there and back in one day. It's cool, traveling with a cop;

when we get stuck in traffic jams, he switches on the flashing light, and we can park anywhere.

I discover a dead old man, but whose ribcage still rises and falls. He's had no brain activity for forty-eight hours. I don't recognize the man in the photo Louis showed me. The snap taken by Mathilde Pinson, with the passerby pulling a shopping caddy in the street. I study his profile, the shape of his closed eyes. No resemblance to the people in my family.

"Are you sure it's him?"

The doctor and nurse look at me suspiciously. I haven't touched him. I refuse to sit near him. This man is a sinister stranger who terrorized his wife and his daughter. Killed Mathilde Pinson and Viktor Socha, beat all his victims to death.

A sheet covers his body, which is wired up to some unbelievable machines. I feel very uncomfortable. I notice his skin, the bruise left by the IV. He's a waxen yellow.

"It's due to the overdose of medication. The liver couldn't take it. He poisoned himself. All the vital organs were affected."

And the vital organs of the women he haunted are now just dust.

It's one of the worst moments of my life. It reminds me of the execution of Ceaucescu. The second death I'd seen, but that one was on TV. You get nothing out of it. Neither joy nor glory. At most, a sense of relief, revenge for the people. But in this case, where's the revenge? Marie and Blanche are buried. This death has come too late.

They wait for my consent to confirm it, make it official. I who am nothing to him, he who is nothing to me. I don't listen to the doctor, who's talking to me as if I knew the lifeless specter lying on this bed. All I hear is that he's brain dead. That it's over. He can't hear anymore, feel anymore, can't breathe on his own anymore. I'm finally asked whether I have any questions. None. I feel like asking again whether it's really him, but don't dare. Paul replies for me:

"Until a few days ago, Madame Septembre was unaware that this individual was related to her."

I don't know why, but the doctor doesn't seem to believe us. We leave the room, and I'm asked to sign a piece of paper. It will be our only link, his death. A piece of paper on which our names are brought together. Before I can get out of the place, I'm given a bag containing his personal effects. I feel like a usurper in a really bad movie. We get back in the car.

"Okay?"

"Okay. D'you think that . . . they've switched him off?"

"Yes."

". . ."

"I wanted to tell you, Liouba Rozov, Levgueni Soudkovski's mother . . . she was a trapeze artist. She died when her son was four-and-a-half."

". . ."

"He grew up with his father, a real brute."

". . ."

"He was found lying on his mother's grave."

"He should be buried with her, somehow. I'll pay for it. At the stage I'm at, one funeral more or less . . . I earned so much making movies that now I finance funerals . . . Should've been a funeral director rather than a film director."

". . ."

"Could you organize that for me, Paul?"

"Yes, chief. But there's something else."

"What now? There's always something else . . . "

"Soudkovski did a lot of research into you these last few weeks. He always deleted his search history, but our digital guys got inside the belly of his computer."

". . ."

"Look in the bag."

Paul indicates the one I'd been given at the hospital and had thrown onto the back seat. We're still in the car park outside.

"D'you think he wanted to kill me?"

"No, I think it's something else."

He adds nothing more. I put my gloves on before reaching for the bag. I don't want to touch what belonged to that man with my bare hands. It's also a way of keeping my distance. Inside, I find gray trousers and a black sweater wrapped in plastic. It all reeks of wood-fire smoke. I recognize my red scarf in another wrapping. I remain speechless while I work out that he must have stolen it the day he got into Colette's house. I looked for it everywhere, thinking I'd forgotten it somewhere. Paul murmurs that he was wearing it when they found him, unconscious, in the cemetery. Why was he wearing my scarf? What did he know about me? Had he worked it out, about Blanche's pregnancy? I'm starting to feel that debilitating heat grip me. The one that strikes me down. That stifles me.

Finally, I find an ancient wallet, very worn, its seams almost torn apart. Colette would've been pleased to have it in her hands, leaning over her workbench. She loved topstitching fine leather goods. She'd say she felt like a goldsmith.

I'm feeling increasingly hot. Increasingly bad. I hear Paul say to me:

"I asked them to throw away his shoes and coat, they were filthy."

A list worthy of the poet Prévert: trousers, sweater, stolen scarf, wallet. My voice comes out muffled:

"Is this all he owned?"

"He stole a car at Valence station, it was found near here. There were some clothes inside it, a moneybox containing banknotes, newspapers, dumbbells, all kinds of shit, and, most importantly, a computer in the trunk. It was all sent to the lab."

"And my pink box? Did you find it?"

"No."

"And my photos?"

"Nothing. No box, no photos."

I open the wallet, trying to control my shaking hands. It contains nothing but a black-and-white picture of a woman. The photograph is in perfect condition. Care has been taken of it. It must date to the twenties or thirties. A dark-haired woman smiles at the camera. By the time my brain processes the information, analyses, understands, realizes, suffocates, rejects, by the time I've studied the hair, eyes, nose, cheekbones, mouth, smile, gala dress, body, hips, legs in spangled tights . . . By the time . . . I can feel myself going. But I refuse to black out, forbid myself to. I close my eyes and press my head into the headrest. I'd like to whisper to Paul, "Tell me I'm dreaming," but

I can't speak, can't get a single word out. I hear my breathing. I hear the siren of a fire truck or ambulance passing by in the distance. I hear his voice. "Breathe."

I breathe. I open my eyes. Look again at the photo. Turn to Paul, manage to say: "It's crazy." And he replies: "Totally crazy."

*

It's eight o'clock. I'm alone in my apartment. Paul dropped me off late-afternoon. Cornélia left me a soup in the fridge. Ana's having supper with her father to settle their disagreement. I've just been doing some research into Liouba Rozov. An hour to find two measly lines concerning her on a website about circuses of the past: "Trapeze artist originally from Russia. The Circus Elliott (France) hires her in 1927. First woman to perform a double somersault." These few words move me. She exists. Existed. She did double somersaults. No new photograph. My eyes are already smarting from the hours I've spent studying our resemblance in the one I have. I feel as if I'm seeing myself in a former life. Or that I've been made up for some period film. I can't wait to show this photo to Ana. It's strange seeing your own face in an ancestor's. Reminds me of the reincarnation stories we'd tell each other, me, Ilyas, Adèle, and Hervé, to scare ourselves.

I have the face of a Russian woman, and I didn't know it. It has been pointed out to me that I look Slavic, and I've always replied that my maternal grandparents were from a Jewish settlement originally from Eastern Europe. Was Liouba Jewish or Orthodox? Were Soudkovski's tears real or dreamed? Did he get into my room at the Monge? I'll probably never know. And even if Paul were to discover that his phone pinged in Gueugnon that night, I don't want to know. I've told him that. I don't want to know anything else. I'm going to do some more research into Liouba, to find more information about her origins. And possibly some other photos. But I don't want to learn anything more about her son. I'm too scared of him. I've never felt as close to Blanche as I do in the terror he triggers in me. Is it because his blood runs in my veins? Because I carry part of his evil within me? His evil and his pain?

I still have the last cassette to listen to, from Blanche's coffin. Who's speaking on it? Blanche? Colette? Mom? All three of them? I have it in my hands. Once I've listened to it, I'll put it away with the others. And I'll make sure they're preserved for as long as possible. They contain our memory, our history.

When I heard Dad's voice addressing Blanche, I thought how extraordinary it is to hold on to voices. Even more so than images. An image imposes itself. A voice lingers and reinvents a face. Apparently, we have the same voice at every age. Was it this first cassette that made Colette want to continue? Probably. Colette must have discovered it when she found my old recorder. And I imagine her giving it to Blanche in 2000. "This is from Jean. He left it for you."

I'm the child of several stories. Powerful stories. I owe it to myself to continue telling such stories.

I take a quick look at my mail, placed on the desk, and am drawn to a parcel. My address is handwritten. It was posted in Paris, from the eighteenth arrondissement. I don't recognize the writing. I open it and find the pink box containing all my photos.

*

BLANCHE

My dear Agnès, I didn't want to. Because I think I don't exist. That I shouldn't exist. That all this is a disturbance. It's March 30, 2007; Colette is beside me. She's always been near me. Thank goodness she does exist. We've just listened to the Goldberg Variations *played by your father. And all that beauty has gone to my head. So Colette is asking me to talk to you, because . . .*

Silence.

BLANCHE

. . . I'm forever talking to her about you, but I never actually talk to you.

Silence.

BLANCHE

"Talk to her about yourself," she repeats. "Tell her," she repeats. I never would've plucked up the courage without her. You're a great lady. I feel like a little mouse who gave birth to a mountain. I only spent one night with your father.

I thought about not saying anything. Staying close to the recorder without uttering a word, so you could hear my silence, the absence of you, of us. All that absence that has haunted me since the day I placed you in Hannah's arms, in the back seat of the car.

Silence.

BLANCHE

The sound of the engine. Jean drove off after kissing me. I heard the car moving away.

Silence.

BLANCHE

If I'd had to speak to you one day, I would've liked to do so in the flesh. But he *is still alive. He's hiding. He's looking for me. And if* he *finds me, I'm scared he'll find you.*

Silence.

BLANCHE

Silence is never beneficial. It can even kill. So here goes. I realized that you were inside me a long time after conceiving you. At five months pregnant, I felt kind of bubbles in my stomach. Your first movements. Your presence. I hadn't put on a gram, or seen my periods . . . but since I rarely saw them, I hadn't twigged. Knowing that you were inside me, understanding that you were inside me, I felt, all at once, immense happiness, universal joy, and sheer anxiety. I never thought I'd keep you, Agnès. I knew immediately that we'd have to separate. That I'd have to get you out of this vicious cycle. If he *found out about it, he'd kill me, and your life would be threatened, or he'd hold on to you. He'd turn you into his plaything, like he did me, a stolen, weakened, isolated soul. There really are beings who terrorize. And more than we think. There really are martyred families living under the control of a tyrant. And more than we think.*

It wasn't Jean I went to see, it was your mom, Hannah. It was women's business. I waited for her after a concert, on Rue des Tables-Claudiennes, in Lyon. I'd found her photo, alongside those of other musicians, in a leaflet. Jean had told me about her during our evening together. I'd asked him lots of questions. He told me how they met. The note inside the piano. And her, a violinist. The story of her deported family and her adoption. I thought, my child will belong to a pianist and a violinist, and not someone like me. It was unthinkable that he *should ever lay eyes on you. If Hannah had refused, I would've given the baby up at birth and killed myself straight after. But I managed to live because one evening, I met Hannah Ruben. She noticed me because of the resemblance. She came over and asked, incredulously: "You are? . . . Colette has a sister? Jean has another sister?" I lowered my eyes. I didn't know if Jean had told her about me. About our night together. I've never felt so ashamed in my life. I can't remember exactly the words I used. But I know that I told her everything out there, in the street, on the sidewalk. I had very little time. I was expected back at the cabaret. I'd requested a rare break. They thought I had a date. Which was true, but not in the way they imagined. And Hannah was looking at me with alarm, clutching her violin case. How pretty she was . . . I could see in her eyes that Jean had told her about me.*

I spoke to your mom on June 21, 1972. The first day of summer, the day Jean died fifteen years later. She could've asked me to leave on the spot, not believed me. But Hannah listened to me, didn't judge me. I think she understood my terror, and the urgency to save your life. She took my hand—yes, took my hand—and promised to help me. She was so tall and so dignified, I felt pitiful, wretched, and sadly dirty. But I wasn't alone anymore. She loved your father so much, she accepted everything from him, even the child he'd created with another woman.

I had spent the night of January 19 with Jean Septembre, so one just had to add nine months to imagine the approximate date of your arrival in the world. Hannah asked how she could contact me. That wasn't an option. I took the phone number she scribbled on a bit of paper. I told her that I'd call her from October 19 onward. Hannah asked me what I would do if the baby arrived before that. But I was convinced that the child would remain with me to full term.

I'd warned the cabaret: "I'm going to be away for four days, but if you tell anyone, I'll never be able to work here again." I took risks. Sam, my boss, would report my every move. But his wife, Arielle, shielded me. I took risks, but I had no choice. I realize today that your top-secret birth was something of a miracle.

I had four months to prepare you for our separation, without ever mentioning it. I told myself that we had four months to live together. During the day, I concealed you under binding, and at night, I caressed you. I'd whisper poems and songs to you, so he *couldn't hear me on the other side of the wall.*

On October 19, 1972, he *told me he was going away for four days, as usual. He threw a few things into a bag and left with my dog, Véra. At first, I was wary. He always left on that date, but I still thought that someone from the cabaret might have given me away. I sat down and waited to hear his steps on the stairs, for twenty-four hours. Nothing. I didn't sleep. He didn't come back. On October 20, I phoned Hannah. We met on Rue des Tables-Claudiennes, like the first time. On the way there, I turned a thousand times to be sure he wasn't behind me. Jean and Hannah were waiting for me in a car. I thought they'd take me to a doctor in Lyon, but they drove out of the city. Jean said to me: "We're going to my sister's, she'll know what to do." His sister . . . The one who'd brought me food at school, pretending that she had too much in her bag.*

I fell asleep in the back seat. It was Colette's voice that woke me. Colette who wasn't expecting us. When she saw me, she recognized me. "Blanche, is that you?" Colette hadn't changed at all. I don't think I had, either. Her place smelled of polish.

I freed my body by removing the girdle that was suffocating me. At that moment, I allowed you to arrive. The four of us had supper in silence. Colette was never a woman to ask questions. I didn't dare look at Jean the entire evening. I was ashamed of the situation; I felt terribly guilty with regard to Hannah. I was in love with him . . . How to put it? Dreadfully and madly in love. Painfully and madly.

Today, I'm sixty-one, and I never saw him again after that October in 1972, except on TV, and I still love him. Like Colette loves Aimé, and Aimé loves Colette. They're clear to see, these things, because they're rare. Seven years ago, when I found Colette again and settled in your room, Agnès, she gave me the cassette Jean recorded in 1985, at Christmas . . . The tape is worn now, I've listened to it so often. I don't know if you'll have already heard it by the time you listen to this, but it's as if Jean had stitched up my broken heart, thirty-five years after we first met.

On the evening of October 20, we went to bed very early. Colette asked if she could touch my belly.

"I'm going to be an aunt."

"The child will call you tata*."*

"I'd prefer to be called Colette."

We held hands to fall asleep. I was so tired. Before closing my eyes, I told her about the night I'd spent with her brother in four words. Piano, meeting, dazzled, love. They say the devil hides in the details; I can tell you that, on the only night I spent with your father, it was God who wasn't hiding anymore.

When my waters broke, I was dreaming that it was Jean's hand in mine, not Colette's. Like your father, I wanted Colette to help bring you into the world. I knew that she'd know what to do. Crazy as it might seem, I felt no pain giving birth. I was too keen to deliver you to freedom, to a life that I wouldn't know. I was breaking the curse of my elders.

My genitor never spoke to me of his mother. He *lived with her photo. No one was allowed to look inside his wallet. And no one disobeyed him. Except me. I still have my grandmother's face imprinted on my retina. It's almost an ailment. When I close my eyes, I see her as clearly as I see the world around me.*

You were born in barely three hours. Far away from violence, surrounded by love. Colette knew exactly what to do, and Hannah never left us. It's Colette I was gazing at when I heard your first cries. Jean stayed in the background. When he saw you for the first time, it was as if he were the child. And of course it was Hannah he kissed, not me.

Silence.

Blanche
On October 23, Jean returned to Colette's with your birth certificate. Agnès Septembre, daughter of Jean and Hannah. You were saved. We could have stayed just as we were for days. But I had to get back before that evening.

Silence.

Blanche
Jean and Hannah drove me to Lyon. I asked them to drop me off far from the apartment, in case he *was already back. They kissed me. Hannah was crying so much, she made my face wet. Jean was silent, distraught. I planted a final kiss on your cheek. You were sleeping. Just as well. You didn't see me leaving you. I walked without thinking. Went up the stairs without thinking. Opened the door.* He *wasn't back. I changed my clothes. If my calculations were right, he'd arrive that evening. On Mondays, the cabaret was closed. I peeled some potatoes. At around 7* P.M.*, I heard Véra charging up the stairs;* he *opened the door,* he *didn't greet me, the dog made a fuss of me, and we ate supper in silence. I cleared the table, did the washing-up, took Véra down for about fifteen minutes. Outside, it had suddenly turned cold. My body was just pain, my head empty. I sat on a bench. Véra rested her muzzle on my thigh, looking at me with infinite sadness, as if questioning my distress. I couldn't answer her.*

I had to behave as if nothing had happened. If he *had discovered that I'd just given birth, he'd have never stopped hunting you down. Like he hunted my mother down, obsessively.*

Life returned to normal. An almost-life. A life under surveillance. With a few brighter moments at the cabaret. Only Colette, Jean, Hannah, and I knew that you were born during the night of October 21, not of October 22. At first, I would phone Hannah, but it was too painful for both of us. I withdrew, but first I gave Hannah the post office details. She sent me photos until you were twenty. The last time I spoke to her was in 1987, after Jean's death. I needed to tell her how much I was thinking of the two of you.

Silence.

BLANCHE

On December 23, 1981, I saw you on Rue des Chartreux. I was with him. *We were coming out of a store. He had fitted me out, like a child. I was thirty-five years old. On the sidewalk opposite, I recognized Hannah and, holding her hand, a pretty little girl. You were in a red coat and had colorful barrettes in your hair. You were skipping. I embraced your joy from a distance. Hannah didn't see me. I followed you with my eyes. He asked me what the hell I was doing, and I replied: "Nothing, just watching the little girl over there." He muttered something. I didn't move until you'd disappeared. Much later, I saw you on TV. How clever and beautiful you are. You're an artist. And your movies are magnificent. I watched them, telling myself that you'd made them for me.*

Silence.

BLANCHE

Colette showed me photos of your daughter, Ana; she looks like Jean. She's a pianist . . . You've made a success of your life and hers, Agnès. Thank you for that. I don't want to stop talking. That's why I didn't want to start. But you've never needed me. Your parents are parents. Me, I'm the wind.

End of the recording.

37

HANNAH RUBEN

December 23, 2004

She is making jasmine tea for Agnès. She has bought chestnut *mont-blancs*, her favorite dessert. Pierre, Ana, and Agnès are back from Los Angeles for the festive season. Tomorrow, as is their tradition, they'll drive to Gueugnon, and back, to celebrate Christmas Eve with Colette. Agnès rings the doorbell and walks in. "Mom?" Whenever Hannah hears her daughter's voice, she quivers. She goes down the corridor to welcome her. She hasn't seen her since last May; it's been a year since they moved to America. She hugs her tall daughter tight, only reaching her chin. "Goodness, she's tall, your daughter."—"She gets it from her father." The set response for years.

At first, Hannah had struggled with tenderness. Every cuddle had made her feel as if she were stealing her daughter's love from another woman. She was almost scared of Agnès. But with time, affection did finally come naturally, especially since she became a grandmother. Once Ana was born, a wall came down; she feels legitimate in her role as a parent.

Hannah thinks Agnès looks tired. Her features are drawn. "It's nothing, just jet lag." Hannah doubts she's happy in the States. Ana throws herself into her grandmother's arms. "Mamina!" A contraction of *mamie*, "grandma," and Hannah that the child invented. "The apple of my eye," that's what she calls her granddaughter, who has the same eyes as Jean. Ana is nine years old. It's the age Agnès was in 1981, when Hannah had spotted Blanche on the sidewalk opposite, in Rue des Chartreux. She hasn't been back there since. Blanche was with the madman. Short, dry, stern, his face weatherworn, craggy like the faces of laborers who work outdoors. The opposite of Blanche, who was always so beautiful. How had she managed to keep her sunny disposition when her daily existence was hell? It was a mystery to Hannah. That day, she thought how that bastard had almost been a blessing for her, Hannah. If he hadn't existed, Blanche and Jean would probably have lived happily ever after. He was the one who'd prevented them from getting to know each other properly. Hannah felt ashamed of that thought. A clammy shame that clung to her for a long time.

Realizing that he must be Blanche's father, and that she must keep moving without looking at them, for fear of the danger, she squeezed Agnès's hand a bit tighter than usual and sped up. In her panic, she thought Blanche was going to shout: "Give me back my daughter!" This fear struck her for a split second. She could feel Blanche's eyes on them but didn't look up. Hannah had known this would happen eventually one day. Where and when, she had no idea; that was up to chance. But they lived in the same city. A city of 500,000 residents, but the same city, even so.

For years, Hannah had feared that Blanche would return to ask her to give Agnès back. She had nightmares about it, always the same one. She'd go into her daughter's room, but she wasn't in her bed anymore; she'd been taken away by her mother. The real one. Years later, when Agnès had turned up at Hannah's, pregnant, proudly flaunting her sweet little bump to surprise her mother, Hannah had almost admitted the truth to her: *there's no photo of me pregnant in the albums and boxes in the sitting room because I didn't carry you.* But then she'd remembered what Blanche had told her: "Never say a word, Hannah. If my genitor found out about her, he could harm her. He really is insane."

Never would Hannah forget the anxiety that had gripped her, then haunted her, between the evening she'd met Blanche for the first time and that phone call on October 20. She was about to become the mother of a stranger's child. It had reminded her of her own story, of the Gravoins who had taken her in, loved her like their own daughter. Thanks to them, not only had her life been saved, but she'd also had a happy and privileged childhood. Of her adored grandmother who would sing "*Insensiblement*" to her and endlessly tell her: "Don't be afraid of anything, only do what you want to do." On the night of Agnès's birth, she had taken off the chain bracelets with her two names on them. In becoming a mother, she was leaving behind her own story to write a new one.

On that evening of June 21, she'd got back to the apartment she'd been sharing with Jean for a few months. He'd returned that very afternoon from Rome, where he'd played at the main auditorium. He was tired but happy. And in the evening, between the pears and the cheese, Hannah had said to him: "The young woman you spent a night with after the cabaret is five months pregnant. She can't keep the child because her private life is very complicated. She lives under the control of a dangerous man, so we're going to raise the child. I'm pregnant by you without being so. Another woman is carrying our child."

She had said all this in one breath, like a speech in a melodrama learned off by heart. Jean had only been able to whisper her name: "Blanche?" He remembered her name. So it wasn't a one-night stand. You don't remember the name of a one-night stand.

The following day, Jean had questioned her: "Where did you see her? What did she say exactly? Where is she going to give birth? Is she well?"

Was she well? No, since she had to give birth secretly and then abandon her child. A pregnancy he'd caused without taking the slightest precaution to protect her. Hannah had thought hard about it. Where could they find a doctor or midwife who would accept the unacceptable? How could they ask even close friends to help a woman give birth when she was giving the baby up, all without going through a hospital? That's how Colette came to seem like the only solution to Jean. Like when they were children. After all, his sister had looked after the ewes, and when a lamb was struggling to be born, their father would say: "We've got the lass." Hannah had exclaimed: "But a woman isn't an animal, for goodness' sake, Jean!" It was the first time she'd raised her voice, gripped by an anger she'd stifled. *For goodness' sake, Jean.* For the first time, she'd doubted her love for him. Had blamed him for his betrayal. While she was in the whirlwind of an orchestral tour beyond her wildest dreams, he was in the arms of another woman. How many more times would he cheat on her? How could her handsome husband show such immaturity? Come up with such an absurd idea? To ask his shoe-mender sister to assist with a delivery? Was he really that fanciful? His head was always in the clouds, it was like he lived on a different planet—but his head wasn't in the clouds the night he got an unknown woman pregnant.

And Jean had explained it all to her. Blanche wasn't an unknown woman. She had been close to Colette. They'd lost touch, but they'd known each other since elementary school. Of course Colette would know what to do, and if there was the slightest complication, she'd call Dr. Labori, her friend.

From October 1 onward, Hannah had cancelled all her trips, claiming to need rest. Later, she'd say that she stopped for the last weeks of her pregnancy. After the ordeal that awaited them, lying would be nothing. So, while Jean continued to travel to give concerts, she had remained beside the phone. And what if Blanche didn't ring? If she'd had a miscarriage? Or found another solution? What if she'd changed her mind? Or worse, admitted everything to her father? Or what if her father had discovered the pregnancy and killed her? What if she'd met someone else? If she'd ended up running away? And what if, what if, what if. Hannah had felt alone. Very alone. But not as alone as Blanche, who was having to hide her pregnancy. Wasn't it the lot of women, to be alone? Hannah had never held it against Blanche. Never. Hannah had sincerely liked Blanche.

The jasmine tea perfumes the sitting room. After Jean's death, Hannah had kept their apartment, the photos on the walls, Agnès's room, the piano. Never would she have parted with Jean's piano. Little Ana sits at it to show her Mamina the progress she's made. Agnès adjusts the height of the piano stool and then joins her mother to enjoy her dessert while listening to her daughter play Mozart's *Symphony No. 21*. Going by her progress since last spring, watching her little fingers flit across the keyboard with a dexterity reminiscent of Jean's, Hannah knows that her granddaughter will become a professional if she keeps practicing relentlessly. She's already at the level of a future concert pianist. Hannah knows musicians well, has mixed with them since she was very young, thanks to Éléonore.

How she'd loved accompanying Jean all over the world, playing, sublimating a sonata with him. The dusty smell of the concert halls, their communion on stage, the nights in hotels, the planes, the trains. Revering some conductors, performing with them again, like finding God again, or good fortune. Dreading others, quick-tempered and unpleasant. The music together. The great joy of a piece you know backward, but feel as if you're rediscovering each time. The resonance within that makes your flesh quiver. To possess the gift of music is to possess something of the divine. And Jean possessed Heaven itself.

In the morning, he would practice his piano, she her violin in the room next door. Sometimes she would stop playing to listen to him. Agnès had always rejected the idea of being, and any desire to be, a musician. "Because you were never there," she had reproached Hannah one day. "For me, music is absence." These words saddened Hannah, making her feel as if she'd betrayed a promise made to Blanche. But Hannah does have to admit, she always preferred Jean to the rest of the world. When he had left her, at the age of thirty-seven—you just don't die at thirty-seven—she thought she'd never get over it. She never did get over it. He'd made her a widow of forty-five years old, a woman in despair. She took this as a sign of divine punishment for having loved her husband too much, to the detriment of others. Including her only daughter.

Agnès preferred to cut out pictures and glue them in exercise books, write stories, record herself, and later, film with her camcorder. Is it because Agnès carries a secret she's unaware of that she's such an outstanding storyteller? Through her screenplays, is she looking for an answer that, unconsciously, she's missing?

Tomorrow will be their last Christmas Eve. Hannah won't say anything to Agnès before she leaves again. She doesn't want to spoil the fun and joy of their reunion. She'll tell her about it later. Make her come back from the States when she senses that it's the end. Death doesn't frighten her. She'll be with Jean again. And will protect Ana and her loved ones. She sees the dead as guardian angels. Her cancer has spread. It's too late to consider any treatment. An oncologist friend will help her to depart with dignity. He's promised her that. For now, she subdues her acute back pains with opium pills. A veritable junkie, she thinks. She continues to practice her violin every day, so she still has the pleasure of making music. She has six to nine months left; it's hard to say, they explained to her. She hopes to see the spring again.

Hannah picks up her violin and accompanies Ana. *Symphony No. 21* is one of her favorites. Agnès smiles. She takes a picture of them with her phone. Now, photographs are taken with telephones.

The following day, they meet up again at Lyon-Part-Dieu station. Pierre will take a later train; he has a meeting with his French agent who wants to introduce him to an important director. Hannah has never really known what to make of Pierre. He is funny and charming, but she wonders if that's enough to keep Agnès happy. With the passing years, Hannah finds her increasingly anxious. She tries to beat records, but not for herself, for her husband. In the train, Ana stays with Hannah. Agnès sits on her own, three rows down; she's writing her next screenplay.

Louis comes to meet them at the Creusot station. Agnès, Pierre, and Ana will sleep at the Hôtel du Centre, and Hannah at Colette's. She informed her by phone: "For once, I'd like to sleep at yours this year." Hannah will tell Colette everything. She knows she can trust her, that she never talks, that she listens without judging.

Lunch is joyful. Colette is happy to see them again and closes the shoe-repair shop for the whole of December 24. "Shoes and keys can wait."

After lunch, Agnès and Ana go for a nap while waiting for Pierre. And Hannah goes home with Colette. They sit in her tiny kitchen, make tea. Colette asks Hannah to forgive her, she doesn't have any "top-quality tea." Hannah gazes at the pictures of various footballers and coaches on the wall. The sound of steps. Hannah starts. At first, she thinks she's seeing a ghost, that it's the effect of all the medication she's taking. Blanche, standing in the doorway, in a purple-and-red dress. Apart from the hair, she looks like Colette in color.

"I've been living here for four years. I ran away when I discovered that *he* had beaten my mother to death. I reported him to the police. I believed he was in prison, but they released him; he must be searching everywhere for me."

"Blanche, it's you . . . How happy I am to see you. You had the courage to leave . . . "

Blanche and Hannah embrace each other for a long time, watched by Colette, who says not a word.

Hannah Ruben dies on June 13, 2005, at the Pompidou hospital, with Agnès and Colette by her side. Ana was allowed to come and kiss her the previous day. Blanche will have a plaque placed on her grave: "Hannah, may your rest be as peaceful as your heart was kind." At the funeral, they'll play Schubert's *Fantasy for Violin and Piano*. A piece that Hannah and Jean loved to play together, and part of an album they recorded in 1982 for Deutsche Grammophon. On the jacket of the record, they pose proudly, against the light, in a studio, she with her violin tucked against her neck, he behind his piano.

One day, Agnès had spotted the record in Madame Bedin's store, when she was there with Colette, and had said to her: "It's crazy how I don't look like my parents." To which Colette had replied, with humor: "Me neither, thank God."

*

Blanche will rejoin Jean, Hannah, and Colette in La Guillotière Cemetery, in Lyon, on February 3, 2011, under her mother's maiden name: Blanche Roman. Her blue shoes will be placed on the tomb.

38

June 21, 2011

My Lina, on this blessed day, I'm giving you two rotten presents: first, my surname. Before signing, I want you to know that, from today on, if there isn't a photo of you beside your new name, many folks will frown. Second, I'll never be able to knock back a whiskey with you. It's love and fresh water for us. And possibly coffee, tea, sodas. But I promise I'll be able to mend things, build dreams for you, houses, gardens, furniture, paths.

"I'm not sure you won the lottery when you met me. Where you haven't done too badly is that I don't like religion. So I can convert to whatever you like, especially to you. As you know, I think God abandoned me when I was seven, but he seriously made up for it last year. As for the Blessed Virgin, she never abandoned me. She's not called Maryam or Marie, but Nathalie. She never let go of my hand and always believed in me. I owe her everything, before you. The name Nathalie means birth. Nat, everything today, it's thanks to you.

"I want to pay tribute to my parents. I imagine my mother up there, saying to my father, "How beautiful our son's wife is," and paying no attention to what I've just been saying, not because she doesn't want to, but because she can't.

"I pay tribute to my darling sisters, Zeïa and Fatiha, who are the pride of our Algerian family. Two brilliant brains to put up with my reckless one. What a great brother!

"I thank all those present and all those who have departed.

"Finally, I'd like to reassure my parents-in-law: don't go on appearances; even if, on paper, it doesn't look great, I'll do everything in my power to be sure Lina's happy. And when someone's as in love as I am, they have superpowers.

"Lina, my love, I hope we have a kid who looks just like you. Thanks for having faith in me; I didn't think anyone could give me my wings back. In fact, I didn't even know I still had any."

"Ilyas, my love, I'll take your two rotten presents. I'll take all of you. I'm so proud to have your surname that I'm going to write it all over the place. I'll tag it on every wall in Gueugnon. Folks will be able to say, 'it's those Arabs again.'

"I hope we have at least three kids, and who cares who they look like, if they're anything like our meeting, if they're as radiant as you can be when you believe in yourself. And I won't be knocking back a whiskey, with or without you, because I want to make the most of you with a clear head. I find you far too handsome to waste my time in 'artificial paradises.' I intend to have too much of you until the end of my days and nights, with my eyes wide open. I want you the way I did that Monday when I saw you enter Flumet's town hall with Agnès, to the extent that, ever since, I've loved Mondays. Thank you to Agnès, who agreed to be my witness. I wanted it to be you because I took you for Ilyas's wife that first time . . . On top of that, you fainted in my office. So, you won't be his wife, but his wife's witness. People asked me: 'Lina, why are you getting married so fast?' Quite simply, because Ilyas is so obvious. Because we have no time to lose.

"And know that we'll be a little old couple, all shriveled up, together. We have big plans: to live the simplest of days here in Burgundy. I've noticed that certain locals roll their 'r's, so I promise, I'll give it a go!

Thank you all for being here with us. Thanks to Zeïa and Fatiha for their welcome and kindness. I'm an only daughter, so I'm gaining two sisters and a husband on the same day. And thank you, Ilyas, my love, for having faith in me, when I didn't think a girl's wings could be repaired."

"In the name of the law, I declare Monsieur Ilyas Otmane Mansour and Mademoiselle Lina Catherine Auzière united in marriage. You may kiss the bride."

Nathalie and I stand up together to sign the register. Our legs are like jelly and our mascara's running. We kiss the newlyweds on our way there. They're so very beautiful.

Ana sits at the piano and plays Rachid Taha's "*Ya Rayah*" with four other musicians: two string-players, two percussionists. The singer has a voice (almost) as beautiful as Taha's. The mix of harmonies is a perfect reflection of the couple. At Lina's request, Ana has been preparing this piece of music in secret with her accomplices.

All the guests stand up, kiss and hug the bride and groom. Fatiha, Zeïa, Nathalie, and Lina's parents all dance together. Adèle, her daughters, Paul, Hervé and his son, Antoine and I dance, too, clapping our hands. Ilyas and Lina join our group. It takes us a while to leave the town hall. Personally, I'd like this moment to go on forever.

The weather is beautiful today. Life feels like a joyous whirlwind. Almost a romantic comedy. The bride is in white and the sun shines elegantly. The groom looks dazed, but smiles his lovely smile.

I'll never forget what Ilyas said to me when we got back from Flumet, although absolutely nothing had gone on between him and Lina: "The hardest thing, when you meet someone, is telling them what happened. It's an unavoidable stage you really don't want to face. That's why I've never stuck around a girl for long, so I wouldn't have to say anything. But . . . I really think that with Lina, I'm going to stick around for a seriously long time."

On the square outside the town hall, the Rue des Fredins neighbor, Cécile Aubert, is among the guests. I watch her chatting with Ana, who's wearing a pretty black dress. She's put make up on her big, pale eyes. My daughter is sublime. The reception is being held at the community center, which the young newlyweds have booked just for their guests, around a hundred of us. We walk over to the center, Antoine brushes my hand, asks me if "the witness is doing well." I catch Louis's arm.

"Daydreaming, Louis?"

"I'm happy for Ilyas."

On Rue Pasteur, the shoe-repair shop is open. Louis doesn't need to walk past it to think of Colette, but I know he gets a twinge of sorrow every time.

"Colette would be happy, too. She was fond of him."

"Yes."

Dad's Steinway still has pride of place on the center's stage, the brass plaque my mother put in the entrance has lost its shine.

We all drift gently toward evening. People chat, get to know each other, eat standing up, sitting down; the doors remain wide open, those who smoke go in and out. Those who don't smoke do, too.

I withdraw a little outside to listen to the hubbub, I can hear the distant laughter. Place de Gaulle is opposite the center; now plunged into darkness, it's where, long ago, Soudkovski's circus erected its big top on two occasions. I imagine Blanche and Colette walking up Rue Saint-Pierre to go to school.

Fatiha joins me, jolting me from my thoughts. I've never really spent time with Ilyas's sisters; the older one was too old to be interested in us and the younger one too young to interest us.

"Did Ilyas tell you about Charpie?"

I'm surprised that she would bring this up with me, and that she knows his nickname. I don't know what else she knows, what Ilyas has confided in her. Fatiha is eight years older than him, and when he was abused, she was a teenager. I thought that Ilyas had never admitted it to his family. Indeed, I was amazed that he alluded to it in his speech: "God abandoned me."

"Yes, he told me about it when I came back to sort things out concerning my aunt. Never when we were teenagers."

She appears to think for a few seconds.

"When I had my son, Sohan, my brother was really happy. He's a super-uncle. He's caring, plays with him, showers him with gifts. Since we live in Fontainebleau, we don't see each other more than three, four times a year, but each time we do, it's really lovely. But the older Sohan got, the stranger Ilyas started to behave. He'd phone me several times a day to know how Sohan was doing, what he was up to, to check that my little boy wasn't isolating himself. Crazy stuff. I'd reply: "Why would he be isolating himself, Ilyas?"—"Okay, but does he cry when he goes to the childminder's? What's he doing when you get there?" Anyhow. Eventually, I stopped answering when he called.

One evening, having dinner at friends', the conversation turned to family. I talked, with stupid amusement, about my overprotective little brother's behavior, his endless questions that I found loony. A shrink who was there listened to me carefully. At the end of the dinner, she whispered in my ear that my brother might have been a victim of abuse and be transferring that onto his nephew. Hence his fear and his obsessive questions. I didn't want to believe her. 'That' couldn't happen to a family like ours. I was sure of it. And I never brought it up with Ilyas. Out of shame, or a fear that he'd feel uncomfortable."

Fatiha takes a pack of cigarettes from her pocket. Offers me one. I realize that it's the first time she's really talked to me. We crossed paths all through our teens, and greeted each other because we were linked by Ilyas. "Hi, how are you?"—"Fine, and you?"

"Last year, I overheard a conversation between Nathalie and Ilyas. I was at my parents' house with Sohan. It was warm and late, all the windows were open. The two were just back from a vacation in Nice. I don't know why, but they stopped at the house to collect something. Before leaving, Nathalie sat in the garden to stroke the neighbors' cat that was forever squatting at ours. I could hear their voices from my bedroom. First, Nathalie said: 'Do you remember, Charpie had a little dog.' And then I picked up other words such as 'young . . . shy . . . only boys . . . you . . . ' I heard Nathalie's endless chatter to my little brother as if I were the target of machine-gun fire. I knew perfectly well who she was talking about; I'd done an internship at the factory's computing department. And it was *him* who ran it. The first thing I thought was: did he know that I was the big sister of the little boy he'd abused that same year? The answer burst into my head, exploded even, a real bullet to the brain: of course he did . . . There aren't umpteen Mansours in Gueugnon. And Ilyas and I look alike. I gathered that they'd just come across him in Cannes. I 'got hatred,' as my cousins would say. A hatred that was unfiltered, unhesitating. From the moment I heard Nathalie talking to my brother, I stopped thinking. Charpie was on the files of my airline company, address and phone number included. I found him in a split second. In any case, he'd never hidden. Never tried to disappear, despite what he'd done. He was even in the phone directory. He simply left Gueugnon abruptly after an event I don't know the ins and outs of. And that was it. The man had never been investigated . . . He surely couldn't die peacefully in his bed. I'm a vegetarian, I hate the sight of blood, I'm anti-death penalty, and I've always voted left, except in 2002, when the only choice was between Chirac and Le Pen. But I told myself I was going to finish the bastard off. Showing that one can betray one's deepest conviction at any moment. I saw myself back at the office, him leaning over me to show me some data to enter into the computer. His cologne, his shirts, his mouth, his nose, his social status, as if he could do no wrong. I thought how that same year, he'd raped my seven-year-old brother, and I hadn't been able to protect him. I booked a Paris–Nice flight for the following week. I intended to get into his home by ringing his doorbell. To make a crime look like suicide. What was I going to use? A firearm? Medication? Defenestration? I had no idea. I never got on that plane. His body was found just days later out at sea, near Cannes. He didn't get murdered by the intern from 1979. I felt such anger when I saw the piece on his death in the paper, with his photo alongside. He was smiling. A picture of him taken at the stadium on a match night; the team must have won. I spent hours poring over maps of Cannes, and he can't have killed himself; it's all flat, stable footing everywhere, he hadn't swallowed any medication, there's no clifftop or bridge over the sea. Unless the sea came and swept him off a strand or jetty. Hard to believe in the middle of July. I felt ashamed, Agnès, ashamed not to have done the dirty work. By dying before I found him, by dying without ever being tried, he sure gave us all the finger."

She stubs out her cigarette with her heel, then picks up the butt.

"Shall we go and dance?"

"We'll go and dance."

*

Zeïa was born three years after Ilyas. Her first smile had been for him. That loving brother who would say to her: "Hold on, I'll help you build the castle. Are you cold, sweetie? If anyone bothers you at school, just tell me, okay?" He was always the buffer between her and her big sister Fatiha, who was annoyingly bossy.

With her deep-rooted sense of justice, Zeïa had become a criminal defense lawyer to defend what seemed indefensible in the eyes of public opinion. It was what drove her. The daughter of immigrants, she'd fought like a lion to get the best grades at school, never believing that anything was inevitable. In the early 2000s, she was the only woman to have chosen criminal law rather than civil in the town of Mâcon, where she lived. The accused were wary of women, thinking that they weren't capable of defending them; they preferred to be represented by men. For a long time, she had dealt with petty larceny as a court-appointed lawyer. Things had changed with homicide case involving the death of a policeman. The accused had been acquitted, due to a lack of evidence, thanks to Zeïa's speech for the defense. A speech that was brilliant and fair. Throughout the trial, which had lasted three days, she had intervened skillfully during the proceedings and had sowed doubt in the minds of the jurors, who had preferred not to put a potentially innocent man behind bars. Three months later, the real culprit had been arrested. Since that event, the entire region wanted to be represented by Maître Mansour.

Zeïa had always wanted to defend and represent those who couldn't, or struggled to, express themselves. She hadn't understood why her brother had suddenly stopped playing football, when he was the best at it, should have pursued a sporting career. When she'd asked him the question, he'd smiled sadly at her. "I'm going to leave. You'll get my room . . . " That had been his only response. When Ilyas left home, she'd taken his departure as a personal failure and had cried for weeks.

In 2009, she was in Ilyas's old room when she'd heard her brother and Nathalie talking in the garden about their awful encounter in Cannes. Zeïa was preparing her files with the help of a flashlight, so as not to attract mosquitoes. Enlightened by Nathalie's words, Zeïa had understood what had caused Ilyas's suffering.

In junior high, a friend had told her that her brother was doing drugs, that he'd been seen buying his dope from someone shady. Zeïa had said: "You're wrong, it can't be him. People can't tell one Algerian from the next here." That's when she'd realized that he'd left home to give himself over to his addictions.

Having only just avoided the cops, Ilyas didn't want to get stopped with drugs on him, for his parents' sake. But with any bottle of any kind of alcohol, he was untouchable. It was legal. Alcohol feeds grief.

As the years went by, Zeïa had finally admitted that he'd hit the bottle some evenings and every weekend. She'd seen what he looked like on Sundays, when he came home for lunch with his parents. He would hide away on his days off to get drunk. He still wanted to be a perfect son. Ilyas had always pretended.

On that night in July 2009, hearing Nathalie, Zeïa had immediately realized that all this had to do with her sister's former boss, in the computing department. She remembered him. Had already heard murky stories concerning him. A friend had seen him in a car with a very young man, "his fiancé," he'd joked. His words had chilled her. She hadn't slept all night. Imagining what her brother had suffered. Intolerable. The following morning, a Sunday, she'd rung directory assistance and been given the address and phone number in Cannes of the man in question.

She'd thought about it all day. Had gone to see her brother. He'd been surprised to find her on his landing.

"Hello, *maître.*"

"What are you up to?"

"Going for a swim in Montceau, at friends of Nat's, fancy coming?"

"No, I'm going away for a few days; I just wanted to give you a hug first."

"Oh, right, where are you off to?"

"Don't know. Maybe to the seaside . . . Was Nice fun?"

"Brilliant."

"Great."

She had hugged him a bit tighter than usual and left. She'd felt his eyes on her back. He was keeping his nose clean now, had quit boozing. Seemed more stable. But not happier. She'd long thought that Ilyas and Nathalie were romantically involved. She'd long hoped that he'd meet someone.

That Monday evening, in Cannes, when the former boss had walked out of his apartment building, Zeïa was sitting at the wheel of her car. What was she doing there? Was she going to behave like the people she represented? The ones society, and she herself, passed judgment on? She'd been parked outside the address she'd been given for a few hours now.

She would have recognized the man's demeanor anywhere. The sight of him made her suddenly feel sick, so she'd half-opened the door to vomit in the gutter. When she looked up again, he was already far away. *Shit*. She'd started the car and followed him from a distance. He walked as far as the Cap de la Croisette and sat down at the terrace of a café.

She knew this place. Had come here with a conquest three or four years ago. She couldn't remember anymore. Rarely remembered dates. At that precise moment, she wondered whether she liked women because her brother had been abused by a man. There would never be an answer to that question.

He was waiting for someone. He checked his watch, frequently. She was parked against the traffic, observing the passersby, the guys in shorts and the girls in short dresses. The local police pulled up to ask her to move. She felt like saying to them: "Instead of bothering me, go see the guy over there, a guy who's never been investigated and who always uses the crosswalk." But she'd zipped it and done what they asked. The last thing she needed was to be noticed. She finally found a parking space, something of a miracle. She'd gotten out of the car. He was still sitting there. Sipping his drink. After an hour or two, he got up to leave. Zeïa had completely lost track of time. She followed close behind him. At the level of a car park, a bit farther along, as he walked in the half-light to get back to the edge of the sea, a car had come out of nowhere and headed straight for the man. As soon as she realized what was happening, she stepped aside to hide behind a van. The car had stopped a centimeter away from its target. Zeïa instantly thought of her brother. Maybe it was him, at the wheel of a Citroën with a Saône-et-Loire license plate. The plates couldn't be a coincidence. She hadn't been able to see the driver clearly. Why would her brother have stopped at the last moment, leaving the predator alone and stunned? Zeïa's heart started to beat abnormally, as if arrhythmic. The Citroën disappeared into the night, abandoning both of them. The sister and the rapist.

She walked determinedly up to him. The man hadn't yet recovered from what he'd just been through. *You, what you've just been through is nothing compared with what you put others through. For you, they're just "others," for all of us, they're our brothers.* Zeïa pulled an iron out of her beach bag. Her mother's iron, which she had taken as she left the house. Premeditation.

He made a strange face, screwing up his eyes, not understanding either the presence of this stranger, or the incongruous object she was pointing at him. A face distorted by surprise. A kind of Picasso, but a bad one. Something that doesn't exist.

"When he was seven, my brother burned himself with an iron. He told us it was an accident, but it wasn't."

Zeïa struck him in the face. With unimaginable force. A horrifying sound. Never had she hit so hard. Never had she hit, period. He fell to the ground. The sea was murmuring a few meters away. The Mediterranean. His Mediterranean. She dragged him. *Splash! Take him. Carry him away.* The dark water had swallowed him up. As it had the murder weapon. Her mother would search everywhere for her iron. Wondering how such an object could just disappear. A storm would come up a few hours later, as if the sea were her accomplice. The body would be found much farther away.

Zeïa had seen her brother burning himself. He was seven, she, four. She had seen him do it, seen him placing the burning-hot object against his skinny thigh, he was wearing blue football shorts. His dark, vacant eyes watching the hot soleplate silently sink into his flesh. He hadn't cried out. She was the one who'd screamed. Their parents had rushed to the emergency department. Ilyas, as if absent from himself, on the back seat, had fainted on the way there. Fatiha had looked after Zeïa during that time. And she, Zeïa, had kept the secret, it wasn't an accident. But mutilation is incomprehensible at the age of four. She'd taken it to be a dangerous game, a forbidden game. *One of those dumb things boys do.*

When she'd heard Nathalie talking in the garden, that painful memory had come flooding back.

Ilyas had talked to his sisters after meeting Lina. Given them a summary, as if they'd always been absent from his life, of his times in detox and his battles, his stays in the Garches hospital that had saved him, thanks to Nathalie and an inner strength he didn't know he had, and maybe, also, so that bastard would stop ruining his life. He intended to live, at last.

Zeïa had said nothing about what happened in Cannes. Would never tell a soul. She, more than anyone, would continue to defend people in the name of innocence.

39

"*Quand j'serai KO*"	When I'm KO'd
"*L'Amour à la machine*"	Love in the Washing Machine
"*La vie ne vaut rien*"	Love is Worth Nothing
"*La Ballade de Jim*"	The Ballad of Jim
"*S'asseoir par terre*"	Sitting on the Ground
"*Foule sentimentale*"	Sentimental Crowd
"*Allô maman bobo*"	Hello Mommy, It Hurts
"*J'ai dix ans*"	I'm Ten Years Old
"*Poulaillers' Song*"	Henhouses' Song
"*Bidon*"	Phony
"*Jamais content*"	Never Happy
"*Le Bagad de Lann-Bihoué*"	The Bagad de Lann-Bihoué

Since I'd drunk a bit too much, I'm not sure what the order of the songs was. Except for the last one. "*Le Bagad de Lann-Bihoué.*" A crazy title that no one can remember. Mention this Alain Souchon song, and people always quote: "*Tu la voyais pas comme ça ta vie*"—You didn't picture your life like this. After the wedding reception, we went to the raffle house. It was four in the morning.

Antoine told me he wanted to plug his phone into a speaker to listen to music. He went to look for his cable in a box full of junk. Meanwhile, I scrolled through a whole load of song titles on his phone, like in a pick-and-mix candy store, just help yourself. I selected only Alain Souchon songs. I was determined to start by singing him "*Quand j'serai KO*" and "*L'Amour à la machine.*" The others just turned up. In no particular order. Because I know them all by heart, Antoine said: "No way, you know them all by heart! I'd love for you to know me like that, by heart." And I'd repeat certain words, explaining to Antoine that Alain Souchon is the greatest genius of this century, to the extent that even Jacques Brel would've been crazy about him. Afterward, we played a game, finding THE gem of a line in each song:

Quand j'serai rien qu'un chanteur de salle de bains
When I'm nothing but a bathroom singer
Pour retrouver le rose initial de ta joue devenue pâle
To get back the pink of your now-pale cheek
Il a joué "Jeux interdits" *pour des amis endormis / La nostalgie*
He played "*Jeux interdits*" for sleeping friends / Nostalgia
Avec elle il voulait un bébé sans rire
With her he wanted a baby, no kidding
On a l'vertige sur nos grandes jambes de bazar
We get dizzy on our long, dime-store legs
Pour demain nos enfants pâles / Un mieux, un rêve, un cheval
For tomorrow, our pale kids / An improvement, a dream, a horse
Moi je voulais les sorties de port à la voile, la nuit barrer les étoiles
I wanted to leave harbors in a sailboat / Crossing off the stars at night
Je vis dans des sphères où les grands / N'ont rien à faire
I live in realms where grown-ups / Have no business to be
Mais comprenez-moi, la djellaba / C'est pas ce qui faut sous nos climats
But you know, the jellaba / Just isn't the thing in our climate
Elle croyait qu'j'étais chanteur, incognito voyageur, tournées, sonos, filles en pleurs, admiration
She thought I was a singer, traveling incognito, tours, speakers, girls in tears, admiration
Construire des tours de carton bleu, pour que les petits garçons mettent leurs jeux
Building towers of blue cardboard / So little boys could put their toys in them
Moi aussi j'en ai rêvé des cornemuses / Terminé maint'nant, dis-moi qu'est-ce qui t'amuse?
I once dreamed of bagpipes, too. / That's over now, tell me, what's so funny?

Antoine and I agreed on each and every gem. To "*Le Bagad de Lann-Bihoué,*" between

Tu la voyais pas comme ça ta vie,	You didn't picture your life like this
Tapioca, potage et salsifis.	Tapioca, soup, and salsify.
On va tous pareil, moyen, moyen,	We all end up the same, so-so,
La grande aventure, Tintin . . .	The great adventure, Tintin . . .

we kissed.
And it was good.

As Bourvil sang in "*C'était bien*":

Ils buvaient dans le même verre,	They drank from the same glass,
Toujours sans se quitter des yeux.	Still not taking their eyes off each other.
Ils faisaient la même prière,	They said the same prayer,
D'être toujours, toujours heureux.	To be always, always happy.
Parmi les gravats ils souriaient	Amid the rubble they smiled
Dans ce petit bal qui s'appelait	At that little dance hall that was called
Qui s'appelait	That was called
Qui s'appelait	That was called
Qui s'appelait	That was called

From Souchon to Bourvil.
And it was good.

40

October 21, 2010

On the night Blanche died, before Dr. Pieri arrived, Colette took down all the photos of Agnès that Blanche had pinned up on the walls of her room, and put them back into their original box. A shoebox that Blanche had covered with pink paper. She placed it beside her collection and closed the cupboard door.

Now Colette puts the recorder and the cassettes into her big suitcase. Blanche's voice and her own will be going on a journey to the most beautiful of destinations, to Agnès and Ana. Then she phones Louis: "Tomorrow morning, come and get my suitcase for Agnès, I'd like it to stay at your house and for you to give it to her when I'm dead." Louis retorts: "Come on, Colette, you're not going to die anytime soon." She replies: "I am."

That night, it was thirty-eight years since she helped bring Agnès into the world. Since she became an aunt. Since she set eyes on her, wrapped her in a blanket, and entrusted her to Blanche and Hannah, although she would have liked to keep her. But she'd never told anyone that. Thirty-eight years since she saw Jean become a father, bowing over the little one as if she were a saint, to kiss her.

She picks up the dictionary that is kept under the TV console, beside Dr. Pieri's bottle of whiskey. It's the first time she's opened her dictionary to the word "*tante.*" Usually, she uses it for her crosswords. "*Tante: nom féminin, soeur d'un des parents; femme de l'oncle; mont-de-piété: j'ai laissé ma montre chez ma tante. Tata (familier): tante dans le langage enfantin.*" (Aunt: feminine noun, sister of a parent; wife of an uncle; pawnshop: I left my watch at my aunt's place.

"Tata"—informal: child's word for aunt, like auntie.) Colette smiles and closes the dictionary.

She returns to her suitcase, checks it's properly closed, automatically brushes off any dust, puts it on the kitchen table where it's obvious. This suitcase is the one she was carrying when she left the mother, fifty years ago, to go and live at Mokhtar's. This suitcase represents Blaise, who slipped money into her pocket when she was in need.

On September 17, 1986, Blaise is in the hospice wing of a Paris hospital. He's in isolation, like a murderer. With banknotes and the signing of discharge forms, Eugénie de Sénéchal manages to have him brought back home, so he can pass away with dignity in his own bed. In France, they talk about AIDS as the "pink plague." Colette, who speaks with Eugénie regularly, has understood the urgency of seeing Blaise again. She hasn't seen him since 1973. Jean often visits him when giving a concert in Paris. Sometimes, they phone Colette. "Here's Blaise," her brother says to her. "How are you, Colette?—Fine, and you?—Nice weather in Gueugnon?—So-so.—And the team's ranking?—We're keeping steady.—I went to Jean's concert, it was breathtaking. Love from me.—From me, too."

The thread is broken, because Colette never read *L'Éternité*. Blaise's first novel. On Sunday, September 18, Aimé, who insists on accompanying her, comes to collect her at seven in the morning outside the shoe-repair shop. In France, people are starting to recognize that the illness Blaise is suffering from is only transmitted through blood and sexual relations, but many refuse to go near the sick.

When Colette sees her childhood friend emaciated and covered in purplish-brown marks, she clings to him as if to hold him back or leave with him. Blaise is pure suffering. Morphine is being regularly pumped into his veins. There's an unbearable smell of putrefaction in the room. Aimé lays a comforting hand on Colette's shoulder.

Blaise opens his eyes, recognizes her, manages a faint smile. He looks toward Aimé. Colette introduces them. Blaise whispers: "He's handsome, your husband." Aimé blushes. Colette has brought *L'Éternité* with her and takes it out of her bag.

"Would like me to read it to you?" she asks, smiling at him.

"Please," Blaise murmurs.

She sits beside him, Aimé takes a seat, close to them.

Colette reads the novel out loud. Blaise occasionally dozes off, frequently opens his eyes, asks Colette to hold his hand. During the final chapters of the book, Eugénie joins them, walks around the bed and holds Blaise's other hand.

"*L'être qu'on adore*"—the person one adores—are the last words of the novel. When Colette says them, Blaise passes away. When they emerge onto the street, overwhelmed and distraught, Aimé says to Colette:

"I'm taking you to the sea."

They say nothing on the drive there. It's just getting dark.

They sleep at the Hôtel Flaubert in Trouville. The following day, they wake up beside the sea, the sky is blue, a watery blue. The tide is low.

It comes back in, right up to them, at around one o'clock. Colette has a swim in her underwear. It was Blaise who taught her to swim. She moves through the waves murmuring "*l'être qu'on adore, l'être qu'on adore, l'être qu'on adore . . .* " Her tears mingle with the salty water.

Aimé and Colette spend the afternoon lying close together on the sand, wrapped in blankets they bought at the Monoprix on Quai Fernand-Moureaux.

She kept them; now she puts them on her bed. Colette is turning in. It's a bit chilly. She pulls the blankets over her. Something's up with the radiator in the room, must talk to Louis about it.

She closes her eyes. Summons a memory. Always the same one: July 19, 1976. She comes out of the bathroom. Her nape and face are wet. Aimé is waiting for her in the sitting room, she's wearing his tee shirt, has untied her hair. Aimé, who was about to place the stylus on the ABBA record, stops still at the sight of her and says these words: "How beautiful you are, Colette."

41

October 31, 2011

Sitting in the sun on the terrace, I survey the countryside as it sketches its first autumn colors, and I still can't quite believe the unreal beauty of this place. My good fortune. My house in Burgundy. I bought it from Antoine last summer. It was July 22 and pouring with rain.

Ana has just left with him, for the station. I'll join her in Paris tomorrow. I'm stretching out my time here, and, most importantly, I have an appointment to keep.

I spent the weekend with my daughter. I'd found an 1889 piano at the Emmaüs charity store, which I'd had entirely restored. She practiced, just as my father did, and Chopin, Mozart, Liszt, and Bach moved in for hours. Suddenly, what Pascal Amoyel, the concert pianist and Ana's prodigious music teacher, once said came back to me: "Thirty-five years I've been playing him, and it's still a mystery. Bach, it's infinity at one's fingertips."

Life, too. We make of our life what we feel like making of it, and are unaware that we possess it to infinity. Until death. Unless we're a composer. A painter. A sculptor. A film director. A writer. A gold prospector. Charlie Chaplin is here forever.

Since the house is very isolated, I see and hear every rare car that turns up around here, where four families, including mine, share thousands of hectares of pasture, forests, paths, and river.

I watch Ilyas's Méhari coming up the road. *He's on time.* We arranged this meeting a year ago, at the Petit Bar. We were supposed to meet again right there in a year, but that was before my house. Ilyas wanted the "handover" to take place here instead.

I've slipped my novel into an envelope. I haven't yet sent it to an editor. I'm waiting until I've seen Ilyas. To know where he's at. I want us to set off at the same time. Like when we were kids and would run a race from a line drawn with chalk. He always won. Followed by Hervé. Adèle and me behind, neck and neck. He gets out of the Méhari, empty-handed. I hide my disappointment behind a smile.

He walks up the steps and kisses me. Lifts up his sweater, and his manuscript is flat against his tee shirt, tucked into the waistband of his jeans.

"Should've seen the look on your face when I got out of the car!"

I yelp with joy. He gives it to me. The pages are bound. I hug it the way one hugs a small child.

"You've finished it?"

"I think so."

"Can't wait! What's the title?"

"*Le jour se lève* . . . Like the song by Grand Corps Malade."

"I love that song. It's also the title of a movie by Marcel Carné."

He smiles at me.

"Jean Gabin."

"Yup, with Jean Gabin . . . And Arletty."

"You're well?"

"I'm well."

"And Lina?"

"Splendid . . . I never thought they existed, people like her."

"Shall I make you a coffee?"

"Yes. How about yours? Have you finished it?"

"I think so . . . "

I hand him the envelope.

"As promised."

"Is it still called *Hannah Ruben*?"

"No. I changed along the way."

"You changed the title?"

"Yes."

"What is it?"

"*Tata*."

Acknowledgments

Thanks to my readers; your breath carries me forward.

Thanks to Mocktar, the shoe-mender on the Rue des Abbesses, who has such grace.

Thanks to Bernadette Degrange for the football and the childhood.

Thanks to my favorite violinist and friend, Anne Gravoin, for your wise advice and the idea of the note slipped under a key.

Thanks to Pascal Amoyel, a brilliant pianist with a huge heart, for all that you brought to me.

Thanks to Nadia Farès and to America.

Thanks to Nathalie V.; Daniel F.; Christophe D.; Thierry D.; Sylvie B.; and Éliane B., for sharing with me their memories of *him*.

Thanks to Maître Denis Fayolle.

Thanks to Stéphane Baudin; to the public records team at the Gueugnon town hall; and to Johan Martin for the archives and your precious help.

Thanks to Papa. To Michel Chaussin and Christophe Trivino for enlightening me on the history of football, the matches, and the factory that has been the beating heart of the foundry town for more than three centuries.

Colette's collection does exist, but it was created by Monsieur Georges Pichard.

Thanks to all those who have raised aloft the Football Club de Gueugnon.

Thanks to gentle "Madeleine" who wandered the streets murmuring, most probably, poems.

Thanks to all of these families: Berthéol, Michel, Soussand,

Chaussin, Bedin, Laroche, Bresciani, Courault, Vezant, Humbert, Carnat, Jean, Berry, Larand, Dantas, Petitjean, Carré, Bondoux, Charles, Degrange, Bernard, Lopes de Lima, Dollet, de Chargères, Duclos.

Thanks to Marie, of the Pomme d'Amour, and to Nathalie and Éric, of the Monge. I "transplanted" you.

Thanks to my dear parents, Francine and Yvan Perrin, who ran the store Shopping, on Rue Jean-Jaurès (among others).

Thanks to the former shoe-menders on the Rue Pasteur, whose names I don't know.

Thanks to Joseph Fasoli for the pizzas on Place de l'Église, and Vincent Surace for the coffees at the Petit Bar.

Thanks to Éloïse Cardine.

Thanks to Frédérique Favre and Marc Bonnetain for the information on Father Pierre Aubry, of whom I was so fond.

Thanks to Doctors Isabelle Sec, Jacques Pieri, Frédéric Saldmann, Thomas Battini.

Thanks to all my neighbors and friends in Armecy.

Thanks to Alain Souchon; you have enchanted me throughout the writing of this novel and throughout life, too. And to Vincent Delerm. As is the tradition.

Thanks to Glenn Gould, France Gall, ABBA, Elsa Lunghini, Clara Luciani, Damien Saez, Alain Bashung, Grand Corps Malade, Léo Ferré, Étienne Daho, Rachid Taha, Véronique Sanson, Marie Laforêt, Bourvil, Daniel Auteuil, Peter Falk, Mathilde Seigner, Jennifer Coolidge, Patrick Dewaere, Guillaume Schiffman, Sempé, Guy de Maupassant, Pierre Bellemare, Ilyas B., David Foenkinos.

Thanks to the team at the Villa des Abbesses and at the Nazir.

Thanks to Samuel and Victor Hadida.

Thanks to Agnès Jaoui, encountered one Sunday in the countryside. Suddenly, everything changed.

Thanks to Marcel Carné, Claude Sautet, François Ozon, Milos Forman, Krzysztof Kieslowski, Henri-Georges Clouzot, Jean-Jacques Annaud, Gérard Krawczyk, Jane Campion, and so many others.

Thanks to Catherine, Carol, and Micka, whom I call (almost) every day to ask a question.

Thanks to Loup Lardot and Nathalie Marchandeau.

Thanks to my maids of honor. Thanks to Amélie for the lunch.

Thanks to my children, stepchildren, grandchildren, *tatas* and *tontons*.

Thanks to my niece Emma, who calls me *Tata*.

Thanks to my Albin Michel clan, for your unshakeable faith since forever. Maëlle, I love your voice choked with emotion.

Thanks to my Livre de Poche clan, for your seriously crucial presence.

Thanks to the *Secours populaire*, to the French Red Cross, to *Secours catholique*, to the Salvation Army, all mentioned in this novel.

adpa-refuge.annieclaudeminiau

Vestiaire Solidarités Saint-Bernard, Paris 18e
solidaritessaintbernard@gmail.com

Sorry to the victims; we can never do enough to protect you.

About the Author

Valérie Perrin was born in 1967 in Remiremont, in the Vosges Mountains, France. She grew up in Burgundy and settled in Paris at the age of nineteen. The international success of her novels *Forgotten on Sunday*, *Fresh Water for Flowers*, *Three*, and *Tata* has made her one of the most widely read and most beloved French authors in the world. *Fresh Water for Flowers* (Europa, 2020) won the Maison de la Presse Prize, the Paperback Readers Prize, and was named an ABA Indies Introduce and Indie Next List title. It has been translated into forty languages. In Italy, both *Fresh Water for Flowers* and *Tata* (Europa, 2026) were the bestselling books of their respective publication years. In 2025, readers of *ELLE* named Perrin one of their top ten favourite French authors of all time. Perrin now lives in Paris.